A qualified parachutist, Har
Intelligence for over ten yea
surveillance in Northern Irel
Berlin during the Cold War w
dragged from his car by KG   _ has lived
a more sedate life in the private sector as a director for an international
company and now enjoys the pleasures of writing. Harvey is married
with four children. For more from Harvey, visit his website at
www.harveyblackauthor.org.

Praise for Harvey Black

"Harvey Black's geopolitical survey is beautifully intertwined with personal stories of his characters. He builds tension relentlessly... looking forward to the next book!" – Author Alison Morton

"... tension, suspense, action, intrigue and moments of tenderness too which are a nice touch. I recommend the book entirely." – Steven Bird

"Factual along with gripping, takes me back to the days of the BAOR and what we all trained for... look forward to the next instalments." – Jon Wallace

"This book needs another one to follow on and complete the story. A similar story to Tom Clancy and his *Red Storm Rising*." – A Jones

"This is the best read I have had in ages very techno and extremely fast moving. It could have happened." – TPK Alvis

"This is a thriller in the style of Robert Ludlum or Tom Clancy. Credible characters and fast pace... thoroughly enjoyed the roller coaster ride!" – Author David Ebsworth

"The build-up is gripping and enthralling." – Author Sue Fortin

"If you have enjoyed *Chieftans, Red Gambit, Red Storm Rising, Team Yankee* etc, then don't miss this. Well written, realistic, unputdownable." – R Hampshire

Also by Harvey Black:

DEVILS WITH WINGS SERIES
Devils with Wings
Silk Drop
Frozen Sun

THE COLD WAR SERIES
The Red Effect
The Black Effect

COMING SOON
The Blue Effect

HARVEY BLACK

THE BLACK EFFECT

SilverWood

Published in 2013 by SilverWood Books

SilverWood Books
30 Queen Charlotte Street, Bristol, BS1 4HJ
www.silverwoodbooks.co.uk

ISBN 978-1-78132-122-5 (paperback)
ISBN 978-1-78132-123-2 (ebook)

British Library Cataloguing in Publication Data
A CIP catalogue record for this book is available from the British Library

Set in Bembo by SilverWood Books
Printed in the UK on responsibly sourced paper.

Dedicated to Michael 'Mick' Comerford (1905 – 1961),
a soldier who survived 3 years 8 months in Japanese PoW camps.
And to all soldiers of the Commonwealth both past and present.

Shimla Hills ©1934. Name: Michael 'Mick' Comerford (sitting).

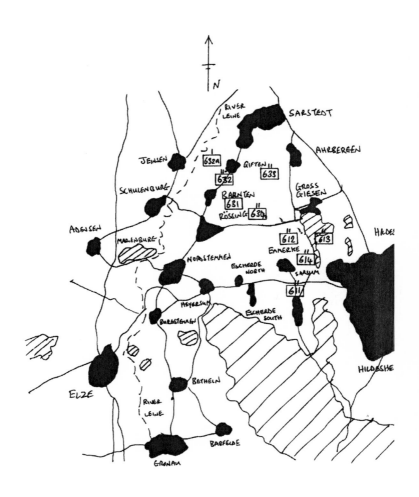

61st and 63rd Guards Tank Regiments Attack 7 July.

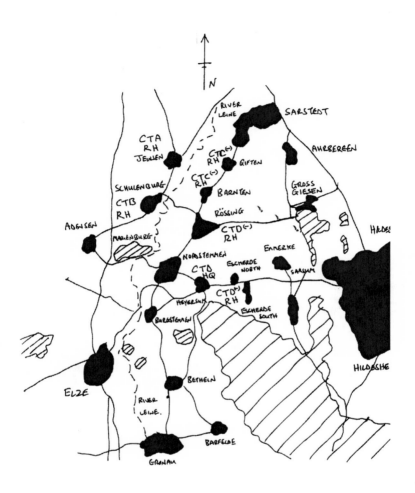

Royal Hussars Tank Regiment Dispositions 7/8 July.

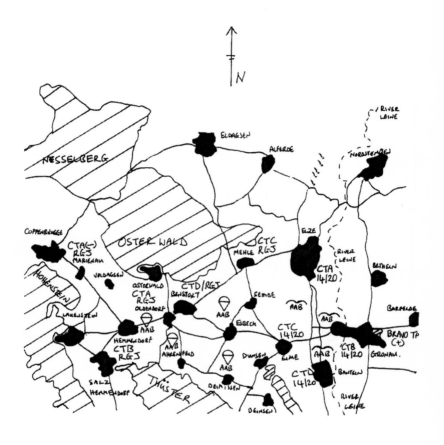

Dispositions 14/20 Kings Hussars and Royal Green Jackets 7/8 July.

Foreword

Nightmare: *a frightening or unpleasant dream*

By definition, a nightmare is an ethereal thing, something to wake up from with a certain amount of relief. The twentieth century turned nightmares into reality for many people across the globe and the Great War was considered a 'war to end all wars' – yet it was not an ending, just a beginning. In 1919, the thought of more serious conflicts would have been the stuff of bad dreams, but that perceived ending had fashioned a man capable of weaving nightmares beyond the subconscious of most. In a mere twenty years, Hitler took Europe to the doors of perdition, wiped out 6,000,000 Jews, and left his homeland, and his people, without hope.

The clearing out of old colonialist empires left the field open to humanity's first real superpowers, each immovable, each unstoppable. Stasis followed in the form of the Cold War. Though cold, it caused all world leaders to have hot nightmares with bellicose events, caused by mighty powers flexing muscles at imagined sleights and paranoid intelligence, increasing in number as the 1980s approached.

I worked in the defence industry from the seventies into the new millennium so was closer to events transpiring then than most. The perception was that John F Kennedy had sent the Soviet Union packing in October 1962 and, no matter what, the balance of power had moved solidly to the United States of America. However, just below the surface, with finances at a critical level, the Soviets were ready to lash out – an old bear unwilling to relinquish territory and still strong enough to use its claws. Stasis remained, held by the energy of things nuclear. But...

In West Germany, allied forces lived in capitalist comfort even though each man and woman knew what lay over the border, over Churchill's Iron Curtain. With the will, with enough idealistic energy, could the Soviet steamroller save its gentle demise by use of a successful pre-emptive gamble? A strike of such velocity as to nullify the souls defending freedom? I did not know. Would we, who according to Oppenheimer had 'become death, destroyer of worlds', use the power of the atom to assert our right? I did not know. Somewhere in East Berlin at the time were soldiers who tried to know as much as possible. Little things. Pixels of information building pictures – some, indeed most, were hopeful. Some were dark – a frightening or unpleasant dream.

Only a soldier knows how it feels when the armour of training is engulfed in fear. In the 1980s, only Army Intelligence lived with nightmares moving in front of them plucking hairs from the old bear's back. Would the Soviets take the gamble? It was not unprecedented: the Normandy landings, Pearl Harbour, Stalingrad – all unlikely victories, all gambles, and all nightmares for many. They never attacked and the Wall came down; the ship of fools had finally run aground. But...

Paul Comerford

Chapter 1

0630 5 July 1984. Combat Teams Alpha and Bravo/Royal Green Jackets Battlegroup. Area of Supplingen and Supplingenburg, West Germany. The Red Effect +1.5 hours.

A puff of smoke left the end of the barrel of the Chieftain's 120mm main gun as the armour-piercing discarding sabot round shot from the muzzle. The sabot petals, having served their purpose, separated from the projectile and the deadly penetrator sped at over a thousand metres per second towards its target. Immediately after firing its main gun, the Chieftain tank fired off its two banks of six electrically-actuated smoke grenade dischargers erupting into a cloud of dense smoke out to the front as the driver gunned the engine reversing the fifty-two-ton giant back, deeper into the tree line. The tank and crew would move to another position in a last-ditch effort to cover the rest of Combat Team Bravo, harassed by Mi-24 Hind-D attack helicopters, who were in the process of withdrawing from Supplingen, their work here done.

Combat Team Alpha, opposite, in the village of Supplingenburg had also pulled out. A few rounds of smoke from their mortar section gave them some cover and a pair of Harrier Jump Jets had made a brief appearance, one shot down, hit by a fusillade of anti-air fire from the four 23mm barrels of a ZSU 23/4, a missile from an SA-9 sealing the aircraft's fate. Combat Team Alpha, badly mauled by the Soviet artillery and a heavy missile barrage that preceded the Soviet Army's assault on the British covering force, were pulling back through the Dorm Forest. Some elements were forced to use the main route, at speed, to Konigslutter, where Combat Team Charlie from the Royal Regiment of Fusiliers Battlegroup would provide the next stopgap.

The T-80, pounding along the left-hand side of the battalion commander's T-80K command tank, swerved left, initiating a zigzag movement to make itself a harder target for the enemy they were assaulting. Hit earlier by a High-Explosive-Squash-Head (HESH) round, that stripped the explosive reactive armour blocks from the front left of the turret, they had now become the target of the hardened penetrator that had just been fired by the Bravo Chieftain tank. The lightweight ballistic cap on the end of the penetrator was crushed and the steel sheath, surrounding the tungsten carbide penetrator which was twice as hard as steel, peeled away as the core pierced the T-80 main battle tank. Breaking up as it penetrated the armour at the base of the left-hand quarter of the turret, an elliptical spall blossomed out inside, the heated fragments ripping into the crew inside. The over-pressure burst their eardrums, and blood trickled from their ears and noses. Hot, smouldering slivers tore into the gunner's right side, gouging into his flesh and peppering his skin with burning fragments, his hands clawing at his face in an effort to free himself from the agony, the smell of his burning flesh making him retch. The rest of the debris ricocheted around the fighting compartment, shredding the tank commander's legs, his screams drowned out only by the louder screams of his gunner. The driver, relatively safe for a fraction of a second longer, continued to drive the tank forward before the ammunition ignited, erupting within the steel confines of the tank with nowhere to go, until it lifted the turret two metres into the air, molten metal and shrapnel killing the crew, before it fell back down, slewed to the left as the armoured giant, now crippled, ground to a halt. The rest of the tanks maintained their advance, pushing ahead, their masters urging them on.

Lieutenant Colonel Trusov, Commander of the 2nd Battalion, 62nd Guards Tank Regiment, 10th Guards Tank Division, both heard and felt the destruction of the tank that had been running alongside his. Although recognising he had lost another of his battalion's tanks, the battle was progressing well. All three of his company's tanks were now racing in between the villages of Supplingenburg to the north and Supplingen to the south. His order from above was to pass between them, bypassing them. The enemy appeared to have withdrawn from the northern settlement and, although they were still receiving potshots from the south, the four Mi-24 Hind-D attack helicopters, from the division's helicopter squadron, were causing havoc, keeping the British Chieftains on the move, making it difficult for them to zone in on the advancing Soviet armour.

"*Two-Zero, Two-Two. Minefield! Minefield!*"

"All Two-Zero call signs, stop, stop, stop. Two-Three take left flanking position, Two-One right."

"*Two-Two, understood.*"

"*Two-One, right flank. Flossgreben water feature, 100 ahead.*"

"*Two-Three, covering left.*"

"Two-One, move up and cover mine clearing and crossing."

"*Two-Zero, Two-One, acknowledged.*"

"All units, Two-Zero. Make smoke."

Kokorev, the driver, called out. "Us too, sir?"

"No, just a platoon per company. That will be enough."

Three tanks per company moved into position and drove in a predetermined pattern, injecting diesel onto their exhaust manifold creating clouds of white smoke, engulfing the rest of the tanks in the unit in a fume-laden screen, but providing them with cover from any enemy tanks targeting them. The 62nd Regiment's artillery unit had also been tasked with dropping smoke shells ahead of the advance, on the western side of the *Flossgreben*, a four-metre wide watercourse, one of many scattered around the area, to enable a safer crossing.

Trusov took stock of the battle so far. He had lost six of his tanks, far less than he had expected. At least two could be recovered: one had hit a minefield and was repairable, and the second had just thrown a track. Four though, along with their crews, had been completely destroyed. He still had twenty-five tanks left. With the tank battalion behind ready to cross the *Flossgreben*, immediately after his battalion had crossed, both had been instructed to race for Konigsburg.

The mine-clearing tanks advanced. The tank-mounted device, attached either side at the front, was lowered, the blades digging deep into the ground as the tanks powered forward, ploughing up and pushing the mines aside, outside the tank's path. The mines, now upside down, would be relatively ineffective, the force of any blast going down rather than upwards. Two safe corridors cleared, the TMM Scissor-bridges moved forward to set up crossing points, to enable the advance to reconvene. Close by, *Boyevaya Mashina Pekhoty's,* (BMP-Mechanised Infantry Combat Vehicles) disgorged their crews, and the Soviet soldiers prepared their SA-14 Gremlins, shoulder-launched, ground-to-air missiles pointed forwards and up at the ready. The tracked, self-propelled-anti-aircraft-gun, the ZSU 23-4s, Shilkas, fanned out, their four 23mm barrels swivelling left and right, aimed up into the air. Each water-cooled auto-cannon, with a cyclic rate of up to 1,000 rounds per minute, guided by the onboard J-band radar, would provide a destructive barrier, out to two kilometres, against any aircraft daring enough to come in low to prevent the crossing. Further back, SA-9s, SA-6s and SA-4s waited, missiles loaded ready to shoot the enemy out of the sky.

0630 5 July 1984. Combat Team Bravo/Royal Green Jackets Battlegroup.
Area of Supplingen, West Germany.
The Red Effect +1.5 hours.

The Combat Team Bravo tank commander, Sergeant King, called to his driver to halt the tank as he peered through the vision blocks, rotating his cupola a few degrees, seeking out any enemy activity ahead of him. The length of the *Flossgreben* ahead was blanketed in smoke and, as there were no targets visible to him, his only task now was to report the fall of shot when the divisional artillery bracketed the area with high explosives in an attempt to disrupt, or prevent, the Soviet forces from crossing the water barrier. King tried to peer deep into the smoke, but could see nothing, although he could hear enemy tanks on the move across the other side.

He reflected on one of the many intelligence briefings he had received as part of his military training. Under the heading of the capabilities of the Soviet army, he had been told that the Soviets didn't even consider the River Weser as a barrier, such was their river-crossing capability. All he had to do now was report the fall of shot; then, along with the remaining tank in the troop, he could pull back. He would not be sorry. The Hind-Ds had been hunting them relentlessly; the Blowpipe shoulder-launched missiles despatching only one, they appeared invincible. The Combat Team and even Brigade seemed to be able to do very little about it. The precious Rapier missile batteries were being kept further to the rear to protect the main force digging in. Without warning, the smoke-filled area suddenly erupted into swirling eddies as the first 152mm ranging round from an M109 self-propelled gun struck. It was bang on.

"Zero-Alpha, this is Alpha-Two-Zero. On target, fire for effect. Over."

"Alpha-Two-Zero, this is Zero-Alpha. Roger, on way. Job done. Get out now. Over."

"Alpha-Two-Zero moving out now. Out."

The rest of M109 battery, belonging to 40th Field Regiment, Royal Artillery, launched their barrage in earnest, the large calibre shells peppering the river-crossing area with hot lethal fragments, killing one of the air-defence units on the ground, knocking out a Shilka and destroying two of the TMMs.

0630 5 July 1984. Combat Team Alpha/Royal Green Jackets Battlegroup.
North-west of Supplingenburg, West Germany.
The Red Effect +1.5 hours.

Looking back, the village of Supplingenburg was not only obscured by a shroud of smoke from a second Soviet artillery bombardment but also from the many burning buildings; pillars of black smoke dominating the skyline. Although the shelling had shattered the British forces using the village as a defensive position, the fug from it now provided them with cover as the Combat Team retreated.

Lieutenant Dean Russell rocked from side to side as the FV432 armoured personnel carrier weaved around the ruts and dips of the narrow track that snaked through the Dorm Forest, taking them west, away from the devastation behind them. Beneath the black camouflage cream plastered to his features, now sweat-streaked and covered in a layer of dust, his face was pale as a ghost. Dug in on the eastern outskirts of the village of Supplingenburg, one of the many British units positioned along the frontline to blunt the initial attack by the Soviet forces, he and his men had been confident that they would give a good account of themselves. Now? He didn't know what to think. He had been proud of the way his platoon had conducted themselves during the attack. But the thirty-minute Soviet artillery and missile bombardment had made it a one-sided battle. After a seemingly endless deluge of explosives smashed into Combat Team Alpha and Combat Team Bravo and the other units of the Royal Green Jackets Battlegroup, followed by an assault consisting of the latest Soviet T-80 tanks and more of the dreaded Hind-D attack helicopters, they experienced a short but decisive defeat, having no option but to withdraw. Yes, they had held up the enemy for short period of time, which was their aim. However, their first encounter had not been a good one, and he, like his men, felt adrift and dispirited. The engine of the 432 growled as the driver pushed the battle-taxi hard as they came out of a dip, the driver careering sideways as he barely missed a felled tree that partially blocked the track. Russell looked back, hanging onto the General-Purpose-Machine-Gun (GPMG) pintle; the next 432 in his platoon was following behind, the third further back again. The fourth had been abandoned back in the village, wrecked and on fire after being hit by a 122mm artillery shell. It wasn't just the destroyed vehicles that had been left back at the village. The wounded had been loaded onto any vehicle that could accommodate them, but the dead had been left behind. There just hadn't been enough time if they were to keep ahead of the Soviet advance and escape being cut off from the rest of the army. That bothered the young lieutenant the most: having to leave some of his men behind, their dog tags and memories the only evidence he had of their existence. His commander of one-section, Corporal Wood, along with two other soldiers and the crews of the two Milan firing posts they were covering, had been lost. The rest of the company had also fared badly. His opposite number, and friend, in command of two-platoon, Lieutenant Ward, had been killed, along with men from his platoon, when his position had been struck by a Scud-B missile. He turned to face forwards again. A 432 from second-platoon was ahead of him, his driver sticking to it like glue, not wanting to be left behind. There was a sense of urgency, a need to get away, find some time and space to reflect on what they had just experienced, a time for the unit to reform. Or was it panic and the desire to escape and lick their wounds? He rose above it, believing that they had blunted the attack and were now withdrawing in good order to dig in further back, allowing other units to take their turn in despatching the advancing enemy forces.

A sudden bright flash ahead blinded him temporarily, his driver pulling hard on the right steering lever as the 432 swung right into the loosely packed trees to avoid the erupting armoured personnel carrier ahead. The deafening sound, as round after round from the Hind-D's 12.7mm four-barrelled Gatling gun punched into the stricken 432, now ablaze, pummelled the lieutenant's eardrums. The sound was then joined by the roar of the helicopter's turbine engines and the downblast from the rotor blades as it shot past, its wingman placing more rounds into the afflicted vehicle, the gunner tracing the track seeking out more targets.

Russell's 432 had ground to a halt, as did the two behind him, the track ahead now blocked by the fiery grave.

"Out, out!" He screamed.

The back door flew open and the 432 disgorged its load of infantrymen.

"Blowpipe, Blowpipe," he yelled to his men.

He was suddenly thrown to the ground by a fierce blast as the burning armoured carrier tore itself apart as the ammunition and fuel exploded.

"Move it," he screamed.

Farrell braced his legs, his oppo helping him steady the Blowpipe, a man-portable, surface-to-air missile, on his right shoulder. He aimed it through the gap in the trees above, searching for another attacking helicopter.

Russell knew it was pointless as the likelihood of the firer locking onto a fast-moving helicopter at treetop height was extremely doubtful. Anyway, the helicopters had done their job and were either going back to their base to refuel and rearm, or were out there somewhere else seeking out more lucrative targets.

"Mount up, mount up," he called to his men. "Find us a route through the trees so we can get round it," he said to his driver, pointing at the still burning 432. *An inferno, a graveyard for more men of Combat Team Alpha*, he thought.

The soldiers climbed back into their vehicles, their eyes drawn to the burning coffin where some of their fellow soldiers had no doubt died. Lieutenant Russell did a circuit of the burning mass, holding his hand up to protect his face from the searing heat, searching for any men that may have dragged themselves to safety. But he saw none. After a few hundred metres, the 432 clawed its way up a shallow bank and was soon back on the track on the other side, and the convoy continued on its way west and to safety. He shook his head to the unspoken question from one of his men: should they go back? They continued their journey, needing to catch up with the rest of their unit.

Chapter 2

Since four in the morning, at the same time the Warsaw Pact launched its devastating opening gambit along the entire European Front against the thinly held NATO covering force, the units of the Soviet 25th Tank Division had been moving into its alert assembly area. Released from their role of encircling Berlin, this mission handed over to the soldiers of the German Democratic Republic, they would now be able to add their weight to the Warsaw Pact forces battling for supremacy on the European battlefield. On hearing the news of their country's attack on the West, the officers of the division drove their men relentlessly, preparing them, and the unit, for the next stage: the start of a long march west. With over 300 kilometres to their final destination, Salzgitter, West Germany, they would have to move at least 150 kilometres during the next twenty-four hours if they were to be in a position to support the battle that by now was in progress.

At the divisional departure areas, columns were already forming up, preparing to begin their journey. The division had been separated into different packets: wheeled, trailer-loads, and tracked vehicles. The last of the 300-plus T-64s were loading onto the semi-trailers, the roar of the Maz-537 tank transporter's engines reaching a crescendo as those already loaded with their cargo pulled away to start their trip west. Often referred to as the 'Beast', the Maz-537G was more than capable of pulling the semi-trailer, rated at fifty tons, powered by its 525hp engine, as fitted to many of the Soviets' main battle tanks. At over nine metres long and able to travel at up to sixty kilometres per hour, it was ideal for the task of moving this key element of the division. An entire transport regiment had been allocated, by the Front Headquarters, to move the main battle tanks, the tracked surface-to-surface missile TELs and some of the surface-to-air missile launchers, to their intermediate assembly area south of Genthin, 150 kilometres away.

On a parallel road, the other tracked vehicles, such as the BMP-2s from the tank regiments, the 142 BMP-2s from the motor rifle regiment, and the remaining tracked vehicles – surface-to-air missile carriers, the self-propelled guns of the artillery regiment and the numerous engineer vehicles, GSPs, K-61s and PTSs – would soon start their journey. Broken down into smaller packets, they too were starting on their long journey towards the front line.

Further afield, an even bigger group was forming up. The wheeled element of the division was in the process of refuelling before they too headed west. They would travel at around twenty kilometres an hour, stopping for a twenty-minute break every three hours arriving at the long-halt area late during the evening of 5 July. The tracked vehicle column would arrive roughly four hours after the wheeled column, their slower speed of twelve to sixteen kilometres an hour making the journey that much longer.

Officers and NCOs could be heard cursing and bellowing at the troops, urging them on ever faster to get their vehicles into the right order and join the exodus west. Others were tucked away into the tree line, waiting their turn to be called forward, adding to the volume of traffic starting to clog the roads. Excluding the three tank regiments and the motor rifle regiment, the division had over 800 wheeled vehicles. A huge logistical tail. Two parallel columns would stretch for up to thirty kilometres each along the road network they would be using, ranging from chemical decontamination and disinfection vehicles to Zil-131 fuel bowsers and ammunition transporters. Soviet Military Police and Traffic Regulators would be responsible for ensuring the roads were kept clear, controlling the speed and the flow of traffic to ensure the divisions needed for the 2nd Strategic Echelon would arrive when needed. This was the logistical element of the division; the lifeblood that was required to feed, fuel, repair and protect the massed armoured armada that was heading to the front to add its weight to the forces pushing the NATO armies out of West Germany.

Aircraft from the Soviet air force circled above, their jets blasting the air as they banked and turned, providing overhead cover should the West decide to interdict this and other divisions, deep inside East German territory, preventing them from reinforcing the Western TVD armies.

After spending two weeks preparing for mobilisation in secret, 8th Guards Tank Division, of the 5th Guards Tank Army, one of many units under the command of the Byelorussian Military District, finally received its entrainment orders. Prior to mobilisation, soldiers brought back to their unit for their annual refresher training were retained, ensuring this Category-A unit was at full fighting strength. The Byelorussian MD had a powerful force at its disposal and was allocated to the Western TVD's, 2nd Strategic Echelon. The headquarters, based in Minsk, Belarus, had two Tank Armies, the 5th and 7th, and a Combined-Arms Army, the 28th, under its command. Between those army-level headquarters, they could field ten tank divisions and four motor rifle divisions; although, apart from the 8GTD and the 120GMRD, which were classed as Category-A divisions, at 100 per cent strength, the remaining units had, historically, only been at Category-B status. This was around fifty per cent of their wartime strength. The Politburo, recognising this weakness, had authorised units to retain those soldiers that turned up for their annual refresher training and, as a consequence, most units were averaging ninety-five per cent of their wartime strength. Any troops still requiring additional training would be transported to the front in the next few days. One other powerful force the Byelorussian MD had was the 1st Tank Corps, made up of three tank brigades, with a force of nearly 500 T-72s, and a motor rifle regiment. The MD also had on call an airborne division, artillery division, Air Assault Brigade, Attack Helicopter Regiment and its own air defence assets. To provide air-to-ground support and high-level air defence, it possessed its own air force, consisting of three air divisions. Two fighter divisions consisting of Mig-29s, a fourth-generation, air-superiority fighter, designated Fulcrum by NATO, and Mig-23s. Reported as Flogger, these older Interceptor fighters were still lethal in the air and would bolster the hard-pressed air divisions battling on the European front. A fighter-bomber division, with 130 aircraft, with Mig-27s, SU-24s and 25s, would support their troops on the ground.

The alert had been received by the divisional commander at one in the morning of the 5th July and, since first light, his large force had assembled, after moving the seventeen kilometres by road march to their dispersal areas. The divisional headquarters was based in Homel, Belarus, its subordinate units at various camps throughout the region.

They weren't the only unit on the move from the 5th Guards Tank Army. The 6th Guards Tank Division at Babrujsk was also moving to railway sidings to entrain, as were the 22nd and 29th Tank Divisions. The fifth division, the 56th Guards Motor Rifle, based at Mazyr, had dispersed, but wouldn't be moving west until the next day. The Byelorussian MD was being moved to a position directly behind the Group of Soviet Forces Germany (GSFG), ready to take over and thrust the knife deep into the perceived soft West German belly.

The Carpathian and Baltic Military Districts were also on the move; a huge war machine that was on its way to grind the hard-pressed NATO forces into the dust.

The tanks, T-72s, moved towards the entraining area; the division divided into packets heading for one of three stations, two entraining points at each one. Hundreds of tanks and mechanised infantry combat vehicles and a mass of wheeled support vehicles were on the move. Not just this division, but others in this Military District were on the move. The division had been allocated thirty-six trains, each one taking three hours to load. The officers were almost in a frenzy, pushing their junior officers and NCOs to keep to the tight schedule. The first train was due to leave at seven in the morning, the rest following, one every thirty minutes. The first of the electric trains pulled out. Its wheels squealing against the tracks, the hum of the engine noise getting louder, and the clank of the chains as the line of flat cars took the strain before being pulled forward. Railroad transport would play an important role in moving the 2nd Strategic Echelon forces to the front. The Soviet command could use the electric trains deep in the rear, generally safe from enemy fire. But the closer they got to their destination, the greater the risk. Then they would switch many of the electric-locomotives for the old-fashioned, but effective, steam train. Enemy artillery and air power wouldn't be the only obstacle they would come across. In the Soviet Union, the railways used a broad-gauge line, 1524mm, whereas in Europe the size of choice was 1432mm, a standard gauge. They had laid some broad gauge in East Germany, but not enough to satisfy the needs of the Western TVD. The Soviet rail engineers were already at work converting standard-gauge railway lines to the Soviet broad gauge.

Chapter 3

Trusov rubbed his eyes, still tired despite a relatively comfortable four hours' sleep. He didn't feel as exhausted as he had expected after twenty-hours of almost constant battle. Although he felt they had made good progress so far, making headway despite a staunch defence by the British covering forces, their long-range artillery and ground-attack aircraft homing in on the advancing Soviet armour, his masters were of a different opinion. Impatient as ever. Wanting more, and wanting it more quickly. But they had made twenty-five kilometres into 4th Armoured Division's covering force area. With that, he felt some satisfaction.

He checked his watch as he heard Kokorev clambering up from his driver's position, Barsukov cursing as Kokorev's boot trod on his leg. Although the extremely low profile of the T-80, particularly when hull-down, like all the modern Soviet tanks such as the T-72 and T-64, made it a difficult target to see and hit, the upshot was it was cramped, and only the installation of the autoloader enabled the tank to carry a crew of three. Kokorev chastised his comrade and handed him a mug of soup, passing a second one up to Trusov. It was a borscht soup that his driver had thrown together, taking advantage of their short break. He had scrounged around the fields looking for fresh potatoes, vegetables or cabbage, and had returned triumphant. It was welcome, and Trusov thrust his body out of the hatch, settled his elbows on the edge, and sipped at the soup, savouring the smell, chewing on the bits of beetroot and cabbage. It tasted luxurious. His thoughts drifted to the frantic briefing called by his regimental commander, Colonel Pushkin, and the next steps of their advance had been agreed.

After thrusting to the north of Konigslutter, brushing aside the Royal Regiment of Fusiliers combat team in Schandelah and a troop of four scimitars in Destedt, they had finally ground to a halt as A-Squadron of the 3rd Royal Tank Regiment, with four troops of Chieftain tanks, a troop positioned in each of the villages of Dettum, Obersickte, Cremlingen and Salzdahlum, had inflicted severe losses on the 1st Battalion who had been taking the lead, giving Trusov and his men a reprieve and a chance to rearm and refuel. Having destroyed seven of 1st Battalion's T-80s, for the loss of only two Chieftain tanks, one of those destroyed by a Hind-D, the British squadron had withdrawn, its task done.

During the night, 62nd Guards Tank Regiment had settled down to rest, rearm and refuel. With the adrenalin no longer coursing through their veins, weariness had started to make itself felt. The tank crews snatched as much sleep as they were able, some of them even too tired to eat. 10th Guards Tank Division, supported by 3rd Shock Army assets, and even assets from the Group of Soviet Forces Germany, were planning and preparing for an extensive artillery and air-to-ground strike on the NATO forces protecting the passageway between Braunschweig in the north and Wolfenbuttel in the south. Huge quantities of ammunition had been brought forward during the night, despite the enemy's artillery and air force attempts at interdicting the movement of the much needed supplies. Stockpiles had been placed close to the self-propelled and wheeled artillery. All they waited for now was the order to commence firing.

10th Guards Tank Division, led by the 62nd GTR and 248th GMRR, had advanced rapidly during the last twenty-four hours, pushing twenty-five kilometres into West Germany, and was now ready to strike again. Trusov had positioned his battalion on the outskirts of Salzdahlum, about five kilometres from Braunschweig and three from Wolfenbuttel. The third-battalion had been deployed in Ahlum and first-battalion on the eastern outskirts of Salzdahlum as the reserve. The regimental recce company had been deployed in Obersickte. The regimental commander had in effect planned to use the three tank battalions as a single echelon, with the motor rifle battalion as a second echelon in reserve. Forcing a breach in the British covering force's final defensive barrier and crossing the River Oker would see the regiment, and the division, up against the British main defensive positions along the River Leine. The next thirty kilometres would place them south of Hanover, deep inside West Germany. Here the division's second echelon would take over: two fresh tank regiments, supported by two regiments from 7GTD to the south. At a meeting with the regimental commander, joined by Major-General Abramov, commander of the division, the message was clear: Attack, attack, attack. Again and again, until they reached Hanover. Then, with the rest of the division committed, supported by 7 Guards Tank Division to the south, they would cross the Leine, break through the main British lines, enabling 12th Guards Tank Division, the Operational Manoeuvre Group, to exploit the breakthrough, striking deep into the British rear area, threatening the flanks of Northern Army Group's other Corps, the German to the north and the Belgian to the south. This time, the artillery and missile barrage would be for a full sixty minutes, the guns of the 700 tanks of the two divisions adding to the volume of high explosive raining down on the defenders.

Trusov jumped, his thoughts interrupted as the artillery barrage let rip, and a deluge of shells and missiles beat down on the defenders, killing both soldiers and civilians alike. Once more, army-level artillery assets had been allocated to this key sector of the front.

Crump, crump...crump.

He was joined by his gunner. "I don't envy the British, sir."

Trusov nodded slowly. "I'm with you on that, Barsukov. It must be bloody hell over there."

"Do you think they'll put up much of a fight, sir?"

Crump, crump, crump...crump...crump.

"They'll fight, but only long enough to slow us down."

"Why don't they make a stand?"

Trusov smiled. "Because there's no point. Their forces are too few to stop us. If they hold their ground, they will end up isolated and will either be defeated or be surrounded and have to surrender."

"Surely, sir, they have to stop running at some point. We'll be at their English Channel in about a week at this rate."

This time Trusov laughed and Barsukov reddened. "Oh yes, they will stop and fight. What they're doing now is just an attempt to hold us up, inflict casualties, force us to extend our logistical tail, burn up fuel and ammunition. They will stop and fight, Comrade Barsukov, and when they do, we'll be the first to know about it."

Schzoom, schzoom, schzoom...schzoom...schzoom...schzoom...schzoom, schzoom, schzoom.

They both ducked involuntarily as wave after wave of BM-21 launched, 122mm rockets streaked overhead. Fifty-four missile platforms sending over 2,000 deadly high explosive packages to swamp the two remaining combat teams of the Royal Regiment of Fusiliers Battlegroup, dug in south of Braunschweig and north of Wolfenbuttel.

"Shit. I'm glad I'm not amongst that lot."

"It's just about to get worse for them, Barsukov. We move out fast, as soon as it stops, using the air–to–ground attack as cover. Make sure Kokorev is ready."

"Will do, sir." With that, Barsukov dropped back down inside the tank and made his way to the front to chat to his fellow crewman.

Crump, crump...crump...crump...crump...crump.

The artillery assault was incessant, and Trusov actually felt sorry for the British soldiers. He knew that many of them were being killed at this exact moment in time. Every time a salvo of shells bracketed their positions, someone was in danger of injury or death.

Trusov stared at the constant flicker of lights dominating the horizon in front of him, mesmerised by the flashes as the high-explosive shells erupted all along the forward line of enemy troops. This would be the second major push they would make.

One Guards Tank Army would also be resuming its push west, threatening the southern flank of 1 British Corps and 2 Guards Tank Army menacing the northern flank; the British Army of the Rhine was under enormous pressure. The German Army was holding well in the north, defending their own area of responsibility and providing the covering force for the 1st Netherlands Corps as it moved rapidly east to occupy the positions allocated to them to defend. But, to the south, 1st Belgian Corps was struggling to get into position, due to delays in calling up reserve units and initiating full mobilisation, resulting in a weak point in Northern Army Group's southern wing. Again, the German forces were obliged to temporarily fill the gap.

Round after round pummelled the soldiers of Combat Team Alpha, dug in amongst the southern fringes of Braunschweig, and Combat Team Bravo in Wolfenbuttel. A scattering of troops also defended the wooded area that lay in between the two conurbations. 62nd Guards Tank Regiment's 2S1s fired shell after shell into the trees of the small wood that lay less than three kilometres in front of Trusov's position. Trunks were splintered and branches were severed; the troops dug in along the edge were suffocated by the sheer ferocity of the torrent that beat down on them. A battalion of eighteen BM-21s had been allocated to fire a full load of 720 rockets at that particular target. Once fired, all 720 of the M-21OF three-metre long rockets would be launched striking their target mercilessly, swamping the entire area with high-explosive fragmentation within twenty seconds of the firing being initiated. When they eventually hit, the entire length of the forest, a kilometre long and to a depth of 200 metres, erupted into a maelstrom of flying splinters of wood and, from the rockets themselves, lethal slivers of metal tore into the ground, trees and flesh alike. Trusov, although safe, held his hand up in front of his face and felt sick at the thought of himself being on the receiving end of such death and destruction. For twenty seconds, the forest and troops dug in along its edge were laced with a lethal cocktail, the onslaught unforgiving. If that wasn't enough, after two minutes of preparation, the BM-21s moved positions so they weren't exposed to counter-battery fire, and prepared to fire again. Ten minutes to reload and, twenty minutes later, Trusov witnessed the utter devastation of the wooded area in front of him. Nothing, he thought, nothing could have possibly survived that. But some did survive. Troops still alive in their holes cowered deep into their trenches, struggling to draw breath, the sound ringing in their ears, the sucking noises as they gasped inside their rubber masks, more than one soldier panicking and ripping off his S6 respirator, cursed by their comrades and NCOs alike. Luckily, the attack was not chemical, but many were killed all the same. Not a single soldier who survived left that wood without feeling shaky and sick.

Wolfenbuttel fared better. Although the rain of shells pounded the buildings into rubble, tore into their quickly prepared positions in the ground around it, the unit was spread over a much wider area. A fully mechanised infantry company, less the platoon defending the forest to the north, along with five Milan firing posts, were still capable of putting up some resistance when the attack they knew was inevitable came. The Soviet High Command had allotted Frog-7, Scud-B and BM-27 missile launchers for the main bombardment on the towns of Braunschweig and Wolfenbuttel. They had only one intention: to smash the covering force once and for all and keep the momentum of the army, of over 1,500,000 men, advancing west.

Barsukov came up alongside, and Trusov felt the shudder as Kokorev started the tank's engines. He looked at his tank commander and tapped his watch, holding five fingers in the air. "Five minutes," he mouthed.

Trusov nodded in acknowledgement. There would be no radio messages, no waving of flags in the air like they did in the early days, but his unit knew to pull out in exactly five minutes and attack.

To the north, Captain Yakovlev's recce company, two platoons of BMP and one of T-80s, would conduct a feint to the south-east of Braunschweig, distracting the enemy, also acting as 62GTR's right flank protection. The scout-car company of BRDM-2s would form a screen on the regiment's left flank, warning the unit of any enemy counter-attack. Lieutenant Colonel Aminev's third-battalion with its remaining twenty-six T-80s would strike south, under cover of a smokescreen provided by a battery of the regiment's 2S1s. His unit would try and filter through the wood to the north of Wolfenbuttel. The motorcycle section from the recce company would help guide them through. The motor rifle battalion would head straight for the centre of the wooded area, fighting their way through the battered British forces there, meeting up with 3rd Battalion's tanks. Once the wood was secured, the infantry would fulfil their role as the regiment's reserve, and remain there.

Unknown to the Soviet forces, the British infantry, the remnants of two platoons, one from Combat Team Alpha in the north and a platoon from Combat Team Bravo in the south, were already pulling back to a safe area in the rear. They had done their job – in spite of the fact that they felt like they were retreating taking their casualties with them. But they had left at least fifteen men behind, dead, some unrecognisable after the battering they had received from the Soviet rockets. The soldiers were asking – no – demanding to know where their help was from their own artillery and air force. British artillery had scored some successes in their counter-battery fire missions, but with so many targets out there and the constant need to move to ensure they weren't targeted themselves, they had little effect in significantly reducing the array of tubes and missiles aimed at their armour and infantry. The air force was in a fight for its own survival. Heavy air and missile attacks on the NATO airfields, along with Spetsnaz sabotage, had disrupted their ability to support their forward troops to any great extent. Protecting reinforcements speeding to the front, preventing their precious airfields from being made unusable and fighting off the Soviet air force that attacked in wave after wave, there was little they could do for their covering force.

The sudden silence was almost disorientating; the artillery bombardment ceased almost as one. A fug of smoke had manifested itself along an entire ninety-degree front ahead of Trusov's tank. He caught a whiff of propellant on the breeze, coming from the mass of Soviet artillery that had been firing for the last hour.

Whoosh, whoosh...whoosh, whoosh.

Trusov and Barsukov looked up at the sky-blue underbellies of two pairs of Sukhoi SU-25s as they shattered the silence that had lasted for a mere few seconds. The shoulder-mounted trapezoidal and conventional tailplane gave the jet a unique silhouette. Weapons were slung beneath the five hardpoints beneath each wing. Two carried 57mm rocket pods, more death to rain down upon the enemy. In addition, a 30mm cannon, with 250 rounds of ammunition, was located in a compartment beneath the cockpit. Nicknamed Frogfoot by NATO, the single-seat, twin-engined jet aircraft was specifically designed to provide close air support for Soviet ground forces. They would be expected to perform between eight and ten sorties a day. This was the first one of today's attacks.

"The bloody *Grachs* (Rooks) will sort them out if the artillery hasn't," crowed Barsukov.

Trusov didn't answer, but checked his watch. Thirty seconds to go. He pointed downwards to Barsukov who then slid into his gunner's position on the left.

Pulling on his padded helmet, he now had communications with Kokorev, the driver and his gunner. *"Fifteen seconds."*

"Sir," Kokorev responded.

Ten seconds. A ripple of 57mm rockets, smoke trails behind them, left the aircraft pods. Two aircraft targeted the southern edge of Braunschweig; two attacked the northern edge of the forest.

Kokorev looked up at the barrel of the tank gun above him, just to his right, and pulled on the hatch handle and heaved the driver's hatch closed.

Five seconds. Over 100 missiles, fired by the Rooks, struck their targets, laying a carpet of high explosives and shrapnel along the periphery where any remaining British troop would be waiting for the expected enemy advance.

"Go, go, go," Trusov yelled into his mouthpiece.

Kokorev peered through the three vision blocks in front of him, his left hand raising the engine-idle lever and his right foot pushing on the accelerator pedal, the T-80's 1,000-horsepower gas-turbine engine powered the tank forward. They pulled out from behind the two-storey house they had been secreted behind; their camouflage netting had been removed earlier. T-80s along the entire length of 62nd GTR front appeared from their hiding places and slowly gathered speed.

As for Trusov's battalion, Vagin's third-company was on his left,

Ivashin's company on the right, and Mahayev's out in front, followed closely by two mine-plough tanks. Earlier, during the hours of darkness, a Soviet reconnaissance patrol had identified a probable minefield. The British had laid a carpet of bar mines between the forest and Braunschweig, hoping to hold the Soviet tanks up while their Milans picked them off from the side. The engineers had just completed their survey when they were bounced by a British fighting patrol. They barely made it back to the Russian lines, losing a third of their small force on the way. Under the cover of a smokescreen, the two mine-plough tanks moved forward rapidly and started to plough a passage, the width of two tanks, through the minefield. The remaining tanks of the battalion would pass through the gap, fanning out either side, the fuel injected onto their manifolds providing additional smoke; much needed cover from the eyes of their NATO enemies.

"*Two-Zero, Two-One. One down, one down!*"

"Two-One, understood. Keep moving."

Another T-80 casualty, thought Trusov. He pushed the hatch open and climbed up so his shoulders were well out of the turret, being met by a swirl of smoke, the stench of diesel fumes nearly making him gag. The tank bounced across the open ground ahead, Kokorev heading slightly north-west as instructed. Neither he nor Kokorev could see very much at the moment. The biggest risk was driving into one of their own comrades. Travelling at about twenty-five kilometres an hour, they would step up to forty once they were through the minefield. Although he could see very little, Trusov strained his ears and could pick out the roar of engines ahead as they negotiated the occasional ditch or mound.

"Slow by five; our boys are just ahead," he informed his driver.

Looking down and to the left, past the other side of the yellow-painted auto-loader, he could see Barsukov, rocking from the hip as he moved with the motion of the tank, his eyes up against the IG42-quantum periscope sight, ready to fire on a target that presented itself. Looking down and right, the visual indicator showed that there was a sabot round loaded and ready.

"*Two-Zero, Two-One. Through the minefield. Over.*"

"Two-One, understood."

On the internal comms, he called to Kokorev, "Stop, stop, stop."

The heavyweight tank came to a halt, rocking on its suspension.

"Two-Two, Two-Three, stop, stop. Two-One, leave unit as marker; then move two, zero, zero west. Over."

"Two-One received, smoke thinning. Out."

The turret swung right as Barsukov lined the tank's gun barrel up with the likely direction of the town of Braunschweig.

"Two-Three, Two-Zero. One minute, then move through. Two, zero, zero south-west."

"Two-zero-zero, south-west."

"Two-Two, Two-Zero, wait two, then two, zero, zero north-west."

"Two-Zero, Two-Two. Yes. One unit dropping out, mechanical."

Shit, thought Trusov. But he couldn't complain. They had been exceptionally lucky in keeping most of their tanks on the road. He scanned what little he could see ahead; but the smoke was definitely thinning out. He felt a slight southern breeze on his left cheek, indicating the smokescreen would move across the town, but expose his left flank to the forest.

Boo,boo,boo,boo,boom. Boo,boo,boo,boo,boom.

A ripple of explosions came from their front left and right flank as Frogfoot ground-attack aircraft laid into the defenders yet again. Any survivors from the previous artillery, missile and air attacks kept their heads well and truly down.

Good, Trusov thought, that would keep the British gunners' heads down. He could see more and more clearly in front of him. Although cover was a good thing to have, they also needed to see where they were going and pick out targets that may threaten their advance. He tapped his fingers sequentially on the edge of the turret hatchway, listening intently for any sound of movement. Off to his front right, he could not only hear tanks moving but could also see the shadowy shapes about 100 metres away, heading at speed for the gap through the minefields.

"Standby, standby," he called to Kokorev.

Barsukov heard the call and turned the turret so it was now at a forty-five degree angle to the left, the likely area where he would find a target and where the smokescreen would disappear first. He was nervous, as was his comrade up front in the driver's seat. Stationary, they would be a sitting target; he would be pleased once they were on the move again.

Off to the left, Trusov heard the whine of gas-turbine engines as Two-Three started their journey towards the gap they must pass through. He caught a flicker of movement out of the corner of his left eye as one of Savva's tanks sped across their front, not more than twenty metres ahead. He resisted the temptation to order Kokorev forward, knowing there would be a high risk of a collision.

"Two-Zero, Two-Two. Through."

Trusov did not acknowledge; too much radio chatter was unnecessary. The tank company raced west, through the gap; then dispersed to their planned positions, spreading out to make less of a target.

"Two-Zero, Two-Three. Through, deploying."

Savva would be taking his company south-west, covering the battalion's left flank.

The turret of Trusov's command tank moved slightly, Barsukov's impatience telling.

"Keep it still," snapped Trusov. "Kokorev, pull forward slowly."

The engine built up power, Kokorev manipulating the accelerator, engine idle and the gear shift on his right, and the tank built up speed. Peering through the vision blocks, he too could see dark shadows ahead as they caught up with Savva's company and made their way through the minefield. One of Mahayev's tanks and one of the mine-plough tanks marked the entrance, the commanders in the turrets waving them forward.

"Go for it," ordered Trusov.

Kokorev didn't need to have the order repeated. He put his foot down, taking the tank up through the gears, the battle tank lurching forwards, ripping up the earth beneath its tracks. Savva's company cut left as Kokorev manoeuvred his tank out of the gap on the other side. They were followed by the guard tank which quickly overtook them to catch up with its mother unit.

Trusov was almost blinded as they drove out of the smokescreen into full daylight. The tanks had now stopped generating smoke, ready to use their engines for their true purpose: to power the T-80s into battle. Leaving the rapidly dissolving smokescreen behind them, Trusov's battalion fanned out. He could see the forest ahead, now occupied by their motor rifle battalion. The battalion had encountered no resistance. In fact, the biggest challenge was not the British army but negotiating the shattered ground with their BMP-2s. The motor rifle battalion commander, Lachkov, would have been astounded if there had been anyone left alive in this hellhole, to have prevented his men from taking their objective: the western edge of the forest where the River Oker would be a mere 2,000 metres away.

The T-80 lifted up as a shell exploded less than twenty metres away and rocked back down, Kokorev fighting with the two steering sticks to get it back in control. Trusov ducked as clods of earth pounded the tank and fragments zinged off the turret, and he quickly dropped down into the compartment closing the hatch after him. He peered through the right-hand vision-block and could see columns of earth being thrown into the air as shell after shell peppered the ground around his battalion. It was the British army's turn to retaliate and hammer the advancing Soviet forces. Reports started to come in from the R-173 radio transceiver. Two-company on the right flank had lost one tank to artillery and a second to a Milan missile.

Trusov urged Kokorev on. If he could get two-company into the northern edge of the forest, facing the southern outskirts of Braunschweig, one-company on the western edge of the forest on the right flank of the motor rifle battalion, the third tank battalion would be to their far left and three-company in reserve behind, he would be in a good position to support the advance and the crossing of the River Oker. The entire 62nd Guards Tank Regiment of seventy-eight tanks, its motor rifle battalion and its twenty-four remaining BMP-2s would support 248th Guards Motor Rifle Regiment in making a crossing. All of the regiment's eighty-two BMP-2s and twenty-six T-80s would be joined by the reconnaissance battalion. Heavy amphibious pontoons, such as the GSP ferries, along with PTS and K-61s, were already speeding to the front, ready to force a daytime crossing. A PMP pontoon bridge company would enable the Soviets to put in place a substantial floating bridge to move heavier units across and get to grips with the enemy. Heavy artillery, air-to-ground support from the air force, missiles and rockets had been committed to make this a fast passage.

It wouldn't be the only crossing. Further south, 7 Guards Tank Division would be doing the same, increasing the pressure on the thinly spread British 4th Armoured Division trying to stem the flow. The British would continue to fight a delaying battle. The combat teams were already withdrawing from Braunschweig and Wolfenbuttel, to take up positions on the western bank of the river, leaving any further fighting to the West German reserve forces. No effort would be made by the Soviet army to enter the major conurbations; not yet, at least. But follow-on forces would ensure the security of the rear. Two additional elements would help swing the day in the Soviets' favour, the dreaded Hip and Hind gunships supporting a full motor rifle battalion, provided by the 61st Guards Tank Regiment that would be landed on the opposite bank by scores of Hip and Hook transport helicopters. Trusov was confident they would be able to continue their advance west by early afternoon.

Chapter 4

0410 6 July 1984. East of Berlin, East Germany.
The Black Effect −2 days.

"Jacko," Bradley hissed into Jacko's ear, his hand close to the sleeping soldier's mouth, ready to clamp it shut should he shout out or make the slightest noise. Jacko's eyes opened and he was immediately alert, sensing the urgency in Bradley's voice.

"What is it?"

"Listen."

They both kept silent and still, the sudden sound of a dog barking in the distance.

"It's just a dog," Jacko hissed back.

Then there was a second bark, deeper, followed by a third.

"Shit."

"We need to bug out, and quickly. Pack your stuff and I'll sort mine and the radio."

"What about this?" asked Jacko, indicating the camouflaged mesh frame that spanned the space above them, keeping the foliage above at bay.

"Leave it, we don't have time."

Two dogs barked again, sounding closer, and Jacko quickly exited his sleeping bag, immediately flattened it and rolled it up, squeezing it into the haversack. Although cramped, they worked speedily side by side. Speed was of the essence, the barking dogs the only motivation they needed.

"How far?"

"Less than a K, I would say. Here in ten," responded Bradley. "Finish up here; then bring your stuff out. I'm going to take a look around."

Bradley poked his head outside and looked to the right as the headlights of a truck flickered by on the autobahn, causing him to flinch. He blinked. He had lost a portion of his night vision, but could see enough until it improved again. The Browning pistol dug into his side as he got up, a comfortable feeling, one of security. He pulled it out of the holster clipped to his belt on the left-hand side of his barrack trousers. It was loaded, with a round up the spout and the safety applied. He dragged his Bergen out of the hide, leaving it at the entrance, and then crept along the upper edge of the railway embankment, making his way west until he came to the edge of the Berlin ring road. It was four ten and there was very little traffic on the road. When it was busy, it was usually long convoys of supplies and troops heading west to join their comrades doing battle against NATO. Civilians were rarely seen on the road, confined to their homes no doubt while the East German military machine went about its business.

Bradley peered across the motorway, turning his head slightly so that his right ear could catch any sound that would be a threat to them. Lights flickered through the trees as the enemy played their torches around the area, making sure they didn't step onto any hazards. They were looking for them; he had no doubts. The noise from the dogs was getting steadily louder. If he had to hazard a guess, he would say there were three tracker dogs on their scent, and he estimated they would be here in less than ten minutes. And to make matters worse, they were on his side of the embankment. They were obviously doing a sweep along the railway line. But why? Were they looking for saboteurs? Or were they looking for him and Jacko? Or were they just plain old Transport Politzei?

His head snapped round as he heard the bark of another dog off to the left. He looked to the front again. It was clear. He raised his body up higher so he could look back along the road to the other side of the bridge that crossed the railway line. He was startled, seeing more lights. Another collection of torch beams stabbed the darkness as a group, probably soldiers along with a couple of dogs, were moving along the edge of the autobahn. *Fuck*, he thought and immediately dropped back down. They were searching both railway embankments. It was the two of them they were after. They must have found the Range Rover.

He duckwalked back to the hide and pushed his head inside. "We need to go now, Jacko. They'll be here in minutes. There's a group practically opposite us."

"How close?"

"Bloody close. Shift."

"I'm done."

Jacko joined him outside, and they both hoisted their packs, considerably lighter now they had used up some of their supplies, Bradley's being the heaviest with the Clansman radio. Jacko dropped down, pointing to the lights of the soldiers crossing the autobahn on the opposite side of the railway line. They were safe for now, but the soldiers' friends on this side of the embankment wouldn't be far away, and the two groups could quickly join up if needed. The two dogs were barking frenetically now, sensing something, urged on by their handlers. They would soon pick up the scent of the two soldiers. Then all hell would break loose.

Bradley grabbed Jacko's arm and pulled him away from the edge and took the lead, taking them east along the edge of the thicket, the same undergrowth where their hide was secreted. It would no longer be a secret, that was for sure. After fifty metres, they found the gap that they had identified during an earlier reconnaissance, when they were logging all the exit routes they could use should they get bounced. Both passed through it, going north, deeper into the forest and further away from the railway line and the dogs. A dog barked, sounding closer, directly opposite the hide they had just left. They could very well be across the railway line in a matter of minutes. The two groups were converging. Soon the hunt would be on.

Bradley picked up the pace, keeping a northerly direction, Jacko tagging along behind him, stumbling occasionally, his lanky legs getting the better of him. The pace got quicker and quicker, speed more important than caution. Bradley broke into double time, his Bergen jumping slightly on his back, secured when he pulled the straps much tighter, shifting the weight high onto his shoulders. The small compass glowed slightly in his hand as he checked they were on course, turning north-west, keeping the autobahn about 100 metres off their left side. East of them were ploughed fields, a stretch of open ground in the centre of the large forest, an area a kilometre long by 500 metres wide. To cross that, they would expose themselves to their pursuers with nowhere to hide and leave a trail of footprints that the dog handlers could easily follow by torchlight. At least in this direction, they would have some tree cover.

Bradley and Jacko stopped suddenly and looked over their shoulders as they heard a commotion, dogs barking wildly with excitement, soldiers shouting, the disturbance coming from the area of the hide they had just vacated. The dogs' noses would be twitching and sniffing, their senses working overtime. It wouldn't take them long to pick up their spoor and start to follow.

"They've found our spot, Jacko. Let's get the hell out of here."

Bradley sprinted off, continuing north-west, now at a run, tips of branches flicking against his arms as he weaved in and out of the trees, the sound of dogs barking growing louder, spurring him on. The shouts of handlers also increased in volume, keeping the dogs, yanking at their leashes, under control. The group had been joined by more canines, no doubt from the other side of the railway line. Bradley pushed his body hard, knowing the soldiers would be invigorated now they had found the hiding place of the spies they had been searching for, for the past twenty-four hours. The soldiers and the dogs would also be in a flat-out run. Bradley's only hope was to keep the two of them moving; keep one step ahead of their pursuers.

A flicker of light caught Bradley's eye; vehicle headlights on the autobahn to their left, at least two or three trucks, he surmised. Reinforcements. Matters had just got worse. They were at least getting further and further away from the railway line, and starting to put some distance between them and the soldiers behind them. There was a squeal of brakes as more vehicles pulled over onto the hard shoulder of the autobahn, disgorging MFS troops to join in the hunt.

Bradley stopped suddenly, Jacko ploughing into the back of him, as they arrived at a road, Buchhorster Strasse. Left along the road would take them under the autobahn, right to the village of Schonwalde. He did a quick scan left and right; then called to Jacko, "Let's go."

They pounded across the metalled road, the sound hollow, turning back on a northern heading, moving away from the roads and deeper into the forest before they got boxed in, although Bradley felt sure it was too late. He could hear Jacko's laboured breathing behind him, the bark of the dogs indicating the hunters had closed the gap again, keeping pace with them.

"They can't be more than 500 metres behind," Bradley called back to him. "Jacko."

"Yeah."

"We stop...in five."

"Right."

"Drop Bergen's...take scoot packs."

"Gotcha."

"We need...to pick up...speed."

"I'm...fucked."

Bradley dropped back alongside him as they made their way down a wide path through the trees. He placed a hand on Jacko's shoulder. "Come on, Jacko...your lanky legs...and skinny frame...can run faster than this."

Jacko nodded his head, spit and froth flying from his mouth as his breathing got faster and faster. Encouraged, he lengthened his stride and picked up speed. Bradley stretched out his stride and returned to the front to lead them both on again. They continued north for another six minutes, crossing a track that ran south-west to north-east, Bradley taking them through and around the trees. His intention was to keep moving, remain under cover of the trees for long as possible. He knew they had to lose the dogs. If the war dogs stayed on their tail, the two runners would eventually run out of steam. Although the dogs and their handlers would also tire, additional troops would already be closing in, with fresh dogs ready to take over the manhunt. If only they could get to the farm he knew was a mere two kilometres away, they might stand a chance. Get amongst some cow muck, or silage, overpower the scent of their bodies, make it hard for even the sensitive noses of the dogs to differentiate between the smell of animal waste and men.

Whop, whop, whop, whop, whop.

"Down!" yelled Bradley.

They both dived beneath the canopy of a tree, the helicopter flying directly over their heads before turning left and flying west. Another could be heard off to the east. The net was closing in; it didn't look good. The Tegler Fliesstal was a large forest for them to hide in, but with helicopters, troop carriers and hundreds of police and soldiers, it was only a matter of time.

But Bradley wouldn't give up. "We dump the Bergens here."

They shrugged the heavyweight rucksacks off their shoulders and quickly extracted their scoot packs: smaller packs containing essential items such as water, ammunition, food and some medical supplies. Bradley still persisted with carrying the radio.

"Come on, let's go." Bradley pulled Jacko up from the floor and they set off again, the sound of a helicopter to their right and the barking of the dogs behind ringing in their ears.

They picked up speed. Although panic had not yet set in, they were starting to feel that they were running for their lives. Having shed their Bergens, the two men were running hard and fast. Bradley heard Jacko stumble, heard the cracking of branches and twigs as he crashed into some low-lying branches, catching a glancing blow off a tree, crying out as his shoulder rolled over the lumpy ground. Turning back, Bradley was soon crouched at his comrade's side and could just make out the grimace on Jacko's face, his bared teeth showing in the half light of the forest, indicative of the pain Jacko was in.

Bradley looked about him, noticing that the dogs were quieter, tiring perhaps, saving their energy for when they got within striking distance of their quarry.

"It's my bloody ankle, hurts like fuck."

"Here, grab my arm." Bradley braced his legs, a smell of mulch and pine reaching his nostrils as he leant over and offered his hand.

"Aaagh, my bloody shoulder!" He hoisted Jacko up, the man crying out again as he put weight on his ankle.

The barking of the dogs suddenly picked up again, seeming much closer now, perhaps getting a whiff of their scent, driving them to pull their handlers ever faster.

"The dogs are getting closer. We need to shift."

"I'm ready."

They headed off again, but Jacko made a mere ten metres before crying out in pain as he jarred his badly twisted, if not broken, ankle. He was going nowhere. Before Bradley could say anything, the soldiers suddenly appeared as shadowy figures not more than 300 metres away, a gap in the trees giving them a view of Bradley's and Jacko's silhouettes.

"Fuck, run, Jacko."

Bradley jogged sideways, watching his comrade's poor attempt at running at speed, his ankle giving way again and sending shockwaves of pain through Jacko's nervous system. Even knowing the enemy were in striking distance was not enough. Shots rang out.

Zip...crack. Zip...crack.

"Run, Jacko," he screamed.

Bradley dropped down on one knee, pulled his pistol from the holster at his side, flicked the safety catch, aimed in the direction of the advancing shadows, tried to steady his still heaving body, his hands shaking, and fired a double tap. Now, at 200 metres, he knew the shot was pointless. But it may give Jacko a chance.

Thunk, thunk. Two more shots rang out, hitting the trunk of a tree.

Zip...crack. Zip...crack.

"Ughh."

Bradley turned his head to see Jacko tumble forwards, the momentum of his attempted sprint forcing him into a forward roll, hitting the ground hard.

Zip...crack.

"*Halten Sie! Halten Sie!*" The soldiers screamed the order to halt. Less than 200 metres away now, the dogs were barking and yelping, straining at their leashes, forcing their handlers into a sprint.

Bradley rushed to Jacko's side. His friend's body was limp. Although he couldn't see Jacko's glazed-over, staring eyes, a hand over his mouth didn't reveal the warmth of his breath, an indicator that his fellow soldier was dead. He couldn't dally, got up from his crouch, fired another two shots, and ran for his life, jinking left and right, changing direction as snappily as he had seen any hare do.

Zip, crack.

"*Halten Sie! Halten Sie!*"

Zip, crack.

He weaved in and out of the trees, trying to spoil their aim, using the trunks for cover, the occasional bullet splintering a tree or chopping off small branches, twigs and leaves showering the escaping soldier. Faster and faster, arms pumping, his breath rasping, lactic acid burning his muscles as he tried desperately to outrun his pursuers.

The firing stopped. The noise of the dogs yelping and barking increased once they got the scent of blood as the soldiers of the *Volksarmee* established the condition of the escapee they had just shot. Leaving a couple of soldiers to watch over the dead body, they continued the chase, fresh dogs having been brought forward from the autobahn, the dogs jumping forwards, dragging their handlers in the direction of fresh quarry. They headed off after their prey, knowing Bradley would be tiring.

He was tired. Only a deep sense of fear kept his legs moving, almost robotic-like, occasionally stumbling drunkenly as his thighs got tighter and tighter. All but sprinting, he was brought to a sudden halt as he stormed straight into an irrigation ditch, throwing his left shoulder hard against the far side ditch, a wall of stacked earth, the water up to his waist. A rank smell assailed his nostrils. His mind worked feverishly as the howls of the dogs got closer and louder. The radio. He needed to ditch the Clansman radio. He clawed his way out of the ditch, slipped off the scoot pack and pushed it, including the radio within, down into the repugnant quagmire he had just left. He turned a sharp right and headed along the ditch, avoiding the clearing to the north, wanting to get back amongst the trees further to the east, now he was beyond the clearing that had prevented them going in that direction earlier. His boots squelched as he ran, his trousers slapping against his legs, the howl of the dogs urging him on. He would run until he collapsed, abject terror now keeping him going. Deep down inside, he felt despair slowly rising to the surface, knowing the German *Volksarmee*, *Volkspolitzei* and the MFS, the military state police, the dreaded Stasi, would be setting up control points on every road or lane in the surrounding area, despatching more and more search teams to close in on him, pinning him down into a smaller and tighter area.

Whop, whop, whop, whop.

A helicopter reared up in front of him as it came to the hover, the downdraught bringing Bradley to a halt as he shielded his face, a powerful searchlight beam blinding him, shifting to keep the runner in its glare.

Thump! A heavy weight struck him between the shoulder blades as the forty-five kilogram Alsatian war dog ploughed into the back of Bradley, knocking him to the ground. The dog immediately bit into his victim's back, gripping clothing and flesh between its large teeth, twisting and dragging the body towards him. Bradley let out an involuntary scream as the dog's jaws shifted position, biting deeper into his back. A second dog joined in the fray, grasping the arm Bradley was about to use to help get himself up; gripping the limb between its teeth, grinding its powerful jaws together in a chewing motion, crushing Bradley's arm with such force, that the radius and ulna actually touched. The noise of the helicopter failed to drown out the growls of the wild animals and his own screams. Bradley grabbed his pistol with his free arm, pointed it in the direction of one of the dogs, his eyes still blinded by the searchlight above, and pulled the trigger. He heard a satisfying yelp as the dog dropped, the bullet having passed through the top of its shoulder blades, and he felt the pressure released from his arm. He didn't hear the soldier or see the boot swinging towards his head, but felt the pain as it struck his temple. Shooting stars and bright lights were the last things he saw as he passed into unconsciousness.

Chapter 5

0420 6 July 1984. 25th Tank Division, 20 Guards Army.
Michendorf, East Germany.
The Black Effect –2 days.

The divisional columns had completed the first stage of their long-distance march, and had settled down for a long halt, if that was what you could call it. Some units had arrived late afternoon, early evening; others had driven into their final rest area at just after ten. But there was no immediate respite for the various packets: wheeled, trailer-loads and tracked vehicles. The wheeled packet was dispersed into various hides around the Potsdammer Wald, part of a large forested area fifteen-kilometres south of Potsdam, that surrounded Michendorf. They were then ordered to check their equipment, refuel their vehicles and complete any servicing requirements. Then, and only then, were the troops provided with their first hot meal in twenty-four hours.

The 300-plus T-64s, transported by semi-trailers, were split across a much wider area, but the areas had good access to the road network as, once rested, they would be back on the road. Stavka were screaming for reinforcements to be in place on time to support the war effort to the west. The pressure was on for the army to achieve what it had promised. A third area had been allocated to tracked vehicles, such as the BMP-2s from the tank regiments, and the tracked surface-to-air missile carriers that were also deploying to protect the convoys from any possible air attack. The self-propelled guns of the artillery regiment and the engineer vehicles, GSPs, K-61s and PTSs, joined them. The largest group of all, the wheeled element of the division, had been allotted a sizeable forested area surrounding Beelitz. The road network was considered to be good, and the trucks would not be held up when it started all over again in the morning.

That time had come and the officers and NCOs, particularly the *Praporshchik*, the warrant officers, drove the men mercilessly to ensure they would be ready. Their next 150 kilometre march would see them in the area of Helmstedt, getting into more dangerous territory, where they would be closer to the enemy and any deep interdiction strikes. Even when in Helmstedt, they would still have nearly seventy-kilometres until they reached Salzgitter. The final deployment area, where the Stavka deemed they would deploy before being committed to the battle.

0430 6 July 1984. 8th Guards Tank Division. Kuznica, Poland.
The Black Effect −2 days.

To say the activity at Kuznica, Poland, was hectic would be an understatement. Here, after a journey of some 900 kilometres, the trains carrying the division had to stop. Here, they were in the process of switching from the Soviet gauge to the European gauge. The process of switching the undercarriages was time-consuming and would take at least two hours per train. For some of the routes, this change was not required. On one route, L'vov, Krakow, Katowice, Wroclaw to East Germany, for example, a wide-gauge track already existed. The first steam train, puffing clouds of black smoke and white steam pulled out of the sidings, a long journey ahead of them. The next stop for the thirty-six trains transporting the division west was the railroad bridge over the Vistula, another 400 kilometres away.

Chapter 6

The M2-Bradley, armoured infantry fighting vehicle, from the 11th ACR changed position again, the Commander on edge and feeling exposed as they watched over the engineers working on the bridge where it crossed the River Fulda, west of the town itself. The turret swivelled and the 25mm Bushmaster chain gun covered the arc that had been allocated to its crew.

The three engineers lifted the eighty-kilogram Medium Atomic Demolition Munition, a MADM, carried in a heavy backpack, off the back of a Gamma Goat, a six-by-six, amphibious wheeled vehicle. This particular type of weapon was a W-45, a multi-purpose nuclear warhead developed in the early 1960s. With its nuclear fission core, called the 'Robin primary', it would generate a half a kiloton yield, equivalent to 500 tons of TNT. German Jaeger, reserve units, had been rounding up German civilians throughout the night, forcing them out of their homes, urging them to move west to safety. Not only was the Soviet army practically on their doorstep, but once this particular bomb exploded, there would be little left of their homes for up to a radius of quarter of a kilometre.

They set it up next to one edge of the bridge, in the centre of the span, and the lieutenant in command set the cypher for the code-decoder component, linked to the firing unit. When it exploded, it would devastate the bridge, tearing it apart and preventing its use by the Soviet armour that was fighting its way to the banks of the River Fulda. It wouldn't delay them for long, such was the capability of the bridging equipment and engineering units of the Soviet army, but it would at least delay the enemy that little bit longer.

Private First-Class Larry Poole applied a touch of power to the tracks
and edged the sixty-seven ton M1-Abrams forward, the 105mm barrel
pointing in between a few saplings along the edge of the railway line
running north to south in front of them.

"Stop," called Staff Sergeant Kyle Lewis, the commander of
the tank and the second in command of the platoon. "That'll do it,
Poole. Shut her down."

The engine was turned off and SSGT Lewis checked his arc
of fire. A-platoon, Anvil, was situated along the western side of the
railway line, on the north-eastern edge of the village Kerzell. Only
three tanks now; one had been destroyed during the initial attack by
the Soviet forces that pushed their way into West Germany and were
now at the very outskirts of the town of Fulda and in places further
north, crossing the River Fulda to continue their advance west. They
had pushed the US forces, the 11th Cavalry Regiment, the Black
Horse Regiment, twenty-five kilometres back and were now on the
doorstep of the Fulda Gap ready to push the final 100 kilometres
that would take them directly to the German city of Frankfurt.
If the Soviet army got in amongst the slowly consolidating US
reserve forces arriving into theatre, were able to attack and destroy
ammunition and supply dumps, and destroy the airfields being used
by the US and West German air forces, the entire war would take a
turn for the worst for US V Corps and split CENTAG, separating it
from NORTHAG and cutting off the 2nd German Corps from its
Army command.

Lewis called down an order to his crew, and the gunner, Corporal
Emery, and loader, PFC Peeger, clambered out and started to unpack
the camouflage netting to spread over their tank and protect it from
the prying eyes of the Soviet air force.

Lewis rubbed his eyes and ran his hands across his stubbled chin.
"The guys could do with a coffee. See what you can do, Larry."

His pale-faced driver joined him on the turret. "Sure, Staff
Sergeant, we're all ready for one, I think."

Lewis looked at his driver, his face even paler than usual, with
sunken eyes and faint black circles starting to form beneath. "It will
do us all good. But don't stray too far. Take it in turns if you need

46

a piss, but be ready to get back in double-quick time. We don't know when Popov will be here, but they won't be far away."

"Sure, Staff Sergeant."

Poole clambered across the tank to acquire the makings of a brew, and Lewis picked up his binos from the turret and surveyed the area ahead. He could hear the thumps and claps of explosions coming from the east. They had been almost pulverised in the initial onslaught. His squadron had suffered badly, his platoon getting off lightly, losing only one tank. The other two platoons had lost two tanks each; one from each platoon had been destroyed by a mixture of artillery fire and Hind-D attack helicopters, and the remaining two were mobile, but incapable of firing their main weapons. At this very moment, the two M1-Abrams were racing back to be repaired so they would be able to get back into the fight. He heard a rustle of netting being pulled up behind him.

"Sorry, Staff Sergeant, can you pull this over?"

Lewis grabbed the netting, pulled it up over his head; then Corporal Emery grabbed it and pulled it down the front of the turret, the other crewman placing long, thin poles beneath to push the netting up and out, disguising the shape of the tank. Once the next fight started, if they had time, it would be secured again so as not to interfere with the tank's ability to fight.

"Once you've finished," he shouted to them, "both of you grab two hours' kip. Poole and I will keep watch."

"Cheers, Staff Sergeant. I'm knackered," responded Emery.

Lewis rubbed his eyes again; then ran his finger round his neck between his skin and uniform, topped with his MOPP suit. The Mission Oriented Protective Posture suit would protect him, and his crew, from the toxic environment of a chemical or nuclear attack. They were currently on MOPP level 2: suit and boots were to be worn, and their gloves and mask carried at all times. Although it would provide him with protection against a chemical attack, the downside was that he was hot, dirty, smelly and uncomfortable. He and his crew were close to exhaustion.

After the massive artillery bombardment conducted by the Soviet artillery guns, missile and rocket launchers, which lasted over an hour, they had withdrawn in a swirl of dust and smoke, shocked and shaken, leaving behind a burning M1-Abrams with their friends inside. They hadn't fired a single shot, and Lewis had had to lambaste his crew and drive them hard to get them back into being an effective unit. They had driven backwards almost blindly, passing through Second Squadron who would hold the ground while they withdrew. They then passed through Third Squadron, and only then could the platoon, along with the rest of the troop, reorientate themselves, pull themselves together, identify which units were missing, and dig in to take their turn to slow the advancing Soviet army that was attempting to brush them aside as if they didn't exist.

After the other two squadrons had pulled back through their positions, it was their turn to be on the front line again. This time though, due to the Soviet advance losing some of its way, and even though the Abraham's 105mm guns had a hard time punching through the armour of the enemy's T-64Bs, they had scored their first hit, the crew elated. Then they again withdrew; Soviet artillery tracking their escape, helicopters hunting them down. The Vulcans, self-propelled air defence vehicles, did their best to retaliate, but half a dozen were taken out by the swarm of Hind-Ds that came out of nowhere, often attacking both them and the tanks from behind. The crew had another success, taking out a T-64B and a BMP-1 Mechanised Infantry Combat Vehicle. Once the battle had moved into the undulating area, deeper into the forests, the Soviet BMP-1 MICVs were finding it difficult to use their AT-3 Sagger anti-tank missiles, which were situated just above the 73mm gun. The confines of the terrain often meant that distances were too short, or the wires trailing behind got caught and snapped, leaving the missile to go out of control. This constant fire, move, fire, move and fire had continued up until nine in the evening, when they finally got a respite from Soviet ground-attack aircraft and artillery. But their work was far from finished: refuelling, rearming, minor repairs and maintenance. On top of that, there was sentry duty, always on the alert for a Soviet sneak attack. They knew that at least one bridge had been destroyed. When they felt, as well as heard, the nuclear explosion that devastated the bridge near Fulda and the infrastructure around it, it gave them a feeling of satisfaction that they had deprived the enemy of an easy crossing. They weren't able to see the iconic plume of smoke and gases, but they certainly saw the flash light up the sky and felt its destructive power.

Lewis peered through his binos, lines of netting and plastic foliage obscuring his vision at times, and he scanned the ground ahead. The other side of the railway line were the built-up areas about five kilometres south of the town of Fulda. In front were

Eichenzell and Loschenrod; immediately south of their position, Hattenhof; south-east, a slab of forest; north and north-west, the large forest of Kerzeller Lass-Wald; and further south of Hattenhof, about four kilometres from Kerzell, more forested areas.

The problem for the Soviets, he knew, was not only the dense forest and undulating ground, but heights of up to 500 metres, impassable by heavy main battle tanks, or even MICVs for that matter. Their troop was covering the approach to Kerzell. One platoon to the south, on the other side of the L3430, were providing a watch over the Bundesstrasse 40 that continued east into the E-45, an ideal route to bring Soviet armour quickly west, his platoon to the north. A third platoon was actually astride Bundestrasse 40 itself and a fourth platoon was in reserve. Two hours ago, a battered cavalry squadron had withdrawn to the rear and the 3rd Armoured Cavalry Squadron, holding the line, was being hit again and again as it fought desperately and bravely to hold the enemy back.

Lewis turned his head as he heard the familiar sound of M1-Abrams moving in the distance.

"Is that 68th Regiment, Staff Sergeant?" asked Poole as he clambered alongside his tank commander, handing him a mug of strong black coffee.

"I reckon. Thanks. The boys got some chow?"

"No, they were too tired to eat."

"Ow."

"It's a bit hot."

"Bugger off."

"They'll make a big difference though, won't they? A full battalion of these babies, I mean," Poole said, patting the sides of the armoured turret.

"Oh, they'll make a difference all right. Blocking the forward part of the Gap will give 3rd Armoured and 8th Mech Division a chance to get into position."

"They hit us and we pull back again?"

Lewis turned and looked at his driver. "Not this time, Larry. It's now time to start digging our feet in. Frankfurt's about 100 klicks from here."

"That's still a long way."

"At twenty-five kilometres a day, providing they can maintain the momentum, they could be at the city in four days."

"Shit."

"Yes, shit. So, we've got to hold them."

"Quite right, Troop," added the voice of Lieutenant Jefferson, the platoon commander, as he clambered onto the tank.

"Coffee sir?" asked Poole. "It's a fresh brew."

"Just had one, thanks, Poole."

"If you'll excuse me, sir, Staff Sergeant, I'll take stag at the front of the tank." With that, the driver slid down the glacis and dropped off the front, turned the corner and rested his back against the tracks of the M1, checking his service pistol was loaded and handy. He should have the tank's only M16, but he would get it once the platoon commander had gone.

"Your track up to scratch, Troop?"

"Of course it is, LT, you know me well enough by now."

"Yeah, yeah. Just asking. Make sure your guys are on the ball. The squadron commander reckons they will be here by tonight, if not sooner. I suggest you keep your crew inside the track. There's going to be a lot of shit coming our way."

Lewis studied his platoon-commander. His face still had the appearance of being soft-skinned, that even dabs of cammo paint could not hide. But the puppy fat seemed to have disappeared overnight. Their first taste of battle, and twenty-four hours effectively on the run, had transformed the boy into an officer in command of a platoon of tanks and their crews.

"Good point, LT, I'll call them in shortly. Seems 1st Battalion are getting into position."

"They've had a platoon here since this morning. The rest are manoeuvring into position now."

"They'll make a difference."

"If they, with our help, can screen the Fulda Gap, it will give the 3rd and 8th a good chance to prepare their positions."

The sound of armoured vehicles moving drew their attention towards the activity behind them and they twisted around to take a look.

"That will be the 533rd MI battalion."

"Think they'll be much use, LT?"

An MLQ34 TACJAM of the 533rd Military Intelligence Battalion made its way north, heading for higher ground where it could jam the enemy's communications. A trailer with a generator onboard was being towed behind, to handle the high electrical demand of the jamming equipment soon to be put to use.

50

"Hey, Staff Sergeant, I'll take whatever they've got. At worst case, they can pull a gun."

Lewis laughed. Maybe the youngster had a sense of humour after all.

0730 6 July 1984. East of the Frankfurt area, West Germany.
The Black Effect −2 days.

The military policeman, standing next to his VW 181 Jeep, waved the M1 Abrams of the 1st Battalion, 64th Armoured Regiment, 3rd (US) Armoured Division, the Spearhead Division, past him. The majority of the division had gone this way the previous day. This battalion was following up the rear ensuring the security of the lengthy logistical tail that was growing ever bigger and ever longer as the battle raged further east, and more and more troops and supplies came from the US and Great Britain. He and the rest of *2 Kompanie, Feldjagerbataillon 70* were helping to facilitate the movement of thousands of American troops now piling into Europe.

Under the control of the United States Air Force's Military Air Command, five Boeing 747s and four C-141 Starlifters had landed at the Frankfurt-main in the last six hours, disembarking over 1,000 men and their personal equipment. At the reactivated Wiesbaden-Erbenheim Air Base, over sixty flights, that had flown non-stop over the Atlantic, including the huge C-5A Galaxy transport aircraft, carrying over 5,000 men and 1,000 tons of supplies, had been landing every couple of minutes, disgorging their loads, refuelling, then taking off again for the return flight. Earlier in the day, ten C-130 Hercules transport aircraft had flown in from Dallas, Texas, and US fighter aircraft were moving to European airfields to be in a better position to defend this vast armada reinforcing NATO forces in West Germany.

Reinforcements weren't just coming in by air; many of America's reinforcements were coming by sea. Sea vessels Meteor, Comet, Callaghan and Cygnus had delivered nearly 100,000 tons of equipment to the European continent and were already on their way back to the States to pick up more. The United States Navy Ship, USNS Algol, a roll-on roll-off ship, with the capability to carry and offload the equipment of an entire armoured infantry battalion, had also just docked in Antwerp. The ship had cruised flat out to deliver its load, taking only four days to get from Texas in the US to Antwerp's port in Belgium. From there, equipment would be transported on railway flat cars to their final assembly areas. One of eight strategic sealift vessels, the cargo hold of the Algol had a series of decks connected by ramps so vehicles could be driven out of the storage areas for rapid loading and unloading. With twin cranes aft and amidships, it was capable of lifting fifty tons and thirty-five tons respectively. At 280 metres in length and capable of carrying 700 vehicles, including tanks, trucks and helicopters, it was a much needed asset for Military Sealift Command.

The US Army was on the move. V US Corps, a key force in Central Army Group, was making headway into its preparations to defend West German soil. CENTAG had to cover the ground from just south of Bonn, down to the Austrian border in the south, with the 3rd West German Corps in the north; then V US Corps, VII US Corps and the 2nd West German Corps covering the entire border of Czechoslovakia and butting up against Austria.

The military policeman's arm was getting weary; the constant flick of his wrist indicating to the convoys that they should keep moving. A new tank battalion started to thunder by. Having received their tanks from the 'Prepositioning Of Material Configured in Unit Sets', POMCUS, depot at Kaiserslautern, the 1st Tank Battalion, 77th Armoured Regiment, 4th (US) Mechanised Infantry Division was also on the move east. The first reinforcements to arrive for V Corps, the battalion were being dispatched to the front line immediately. The rest of the division was either offloading, drawing their equipment from a POMCUS site, or still on the water or in the air.

The tank commanders waved confidently at the German military and civilian police as their M-60s growled past. The occasional German civilian returned the wave. But, if the tank crews could see their faces close up, they would see the fear in their eyes. Another M60A1 rattled past, closely followed by an M113A2 artillery observation APC.

Chapter 7

The sentry in full battledress, combat DPMs bedecked with foliage, emerged from behind a tree, his self-loading rifle, SLR, unwavering as he challenged the soldier approaching the complex he was guarding. "Halt, who goes there?"

"Friend," responded the soldier.

"Advance one, and be recognised."

The soldier moved slowly forward, his SMG machine gun held in his right hand, pointing downwards so as not to spook the guard.

The sentry hissed more quietly, "King of Clubs."

"Ace of Spades," responded the soldier.

"Pass," answered the Royal Signals infantryman who was guarding the entrance to the 22nd Armoured Brigade Headquarters complex, situated in the forest of Osterwald, north-west of the village of Elze, seven kilometres north-west of Gronau. The soldier made his way forward towards the entrance, and the sentry, recognising Lieutenant Wesley-Jones as an officer, saluted.

Wesley-Jones pushed his way through the tent flap of the entrance to the complex, a three-by-three-metre green tent, and was challenged again, this time by a Royal Military Police Lance-Corporal getting up from his seat behind a small square table inside.

"Could I see some identification please, sir?"

Wesley-Jones shouldered his SMG, returned the corporal's salute and showed his identification card.

The RMP checked it. "Thank you, sir. The briefing starts in about five minutes if you would like to make your way in, sir."

He thanked the young corporal and passed through the second tent flap on the other side, stepping out into an enclosed area, buzzing with the sound of activity, comms chatter, soldiers rushing to and fro, generators humming in the background. A brigade headquarters was significantly larger than that belonging to a battalion, regiment or even Battlegroup HQ. Scanning the complex, he familiarised himself with the layout. To his immediate right, perpendicular to the tent entrance, were three FV436 armoured command and control carriers, basically 432s with additional communications equipment installed within. The rear door of each one was facing inwards, each with a two-metre by two-metre penthouse tent fixed to the rear, making up the right-hand side of the oblong headquarters nexus. Each of the rear compartments of the 436s, and penthouses, were laid out differently, but most had a table and map boards, officers and men going about their business supporting the brigade that was forward, digging in to defend the River Leine. The first vehicle held the Air element, containing Air and Air Defence Liaison; the second was for artillery; and the third for the commanding officer of the close support engineer regiment. To the left of the entrance tent was a second nine-by-nine tent, occupied by clerks and more Royal Military Police. Perpendicular, on the left, was another line of 436s, making the left-hand side of the complex. These accommodated the commander of the brigade's Signals Squadron and Yeomen-of-Signals in the first, G3-Operations in the second, the control station of the Brigade Commander, where his watchkeepers would be monitoring the brigade and divisional command networks, manned by the SO3 G3 and watchkeepers from a Territorial Army pool. The third vehicle contained G3-Plans, home of the Brigade Commander where, aided by the Brigade Major, arms advisers and visiting commands, he planned and conducted the battle.

At the opposite end, two further 436s were backed up to the headquarters complex, enclosing the entire HQ in an oblong secure area, accessible only through the main entrance. In one was the SO3-G2 Intelligence, supported by an Intelligence Corps Staff Sergeant and the NBC JNCO. The Full Corporal was responsible for plotting the fallout from any nuclear, chemical or biological attack, guiding the brigade command as to where they could move troops to safety, or move troops away from the path of any contaminated cloud or fallout. The second 436 contained the SO1, G1 and G4 watchkeepers, along with logistics operations. The entire complex measured roughly six metres wide by fifteen metres long; a target the Soviet air force, or Spetsnaz operation, would love to get their hands on. The HQ would not stay at this location long, keeping on the move and keeping the Soviet Electronic Warfare units guessing as to where they were.

Wesley-Jones headed for the nearest of the two large inner tents, the first one containing the operations bird table, the second the plans bird table. He bent down and thrust his head and shoulders through the flap and was met by a buzz of chattering that quietened as all eyes turned towards his entrance. The tent was packed with officers from the various elements that made up the 14/20th Kings Hussars Tank Regiment Battlegroup. The buzz of conversation restarted. Officers, from various forces and arms, were lined along each side of the table in the centre of the dimly lit mini-marquee.

"Come on in, Alex, don't be shy." Major Lewis, Commander of B-Squadron, also designated as Combat Team Bravo, laughed.

Red-faced, Alex made his way towards his Officer Commanding and was greeted by his fellow troop commanders and his Commanding Officer, Lieutenant-Colonel Lawrence Clark. He was just one element of the combat team that had been brought together to be briefed by their CO and the Brigade Commander, Brigadier Terence Stewart. On the left-hand side of the tent, leaning up against the tables and chairs that lined that one side, normally manned by signallers and clerks, were the four squadron commanders, and on the opposite side, the fifteen troop commanders Alex would shortly join. Mixed in with the officers of 14/20th Kings Hussars were representatives of the Infantry, engineers, artillery, signals, air force and Army Air Corps.

Major Lewis moved alongside Alex.

"Is this a routine update, sir, or something special?"

"Just an update, Alex, keep us abreast of what's going on around us." The buzz was in full swing again, the soldiers also discussing what the briefing was likely to reveal.

"Do we have any idea of what's happening, sir?"

"I'd like to think so. We have a big problem if we don't. Look, the Brigadier will be with us in a minute, so I suggest you join your fellow officers over there. We'll all know soon enough."

"Will do, sir."

Just as Alex had negotiated his way around the end of the table and over to the other side where he was greeted by his fellow troop commanders, an officer thrust aside the tent flaps allowing another figure to enter. Someone called the room to attention as the Brigadier and the Brigade Major made their way to the far end where the Brigade SO3-G2, the Staff Officer, Intelligence and Security, Captain Edward Rees, was pinning a large map of West Germany to a board resting on an even larger easel. Other map boards were pinned along, at certain points, on the tent's sides. Brigadier Stewart turned to face the group. Slightly behind, and to his right, stood the Brigade Major, the officer equivalent to the Regimental Sergeant Major of a battalion or regiment; not a man to cross, whatever your rank. To their left were Captain Rees, Captain Neil Allen, SO3-G3 Ops and Staff Sergeant Douglas Owen, Intelligence Corps.

The Brigadier cleared his throat. "At ease, gentlemen."

The assembled men relaxed slightly, waiting to receive the update from the Commander. Although some had an inkling of what had transpired, picking it up from snippets of radio conversations and discussions between the various command elements, this would be the first time they would collectively know what had occurred, what was still occurring in this battle, this war that had been thrust upon them.

"Welcome, gentlemen. It is good to see you have all arrived safely, notwithstanding that I wish we were meeting under very different circumstances. We have met under canvas like this on many occasions in the past, but always as part of a field or command post exercise. On this occasion, the circumstances are much more grave."

He caught the eye of as many of his officers as he could, subject to the lighting. He wasn't a big man, but had presence. With his sandy-coloured hair, sometimes slightly tufty as if the barber had missed a small section, and a ruddy complexion, he looked almost paternal. Until a scowl froze you on the spot. He was a soldier's soldier. A warrior. He would get actively involved in the training of his brigade and, when time allowed, had been known to participate in their fitness training.

"Before I say my piece, I will hand you over to Staff Sergeant Owen. He has been tracking the enemy movement to our front and keeping abreast of the bigger picture from Division and Corps. Staff Owen."

The Brigadier, and the rest of the officers at the end of the table, stood to one side allowing Owen to come to the front.

"Sir."

"Come on, squeeze up, squeeze up. Get as close as you can," instructed the Brigade Major with marginal impatience. "We'll issue you with a briefing document and your orders before you leave, but in the meantime having a view of the maps will help."

The officers shuffled forward as best they could. The Staff Sergeant tapped the first map on the easel, using a stick he had stripped from one of the trees outside.

"First I will cover the bigger picture." At six foot two, he could almost look over the heads of his superior officers lined up with him. "I will work from the south to the north."

"It is important that you all understand the overall situation that AFCENT finds itself in. Whatever affects the Allied Forces in Central Europe will impact on our Northern Army Group," added the Brigadier. "If NORTHAG has to respond then 1 BR Corps will potentially have to respond. So, dig in well, but always be ready to move when called upon."

He nodded to the Staff Sergeant to continue.

"In the south, in Central Army Group's southern area of responsibility, they are up against the Czechoslovakian army, the CSLA. A division from the CSLA's eastern district has reached as far as the River Danube, as have elements of the 4th CSLA Army. Central Group of Soviet Forces is also advancing on Austria and Southern Germany."

He tapped the map. "Here, further north, the 1st CSLA Army has reached as far as the River Regen and the River Naab. Further north still, they have advanced as far as Bayreuth. The Austrian army, along with the 2nd German Corps, part of CENTAG, is under severe pressure. This is the southern boundary of the American VII Corps' sector."

He paused to catch his breath, taking in the expectant faces. Normally briefings like this would be met with stifled yawns: being told about Orange Force movements, British units acting in the role of the enemy. This time, their life may well depend on the information that was being imparted to them.

"Further north again, 1 Guards Tank Army has already reached Schweinfurt. Elements of US VII Corps is holding its own and reinforcements are on their way. The Soviet 8th Guards Tank Army has breached the Fulda River and has occupied the town of Fulda itself, along with Bad Hersfeld. Soviet Air Assault Battalions have been in support, and the US cavalry regiment, acting as the covering force, has withdrawn in good order. But, they have suffered heavy casualties. The 3rd German Army, the *Volksarmee* that is, is crossing the River Fulda at this very moment."

He shifted his stick to the upper section of the map. "I will come back to 1 BR Corps in a moment. The Soviet Northern Group of Forces have also made good headway, reaching as far as the western outskirts of Luneburg. The 8th Germany Army, the DDR, under command of the Northern Group of Soviet Forces, has taken Lubeck and have reached the gates of Hamburg itself."

There was an intake of breath. The soldiers knew that the Warsaw Pact would advance quickly, but to already be at the fringes of Hamburg was a hard fact to swallow.

"Elements of the northern force are also moving north into Schleswig Holstein. A Bundeswehr panzer division, acting as a covering force, is doing its best to slow them down, but the enemy numbers are overwhelming. Although Warsaw Pact forces haven't crossed the River Elbe to the north, they have crossed it to the south."

He swept the pointer in an arc across the upper section of map. "Crossing the Elbe, the Warsaw Pact forces would then have the option of swinging north and cutting behind the second Bundeswehr panzer division covering force, cutting them off and isolating Hamburg. Hamburg's only link with the rest of West Germany would be by the sea."

He paused and pulled a notebook from the front pocket of his NBC suit. "To NORTHAG. 1st Netherlands Corps is moving into position around the Bremen area. Another Bundeswehr division is covering that sector until the Dutch are there in strength. 1st German Corps, south of the Dutch and north of 1st British Corps, are in position, with their covering force withdrawing, slowing the enemy down. Our area of operation, from south of Hanover to north of Kassel in the south, I will cover shortly. South of us, and the last Corps of NORTHAG, 1st Belgian Corps, is moving through the dense forests north of Frankfurt. A Bundeswehr panzer division is holding the Soviets back until the Belgians are there in force and able to dig in."

The Brigadier held up his hand. "The three German Corps are extremely powerful, but the three divisions acting as a covering force can only conduct limited operations until the Dutch and Belgians take up the slack. So we do need them to get their act together quickly. I will cover our positions when Staff Sergeant Owen has finished his piece, which I think is nearly done. But, generally, 1 BR Corps and 1 German Corps are in position, but our northern and southern flanks are vulnerable. Carry on, Staff."

"Sir. Enemy positions, 1 BR Corps sector. As expected, we are up against 3rd Shock Army."

"As expected," the Brigadier said with a chuckle, eliciting a response from the group, most of their faces breaking into a smile.

"It appears, as expected, that we have 2nd Guards Tank Army to the north and 1st Guards Tank Army to the south. At our immediate front, the two 3rd Shock Army units we are up against are the 10th Guards Tank Division and the 7th Guards Tank Division. These are the Army's 1st echelon divisions and we have been fighting those divisions' 1st echelon regiments for the last twenty-four hours. They are currently in the process of forcing a crossing over the River Oker."

That brought a gasp from some of the officers, astounded that the Soviet army had penetrated so deeply already.

"We have had significant Spetsnaz activity in our area of responsibility, consisting of sabotage and supporting assaults in the areas south of Bielefeld, Herford, north of Salzgitter, west of Braunschweig, Bad Pyrmont, Guterslough, Bruggen, Blomsberg, Munster, north of Springe, and Rhoden."

"And these types of attacks will continue," imparted the Brigadier. "So, don't just keep a watch to your front. There could be helicopter or parachute assaults to your rear, and even attacks by Spetsnaz units already in country."

"And these are only the ones we know about," added Captain Rees.

"That's my briefing concluded, sir," informed Staff Sergeant Owen.

"Thank you, Staff, a good brief. Right, gather around the bird table, gentlemen, and I will take you through our current positions and my intentions."

The assembled officers congregated around the two-metre by two-metre map table, the clink of their weapons audible as they moved.

"Someone at the back there, open the tent flaps," called the Brigade Major. "Your hot, sweaty bodies are turning this place into an oven."

The group laughed, and a couple of junior officers peeled back the tent flaps, tying them into position, the slight breeze cooling the air inside, which was much welcomed.

The Brigadier leant over the map and pointed at it with a pen. "Our brigade's area of responsibility runs from just south of Nordstemmen, here in the north, our brigade boundary line with

7th Armoured Brigade, and to the south our brigade boundary line is with the 12th Armoured, at Alfeld. Our stop line is the River Leine. That's a twenty-kilometre front we've been given to hold. No easy task, gentlemen. Our dispositions are as follows: the 2nd Royal Tank Regiment Battlegroup have got the south of Banteln to Bruggen, and the 1st Battalion Royal Green Jackets Battlegroup will hold the line from south of Nordstemmen to just north of Elze. You have what's in the centre, Lawrence," he said looking at Lieutenant-Colonel Lawrence Clark, Commander of the 14th/20th Kings Hussars Tank Regiment and now the 14th/20th Battlegroup. "Elze is your northernmost boundary. You must monitor the RGJ's position closely. If the enemy manage to push them back north of Elze, the Soviets could cut them off from the brigade and come at you from behind."

"When the recce troop pull back from Barfelde, sir, I could position them to the west of Elze." The Colonel tapped the map. "I have Combat Team Charlie as my reserve near Eime. I could dispatch a troop to support the Scimitars and cover my left flank."

"Good, good. What about Elze itself?"

"Combat Team Alpha is covering the Leine east of the town, and the Germans have at least a company of *landwehr* troops in the town itself."

The Brigadier nodded. "The rest of your Battlegroup?"

"As I said earlier, sir, Combat Team Alpha, three tank troops, and a mechanised platoon, will hold the Leine east of Elze. The eastern bank to their north has some copses, but none right up against the river. I have liaised with arty, and for the wooded areas we have some pre-planned strikes set up. Major Cox's tanks have a good view north-east, east and south-east, so will be in a position to pick off any advancing armour."

Major Thomas Cox, Commander of Combat Team Alpha, nodded in agreement, chewing on a pipe that he never smoked, but was rarely out of his mouth or his hands.

"Gronau." The Colonel tapped the map near the small village that straddled the River Leine further to the south. "The main defensive area will be west of the stop line, where Alpha and Delta troop are digging in. They each have an infantry section. Combat Team Bravo is digging in west of Gronau, covering the western end of the bridge. But, I have taken Bravo-Troop from them and pushed them forward across the water along with a recce troop. Bravo-Troop are dug in along the outskirts of the town, with two 438s to the north. Anything coming from Barfelde, or a 180-degree front, will walk into Bravo-Troop's tanks and the swingfire-missile carriers. They have an infantry section on the edge of the village with two Milan firing posts plus a Forward Mortar Controller. The Scimitars have been withdrawn and a recce troop of Scorpions have settled around Barfelde itself, which is just a scattering of houses, so they won't hang around. Half the troop will watch over Gut Dotzum." He looked up at the Brigadier. "Once they come flying back, the next thing the Soviets come across is my tanks."

"Where's Alex?" asked the Brigadier.

Lieutenant Alex Wesley-Jones brought himself to attention. "Here, sir."

The Brigadier acknowledged him and then turned to the Colonel again. "Don't keep them on the other side of the water too long, Lawrence. Give the Russians a bloody nose; then get them back fast. Only keep them there if you think there is a risk of the Soviets capturing the bridge intact."

"Understood, sir. The engineers have it wired?"

"Yes, they do, or they'd better."

"We have two pallets worth of explosives wired up on the bridge," informed the Engineer's commander. "When we get the word, no one will be crossing that bridge."

"I expected nothing less Patrick." The Brigadier smiled. He turned back to Lieutenant Wesley-Jones. "Make sure you keep your squadron commander up to speed, Alex."

"Sir."

"Major Lewis."

The commander of Bravo squadron answered, "Sir."

"I don't want you on the wrong side either." The Brigadier laughed.

"Understood, sir."

"Carry on, Lawrence."

"Sir. Delta troop, as you know, is with the Green Jackets. Combat Team Delta, the rest of Delta squadron, is based in Banteln."

"Minefields?"

"The bulk, sir, have been laid in front of Gronau, along with some off-route anti-tank mines along the road."

"Thank you Lawrence. All I want to add is that I've held back a Combat Team each from the Royal Green Jackets and 2RTR. They

61

will be our brigade reserve. Not a big reserve I know, but we have a wide front to defend. I have been given the command of a number of Bundeswehr Jeager units. They won't contribute a large force, a battalion-plus in total. But, they can fill in some of the gaps and give us the flexibility of shifting our forces to where we need them. I will make sure each battlegroup is aware of their locations and call-signs. So, what else do you need from me?"

"Nothing, sir, but I do need to tie up with air and arty before I go."

"Right. Well, we'll finish up here. Then I need a few words, Lawrence. Then we can go and stir up the air boys."

Brigadier Stewart pulled back his shoulders and caught as many of the pairs of eyes that were staring at him as he could. "Gentlemen, the enemy is less than twenty-four hours away. When they get here, it is going to be a bloody battle. We have to hold them here." He slapped the table, making it rock slightly. "Pulling back from here, we will be west of Peine and then the Weser. We're not ready for that yet." He tapped the table in synch with his words. "We...have...to...hold. Give 2nd Division a chance to get in theatre and the rest of our reserves to cross the Channel. The enemy are already pushing across the Oker. 4th Armoured can't stop them. They will be banging on our door tonight and will no doubt attack at first light. Questions?"

"Won't they need to rest up, sir?" asked a squadron commander.

"No, they won't. We estimate that they will throw two fresh regiments at us; that's nearly 200 tanks. Following that, they will have two full second echelon divisions. They won't stop. They can't stop. Momentum is their best option. Keep us on the move; don't give us time to dig in; hit us before reinforcements arrive from the UK and US. That's why we have to stop them here."

"What have we got, the brigade that is, sir, in support if we have to pull back or get flanked?"

"A good question, Lawrence. I am led to believe that 24th Airmobile has been released as a Corps' reserve, available for either the 1st or 3rd Armoured Division, depending who needs them the most. I've also asked for a 'Helarm' to be on standby. Because of their flexibility, their ability to move to a threatened sector quickly, the choppers will give us the means to break up any tank concentrations that are trying to outflank us."

"Are we getting good intelligence on the enemy's troop

movements, sir?" asked Major Mike Hughes, Commander of Combat Team Charlie.

"Yes, we are. Now the Warsaw Pact are on West German soil, our Corps Patrol Units have started to report in. We are getting some bloody good intel from them."

"How many CPU units are there out there, sir?" a young lieutenant at the back of the group asked.

"That I can't divulge. To be truthful, I'm not even sure I know the actual number myself. They will feed us with information for as long as they are able."

"We also need to be on the lookout for their opposite numbers," added the Brigade Major. "I can guarantee you there will be more Spetsnaz activity before the day is out."

"Right, gentlemen. Any more questions, save them for your CO or OC. It's time you got back to your units."

"'Shun," called the Brigade Major.

"Take a walk with me, Lawrence," instructed the Brigadier.

The group of officers moved aside; then stood to attention to allow their Brigade and Regimental Commander to pass. Once their seniors had left the tent, they too exited and headed back to their various units, Land-Rovers and Ferret scout cars providing the transport. They left feeling confident, but knew they were about to face the biggest battle of their lives.

Chapter 8

The Royal Air Force Nimrod taxied towards the runway, its four Rolls-Royce turbofan engines whining, impatient to go to full power and launch the aircraft into the skies above.

"Whiskey five, on taxiway two-one."

"Runway approach is clear."

The pilot turned to his co-pilot. "This will be a flexible thrust, navigate Vector one-one-two, rotate one-three-five."

"Roger."

The white lines down the centre of the runway became visible to the pilot as he peered through the cockpit window, the aircraft swinging left onto the levelled strip of tarmac along which the Nimrod would take off and land. On instruction from the pilot, the co-pilot pushed the throttles forward, the four thrust dials moving to show 100 per cent as the engines powered up. On reaching full power, the brakes were released, and the thrust of the four engines pushed the aircraft faster and faster down the runway, the white lines flashing by rapidly beneath the plane as it accelerated down the runway. Once speed was at the optimum, the pilot pulled back gently on the stick, and the heavy plane started to climb, its wheels parting from the tarmac.

"Control, airborne."

The pilot slanted his head towards the co-pilot. "Wheels up."

"Gear up," he acknowledged.

The aircraft banked left, straightened up, then climbed higher and higher, passing through the cloud layer above them, heading for its patrol station. The radar and electronic networks on board, its airborne-early-warning system, scanned the skies ahead and about them, looking for both friend and foe alike. The higher they climbed, the greater the volume of data being fed into the systems computers onboard. Although not without its problems during the development stage, the Nimrod AEW3 was more than able to fulfil the role it was intended for: watching the skies for any Warsaw Pact air force intrusion into British airspace. Soviet air force TU-95s had already attacked British air force bases, airborne–early–warning sites and naval bases along the east coast of the country. The Tupolev, TU-95, NATO codename Bear, could carry conventional weaponry, or the *AN602 Tsar Bomba*, the largest and most powerful nuclear bomb ever detonated. The current ones were fifty megatons, derated from 100 megatons available in the sixties. It was the AEW3's task to spot Soviet squadrons of bombers, and their accompanying fighters, heading for the British coastline, or picked up swinging around behind the continent and attacking the mass of reinforcements steadily pouring into Germany, Holland and Belgium. If seen, they could vector in British RAF fighters to seek and destroy them before they could jettison their deadly cargoes. Attack after attack had been made on the Island of Iceland from the air, and only the presence of both British and American nuclear submarines were preventing the Soviets taking the Island from the sea. Capturing the island would give them a forward airbase and allow their fighters to command the airways, providing protection for their bombers as they targeted the British mainland, or even the convoys moving troops and supplies across the Atlantic Ocean.

"*Captain, comms. Routine navigation. We have our waypoint. Steer two-nine-zero.*"

"Roger."

The radar operator, sitting in the rear of the plane, hunched over his consul and peered at the circular radar screen, the light from it bathing his face with a green tint. He watched as a set of bright green digits lit up.

"*Captain, radar. I have a contact. Zero-three-zero, thirty-eight miles.*"

"Roger, radar. How does that information compare with ground radar?"

The radar operator adjusted the white cloth–covered headphones of his headset and spoke into the boom mike that curved around the left of his face ending up in front of his mouth.

"*Captain, radar. It ties in. I have taken the bearing on the contact. Do you accept my steer?*"

"Roger."

The captain turned to his co-pilot. "It will be on our starboard beam."

"*Captain, radar. It is a large target, probably a Bear.*"

"Roger. Has an intercept been launched?"

"*They're going up now.*"

0840 6 July 1984. RAF Buchan, Scotland.
The Black Effect −2 days.

"Leuchers, launch two Phantoms. Mission number two-eight. Vector zero-three-zero. Climb three-four-zero. Call Buchan as stab two-one. X-ray-zero-two-zero-four. Scramble. Scramble. Scramble."

0840 6 July 1984. RAF Leuchers, Scotland.
The Black Effect −2 days.

The two pilots and their respective navigators raced out of the dispersal room, their green flight helmets swinging in their right hands as they ran at speed towards the aircraft waiting patiently on the runway apron. Light glinted off the clear plastic map-pockets, just above the knee of their green flight suits. Half a dozen ground crew, plonks, raced behind and alongside them, white ear defenders clamped to their heads, ready to be pulled down to protect their eardrums from the noise of the Phantoms' engines once they had been started. A couple of the ground crew split off and headed for the power supply, disconnecting the power lines from beneath both aircraft, while others removed the yellow caps off the two Sidewinder missiles, suspended from wing pylons, and the four Sparrow missiles situated in the fuselage recesses. The pilot and navigator of the nearest Phantom FG.1 scaled the two short metal ladders, hung from the sides of the dual cockpit, and clambered inside: the pilot to the front, navigator to the rear. They shifted and adjusted their positions until comfortable. Each had been followed by a member of the ground crew, who helped them to strap in and carry out any final instructions given. Once complete, the ladders were unhooked and removed, and the twin Rolls-Royce Spey turbofan engines were started. The Phantom Interceptors were now ready on the starting blocks. Two squadrons of Phantoms, thirty-two aircraft in total, were based at RAF Leuchers on the Scottish east coast. These two aircraft were part of the Quick Reaction Alert, the QRA, ready to defend Britain from attack.

Systems on, weapons locked. The lead pilot signalled with a twist of his hand that they were ready to roll, and his perspex cockpit lowered electronically, sealing him in his domain. They both cast their eyes over the controls and dials, ready to move. A member of the ground crew dragged the yellow blocks from in front of the aircraft's wheels, leaving it free to move forward. The pilots of both aircraft powered their engines bringing them up to eighty per cent power, and the two Phantoms, now alongside each other, steadily gained speed, the ground crew ensuring their ear defenders were on correctly as the noise from the four engines steadily increased. An RAF corporal, indicating with two paddles, bringing them both to his shoulders, beckoned the aircraft forward, then changed his action to a sweep of his left-hand paddle down and to the right, letting the pilot know he could sweep left and make his way towards the runway.

The pilot keyed his mike. "Runway, Two-One."

In the control tower of Leuchers RAF base, a Squadron Leader looked through the glass of the 360-degree tower window and clicked on his mike.

"*Bravo-Two-One, Bravo-Two-Two. You are clear for take-off. Wind two-twenty at fourteen knots.*"

"Roger. Two-One rolling now."

"Two-Two, rolling."

The engines flared as the pilot pushed forward on the levers, the thrust forcing the aircraft ever faster down the runway. Two surges of hot flame were emanating from the rear by the tailplane, the distinctive pulse-like pattern, vibrant with heat and energy surged out, the acceleration forcing the pilot and navigator back into their seats. Eighty knots, 100 knots, 120 knots. The wheels of the first Phantom Interceptor left the runway as the pilot rotated the aircraft, closely followed by his wing man.

"Two-One. Bravo-Two-One. Airborne."

"Two-One. Bravo-Two-Two. Airborne."

"*Roger. Steer zero-eight-zero.*"

"Two-one Roger."

"Two-two Roger."

The pilot of the lead aircraft spoke into his face mask, an internal message for his navigator. "Wheels up."

Both aircraft climbed up through the cloud layer before turning north in search of their target.

The RAF base at Buchan, the home of an Air Defence Radar Unit, was located some two and a half kilometres south-west of Boddam. Responsible for coordinating all aspects of Britain's air defence in the northern sector of the country, it would now take over control of directing the Interceptors in their quest to clear the skies of enemy aircraft.

The radar operator, deep down in the R3 underground operations block, studied his radar screen, fed from the TPS-34 radar system above and the GL-161 computer system. The faint green background of the circular scope was lit with bright green flickering points of light, numerals and letters tracking aircraft in its region of control. Twice, they had received a visit from Soviet bombers from Murmansk. The first wave of bombers were hit hard; first by aircraft from Iceland, then by Britain's air defence forces, and again from Iceland on their return. The second wave was more successful and managed to score some strikes on the base, but failed to hit any critical installations. For the sergeant staring at the screen, it had been a nerve-racking experience. Seeing the enemy aircraft on the radar getting closer and closer to their target and hearing the eventual explosions above had brought home the reality of the situation.

"*Bravo-Two-One and Bravo-Two-Two. This is Juliet-One.*"

"Juliet-One, Bravo-Two-One."

"Bravo-Two-Two. Go ahead."

"*Bravo-Two-One, Two-Two. Standby.*"

"Roger."

"Roger."

"*Punch, Punch, target bearing zero-two-zero, angels two-zero.*"

"Roger. Looking level on radar. Nothing yet."

"*I have target heading one-eight-zero, two-thousand.*"

"Roger Juliet-One."

"*Whiskey-One has track and will talk you in.*"

"Understood."

The pilot of the lead Phantom looked right and gave his wing man the thumbs up. His fellow pilot reciprocated. Then, looking out and down through his cockpit, he could see a carpet of white cloud laid out below, appearing solid enough to walk on. Above, the skies were clear and a pale blue.

"Juliet-One, permission to intercept."

"*Two-One. Jinx starboard ten.*"

"Roger."

"*Intercept and identify.*"

"Roger."

"Whiskey-One, this is Bravo-Two-One. You have some business for us?"

"*Yes, yes. Probable Bravo-Echo-Alpha-Romeo.*"

"Roger. Steer us in."

"*Turn one-zero-four left; take three-one-zero.*"

"Roger."

"*Good hunting.*"

The pilot talked with his navigator, then his wing man, and then the aircraft banked left ten degrees, additional fuel was injected into the jet pipe downstream of the turbine, and the afterburners provided significantly increased thrust, taking it from its cruising speed of 900 kilometres per hour to Mach 2.2, twice the speed of sound. Below, those on the ground would have heard the two supersonic booms as the two fighters shot through the sound barrier. Within a matter of minutes, the large silvery Soviet Bear aircraft came into view in the crystal-clear air of the now cloudless skies.

The Bear aircraft, its eight-bladed propellers clawing it through the skies, was impressive and dominating. On the ground, it stood at least to the height of four average men. In the air, its length of forty-six metres and wingspan of fifty metres was impressive as it started to climb higher, its maximum ceiling being nearly 14,000 metres. The Bear's four engines, powering the four contra-rotating propellers, left four white vapour trails in the freezing atmosphere as it climbed at a rate of ten metres per second. Its distinctive wings were swept back at a thirty-five-degree angle. The large bulge beneath the front of the nose of the aircraft, which housed the aircraft radar, helped to confirm it as a TU-95T, a maritime surveillance, intelligence gatherer and targeting aircraft, known to NATO as a Bear-D. Its sister aircraft, the TU-95, was even more sinister, able to carry and drop the AN-602 *Tsar Bomba*, the world's largest and most powerful nuclear bomb available.

"Juliet-One, I have a contact at one-zero left."

"*Juliet-One. Roger.*"

"Juliet-One, Two-One. We have Zombie identification. One, Bear-Romeo-Tango."

"*Juliet-One. Roger. Any sign of an escort?*"

"Negative."

"*Two-One, Whiskey-One. Two Zombies, five miles west, inbound to you.*"

"Roger that. Permission to engage Bear."

"*Weapons free.*"

"Two-One. Roger."

"Bravo-Two-Two, Bravo-Two-One. Take top cover."

"*Roger.*"

Bravo-Two-Two, the wing man, pulled up, into a steep climb, ready to protect his fellow pilot while he went in for an attack.

It wouldn't be difficult. So long as the pilot avoided the gun in the Bear's tail, it would be a simple takedown.

Two air-to-air missiles fired by Bravo-Two-One, soon despatched the large Soviet Bear, the aircraft spinning out of control as a shattered wing dragged it round. At least two chutes were seen leaving the stricken plane. The two aircraft then turned to face the first of many fighters that the RAF would come up against that day.

"*Juliet-One, Whiskey-One. Zombies identified. One hundred miles out. Estimate two-four, over.*"

"Roger that. Out to you. Leuchers, launch all available Phantoms. Mission number, two–nine. Vector zero-three-zero. Climb three-four-zero. Scramble. Scramble. Scramble."

"*Juliet-One, Whiskey-One. Zombies identified. Second flight. Estimate Three-four. Expected target, your location. Batten down. Out.*"

Chapter 9

1030 6 July 1984. Corps Patrol Unit. South-east of Hanover,
West Germany.
The Black Effect −2 days.

The Harrier pilot, Flight-Lieutenant Joseph Tate, flipped his left wing up and banked for a few seconds before straightening up again. Looking right, and down, through the cockpit canopy, he could see the E30 autobahn running east to west. He could make out vehicles travelling along it, but couldn't identify them specifically by type, but one thing was for certain: it was swarming with military traffic. There were certainly main battle-tanks and mechanised infantry combat vehicles amongst the probable supply vehicles and other troop carriers. His job was to photograph what he could see, then get the hell out of the area and head back home.

Originally from RAF Wildenrath, an airbase in West Germany, his squadron had dispersed, as planned, to sites out in the countryside. Fear of a major strike on that airfield, and other NATO bases, by the Soviet air force, had forced the Harrier units to find alternative sites. The Hawker Siddeley Harrier GR.1, known affectionately as the Jump-Jet, was the first generation of its kind. It was the first close-support and reconnaissance aircraft that had the capability to complete a short take-off and landing (STOL) or even a vertical take-off and landing (VTOL). With its unique fuselage-mounted engine, fitted with two air intakes and four vectoring nozzles, the pilot could direct the thrust vertically allowing for a vertical take-off or, when loaded down with weaponry and to conserve fuel, the aircraft's nozzles could be angled to give it forward and downward thrust enabling it to take-off on a short runway. If needed, the Harrier Jump Jet could operate from ad-hoc facilities such as forest clearings, like the one he had flown from, car parks and motorways, avoiding being exposed to potential Soviet missile and, even, nuclear strikes. As a consequence of the unique capabilities of this aircraft, Flight-

Lieutenant Tate had been able to take off from a heavily matted, but short, runway, in a large forest clearing. This enabled the Harrier Jump Jet to take off with a full weapons' load, conserving fuel to enable it to fly further afield or stay longer over the target area. On his return though, he would be able to land vertically.

Out of the corner of his eye, Flight-Lieutenant Tate spotted four trails of anti-aircraft fire, the intermittent tracer rounds glowing as they curved up from the ground, almost lazily, yet the 23mm rounds were leaving the four barrels of the ZSU-23-4 Shilka, at the rate of nearly 4,000 rounds per minute, travelling at over 900 metres per second. The Soviet Shilka fired short bursts, its onboard radar tracking the intruder. Tate pulled back on the stick, climbing slightly as he pushed the Pegasus turbofan engine harder, leaving the tracer trail behind him. He dropped down again, needing to keep the Harrier at the right height so the position of the aircraft was at the optimum if the photography he was about to take would be at its best. As this was a reconnaissance mission, fitted beneath the fuselage, mounted on the centreline, was a low-level daylight reconnaissance pod. The pod was fitted with four oblique F.95 cameras, set at a twenty and thirty-degree angle, one pair fitted with six-inch focal length lenses and a second pair with three-inch lenses. A fifth camera was fitted in the vertical mode, an F.135 mount, loaded with five-inch film.

He checked the aircraft's height again and confirmed his bearings. The Harrier was just passing over a wooded area, about midway between Peine and Lehrte. This aerial photography would give 1 British Corps a better handle on what was coming towards their defensive line on the River Leine. He clicked the button and the cameras started whirring, the rapid shutter movement allowing clear pictures to be taken for up to 500 frames.

The SA-6, NATO codename Gainful, a triple-missile Transporter, Erector and Launcher, TEL, received its tracking data from the battery's 'straight flush' radar, and the missile launch platform turned and elevated the three large missiles.

The curved radar spun round and round on the tracking vehicle, and the operator hunched over the circular scope, watched the rapidly sweeping arm repeatedly showing the blip of the enemy target. More data was transmitted to one of four SA-6s in the battery.

The TEL adjusted the launcher again, ensuring it was tracking the aircraft as well. On command, the crewman launched the 2K12

Missile, a white streak leaving the back of the 600-kilogram rocket as it sped towards its target at Mach 2.8.

The radar warning receiver burst into life, indicating his aircraft had been lit up by the enemy, probably a surface-to-air missile tracking radar.

"Shit." Pushing forward the throttle lever, Tate checked his head-up display and confirmed the plane's heading, then rotated his head wildly, looking left, right, up and down, and over his shoulder, desperately looking for the telltale signs of a missile heading his way.

"Damn." He saw the streak of the missile heading towards him, arcing round and heading straight for the Harrier. He stabbed the chaff button, praying he wasn't too late and pulled on the nozzle angle lever, rotating the vectored thrust nozzles into a forward-facing position: VIFFing, a dogfight tactic he had learnt when fighting against the Argentinian Dagger, a multi-role fighter aircraft, during the war in the Falklands. He used it now to drop his speed and go into a tight turn as a second chaff dispenser was fired. He pulled back on the stick, and his feet controlled the pedals as the G-force applied pressure to his body, tensing his muscles in return to help counter some of the effects. Seconds later, the plane rocked violently as the close-proximity fuse of the missile triggered an explosion, tearing off a section of the wing, ripping open the side of the fuselage, smashing the turbine blades, the engine losing power.

The power loss was almost instant and, as he began to lose height, he spotted a second white exhaust trail leaving the ground. His aircraft was finished, as would he be if he didn't get out, and quickly. Checking his leg straps, he pulled on the firing handle, and the explosive charge of the canopy-breaker shattered the canopy, splinters flying upwards, wind whistling around his face and helmet. The leg straps and harness automatically tightened and the ejection gun forced the seat up the guide rails, clearing the cockpit, followed by the blast of the rocket pack, speeding the seat clear, flinging him forward violently as the ejector seat forced him skyward. As soon as he was able, he undid his seat belt and kicked himself away from the seat. Within three seconds of pulling the firing handle and leaving the aircraft, the canopy had deployed.

Woompf. Behind and below him, he heard and felt his aircraft tear itself apart as the fuel tanks erupted, blasting the airframe into hundreds of pieces that would be scattered over a wide area of the ground below. He looked down; the ground was rushing towards him and he braced himself for the impact.

★

Wilf signalled for Badger to come forward, and they both flinched as the Harrier Jump Jet exploded above and to the right of their position.

"Shit. Look, there he is. Thank God he got out of that in time," exclaimed Badger pointing at the pilot's chute that was filling out to support the pilot's body dangling from the harness below it.

"We need to get to him," responded Wilf.

They both ducked as two SEPECAT Jaguar Jet ground-attack aircraft screamed by at low level, targeting the tank column that was travelling west along the E30. The first one let fly with its SNEB rockets. Each of the eight Matra rocket pods the aircraft had on its under-wing hardpoints carried eighteen of those 68mm rockets. Wilf's team had reported the convoy, and the RAF had managed to conjure up these two aircraft that had then, amazingly, got through the Soviet air-defence umbrella by flying extremely low. What remained of the Harrier, a plume of smoke trailing behind it, exploded again, struck by a second missile, pieces of the shattered fuselage and engine landing not more than 300 metres away.

Wilf, deliberately avoiding the temptation to switch his attention to the stricken Harrier, kept his eyes on the pilot and watched as the pilot's parachute canopy dropped lower and lower until it disappeared from sight. He tracked the last visible position as best he could, mentally calculating on his internal map where he was likely to have come down. The two Jaguar attack aircraft were causing mayhem amongst the Soviet convoy, tens of rockets exploding amongst the armour and trucks. Wilf swung the binoculars round, looking to the south-east, picking out the orange and yellow flashes of the strike followed by plumes of smoke, the sound bombarding his ears seconds later.

"That'll teach the fuckers," growled Badger.

"Did you get his bearing?"

"Yes, about three-twenty, north-west."

He turned to Badger. "Come on then. Let's go."

Wilf led the way, picking up Hacker and Tag on the way.

"Going for the pilot?" asked Tag.

"Yes, but we need to move sharpish."

"Yeah, while they're a little occupied," added Tag with a laugh.

"Hacker, point," instructed Wilf.

Hacker readjusted his M-16, the barrel mimicking the direction of his eyes as he scanned their route ahead. He took them back into the trees of the forest that straddled the E30, and headed north-west. They were at the south-eastern end of a smaller forest that jutted out to the east, a limb of the much larger one, pointing in the direction of the village of Aligse. Their hide was a mere two kilometres north from their current position.

Hacker forced the pace, knowing they needed to get to the pilot quickly. Although the two Jaguars would be ensuring the enemy kept their heads down and focused on surviving the onslaught, others may be tracking the progress of the pilot's chute and following him down. At this very minute, they could be homing in on possible landing sites. Anyway, the Jaguars wouldn't hang around too long.

Hacker weaved through the trees, Badger following behind, then Tag, with Wilf as tail-end-charlie. Wilf would have preferred the patrol to be moving more slowly, but he knew they would have to sacrifice some caution for speed. Options and outcomes swam around his head. They were in an ideal location for monitoring enemy troop movements. The E45, to their west, ran north to south. South of them was the E30 running east to west, where the Jaguars were still causing havoc. The aircraft wouldn't stay in the area for much longer, thought Wilf. More and more surface-to-air-missiles would be tracking the RAF strike aircraft, and Soviet fighters wouldn't be too far away. To their north, running south-west to the north-east, was a further autobahn, Route 3. He didn't want to leave the RAF pilot to the mercy of the Soviet army, but with troops potentially moving in on the area, they were at risk of being compromised. And if the Soviets brought in dogs to track down the enemy pilot, they could well come across their Mexe-hide. Although deep and well hidden, they had learnt from trials, and experience, that dogs had the knack of finding the most perfectly disguised hide. If not the hide, they would pick up on the CPU's trail at and round about their base. The thought of their primary mission being aborted and potentially the team ending up on the run was not a promising prospect. After about a kilometre, they arrived at the northern edge of the forest, and Hacker waved them down. Tag and Badger kept watch to their rear and flanks whilst Wilf made his way to the front.

"Clear?"

"Yeah. I suggest we go left, keep in the forest, cut across the k122, then north along that hedgeline, that will take us across to the opposite edge." Hacker pointed ahead of him.

"Going even further west, staying in the forest, then hanging north, but keeping inside the trees would be better," Wilf countered, scanning the fields to their north-west and north-east, looking for a sign of the enemy, and at the same time looking for the moving pilot, or the flutter of a parachute.

"I know, Wilf, but we haven't got the bloody time. That pilot is going to be up and away pretty quickly once he's got his bearings."

"You're right as usual, Hacker." Wilf grinned, slapping his friend on the shoulder. "Let's go."

Hacker adjusted his webbing belt; the twenty magazines of 5.56mm ammunition for his M-16 were quite a weight, along with a Claymore mine, grenades, two small packs of plastic explosive, not forgetting food and water. He marched at a pace along the edge of the tree line, completing a recce of the minor road before leading them across it. Once he was satisfied they were opposite the hedgerow, he beckoned the patrol forward and slipped out of the forest, leading the way. Looking left, across the open ground, scanning for any enemy soldiers, he kept close to the thick hedgerow that separated the two fields it crossed. Tag stepped out after him followed by Badger with Wilf following on. Hacker led them at a brisk pace, conscious that all the time they were out here in the open, in broad daylight, they were at risk of discovery by the enemy who were swarming all around this area in preparation for continuing their drive west. The hedgeline ran north for about 400 metres before switching to the north-east, where they crossed over the Bruchgraben, an irrigation canal. A convenient log, probably left by a farmer, acted as a bridge enabling them to cross it and remain dry. Another 500 metres found them back under the cover of trees, to the relief of all four of the SAS troopers.

They lay down in the inner edge of the tree line, each facing outwards towards one of the cardinals, their boots touching. Just waiting, watching and listening, ensuring they weren't being followed by an unseen force.

"Any suggestions?" asked Wilf, inviting a Chinese Parliament.

"This is fucking mad, Wilfy. We need to do a bunk now. We couldn't help him even if we can find him in this bloody lot."

"What do the rest of you think?"

"Badger has a point, but we have to at least try."

"I agree with Tag," added Hacker.

"You're outvoted, Badger," Wilf informed him.

"Wankers, the lot of you," Badger grumbled. "But, if we're going to do it, let's fucking well get on with it."

"We split into pairs," ordered Wilf. "I'll take Grumpy."

"Don't you start," responded Badger, but with his face cracking into a gentle smile. Deep down, he didn't really believe in his suggestion: leaving a British pilot to fend for himself.

Wilf got up, followed by the others. "There's quite a gap between trees, so we go at fifty metres apart. We follow a bearing of three-twenty, but as soon as we get near Route 3, we back off and call it a day. If we're bumped, RV-one is the eastern edge of the lake, south of Alte Schanze. You all know it. RV-two, southern edge of the smaller lake north-east of Unter-den-Linden. Clear?"

They all acknowledged.

"Let's go."

The patrol split up, moving until the pairs were about fifty metres apart. Then, heading on the bearing agreed, they started to make their way through the trees. Within their pairs, they drifted a further ten metres apart from each other, maintaining visual contact at all times, scanning for the enemy, searching for the downed pilot. The diagonal distance of the forest was about four kilometres. It would take them at least an hour to do a reasonable search on their current heading. The sound of two helicopters tearing past, over their heads, caused them to hit the deck, but the sound of the rotor blades soon disappeared as the aircraft headed south. There was no sound of the helicopters stopping or turning back, so they continued their quest to find the downed RAF pilot.

Wilf saw Tag signalling to get their attention, indicating they should join him. They had been searching for nearly thirty minutes, and even Wilf was beginning to doubt the sense of their decision. He hissed to Badger, and the two SAS troopers made their way to where Tag and Hacker were staring up into the trees.

"Hacker, Badger. Cover." The two soldiers moved out to about twenty metres distant and kept watch while Tag and Wilf examined the white parachute canopy, torn and entangled in the branches halfway up the twenty metre tree. Suspended from it, still strapped into his harness, his neck and one of his arms at an impossible angle, was the pilot they had been seeking.

"It's no good, Wilf, he hasn't made it. Shall I shin up and cut him down? Get his dog tags?"

"No, leave him. The Sovs will find him eventually. Best they find him as is."

"What now?"

"We continue with the original task."

Wilf called the team back in and ran through the next set of actions they would need to follow. The original task had been to lay up and monitor armour and troop movements along the E30 autobahn, reporting back to 1 BR Corps to assist them with their intelligence build-up, enabling them to decide troop dispositions to meet the massive force coming towards them. They also helped bring in the two Jaguar SEPECATs. The explosions and roar of jets had ceased, indicating that the British ground-attack aircraft had done their job and were running the Soviet air-defence gauntlet again in an effort to return to their base. The team had been taking it in turns to sleep, two on, two off, keeping as fresh as possible for the next stage of the mission. Although it had been disrupted, as a consequence of the downed pilot, they could still continue with their mission. The team had been tasked with approaching and identifying a tank division headquarters, its likely location picked up by an Electronic Warfare unit west of Hanover. They would eventually need to move south, passing beneath the E30, and locate this headquarters, report back and potentially initiate some sabotage.

"Shall I call in about the pilot, Wilf?" asked Badger, the patrol's signals specialist and the team member who carried their Clansman PRC-319 radio, an additional five kilograms on top of his other equipment.

"No, we can send it as part of a routine message later. I want to get us out of here and back on track."

"Route?" asked Hacker.

"Take us to the E30, but keep this side of the 122. I want to have a look at the junction."

"That's going to be like a bloody hornets' nest," proclaimed Badger.

"I know, but we might as well take a look-see while we're in the area."

"We'll need to keep tight, guys," added Tag. "We're right in the middle of one of GSFG's main access routes."

Nods of heads confirmed that they all understood the risk they were about to undertake.

Hacker led off again, taking them south; more slowly this time, knowing that the Soviets could be anywhere in the area, and there was always the potential that a much larger force than theirs could come looking for the pilot. After recrossing the *Bruchgraben*, Hacker steered them along a different hedgerow, bearing south-west, where, after 600 metres, they re-entered the forest, much further to the west. After nearly a kilometre without interruptions, apart from two more helicopters roaring overhead, the sounds had disappeared into the distance. The indication was that they weren't going to land close by. Hacker brought them to within spitting distance of the E45 off to their right and the E30 to their front. The growl of tanks and the noise of other armoured vehicles could be heard moving east to west, the Soviets building up their forces ready to strike at the heart of northern Germany.

Wilf was concerned. Had they been drawn out of their hide too soon? They were right in the middle of a vortex, an enemy build-up, and it wouldn't be long before advanced units started to occupy the very forest they were now in. There was also a danger of NATO artillery strikes on this very position. That frightened him the most, spurring him on to complete this task and get the hell out of here.

"Take us a little closer," instructed Wilf. We need to do a damage assessment."

"OK."

The raised slip road, connecting the E30 with the E45, was directly in front of them. The large intersection, where the two major motorways crossed each other, covered an area of two kilometres by two kilometres and was heavily wooded, providing the team with lots of cover.

Wilf turned to Tag. "You and Hacker stay here. Badger and I will do a recce."

"How long?"

"Thirty minutes tops."

"OK."

The two men made their way to the top of the embankment, waited while a convoy of three Ural-375 troop transports drove by, then, ensuring the road was clear, ran across to the trees on the far side.

"Where to?"

"Go right," whispered Wilf.

Badger led the way. Bearing right through the trees, they came across the loop that allowed northbound traffic to come off the E45, turn in a tight circle, almost driving back on themselves, and get onto the east bound E30. There were four of these loops in total, one at each right angle where the roads crossed.

"It's like bloody Spaghetti Junction," hissed Badger, referring to the M6 junction near Birmingham, his home city.

Wilf knew exactly what he meant, but didn't respond. They made their way to the top, lying down along the edge, watching out for enemy traffic on the loop, but it was quiet, the noise of military convoys still to their south. Up and over and they were soon inside a dense copse, taking their time now as they got closer and closer to the intersection of the two motorways. Both their heads snapped to the left as they heard an engine revving, followed by the distinctive sound of caterpillar tracks. Hunched over, they moved to the edge of the copse, stepping around and over lumps of reinforced concrete and bits of steel, towards the southern edge of the slip road loop. Far off to the left, a ZSU-23/4, self-propelled anti-aircraft gun was adjusting its position, the crew buttoned down inside for the moment. Ahead was a tangled mess. The entire upper section of the six-lane E45, along with the two slip road feeds, had collapsed on top of the E30. Now it was an entangled mass of chunks of concrete, longer broken sections of reinforced concrete, mixed in with bits of overhead gantries and twisted steel barriers. No one would be using this interchange for some time to come.

"Now we know why the feeders are so bloody quiet."

"Yeah," responded Wilf. "The Box-heads have done a good job of blowing this lot up."

"This'll slow the buggers down."

"We've seen nothing north, so they must have built some sort of bypass to the south, to take traffic around it. We can check it out on the way to our lay-up point."

"Yes, and radio it in. Tell the RAF boys to get their asses over here."

"Do that at our next stop Badger. At the same time we can let them know how effective their strike was and how the Soviets have got round it. Maybe they'll want another crack at it."

"Time to go?"

"Yeah, come on."

They made their way back to where they had left Hacker and Tag. Then the SAS CPU patrolled carefully east through the forest where they had identified a lay-up point, where they could wait until darkness. Once last light was upon them, they could head south and carry out their task of locating the enemy headquarters. In the meantime, sleeping two-on, two-off, they could continue to monitor the steady build up of Soviet forces.

Chapter 10

1800 6 July 1984. 62 Guards Tank Regiment. South-east of
Hanover, West Germany.
The Black Effect −2 days.

"I hope you've brought some decent vodka with you, sir?"

The two officers who had just entered the tent stood over
Lieutenant Colonel Trusov, Commander of the 2nd Battalion, 62nd
Guards Tank Regiment, 10th Guards Tank Division, as he twisted
a map around on a small collapsible table, peering at it in the dim
light provided by two oil lamps. He had been the only occupant after
throwing out the rest of his officers, needing time to reflect on what
he needed to do to ensure his unit was ready for any further tasks,
although his men, and machines, were badly in need of a rest.

"I thought it was you that should be offering your divisional
commander a welcoming drink, Colonel Trusov."

The flimsy foldable chair shot back as Trusov leapt to his feet,
seeing not only his regimental commander but also Major-General
Abramov, the Commander of the 10th. He saluted quickly. "My
apologies, Comrade General, Comrade Colonel."

"Sit down, sit down, Trusov."

"Sir." Trusov picked up his chair, pulled additional chairs from
the side of the battalion command tent, and offered one each to the
two senior officers.

"You are lucky, Colonel Trusov. I have brought my own vodka
on this occasion," the General responded, smiling.

"And some glasses," added Colonel Pushkin.

Trusov looked at the two senior officers quizzically as Pushkin
placed three small shot-size glasses on the map that was laid across
the square table. Trusov tried reading his commander's eyes, looking
for a hint as to the purpose of this sudden interruption. But Colonel
Pushkin was giving away nothing. Trusov had spoken to his divisional

commander often, and had been presented with two awards by him: one for his military skill and a second one for bravery when he spent nine-months on a detachment in Afghanistan. However, today, Major-General Abramov wasn't giving anything away either. The General, usually of good humour when briefing his officers or soldiers, could switch to a demon when berating a subordinate for incompetence. Then his humour would evaporate rapidly. On this occasion, the General's expression showed neither humour nor tolerance; it was completely blank. What little light there was from the oil lamps didn't help, casting dark flickering shadows across the two officers' faces. The four-metre by four-metre tent was Trusov's main battalion headquarters' tent; maps suspended from hooks hanging from the tent sides; the table in the centre and another along one side strewn with maps; ammunition and supply requests ready to be transmitted to Regiment and Division. All his communications were with the MTLBs and his own personal T-80K.

Pushkin topped up the glasses, pushing one towards the General and one towards Trusov, keeping one for himself. The General picked up his glass, Pushkin his.

"Well, Colonel Trusov, I would like you to share a toast with us. So pick up your glass," ordered the General.

Trusov did as he was ordered.

"You are no doubt aware that my Chief of Staff, Colonel Rykov, was killed by one of those damn NATO airstrikes."

"He was a great soldier, sir."

"True, true. Well, meet my new Chief of Staff," the General informed Trusov, turning to look at Colonel Pushkin.

Trusov's eyebrows shot up. He stuttered out a congratulation and raised his glass. "To Colonel Pushkin's new position."

"*Za Vas!*" they chorused.

Glasses were slammed down on the table and were quickly refilled by the General. Trusov's mind was racing. A new regimental commander. God, he would have to train another one all over again. Although pleased for his ex-commander, there was some disappointment. Pushkin had been tolerant of Trusov's methods and ways, and his occasional insubordination. They could almost be classed as friends. A new commander may not be so accommodating.

"Congratulations, Comrade Colonel."

"Thank you, Comrade Trusov, but the General hasn't finished." Pushkin turned to the General, his cue to continue the story.

"Colonel Trusov, you are to take over command of the 62nd Guards Tank Regiment with immediate effect."

Trusov looked stunned. "But—"

"No buts, Colonel Trusov. Colonel Pushkin assures me that you are more than up to the task. Also, your actions since the start of hostilities with the West have been exemplary, so I am inclined to agree with him."

"When, sir?"

"You are in command of the regiment as of now, Colonel." The General raised his glass, as did Pushkin, and they in turn congratulated the newly promoted officer.

"*Za Vas!*"

"Right, down to business, young Trusov." The General pushed the glasses to one side, Pushkin gathering them up and placing them on the canvas-covered ground. Abramov peered at the map, got his bearings, spun it around and stabbed a spot with one of his slim fingers. Most senior Russian officers tended to be on the heavy size, and often dominated their men and officers by their sheer magnitude and presence. Abramov, on the other hand, looked almost underfed. Anyone who misinterpreted that for a weakness would soon find themselves on the receiving end of a guillotine tongue. He exuded enormous power and had quickly earned the respect of both his juniors and seniors.

"Nordstemmen to the south, Rossing to the north." He dragged a finger between the two. "I intend that we push right through the centre of these two and across the Leine."

"These two bridges," added Pushkin. "This is where we'll cross."

Trusov studied the area where his ex-commander was indicating.

Pushkin continued. "The first bridge is north-east of Schulenburg, the second next to the high ground further south."

"They'll be primed ready to blow," exclaimed Trusov. "They'll be blown and down before we can get a tank near them."

"More than likely," added the General with a sly smile. "But there is a bigger picture, Colonel. The Tenth and Seventh Guards Tank Divisions have one major task left before we are pulled out of the line and given time to rest and refit. We have to smash the British division that is defending this sector of the River Leine into submission. Cross that river and destroy this key line of defence, giving no quarter. Our main aim: to destroy as much of their force as possible."

Pushkin took over from the General. "The 61st Tank Regiment will target Nordstemmen and the 63rd, Rossing."

"But they'll defend these towns or villages and blow the damn bridges, sir."

"Have faith, Trusov," interposed Abramov. "We will bypass those built-up areas quickly. I don't intend to have my tanks bogged down and my men tangled up in house-to-house fighting. We will try for those two bridges, but a key focus will be on putting our own bridge across the river right in between Schulenburg and the high ground to the south. There is also a rail bridge further south. We'll keep an eye on that as well. Our division will conduct a battalion airborne assault to secure that high ground here, Sel Marienburg. I have also been promised some assistance from the Spetsnaz prima donnas."

Trusov nodded, running the scenarios through his head.

"You see now, Pavel."

"Yes, Comrade Colonel. What about my battalion – uh – regiment?"

"How many tanks do you have, Colonel Pushkin?"

"Forty-nine, Comrade General."

"Hmm, nearly fifty per cent casualties. But your men fought well to get this far."

"Many of the tanks need maintenance, sir, and the crews are tired."

"I understand that, Colonel Trusov," said the General as he leant over the table. "All they have to do is make one last effort for the Motherland; then they will be off the line." He locked eyes with Trusov for a second before sitting back up. "Anyway, the 61st and 63rd will take the brunt. Should we need your regiment, Colonel Trusov, you and your men will be ready."

"Yes, Comrade General, my men will not let you down."

The General stood up, followed closely by his junior officers. "I know, Comrade Colonel. That is why you have this promotion and the responsibility that goes with it."

He turned to Pushkin. "I'll leave you with Colonel Trusov so you can hand over command, but I will want you at headquarters by ten. I will be briefing the division. You will need to be there too, Colonel."

"Sir."

The two junior officers saluted and the General left them to complete a handover. Less than two hours to hand over a full Soviet tank regiment; not a small task.

"The General certainly has a lot of faith in his regiments."

"He does, Pavel. Had the 62nd been at full strength, it would be you leading the attack tomorrow."

"I see he left the bottle behind...do you mind?"

"Pavel, as a regimental commander, you are going to be an even bigger pain in the ass."

Trusov topped up their glasses. "Here's to luck, sir."

"For once I am in agreement with you. The General knows it's not going to be a walkover, so make sure your men are ready."

"*Za Vas!*"

Chapter 11

1800 6 July 1984. Royal Hussars, Combat Team Delta. Rossing, West Germany.
The Black Effect -2 days.

The three tanks of Delta Troop, of Delta Squadron, The Royal Hussars had all returned to their positions on the eastern edge of the village of Rossing. They had pulled back, one at a time, across the River Leine to receive some minor maintenance and to refuel. Many were now fully camouflaged amongst the buildings of the West German village. One of the tanks was using a barn on the edge of the village, straw bales piled up in front to provide cover. A second tank had sheets of hessian, with pale orange bricks painted in the appropriate pattern. From a distance, the sheets of hessian genuinely looked like the wall of a building. Delta Squadron, designated Combat Team Delta, had two positions to defend: Rossing and Escherde. One troop was at the eastern tip of Rossing, at the junction of the minor road that came from the east, from the direction of Giesen, and met with the two roads that skirted the village of Rossing to the south-west and the north-west. Two of the tanks were dug in 300 metres further east on some higher ground, giving the two tanks a full 180-degree arc of fire out to three to five kilometres. A killing ground. A second troop was deployed in the northern sector of the village, giving the tanks a five-kilometre view out to Sarstedt in the north, Ahrbergen to the north-east, and Giesen to the east. Any Soviet armour or armoured infantry combat vehicles would have to cross four kilometres of relatively open ground; not a prospect they were going to relish. In Escherde, three kilometres south-east of Rossing, a third troop was north of the road that ran through the centre. The village straddled the road, the larger element to the south and slightly east. There sat the fourth troop. The two tanks of the squadron headquarters were two kilometres back along the road, in Heyersum. The Royal Hussars Battlegroup was all tanks. This gave the four combat teams high maneuverability to hit the enemy hard, withdrawing slowly, then dash back across the River Leine to act as 7th Armoured Brigade's reserve. The other two Battlegroups, the 3rd Battalion, the Queen's Regiment, and the 1st Royal Tank Regiment, had combined forces to form a Mechanised Infantry Battlegroup; the 3rd Battalion, the Queen's Regiment, with two companies and a tank squadron, and the 1RTR Battlegroup with three tank squadrons and a mechanised infantry company.

Lieutenant Barrett had gathered his men around his troop tank to pass on the briefing he had received from the Squadron OC, Major Carrigan. He was sitting on the engine deck, his men gathered around him, sitting on the ground of the garden owned by the house they were now occupying. The occupants had left three hours ago, but not before making the tankers a hot drink and plying them with freshly cooked, hot food. The soldiers had eaten it with relish, stuffing down as much as they could, a reprieve from their tinned COMPO rations. The locals had even left food for the men, destroying the rest, wanting nothing to be left for the advancing Soviet army. Most of the villagers had now left the village, although a few insisted that they stayed with their homes, where they and their families had been since they were born. They wouldn't leave now, not even for the Russians. The ones that did leave added to the problems for the NATO troops; columns of refugees clogged up the roads. West German Civilian and Military Politzei had to use force on occasions to make room for troops and supplies moving to the front, and injured soldiers being evacuated to the rear.

Barrett's tank was positioned in between two houses. One of two dozer-blade mounted tanks of the squadron had pushed a mound of earth forward, creating a deep berm in front, just ahead of the houses. When the enemy attacked, all the Lieutenant would need to do was drive forward and he would have a 180-degree field of view out to the east, protected either side by the outer walls of the houses and a solid berm in front. Behind, further into the village, two additional prepared positions lay ready and waiting. After the last position was compromised, if they survived that long, they would cross the river to their new positions further back. He looked down at his men, cups of hot tea being passed around by the troop-sergeant, the BVs being kept topped up for that very purpose. A warm feeling passed through him, and he now looked upon them as family. Many a time he had been asked to intervene with a domestic issue that could potentially get out of control, or deal with a soldier who had spent too much money and was now being chased by the Sparkasse Bank for funds; a soldier who had family issues back home and needed to fly to the UK; or one that went out partying and let his behaviour get out of control and had been brought back to barracks by the German Politzei. There has always been a loose bond between an officer and his men. As the troop-sergeant had a foot in both camps, this bond was even more solid between him and the men of his troop. In these difficult times, the bond was now even tighter. It was driven partially by fear, fear of the unknown, fear that they would fail and let their comrades down, and fear of the enemy with their massed tank armies lined up against them. The small unit now recognised the importance of each other, the mutual dependence that was required if they were to function as an effective unit.

"I have just been updated by the OC, and it appears that the enemy is now en route to our location. I'm sure that doesn't come as any surprise to you all." Barrett smiled and the group laughed, a little nervously. "They have crossed the River Oker in force and are not stopping to regroup. It's as if the devil himself is behind them."

There was a short buzz of chatter which soon died down as the troopers wanted to know more about the situation and what was coming their way.

"That would be the KGB close behind them with pistols," said Sergeant Glover as he passed a mug of tea up to his troop commander.

The group laughed, less nervously this time.

"Thank you, Sarn't Glover. Our lads have put up a good fight, but they have been up against significantly superior forces. When I say superior, I mean in quantity, not necessarily quality. Four-div's job has been to delay the enemy, not take them on in a head-to-head. That is our job."

"Shit, sir," spluttered a corporal, Commander of Delta-Four-Charlie. "That means they've gone about seventy Ks in two days?"

"It's what we expected, Corporal Mason. We don't want to squander the forces we have out there with pointless stands. We just want to slow them down. Blunt their attack. Then they come up against us, and we stop them dead in their tracks." He had spouted that phrase numerous times. Did he believe it? He wasn't sure. He understood the concept of defence in depth and only having forces to the fore to slow the enemy down, but just as the corporal had blurted out: seventy kilometres in forty-eight hours. He continued.

Propaganda, he thought, or the truth. "Every kilometre they advance, we are inflicting casualties, forcing them to use up precious fuel and ammunition. Don't forget, their supply lines are longer than ours." Providing, he thought, they survive the Soviet air and missile strikes along with the Spetsnaz doing their best to destroy or disrupt their logistics.

"Have our dispositions been finalised yet, sir?" asked Sergeant Glover, Commander of Delta-Four-Bravo.

"Yes, pretty much. Our combat team has Rossing and Escherde. Charlie has a line north-east to Sarstedt. Alpha covers Jeinsen and Bravo Schulenburg. North of us we have the 3rd Battalion, the Queen's Regiment and, to the south, 22nd Armoured Brigade. 1RTR in reserve."

"Having a picnic, no doubt," commented one of the troopers, which brought a smile to everyone's face.

"Quite. So, the Soviets are going to walk into over 100 tanks. Just sitting and waiting to hit them where it hurts. And with these new babies," the Lieutenant said, patting the Challenger tank beneath him, "they won't know what has hit them. They've not had an easy ride so far, but when they meet us, they'll wish they could turn the clock back."

"They have a huge wake-up call coming to them, sir," added Sergeant Glover.

"Too bloody right, sir," came one comment from the troops.

"Kick arse," came another. Their confidence in themselves and their equipment was undampened.

"What about the Hinds, sir?" asked Sergeant Glover. "Are we going to get some help?"

"The OC has assured me that we will. Tracked Rapier units are being brought further forward and a Blowpipe section will be moving into the village. So, we'll have some overhead cover."

"The Crabs? Been kind of invisible so far."

"I agree with your sentiments, Sarn't Glover, but the RAF has been hit pretty hard. They've had to move between bases and some of the bases have been put out of action by airstrikes and Spetsnaz activity. There is an invisible battle going on overhead and, at the moment, it appears to be stalemate."

"We'll win though, won't we, sir?" Trooper Mann asked.

"Our fly boys, along with our Allies, won't let us down, I'm sure."

"Who are we up against then, sir?" Sergeant Glover steered the conversation back to their immediate issues.

"To our immediate front, we'll have 10th Guards Tank Division. They've been in contact with our covering force from the beginning. Further south, the 22nd are up against 7th Guards Tank Div."

"Won't they have been knocked about a bit, sir?"

"Yes, Corporal Tompkins, that is our hope." Barrett laughed. "But they will have fresh regiments pushed forward now. One or two of the regiments that have been fighting so far will rest and refit and probably be downgraded to the divisional reserves. South of us, Intel think they will have a tank regiment and a motor rifle regiment up front. Between the four, that is still nearly 400 tanks." Seeing the worried look on some faces, he quickly added, "Our regiment has fifty-six Challengers alone, and the enemy has got to come to us. They will get a bloody nose. This is where we will stop giving ground easily."

"Infantry as well, sir?"

"South, there will be a full regiment and a battalion from the tank regiment. If we have two tank regiments in our sector, we'll be up against a battalion from each of the two tank regiments. They have BMP-2s, so don't ignore them. If they stop, it's likely they're going to unleash a Swatter or Sagger missile."

"T-80s?"

"Yes, Sarn't. Don't forget, men, we're dug in and they have to come to us. After, that is, they've negotiated our minefields. The Gunners are going to lay some more FASCAM mines later today."

"Approach routes?"

"Yes, the bar mines will cover the open ground. So, we need to target any mine roller or mine plough tanks as a priority. If they're hit, it will slow them down, and we can pound them as they bunch up."

The sergeant looked uncomfortable as he spoke, not wanting to dampen the troop commander's, or the troop's for that matter, enthusiasm. "What's behind us, sir? Have 2-Div turned up yet?"

"Not quite. Some elements have and they're digging in further back, covering 1BR Corps rear area. So, if we do have to pull back, we'll at least have some cover to watch our backs. The majority of the division will probably be in position by end of play tomorrow. So, we have to hold this position."

"Surely we must have more, sir?"

Barrett looked at his troop sergeant, then at each of his men in turn, knowing the sergeant was voicing the concerns of all his men.

"We still have 4th Armoured Division. They've taken casualties, but are being withdrawn. They will have a chance to refit and rest ready to take up the fight again. No doubt they will receive some reinforcements from the UK. They will be our Corps reserve.I have also been informed that 24th Airmobile has been assigned as a reserve. They will be used to block any breakthroughs that occur."

"With those para nutters coming into the fight, the Soviets best look out," piped up Trooper Deacon. The group laughed.

"The crap-hats are no bad either," added Lance Corporal Frith, an ex-para who had decided to become a tankie rather than staying in the Parachute Regiment and jumping out of aeroplanes.

"Look, guys, we have some of the best troops in the world, including yourselves, heaven forbid." The men laughed, but also bristled with pride. "Our Challengers are a match for any of the Soviet tanks, including the bloody T-80s and T-64s and all the crap they have pinned to it. As for any T-62 or T-72s we come across, they'll be scrap iron by the end of tomorrow."

He cast his eye over his men. They had been together as a troop for over a year. His gunner, Corporal Farre, was the longest serving member of the troop, having joined four years ago. He joined as a driver, then moved to gunner, and finally to command his own tank. Now he was Barrett's gunner, able to take over the tank should the Lieutenant be killed or need to concentrate on troop tactics.

"We keep a grip on our fear. Yes, we will be scared, I will be scared. But if we keep it under control, channel it, we can use those emotions to help us destroy the enemy."

He caught the eye of every one of his men, his confidence and smile infectious, and slowly every man's frown disappeared. He slapped the engine deck of his Challenger. "We load, we aim, we fire. We load, we aim, we fire."

The rest of the troop joined in the mantra. "We load, we aim, we fire."

"Focus on your specific tasks and hit the enemy for six, and we'll come through this." He paused to allow his words to sink in.

"Right, back to your tanks. Delta-Four-Bravo and Charlie you need to move forward to your positions. I have an FFR Land-Rover assigned to take you there."

He slipped off the rear of the engine deck, bending his knees as he hit the ground. He turned round and grabbed his SMG. "So I'll be along to each tank to check your camouflage and your fields of fire. Let's get to it, Sergeant. We'll check mine before you go."

"Sir."

The troopers and NCOs got up off the ground, automatically brushing any dirt or debris off their Noddy suits, not wanting to take any into the fighting compartments of the tanks, their living quarters.

Chapter 12

2100 6 July 1984. 62 Guards Tank Regiment. South-east of
Hanover, West Germany.
The Black Effect −2 days.

Lieutenant Colonel Trusov, soon to be a full Colonel now he had
command of a full tank regiment and not just a battalion, shuffled
through the maps and notes he had made earlier. He was disappointed
that his regiment, 62nd Guards Tank Regiment, 10th Guards Tank
Division, had been put in reserve, although he and his men could do
with the rest, as could their equipment. The T-80s were starting to
become troublesome. Breakdowns were becoming more frequent,
and even Barsukov was getting impatient with the tank's auto-loader.
He had a knack, as did his driver, of keeping the main battle tank
in tip-top condition, but even they were disadvantaged by the lack
of spare parts. He had given permission to completely cannibalise
one of the T-80s, using as many elements as possible to keep others
in his regiment operational. This decision had not been received
well by his divisional commander, but Major-General Abramov,
the Commander of the 10th, the Uralsko-Lvovskaya Division, had
relented, knowing the realities of the situation. He had put a bomb
under the supply officer and had even solicited the support of his
political officer in order to speed up the shipment of badly needed
spares to the front.

Trusov looked over the map, tracing the route 61st Guards
Tank Regiment would be taking in their assault. The low-watt
bulb flickered as the generator hesitated for a fraction of a second,
the radio behind him silent apart from the occasional hiss of static.
The division was on radio silence; communications would only be
allowed once the attack commenced. He grabbed the flask of coffee
from the rack in the rear of his command vehicle, and poured himself
a drink. It was tepid, but he didn't mind. It might help to dilute

the vodka he had shared with Colonel Pushkin earlier. Pushkin, promoted to Chief of Staff, as a consequence of Colonel Rykov being killed by an airstrike, had recommended Trusov to replace him as regimental commander. A private celebration had followed. The MTLB-RkhM-K command vehicle, although low and cramped inside, gave him some peace, some time away from the regimental command tent, time to think. There was also a strong taint of diesel in the air, a damaged fuel line had been rapidly repaired earlier that day. After a whistle-stop tour of his new command, he felt weary and could quite happily pull his legs up on the wooden bench seat, close his eyes and fall into a deep sleep. But he had too much to do. He knew the battalion commanders, who up until recently had been his peers, would be watching him closely. That relationship had suddenly changed. Now he commanded them, their equipment and their men. He had been plagued with questions about spares, fuel, ammunition, promotions, and had delegated as much of it as possible. He sensed that one or two of the battalion commanders were testing him, envious that it was he, and not them, that had been promoted. But now he needed time to fully appreciate the status of his new command if he was to lead it into battle when called upon. He went back to sifting through the status reports from his battalion commanders.

Chapter 13

0330 7 July, 1984. 34th Airborne Assault Brigade. East of
Hildesheim, West Germany.
The Black Effect −1 day.

The soldiers were grouped together in lines, the numbers dependent
on which aircraft would pick them up. They were checking and
rechecking their weapons and equipment, some nervously. They had
trained for this, many times over. Some had even done it for real,
fighting the Mujahideen in Afghanistan. Lieutenant-Colonel Averin,
the battalion commander checked his watch: sixty minutes to go. It
was three thirty in the morning; dawn was slowly breaking, giving him
a view of the many clusters of men waiting patiently to be collected.
His battalion was one of four, all belonging to the 34th Air Assault
Brigade. A second battalion, seven kilometres away, was going through
the same level of preparation. Further back from the front line, two
more battalions were at this very minute loading up onto a mix of
AN-12 Cubs, IL-76 Candids and AN-12 Cocks in preparation for a
full assault on the NATO forces dug in along the River Leine. Two
company-sized forces would very soon be in the air, two advance
forces on their way to secure the landing zones for the rest of the Air
Assault Brigade of over 2,500 men.

Averin called out to his men nearby, giving them the sixty-
minute warning order, the message passed out to all the platoons
waiting. Before they went anywhere though, the army's artillery
divisions would hammer the British positions with a barrage that
would feel like a seismic event. He was feeling decidedly impatient.
For forty-eight hours, the Soviet army had been pounding the
NATO forces, pushing them further and further back; up to eighty
kilometres in places. It was being said that it had been relatively easy
so far, although the Soviet forces had lost much equipment, and
many lives given for the cause of the Motherland. The British had

fought well, but had been rolled back. Averin understood that the British Brigades they were up against had no intention of digging in; they were but a covering force, their intention to disrupt and delay the Red Army, trading ground for time, providing the rest of the British forces with a chance of digging in; building up their forces, or at least allowing reinforcements to arrive in theatre, to meet the tidal wave that was approaching. His men were finally going to get the chance to test their metal against the capitalist armies. An opportunity for his battalion to shine. All he and his men had to do now was wait. Thirty-seven Mi-Hook helicopters, along with a flight of Hips, would soon be en route to pick up his battalion, along with their BMDs, mechanised infantry combat vehicles, and fly them the twenty kilometres to their landing zone.

The Air Assault Brigade had two missions. The primary mission was to secure the bridge that crossed the River Leine to the west of the town of Gronau. One parachute battalion would land south-east of Esbeck, and a second south of Oldendorf. The two heliborne assault battalions would strike at Gronau itself; one battalion to the north-west and his to the south-west. The supporting units, such as the artillery battalion of D-30s, anti-tank battery with its 85mm ASU-85s, anti-aircraft battery of SA-9s and hand-held SA-14s, along with engineers, supply and signals, would land in the triangle formed by the villages of Esbeck, Sehide and Eime. *The enemy won't know what has hit them*, he thought. Two and a half thousand aggressive airborne soldiers bent on taking their objectives and intent on causing the total destruction of the defenders would create havoc behind the enemy's lines. His was the most important mission, along with his sister battalion: to take the bridge itself. Even if the British managed to destroy it, they would succeed in isolating the troops on the eastern bank and secure the bridge foundations enabling the Soviet engineers to throw a bridge across quickly.

0330 7 July 1984. Bravo-Troop (+). Gronau, West Germany.
The Black Effect -1 day.

Lieutenant Wesley-Jones turned, slightly startled as he heard someone clambering up the front of his Chieftain tank. He raised his SMG to his shoulder, peering into the slowly gathering light at the shadowy figure making its way towards the turret hatch where he was sitting. Had he been asleep? He was on stag and should have been alert. No, he hadn't been asleep even though deep tiredness had been dragging at his eyelids.

He pulled the butt tighter into his shoulder. "Who's that?"

"Relax, Alex, it's just me."

He let out the breath he had been holding, sighed gently and lowered his machine gun. "Sorry, sir."

"Don't be sorry, Alex. You don't know who it may have been," responded Major Lewis, the Squadron Commander. "Crap challenge though."

The OC clambered over the turret, careful not to catch the camouflage netting just above him, and lowered himself into the turret hatch next to the Bravo Troop Commander.

"Sorry, sir, still doesn't seem bloody real."

"It's bloody real all right, Alex. Ground radar and the fly-boys are picking up movement out to the front. The Sovs are getting ready for something."

"Don't they ever rest?"

The question was rhetorical. Major Lewis didn't answer.

"What have we got left still to pull back?"

"Just one recce troop and the remnants of a combat team, a couple of Chieftains and three 432s by all accounts. Oh, and some engineers. They've been laying a few last minute surprises. They're about two klicks away in Barfelde and Gut Dotzum. They won't be there for long."

"What are their latest reports?"

"Lots of movement. Heavy concentrations of enemy formations in the Hildesheim forest. Our latest air recce showed troop concentrations around Sibesse, Westfeld, Diekholzen, anywhere they can find space. There's just so damned many of them."

"Did Four-Div make a dent?"

"Oh, they've hurt the enemy all right, but certainly not enough to stop them."

Alex reflected on the battered units returning from the east. Ambulances had been crossing throughout the day, the wounded being rushed to the rear where they could get better treatment. Not all of the Chieftains had returned; dozens must have been left behind: some completely destroyed, along with their crews; others couldn't be recovered as they were under the guns of the enemy. Some had been hauled back on tank-transporters in the vain hope that they could be reconstituted and brought back into the fight. That was not all that had passed through the village and across the bridge. Thousands of refugees had thronged the bridge, shuffling by with fearful faces, many carrying or supporting older or infirm friends or members of their family. They had good reason to be scared: the reputation of the Soviet soldier at the end of the Second World War had been passed down by the previous generation. There was a feeling that the Soviet Union wanted its revenge on the West German population, thinking that they had not been punished enough. Let off lightly by the soft Western capitalist countries. Some of the refugees were lucky, having cars or lorries to travel in, many with their entire worldly goods piled so high that the load was in danger of toppling. Their speed though was no faster than the walking pace of the hundreds that walked alongside or around the mechanical means of transport. The army had allowed them to cross until midday, when a local West German unit was tasked with diverting them to a bridge further south. A military bridge had been placed there deliberately to pull the refugees away from Gronau, to allow the retreating British a free passage across the river to relative safety.

```
0330 7 July 1984. Bravo Troop (+), call sign Two-Two-Delta.
Gronau, West Germany.
The Black Effect -1 day.
```

Lance Corporal William Graham slithered into the foxhole, watching he didn't catch his helmet on the overhead cover. The Milan team of two men had improved their position over the last twenty-four hours, knowing that, when the enemy came, they would need every scrap of cover they could find as their fighting position would be the only barrier between a potential major injury or even death. A bunker would have been better, but the prefabricated, curved interlocking sections had given the hole some shape, some stability enabling the soldiers to make a relatively safe defensive position. It was deep enough to serve their purpose, the upper edge just below the tops of their shoulders, and wide enough so they could lean back against the opposite wall. They had a good view out of the front, and had quick and easy access to the Milan firing post. The top cover consisted of pieces of a broken pallet, layered with earth and some turf on top to help hide their position. Graham's feet touched solid ground, and he avoided spilling any of the hot liquid from the still steaming mug of tea he had brought to share with the Milan crew.

"Cheers, Will, you're playing a blinder there."

Alan Berry grabbed the black plastic mug, savoured the smell of the hot sweet brew, and took a sip before passing it to his oppo, Rifleman Michael Finch, on the other side of the Milan.

"Here you go, buddy, the Corp's spoiling us at last."

"Fuck off, Al, you have the life of Riley."

"Of course I do. Look at this lovely five-star accommodation for a kick-off."

The three soldiers laughed quietly.

Corporal Graham rested his elbows on the front edge of the trench and peered into the gloom, although he could now see the landscape slowly taking shape, but still without colour.

Berry propped his elbows alongside. "They're going to come today, aren't they?"

"That's what we've been told, mate. I see no reason not to believe them"

The mug was passed back over, and they both took it in turns to take a swig of the now half-full mug before passing it back.

"Take as much as you want, Mike, don't worry about us," whispered Berry.

The two continued their conversation.

"You've seen some of the units pulling back?" asked Graham.

"Yeah, some of them were in shit state."

"They've taken a bit of a hammering, that's for sure."

"Our turn next."

There was a pause as the rapidly emptying mug did the rounds again.

"You scared, buddy?"

"Yeah, bricking it," Graham confided.

"Why have they left us alone so far?"

"Dunno, but they've been knocking ten bells of shit out of the guys back there," said Graham, pointing back over his shoulder.

"Probably to wake the fucking REMFs up," hissed Finch.

This brought another gentle laugh.

"Nah, although they deserve it," continued Graham. "They're just hammering our supply lines and reserves. Making sure they aren't getting through to us."

They had listened to the whine of large calibre shells flying high overhead as the Soviet artillery pounded 1st British Corps' rear area. There had been many false alarms as Soviet fast ground-attack aircraft had shot past, but again their targets were NATO forces to the rear; disrupt supplies and reinforcements getting to the front, interdicting the men and equipment badly needed to shore up the defence line being assembled to hold back the Warsaw Pact juggernaut. A huge cheer had gone up when a Tracked Rapier, from across the River Leine, had launched a missile that had torn one of the intruders out of the skies above. The pilot, not having a chance to eject from his stricken plane, went down with his aircraft which exploded in a ball of flame somewhere behind Bravo-Troop's position. The soldiers watching cheered, but for some reason their hearts weren't in it. Many had served in Northern Ireland, sniped at by the IRA, losing close friends from a burst of M-60 fire or a sniper's bullet fired from an antiquated Lee-Enfield. But this was on a different scale. Ambulance vehicles had been crossing the bridge throughout the day. Soon it would be their turn.

"But some are getting through to us, aren't they?" asked Berry, seeking some reassurance from his NCO.

"Yeah, yeah, of course they are. Where do you think this NAAFI tea comes from?" he suggested, holding up his mug that had made its way back into his hand, but was now empty. Hot, sweet tea was pretty much the only luxury they regularly had, although the occasional hot meal was a welcome relief. Graham peered at the luminous dial of his watch, a gift from his girlfriend, Sarah, given to him on the day he was promoted to Lance Corporal, the first step on a very long ladder. It was a proud day for him, and his family. Now he was second in command of a ten-man infantry section.

It was 0330; they had been on stand-to since three, higher command convinced that an attack would come today. A full scale assault or just a probe? No one really knew. He heard a rustle off to the left, his SLR rifle swinging round in the direction of the noise. The figure of a British soldier loomed out of the gloom, and Corporal David Carter, the section commander, crouched down at the rear of the Milan firing position.

"All right, lads?"

"Fine, Corp, so long as you've brought us a brew."

"Fuck off, Berry."

"Corporal."

"Just heard from HQ. They reckon we're going to be hit within the next hour or so, so keep your bloody wits about you. You, in particular, Finch. Before that though, we'll see an infantry platoon and a couple of Chieftains making hell for leather towards the bridge, so keep your fingers off that Milan trigger. Understood?"

They all acknowledged, their mouths suddenly dry, even after the drink. Finch couldn't help but lick his dry lips, a knot building up in his stomach. There was no malice in the Corporal's voice, just banter in an attempt to keep his men alert, but at ease, not tense. If they felt anything like he did, they would be shitting themselves. But he couldn't show it, needing to set an example to the small force under his command. If they sensed how he really felt, it would dent their own confidence. He had ten firing positions in total: seven in a line along the edge of the field in front of the small village behind, and three behind those. One he had just left to the north with two men; this Milan firing point; next another foxhole with two soldiers, one being LCPL Graham's position; then a second Milan Post; then a Gympy team of two, the general-purpose machine gun, the main weapon of the small section; and one more foxhole to the south with the mortar fire controller and forward air controller, although they hadn't seen much air support. They had been told that the RAF were still trying to gain air superiority, and due to the many airfields being hit by missiles and bombs, and some being attacked by Spetsnaz, squadrons were having to shift position. In the last one he had positioned the sustained-fire GPMG, attached from the support company. The three holes further back, maintaining a defence in depth, would be manned by himself and the rest of the section. Two of those men were in the house further back, but he would pull them out of there shortly. The two Milan firing posts came from the battalion's anti-tank platoon, from support company. The platoon commander had also given him two LAW 66mm anti-tank rockets, useful for close protection should the Soviet armour get too close. It didn't seem very much, but he had been reassured when he passed the solid, powerful-looking Chieftain tanks off to his left. If he listened carefully, he would just be able to make out the throbbing engines. Only three tanks though, and a couple of 438s, he thought. He wouldn't be sorry when they were pulled back across the water, back amongst the rest of the battalion. At least then, he and his men would have a river flowing between them and the Soviet army.

"Keep your wits about you," Carter encouraged. "Once you've fired two Milan missiles, pull back to your alternate position. It won't take them long to zone in on your original position. And, for fuck's sake, take your time. Don't be rattled. Better to take a couple of seconds longer and take one of the bastards out. Don't forget, we're not here to stay, so be ready to bug out when we get the word. The 432s are right behind you, just south of the village. I may bring the Peak-Turret forward if we need more support. If we have to pull right back, don't go through the village itself," he advised. "By the time the Sovs have finished with it, it'll be a rock pile. OK?"

"Yes, Corp," they all responded.

"Get to your hole, Will," he said to his second in command. "I'll be in the one behind you once I've been along the line."

With that, he got up from his crouch and made his way along the line of the forward firing positions, talking to his men, cracking jokes, pulling them up if their kit needed sorting, confirming their arcs of fire. Once complete, he felt a little more confident now he had exchanged some jokes with his men. Sergeant Thomas had been called back across the river, his task to make sure the rest of the platoon were well dug in. His platoon commander, Lieutenant Chandler, had also paid them a visit before being called to a combat team brief. The Lieutenant in command of the tank troop, Lieutenant Wesley-Jones, was in overall command on this side of the river. He seemed a decent enough bloke for a Rupert; in fact he came across as quite switched on. That made him feel better – although, in reality, he and his crew would be battened down under fifty tons of armour, fighting their own battle to worry too much about a handful of grunts. He was determined to do his best for his men, his mates. Yes, they were his mates. Finch got on his tits at times and Will could dither a bit, but he wouldn't want to fight alongside any others. He was in command, and he would keep a grip of his section and those attached, get them back safely, or at least die trying.

0340 7 July 1984. Bravo-Troop (+). Gronau, West Germany.
The Black Effect −1 day.

Sergeant Andrews and Corporal Simpson were crouched down at the rear of Two-Two-Alpha, Lieutenant Wesley-Jones, their troop commander, whispering last-minute instructions to his two tank commanders. He was kneeling down and, even through the layer of his combat trousers and Noddy suit, could feel the cool ground, cooled as a consequence of a fine dew that had freshly formed during the night. He caught a faint whiff of the ground beneath, but generally it was overpowered by the smell of the Chieftain's engine as it ticked over, and even, although not too bad at the moment, the smell of his own unwashed body. He had removed his woolen jumper earlier in the day. With the jumper, a combat jacket and the NBC smock, he had found a film of sweat forming on his body every time he moved. It was pretty cool in the early hours of the day, but as dawn broke and the sun rose higher in the sky, so did the temperature, sometimes reaching as high as twenty-four degrees Celsius. His tank was pulled up to the edge of the berm, the OC calling a stand-to. With the trees behind them, a heavily camouflaged turret and main gun, the enemy would struggle to see them until it was probably too late. The small forest they were in front of was less than half a square kilometre, a prominent outcrop on the eastern edge of the German village of Gronau. His tank was at the northern part of the small forest, where he could cover the open fields to their front, as far out as Betheln, a village three kilometres to the north-east. South of Betheln and about a thousand metres closer lay the village of Barfelde, linked to Gronau via a metalled road, Barfelde Strasse. There were four Scorpions, from the regiment's reconnaissance troop, situated around Barfelde and Gut Dotzum, watching and waiting for the enemy to move. The rest of his troop, Two-Two-Bravo to his left and Two-Two-Charlie to his right, had pulled forward into their berms, and soon their respective tank commanders would be joining them. Further left, the ground to the left of the road was raised slightly, providing a shallow plateau, and close to the western edge of it, two FV438s had dug in. Any enemy armour approaching from the east between Gronau and Betheln, across open ground, could be picked off by the two FV438s and their Swingfire anti-tank missiles. The crew had a foxhole about fifty metres from each vehicle, linked by a control unit, in a position where they could watch any approaching armour. With the Swingfire missile capable of making a ninety-degree turn once launched, the vehicles could be hidden and the crew firing it from a safe location. He was in command of the entire force on this side of the river. It wasn't large, but they would still hit the enemy hard.

Wesley-Jones spoke. "If I can't get you on the radio, or even if Squadron can't get me, they will fire two red flares. That will be our signal to bug out."

"The Sovs will know that as well, sir."

"I know, Sarn't, but staying here and getting cut off once they've blown the bridge will be far worse."

"Flare it is then, sir," Sergeant Andrews responded with a smile.

"So keep your eyes peeled, both of you. There'll be all sorts flying around."

"How long will we have, sir?" asked Corporal Simpson.

"Ten minutes notice. So there will be no drills. Blow your smoke dischargers and head for the bridge in double-quick time."

"Sir," they both acknowledged.

"I hope they choose another bloody troop for point next time."

"I'll make sure of it, Sarn't." The Lieutenant laughed.

"Sir...sir."

Wesley-Jones looked up to see the silhouette of Corporal Patterson on the engine deck of the Chieftain, leaning over.

"Corporal?"

"We've got movement out there, sir."

Alex was up in a flash and quickly shook hands with his two tank commanders who then sped off to join their own tank crews, ready to take on the inevitable Soviet tank advance. Alex ran round to the side, then the front and climbed up onto the glacis plate, then onto the turret before slotting into his commander's position.

"Where?"

Patsy handed his troop commander the binoculars and pointed. "About one o'clock, well over 1,000 metres, I would imagine." He then dropped down into the fighting compartment, grabbed his headset, settling into his seat, face up against the sights of the one-twenty-millimetre gun, and awaited orders.

Alex quickly zoomed in on the area and immediately picked up the shape of moving armour clawing along the road. "Two-Two-Bravo, Two-Two-Charlie. Standby. All Two-Two call signs, standby, standby. Movement, direction Barfelde, 2,000 metres."

The turret moved to the left by about ten degrees as Patsy tracked the oncoming vehicles. Alex's crew were on the ball. He couldn't quite make out the shape, but was sure the lead vehicle was a tank like his, a Chieftain. If the group did a dog-leg off the road, to avoid the mines laid alongside the road, it would more than likely be a Brit unit, probably the remnants of 4th Armoured Division, the final units limping back.

The lead vehicle dropped off the road, closely followed by the rest, and Alex allowed himself a sigh.

"I think they're ours, but don't relax just yet." He spoke into his mike boom in front of his mouth. "It could be a trap, or there are Sovs close behind hoping to be led through our minefields."

He could hear the roar of the straining engine as the lead Chieftain made its way back up onto the road, the sound distinctive, the vehicles following now coming into view: two Chieftains and three 432s. The last Chieftain in line looked OK, its turret and gun facing backwards over the engine deck, covering the withdrawal. The lead Chieftain, in front of the 432s, sounded and looked very different. The engine was cutting out intermittently, the driver going quickly through the gears in an attempt to keep the fifty-ton monster on the move. The tracks squealed loudly, more than was normal, and the turret appeared frozen at a forty-five-degree angle, the barrel twisted and bent over the rear engine deck.

"These guys have been in the thick of it," Alex said to himself.

The growling of the engines grew louder as they headed for the bridge, clouds of black smoke now visibly emanating from the engine of the lead tank. The engine screamed louder, fighting against the driver's efforts to keep it running and the tank moving as he desperately tried to get across the bridge and home. Home being safe across the river amongst a more powerful force, protected.

Alex could still smell the lingering fumes from the lead tank after it had passed, smoke pouring from its engine. He hoped they would make it to Gronau.

"They're ours," he called down to his crew. "But standby. We don't know what's coming in behind them."

0350 7 July 1984. Recce-Troop (-). Barfelde, West Germany.
The Black Effect −1 day.

Lieutenant Baty lowered the binos and rubbed his eyes before raising them again. He felt slightly afraid that, if he took his eye off the ball for only a second, the enemy would be on top of them. He tried his best to discern any distinctive shapes on the edge of the Gronauer Holz Forest, an indication that the enemy were preparing to leap forward and continue their assault west. He was covering an arc from ten o'clock to nearly two o'clock. He had definitely seen some signs of movement and had reported it back up the line. But, for the moment, it was quiet. His Scorpion was in an open-ended barn, stacks of straw bales across the front and the sides hiding his armoured reconnaissance vehicle from the eyes of the enemy, fulfilling their motto: 'to see without being seen'. His task was not to fight the enemy, although their 76mm gun could pack a punch, but to be the eyes and ears for the regiment, so the

105

Chieftain tanks could deliver a deadly blow to any advancing armour. He knew the enemy were out there somewhere, close on the heels of the battered unit that had just passed through. The term higher command were using was that they were pulling back, to consolidate a better defensive position. In reality, thought Baty, they were on the run.

He shifted in his turret, the NBC suit chafing the skin of his neck, making it itch, no matter how well he pulled up the collar of his shirt beneath it. The inside black charcoal layer always managed to irritate somehow. He was hot, sweaty and tired; the thought of a shower under hot running water a mere dream. They had not experienced any chemical strikes to date, but now was not the time to relax their guard, and orders from on high had stated they were to remain at NBC level Romeo-four.

"*Two-One, this is Two. Orders. Over.*"

"Two-One, send. Over."

"*Move to grid Yankee, Delta, Two, Charlie, Echo, Five.*"

"Roger, moving now. Out."

Baty informed his driver, and the engine of the heavily camouflaged Scorpion increased its revs as the driver backed the vehicle out of the barn.

"Stop. Left stick," he informed the driver up at the front of the vehicle. "Forward. Stop."

Baty checked the map, shielding the red filtered torch, but the ambient light was improving every minute. He then guided the Scorpion to their next position; higher command no doubt wanting a report on what could be seen from this new location. On instructions from himself, the second Scorpion followed at a safe distance behind. The two vehicles of the recce troop were on the very eastern edge of the village of Barfelde, and they followed the road, Burg Strasse, as it tracked around to the right until they found themselves on An der Schmau. With houses either side of the street covering their left and right flanks, they remained unseen. The streets were deserted as were most of the houses. Most of the German population had fled west, although they had seen at least one elderly couple who had no intention of leaving their home, even for the Soviet army.

"Right stick, take us through the gap then left. Take us up to the edge."

The Scorpion spun on its tracks, turning right, in between the two houses, flattening a small picket fence, turned left and stopped after seventy-metres, up against a dense line of thicket and a few small saplings. This would provide good cover while they conducted surveillance of the northern part of the village and the open ground out front. The other Scorpion pulled into a hedgeline, but further south, closer to Schul Strasse. Baty's troop was responsible for watching the approach roads and ground to Gronau, and reporting back.

"Stop, stop."

The Scorpion rocked gently on its suspension as it came to a halt. The crew quickly spread an array of foliage across the glacis and turret, completely softening the hard lines of the armoured vehicle. It blended in well with its surroundings. The binos were up to his eyes in seconds, a quick scan left to right to identify any immediate threats. Nothing. Perhaps as the light improved, he would be able to see more. It was three-fifty. In the meantime, they would have to wait.

Chapter 14

0350 7 July 1984. 25th Tank Division, 20 Guards Army.
Helmstedt, East Germany.
The Black Effect −1 day.

After arriving at Helmstedt the previous evening, and after a very
short rest period, the division was again on the move. The next stage,
taking them to the area of Salzgitter, would have to be handled very
differently. Although still some way from the battlefield, there was an
ever greater risk of NATO airstrikes; deep strikes in order to disrupt the
Soviet flow of ammunition and other much needed supplies. But one
additional target, reinforcements, would also be on their list. Although,
in some cases, the reinforcing units were of an inferior calibre, what
they lacked in aggression and expertise, they certainly made up for in
sheer numbers. But not the 25th Tank Division. This unit had trained
hard and was more than ready to give a good account of itself. Now
the division had been split into three independent columns. Each
column would march along one of three separate parallel routes, in the
region of six to eight kilometres apart. The total width of the march
sector taken up by the 25th Tank Division would be in the region of
thirty-two kilometres wide. Each of the Division's regiments, and even
down to battalion, would need to be prepared to deploy into a battle
formation as soon as ordered. They would halt for up to an hour, every
three to four hours. Once they reached Salzgitter, sixty kilometres
west, they would be at their departure line; ready to receive orders as
to when and where they would be committed to battle.

0350 7 July 1984. 8th Guards Tank Division. Torun, Poland.
The Black Effect −1 day.

After a journey of nearly fifteen hours, travelling for 400 kilometres, the
division came across its first obstacle. The railroad bridge and the road

bridge at Torun had been destroyed. NATO bombers had flown in low, keeping well below Soviet radar, and attacked both. Thinking that was it, Soviet engineers immediately began to throw another bridge across, using the infrastructure that was already there as the foundation. But a follow-on attack prevented the reconstruction, killing many of the engineers in the process. The trains started to stack up, there being no route for them to continue their journey. Yes, they could turn back, but the parallel railway lines were already at congestion point with so many units moving reinforcements to the front, along with essential supplies. A local commander, a Polish officer, an engineer, had been charged with finding a solution. Local and Soviet engineers were pooled and tasked with getting this badly needed division across the water. The solution, although difficult, was obvious. They brought together as many ferries as they could lay their hands on, and with pontoons and floatable makeshift platforms, they started the long, drawn-out process of getting the unit across to the other side.

Chapter 15

0400 7 July 1984. Bravo-Troop (+). Gronau, West Germany.
The Black Effect −1 day.

"All Two-Two call signs. Incoming! Incoming!"

Alex dropped down into the turret, pulling the hatch down after him. "Gas, gas, gas!" he yelled, pulling his respirator on, followed by the hood of his suit, his rubber neoprene gloves already on. Although the Chieftain tank had an NBC protection system, attached at the rear of the bustle, he knew that any rupture of the fighting compartment would leave them exposed.

"All covered?" he called to the crew.

All three responded positively, a slight tremor to their metallic-sounding voices.

Oh God, thought Alex, *it's finally come.*

0400 7 July 1984. Bravo-Troop (+), call sign Two-Two-Delta.
Gronau, West Germany.
The Black Effect −1 day.

Corporal Carter pulled his body down as low as possible in the confines of the slit trench, two soldiers of his section doing the same. His vision seemed to suddenly turn dark as over 1,000 122mm rockets landed along the full length of the thin line of the Bravo Troop element of the British troops defending this sector of Gronau. The entire stretch of ground appeared to lift up as one as the combined weight of explosives tore into the ground, a dense cloud of dust and debris forming a layer, as if levitating, ten-metres above the ground. No sooner had it levelled at that height than a continuing ripple of explosions maintained it, a screen of debris and shrapnel smashing everything it touched. Those on the other side of the river looked on in awe, seeing nothing but a blanket of death that shielded their eyes from anything they might recognise as landmarks. The enlarged foxhole sheltering the Mortar Forward Controller and Forward Air Controller was hit by two rockets, one after the other, that tore the trench apart, sending chunks of prefabricated panels skyward like misshapen Frisbees; the bodies of the soldiers they had been trying to protect were not far behind them, crashing to the ground, torn apart and unrecognisable. No sooner had the ripple of rocket strikes and explosions started to die off than the crews were already preparing the reload for the next launch, but in the meantime, heavier calibre shells took over the onslaught.

0400 7 July 1984. Bravo-Troop (+), call sign Two-Two-Bravo.
Gronau, West Germany.
The Black Effect −1 day.

Two-Two-Bravo's crew pressed their rubber-gloved hands to their ears as shrapnel from the exploding shells gouged their Chieftain tank, spattered it with flying masonry and bricks from as far afield as the village. Other objects that got in the way of the barrage, added to the debris as the shelling pounded the ground around them.

Clang...ting, ting...clang...clang, clang...clang. Shrapnel eat away at the armour, gouging rents into its outer skin, stripping off anything it could find such as the Gympy, aerials and stowage bins. *BOOMF!* The one side of the tank was lifted completely off the ground, as a 152-millimetre shell exploded right next to it. The track shredded, stripped away from the bogie wheels as if a zip ripped from a garment. The crew as one cried out in fear as a second and third shell ensured the upward momentum of the fifty-ton giant was maintained, flipping it onto its side as if a mere toy.

Sergeant Andrews smashed his head against the hard metal of the turret, his bone-dome saving him from a more serious injury, but a smashed hand put paid to him operating in a tank again for some time – providing he was able to get out.

His gunner, Lance Corporal Owen, fared worse. His body was thrown violently against the breach of the 120mm gun, crushing his ribs and piercing his lungs with splinters of the now exposed ivory bone, his gasps for breath suffocated by the frothy blood, flecking the lens of his respirator with pink spots as it slowly engulfed the inside of his mask. A cry of agony was drowned out by the cacophony of sound outside as the tank continued to be buffeted by the barrage. He tried helplessly to move a broken arm to relieve himself of the mask that was preventing him taking the urgent, deep breath his body and mind craved for. Now distraught, he frantically tried to remove his mask, rubbing its surface against the front of the fighting compartment, desperate to dislodge the respirator that was slowly sucking the life out of him. One last attempt failed as his lungs collapsed, and the very mask that was designed and issued to save his life in the event of a chemical attack, killed him.

The Chieftain, stripped of everything that had been attached to its exterior, the barrel buckled and useless, settled at an uneven angle on its side, the battered gun barrel and the sides of the berm having prevented it from being turned upside down completely.

Trooper Lowe was pinned horizontally in the driver's compartment, on his side, in a space that could barely take a small man in normal circumstances, let alone when on its side. Lowe just stared into what little room he had, stunned. The vision blocks that he had depended on for an external view were now chipped and coated with earth, blinding him, having the effect of magnifying the sound of the shells that continued to explode around them. Tears ran down his cheeks; the urge to tackle the itch beneath his respirator almost as great as the need to escape his current position.

For fifteen minutes, the artillery strike battered the defenders on the eastern banks of the river before switching their interests to those troops watching from the western bank. The sounds and vibrations slowly faded as the guns and rocket launchers adjusted their aim to hit the rest of the defending forces.

0420 7 July 1984. Recce-Troop (-). Barfelde, West Germany.
The Black Effect −1 day.

Rocket after rocket, shell after shell flew over the heads of the two Scorpions in Barfelde. Lieutenant Baty risked poking his head out of the hatch, the tumultuous barrage going on above and behind him. He swallowed and, although in his heart he felt for his fellow soldiers further back, he was thankful that he and his men weren't on the receiving end. The soldiers on the east and west bank of the River Leine, however, were getting the full attention of the massed Soviet artillery, the intention to smash the British army's resistance. For now, though, he and his men were safe. Although a worry filtered to the surface of his thoughts. If they weren't hitting Barfelde, it could mean the Soviets were going to move troops to the immediate area under cover of the shelling, using the L482 road to the south-east, or coming across the open ground from the east. Either direction, he and his second recce unit would be able to see them and report. His gunner, Lance Corporal Alan Reid, called up, "Is it bad, sir?"

"The lads behind are getting a pasting, I should imagine. Thomas OK?"

"Needs a piss, but I told him now is not the time."

This brought a laugh from them both.

"No, he needs to stay put. Something is going to happen as soon as the shelling has stopped, if not before."

"We'll be ready, sir." Reid went back to his gun sight, ready for whatever was to be thrown at them. He had confidence in his troop commander.

The young officer, on the other hand, was not so sure. He shifted his slim frame as he mulled over the likely options of what could transpire. He patted his respirator case, making sure it was on hand should he need it urgently. He had contemplated ordering his men to mask up as the first salvos had flown overhead, but relented. He needed his vision to be clear and unobstructed if he was to observe the slightest of movements from the vicinity of the forest in front. The explosions were occurring at least two kilometres back, and the wind was from the east, so he was confident that he had made the right call. His watch told him it was four-thirty, as the ordnance continued along its westerly flight above him. Picking up his binos, he scoured the horizon, looking for any sign of enemy activity – any activity for that matter. Once spotted, he could report it back and bring down some of their own artillery and start hitting back. Minute after minute, Soviet missiles and shells arced overhead, impacting on his comrades, the bombardment unrelenting.

Thump...thump, thump...crump...boom...crump, crump, crump... thump.

His head started to throb; the heat of the turret's confined space; the uncomfortable Noddy suit; barely a few hours' sleep in the last forty-eight hours; the constant drumming behind him. He suddenly felt disorientated and somewhat isolated, wishing he was back home in England, or even back at Regimental HQ, preparing to go to a mess dinner. He knew they were the furthest unit east, the last of the battered 4th Armoured Division in their area, having passed through the village about an hour ago. His ears perked up as he recognised a change in the sound of the barrage: the torrent of missiles and shells were still rolling west, but now across the river, targeting the troops on the west bank, headquarters' formations and those reserves dug in further back. It continued unabated for another fifteen minutes; then silence. When the silence came, it was eerie, almost disconcerting.

Baty shook his head and spoke to his crew through the intercom. "Standby, lads. This quiet won't last for long. All Two-One call signs report. Over."

"*Two-One-Alpha, all OK.*" His second in command was in one of two Scorpions watching the approaches from the village of Gut Dotzum.

"*Two-One-Bravo, all quiet. Out.*" The second Scorpion in Gut Dotzum was reporting all quiet.

"*Two-One-Charlie. All OK.*" The southern part of Barfelde was quiet as well.

"Bugger."

"What is it, sir?" asked his gunner.

"Watch your front, enemy movement. 1,500 metres, ten o'clock, Track 2, BMP-2."

The turret whirred as Reid slowly turned the turret, moving it gently so as not to cause any sudden movement that could be noticed, the 76mm gun soon aimed in the direction of the Soviet mechanised infantry combat vehicle.

"All Two-One call signs. Enemy movement 1,500 metres, north-east Barfelde."

The BMP-2 had emerged from the western edge of the forest in front of them, creeping forward, sniffing out the territory that lay ahead of it.

Baty kept his gunner informed of the enemy's movement. "First BMP-2 moving north-west, second BMP-2 following."

"Roger. Ready to fire. First BMP, then the second."

"Two more BMPs, moving south-west. Stay with the ones to the north, but hold your fire."

"Roger."

"Two-One-Charlie. You have two Bravo-Mike-Papa-Twos, 1,500 metres out, heading your location. Over."

"*Understood. Have visual. Southern sector quiet. Over.*"

"Roger."

More vehicles emerged from the forest. A couple of BRDM-2s, an SA-9 to provide air cover, and a T-80 fanning out and picking up speed, heading towards Barfelde.

"Two-One, this is Two-One-Charlie. Three Bravo-Mike-Papa-Twos and one Tango-Eight-Zero heading north-west towards my location. Over."

"Roger. Their start point? Over."

"Direction of Eitzum, north-west along Lima, four, eight, two. Over."

"Roger, Two-One-Charlie. Standby. Hello Two, this Two-One. Contact to my front. Two, Bravo-Mike-Papa-Two's and one Tango-Eight-Zero, two, Bravo-Romeo-Delta-Mike-Two's and One, Sierra-Alpha-Nine, fifteen-hundred metres, advancing my location. Need to move in two-mikes, over."

"Two-One, this is Two. Standby for outgoing. Out." The squadron headquarters had acknowledged his report and had also informed him of the anticipated strike from 1st Division's artillery assets.

"Hello Two, this Two-One. Two thousand metres south-east of Two-One-Charlie's position, three Bravo-Mike-Papa-Twos and one Tango-Eight-Zero."

"Two-One, this is Two. Roger that. Out."

0425 7 July 1984. 40th RA. South of Oldendorf, West Germany.
The Black Effect −1 day.

The triangular piece of land, bordered by trees and hedgerows, 600 metres east of Oldendorf, was an ideal spot for the one of the batteries of 40th Royal Artillery Regiment to use as a firing base. The eight M109A2s had lined up in two troops of four, ready to complete a fire mission to support the beleaguered troops to their front. M109A2, a Self-propelled Howitzer, was the indirect fire weapon of the artillery regiments of the British army, and for many artillery regiments and brigades of other NATO forces. The twenty-seven-ton SPH, with its 152mm gun, could pack a punch that would go some way to interdicting the Soviet advance that had just kicked off on the eastern side of the River Leine. The crew of six – the vehicle commander, driver, gunner, assistant gunner and two ammunition handlers – were preparing their particular gun ready for combat. This would be the first time they would have fired in anger. To date, 4th Armoured Division had taken the brunt of the Soviet advance. But, today, the Soviet army was going to be hit by fresh troops, fresh artillery, and more of it. They also had a little treat in store for the advancing forces: the M109A2s would be firing the new lethal round, the M483. This dual-purpose round would deliver sixty-four M42 and thirty-two M46 grenades.

The Corporal sat perched on the metal fold-down seat in the

back of the FV105 Sultan artillery command vehicle, his headphones pulled over his beret, listening intently to the message being received. He tapped on the numerical keys of the Field Artillery Computer Equipment (FACE) console, entering the setting up data for the gun positions. The Command Post Officer (CPO) was watching over him, clutching the remote enter button. The CPO was also checking that the correct data had been entered, comparing it and the target location against his check map, also confirming their own British unit locations. The meteorological and gun muzzle velocity data had been entered earlier via the punched tape reader. Satisfied the data entered was correct and that he was sure of the target location and the location of friendly forces, the CPO depressed the enter button. The counter-penetration fire mission was now ready. The officer gave the NCO the nod and the Corporal started to transmit.

"Zulu, this is Romeo, fire mission."

"*Zulu. Send, over.*"

"Sierra, Zero, Three, Two. Bearing Two-Six-Five, angle of sight one-oh-five. At my command, elevation Three-Eight-Nine mill, three rounds, fire for effect."

There was a pause while the gun battery finalised their own procedures.

"*Roger.*"

"Fire."

The entire battery of eight M109s opened fire, the chassis' rocked violently on their tracks and suspension as the barrels jumped upwards, the barrel and breech forced backwards as the shell exited the barrel, a blast of hot gases bursting out from the muzzle brake. The barrels lowered and, inside the turret, the breech was raised, presenting itself to the crew for reloading. One of the crew pushed the shell into the breech; another gunner pushed a red bag charge after it. The breech was secured, the gunner yanked on the lanyard, and the breech rocked back a second time.

0430 7 July 1984. Recce-Troop (-). Barfelde, West Germany.
The Black Effect −1 day.

Two-One and Two-One-Charlie watched the first salvo land directly on top of the rapidly growing force of armoured vehicles advancing towards their respective positions. One Royal Artillery battery was targeting the area directly where elements of a Soviet tank battalion, at least company strength so far, was advancing on a broad front towards Barfelde. A second battery targeted the road between Barfelde and Eitzum, and a third battery pounded the road that led from Eberholzen to Heinum, about two to three kilometres south of Barfelde. Lieutenant Baty watched incredulously as the first rounds struck the advancing T-80s and BMP-2s. Above the targets, the eight dual-purpose, Improved Conventional Munitions descended on their unsuspecting victims. A fraction of a second before they hit the ground, the thin-walled cargo rounds disgorged their sub munitions; the small burster charge ejecting them, scattering the lethal charges over a wide area. A small ribbon unfurled behind each grenade, stabilising their flight as over 700 plummeted towards their targets. Baty watched as some of the grenades struck the tops of the BMPs, the one-kilogram shaped charges detonating, penetrating the thinner top armour.

At least two of the mechanised infantry combat vehicles ground to a halt as a lethal charge punched through the thin upper layer, causing devastation inside. One went up on its back end as it ground to a halt violently, the driver's body torn apart by molten metal and shrapnel. Further back, one tank was hit three times; initially protected by its reactive armour, but only to be struck again and again as the next salvo of over 700 grenades arrived, two punching through the areas recently stripped of the reactive armour blocks. Fifteen seconds later, a third swarm of munitions blanketed the battlefield in a lethal rain of death. Soviet soldiers, fleeing their stricken armoured vehicles, ran into a rain of metal shards as those grenades that struck the ground detonated in a lethal shower of hot fragments. The Soviet advance was stopped dead in its tracks. But they would be back. Baty knew it was time to move out. They would travel, at speed, back to Gronau and the relatively safe western bank of the River-Leine. But the Soviet armour would be hot on their tail.

0450 7 July 1984. Bravo-Troop (+). Gronau, West Germany.
The Black Effect −1 day.

"Is everyone OK?" called Lieutenant Wesley-Jones, his voice muffled by the black respirator.

"Ellis and me are OK, sir," Patsy responded.

"Trooper Mackinson?"

"Apart from a ringing in my ears, sir, I'm still alive."

"Good, good. Standby. They're bound to be close behind their artillery." Wesley-Jones released the hatch cover, pushing it up and out of the way as he gingerly climbed up, taking a tentative look over the edge of the hatch. The immediate surrounding area was completely churned up, and he was amazed they had come through relatively unscathed. Looking over his shoulder, he saw the whites of splintered trees and branches, shredded by the myriad of explosions that had gutted the area. The berm, a key part of their defensive location providing them with a defilade position, had, in the main, survived, although to the rear of the tank there were two craters they would have to negotiate when they pulled out. The Chieftain hadn't come through it completely unscathed though. Numerous scorch marks and gouges covered the glacis, and the left-hand set of smoke dischargers had completely vanished. Further out, the view of the horizon was blocked by a swirling fog of smoke, dust and fume, the air still full of dust and debris as it slowly settled back down to the ground. The turret jerked slightly and the barrel moved a fraction as Patsy checked that the tools of his trade were in working order. Alex checked the detector paper on his Noddy suit. It was clear; no evidence that there were chemical substances in the air. He took a chance, pulled up the front of his respirator and did a quick sniff test before pulling it back down. If his memory served him right, some smelled of garden plants whereas some smelled of almonds. But, he knew that the highly toxic Sarin and VX nerve agents had no smell. The wind was easterly, so any residue would be blowing to the west. But, to be safe, he would keep his gloves on just in case there was a residue on the surface of the tank. He tugged at the NBC hood and pulled his sweat-soaked respirator up over his face and off, taking shallow breaths to start with.

Crump, crump, crump...crump...crump, crump...crump, crump... crump.

The barrage continued behind him, not letting up on its pounding of the British defenders. He grabbed his bone-dome from inside the turret and settled it on his head, blocking out the sound of the explosions.

"All Two-Two call signs, radio check. All Two-Two call signs, this is Two-Two-Alpha. Over."

"Two-Two-Alpha, this is Two-Two-Charlie. Crew OK, engine deck partially buried, but should be clear to move. Recce element through our location. Over."

"Roger. Two-Two-Charlie, out to you. Two-Two-Bravo, this is Two-Two-Alpha, acknowledge. Over."

Apart from a slight trace of white noise, the network was silent.

"*Two-Two-Alpha, shall I check them out? Over.*"

"Negative. Watch your front."

"*Two-Two-Alpha, this Two-Two-Delta.*"

"Send. Over."

"*Two-Two-Delta. Have casualties, but still operational. Over.*"

"Roger that."

Alex was about to contact the Striker teams when...*crump, crump, crump. Crump, crump, crump.* Small mushroom-shaped clouds erupted along the entire front that was under the protection of the Bravo team, the rapidly expanding clouds of smoke taking the place of the dust, continuing to block out any visibility of what was beyond. Alex's ears pricked up as he heard the distinctive sound of helicopters, not just to his front but off to the right. An explosion occurred somewhere amongst the smoky barrier, followed by a second somewhere down the road between Barfelde and Gronau.

The roadside mines have gone off, Alex thought to himself. A vehicle had been coming straight down the road; the other explosion either an armoured vehicle had run into the minefield placed there the previous day or...

"Stand by, stand by," he yelled into the intercom. "They're breaching the minefield! All Two-Two call signs, they're on their way."

"*Roger,*" responded Two-Two-Charlie.

Still nothing from Two-Two-Bravo. Alex feared the worst.

"*Two-Two-Alpha, Two-Two-Echo. We don't have a visual, but both units intact.*"

"Roger that. Watch your front. There's movement in the minefield. Out."

Thank God, he thought, the 438s had come through it. They would need them before the day was out.

Another explosion. He could now see shapes and shadows through the murk that had been created by the Soviet smokescreen. The wind was not blowing in the Red Army's favour. Although it wasn't strong, the draughts, influenced by the high ground of the Hildesheimer Forest, running south-east to south-west, twisted the currents of air, now blowing in a northerly direction, pulling the smokescreen apart.

Alex's binoculars flicked from left to right and back again as he desperately searched for a sign of the enemy. *Boom.* Another explosion. They had to be using mine roller attachments, specially fitted to the front of certain tanks, the heavy steel rollers setting off the mines, leaving a clear path for the tanks following on behind. Or maybe it was a mine plough. They were coming through. He estimated where the sound had come from: maybe south of the road, ten degrees left. The road was probably temporarily blocked. Whatever was moving along it would need to be shoved off the road. If they went off the road to bypass it, they would stumble into the minefield either side. He dropped down inside and turned the commander's cupola ten degrees to the left.

"Possible target, eleven o'clock." He rested his head on the brow pad and peered through the binocular sight, ready to get the range of the enemy armour, or engage the enemy should Patsy have a problem. He pushed the rocker switch up, selecting the laser option ready to use the laser rangefinder, the input going directly to the ballistic computer. The turret whined and traversed as Patsy followed his orders, aiming the main gun in the direction given by his commander.

"Load sabot," Alex ordered.

Ellis grabbed a sabot projectile, slammed it into the breech, quickly followed by an explosive bag charge from one of the bag-charge containers. He pushed in the small charge, closed the breech and slid the safety shield, the loader's firing guard, across to protect him from the recoil of the huge 120mm gun's breech.

"Up," Ellis shouted. The main gun was now armed.

Patsy checked the ammunition selector was set for sabot, the red light showing the gun was ready to fire. He traversed the turret a bit further via the control handle and elevated the gun slightly. Once fired, the armour-piercing round would leave the barrel at over one and a half kilometres per second.

"Here they come." Lieutenant Wesley-Jones turned the cupola, enabling him to track the BMP that had just appeared out of the smoke. "Contact, 1,000 metres."

Alex pulled the hatch down above him, immediately looking through the frontal vision blocks. "Two-Two-Charlie, watch your arc."

"*Roger.*"

"On," called Patsy, his head up against the binoculars, his finger lingering over the red fire button.

"Fire!" Ordered Alex.

The Chieftain jolted, and the breech shot back violently to the rear of the fighting compartment as the armour-piercing, fin-stabilised discarding sabot round left the barrel, a puff of smoke following close behind it. Travelling at just under two kilometres a second, the penetrator slammed into the mechanised infantry combat vehicle, practically lifting it off its tracks, stopping it dead, smoke pouring from the back as the two surviving soldiers clambered out, collapsing to the ground, disorientated and choking on fumes. Alex didn't hesitate, pressing the selector button to switch from the main armament to the coaxial machine gun. Pressing on the elevation hand wheel for the commander's GPMG, he hit the red Bakelite firing switch, two short bursts killing the two soldiers.

A second round hit another tank, the extremely dense, long, slender dart, a long-rod penetrator driven by a high level of kinetic energy, drilled through the T-80's armour. Even the ceramic properties of the armour were unable to prevent a full penetration.

"Contact, 1,000, sabot." Alex spun the cupola to the left, tracking the next target, the turret going with him as he targeted the T-80 suddenly appearing out of the smoke. Then he started his search for the next mark, leaving Patsy to finish his task as the gunner.

"Up," yelled Ellis.

Patsy depressed the button, and another round headed for its target, this time something bigger. It struck the tank just to the right of the mantle, the force of the blow making the armoured giant shudder, but the exploding reactive armour blocks, initially designed for defeating shaped-charged weapons, still did a good job. Apart from some damage to the smoke dischargers, the tank kept rolling.

"Sabot," ordered Alex, his voice almost shrill as the pace of the battle picked up. Recognising this, he forced himself to calm down, setting the appropriate example to his men.

"Up."

Patsy fired again, the penetrator striking the Soviet tank in less than half a second from firing. This time, the strike was right in between the turret mantle and the main body of the tank, the hardened tungsten-carbide penetrator punching through the thick armour, smashing the auto-loader apart; then breaking up into fragments that ploughed into armour and flesh alike. Moments later, heat turned into fire, fire turned into an explosion as it ignited the ammunition, literally ripping the tank apart.

"A hit!" yelled Patsy.

"Steady, Patsy," coaxed the commander as he turned the cupola left, taking the turret with him. "Target, BMP, 700 metres. HESH."

Patsy again focused on his gunnery, his mind logging that the lieutenant had referred to him by his nickname. Ellis loaded a High Explosive Squash Head (HESH) round. "Up."

Patsy fired. The BMP, that had suddenly swung right as it zigzagged towards them, was struck full on the side, engulfed in a cloud of smoke and flame as it was literally pulverised. To the right, a second T-80 lurched into view, immediately taken out by Two-Two-Charlie. To the left, two striker missiles flared into view, launched at a ninety-degree angle, the gunners tweaking the controllers, keeping the 555-kilogram missile on track as the two rockets levelled out heading towards the two selected targets. All the controllers had to do was keep the target in the crosshairs, and the SACLOS would do the rest. The first went wildly off course, suddenly lurching upwards and flying vertically, no longer interested in its target. The second one, capable of penetrating up to 800 millimetres of armour, ploughed into a BMP, bringing it to a halt.

Another T-80 appeared out of the gloom, its barrel swinging towards Two-Two-Alpha's location. A bank of earth and debris splattered the glacis and turret as a Soviet armour-piercing round came in low, displacing part of the berm before ricocheting off the side of the Chieftain. Its force was badly depleted, but the crew knew that it had been a close one.

Alex saw the offending tank and took control of the turret, swinging it round to the right, on target in less than a second. "Sabot!"

Ellis went through his loading procedure, now completely in the swing of it. Round, bag charge, breech, firing charge, shield. "Up."

"I've got this," informed Alex. Head up against the tank laser sight, satisfied he was on target, he pushed the red firing button. The tank rocked and, in less than a second, the round struck, careering down the right side of the T-80's turret as the driver had veered right at the last minute. Thinking he was safe, the driver maintained his direction of travel, the gunner ready to hit Two-Two-Alpha again, only to be hit on the flanks by a Milan missile. Still not halted, it took Patsy's shot to finish the beast off, grinding to a halt less than 700 metres away. The breeze gathered strength, disrupting the smokescreen completely, allowing the Chieftains on the west bank of the river to join in. Although at an extreme range of 3,000 metres, the additional support was welcome, putting further pressure on the Soviet tank crews.

"Well done, Corporal Patterson."

"Leave the firing to me, sir." Patsy laughed almost maniacally as he depressed the firing button again, tearing a BMP-2 apart.

It's going well, thought Alex, although he knew they had been lucky. Their luck would run out if they didn't move to their alternate position soon. It was tempting to stay in this location, picking off the advancing enemy one at a time. The Soviets would not be so accommodating for long. Already BMP-2s were being ordered to unleash the AT-5 Spandrel anti-tank missiles, suppressing the enemy, allowing the armour up front to get close, then through the British line.

Some artillery erupted around the tanks, stripping off some of the protective blocks. A long-rod penetrator sliced through the upper section of a glacis, disabling the tank's firing systems and killing the gunner. The commander and driver desperately tried to get out of the stricken tank, only to be cut down by a British Gympy, waiting for this very moment to kill off the tank crew that had been trying to destroy them.

0500 7 July 1984. Bravo-Troop (+), call sign Two-Two-Delta. Gronau, West Germany.
The Black Effect −1 day.

Alan Berry settled into position behind the Milan firing post, his eye up against the sight as he tracked the target through the Milan's optical sight. He steadied his breathing and pulled the trigger. The missile burst from the launcher, ejecting the missile container tube from the launcher as it left, a white flare of its solid-fuel rocket clear to see as it headed for its target at 200 metres per second. Berry focused, all his thoughts on keeping a steady control of the launcher, keeping the crosshairs dead centre of the BMP-2 as it rumbled towards them, its 30mm cannon firing wildly as the driver jerked the vehicle left and right to make them a harder target. But, within four seconds, the stand-off probe of the shaped-charged warhead struck, huge clouds of smoke and fume blocking any further view of the vehicle as the Milan missile obliterated the BMP. Finch, on the other side of the Milan, immediately placed a fresh tube, with a new Milan-2 missile inside, on the side of the firing post ready to fire again. After this, they would change location. The other firing point should have already moved.

A platoon of three BMP-2s came to a halt 300 metres out, firing round after round of 30mm high-explosive shells at over 200 rounds per minute into the defending infantry. The Milan firing post further to the south, their position broken up by artillery shells and the crew in the process of picking up the launcher, took half a dozen hits, smashing the launcher and killing its crew. More BMP-2s pulled to a stop in a line facing the British defenders and the Soviet soldiers, sitting back to back on padded bench seats inside, pushed the two heavy rear doors open and started to climb out ready for action. Even after losing at least eleven BMPs and four T-80s to the British anti-tank fire, the two first echelon motor rifle battalions and the two supporting tank companies of the attacking motor rifle regiment, still had forty-nine BMPs and sixteen tanks to do battle with the small force they were up against. The six soldiers from each one came around the side of their infantry combat vehicles, AK-74s blazing. Behind them, spread along in a line, two platoons of three BMP-2s came to a halt, 200 metres further back, each disgorging two-AGS-17 teams. Within less than a minute, the twelve AGS-17s were set up on their tripods and, on the command, opened fire.

The onslaught was shattering. The British sustained-fire GPMG, supported by a sturdy tripod, sprayed the advancing Soviet soldiers with over 600 rounds a minute, the belt of 7.62mm rounds sliding quickly through the assistant gunner's fingers. The gunner attempted to create a 'beaten zone', the firer wishing he was part of a larger force with additional Gympys' in support. Then they could really give the Soviet infantry something to think about. His thoughts weren't to worry him for long.

The 30mm grenades from the AGS-17s started to land amongst the defending soldiers. The thirty-round boxes, one for each of the heavy infantry support weapons, fed the launchers and, within six seconds, nearly 400 grenades exploded amongst the defenders. The SF-Gympy was straddled by half a dozen, plus two arching directly into their fortified position. Both soldiers were killed instantly and the heavy machine gun destroyed.

Corporal Graham, situated in the rear line of foxholes, tried to maintain contact with his small force, but quickly realised he had lost a Milan-FP and the SF-GPMG, and another foxhole had gone quiet. He heard the whine of shells passing overhead towards the troops on the west bank of the Leine, the enemy swamping them with smoke to reduce their effectiveness in supporting the soldiers on the east bank. The 30mm rounds tore up the ground in front of him, high-explosive shells bracketing the village buildings behind as the T-80s joined in to support at least two Soviet infantry companies that had been ordered forward to take the village and secure the eastern end of the bridge that crossed the river at that point. Graham urgently needed some help.

He called forward the 432 from the outskirts of the village, rounds from the 7.62mm gun in the peak-engineering turret forcing the Soviet infantry to drop down and take cover.

"Alpha-One, Alpha-One, this is Two-Two-Delta. Where the fuck's our mortar fire? Over." He had to shout above the noise of another batch of 30mm grenades exploding off to his left.

All he got back was a hiss of static.

"*Two-Two-Delta, Alpha-One-One. We can't make contact with the MFC either. Give us a grid and range. Over.*"

"Wait, out."

A sudden explosion erupted behind him and off to the right as a succession of 30mm rounds from a BMP-2 annihilated the 432 he had brought forward for support.

With his finger on the map, he keyed his radio. "Alpha-One-One. Grid, Charlie-One-Seven, Mike-Two-Five. Fire for effect."

"*Roger.*"

He hoped to God the mortar rounds came soon while he still had some men left. He could hear the standard Gympy firing off to the left and the crack of SLRs. Peering through his binos, he a saw a Soviet soldier go down and suspected it had been a bullet from Jones's SLR. Only he could hope to hit someone at over 200 metres while under fire. He pulled his head down as a strip of ground twenty metres in front erupted, a piece of metal casing zinging off his helmet.

The crews of the two FV432s, manning effectively a self-propelled mortar carrier, adjusted the 81mm mortars, ready to support their beleaguered colleagues. The armoured vehicles, the rearmost part facing the enemy, the barrel of the mortars jutting out of the circular hole in the centre of the vehicles' fighting compartment, were ready. On orders from the corporal in command, two 81mm bombs were dropped into the tubes, the loaders ducking as the first of three rounds per vehicle were fired. The loaders bent down, picking up another bomb and, almost in unison, dropping two more rounds.

Graham watched as two mortar bombs landed just in front of the BMP-2s, the explosions causing no damage but disrupting the BMP-2 gunner's aim. A stream of smoke from each explosion drifted north, blinding both the BMP-2 gunners and the Soviet infantry. Four more rounds landed in front of the enemy line. He needed a direct hit. He knew it was only a matter of time before more BMP-2s arrived and, under cover of 30mm rounds and 30mm grenades, the Soviet motor rifle troops would assault his position. He doubted they would be able to hold them. They would be quickly over run.

"Alpha-One-One. Up fifty, five rounds, fire for effect. And make it fucking quick."

"*On way*," responded the mortar team commander.

Within fifteen seconds, two rounds exploded on top of the BMP-2 line, quickly followed by two every three seconds.

That'll fucking sort you lot, thought Graham. Now was the time to pull his men back to his line of foxholes, and he contacted them by radio and screamed down the line, the volume of fire from the enemy dropping off as more rounds exploded amongst them.

"Alpha-One-One. Fucking great. One tube, left fifty metres three rounds, then right fifty metres three rounds. Second tube up 200 then spread left and right. Got that?"

"*Roger, Two-Two-Delta.*"

If they could keep the pressure on the BMP-2s, give the AGS-17 teams something to think about, and get his men twenty-five metres further back, they had a slim chance. Graham heard the screams for a medic as his men pulled back to consolidate further to the rear. He leapt out of the foxhole, running low, guiding and helping his men back to relative safety. One badly wounded soldier struggling to keep up was quickly thrown over Graham's shoulder in a fireman's lift, finding the strength to run back and place the wounded man in a hole.

0510 7 July 1984. Bravo Troop (+). Gronau, West Germany.
The Black Effect −1 day.

Alex called to his driver. "Mackinson, we move in thirty seconds."

"Roger, sir."

He peered through the forward vision blocks as another Swingfire missile streaked across their front, the missile striking the T-80 perfectly, but the explosive reactive armour defeating the missile's attempt to penetrate the tank's protection.

One more, he thought, knowing he was taking a big risk, *then we must move*. Although he was loath to stop firing. The poor bloody infantry were getting a pounding and needed his firepower.

He adjusted his hydraulically operated seat slightly, then held the commander's grip switch, pushing it in giving him complete control, overriding the gunner. He pushed the button selector switch ensuring it was set for sabot and gave his orders.

"Sabot. I've got this one, Corporal. Standby to move, Mackinson."

Ellis did his job efficiently. "Up."

Alex hit the firing button and, within seconds, the T-80 that had been moving to outflank the 438s on the higher ground shuddered as the penetrator cut straight through the tank's thinner side armour, wreaking havoc inside, stopping the main battle tank in its stride.

Suddenly a Hind-D, one of a flight of four, appeared out of nowhere, a flying tank. It hovered about 2,000 metres out, its characteristic tandem cockpit with double-bubble canopy pointing directly at Two-Two-Alpha. Beneath one of its stub wings, an AT-2C, a Swatter anti-tank missile dropped, rocket motor firing and, at 150 metres per second, it came straight towards the now vulnerable tank. Alex knew that firing at it with the GPMG would be pointless: the titanium-protected cockpit could shield the pilot and weapons officer from up to .5o calibre weapons. The 7.62mm Gympy just wouldn't be enough.

"Hind! Back, back!" he screamed into the intercom. Mackey didn't need to be asked again, hearing the urgency in his commander's voice. Then he hit the single set of smoke dischargers, laying a blanket of smoke on the right front of the tank. Mackey floored the accelerator, the gearbox already in reverse, rapidly gaining speed, dipping into the crater behind them, the engine wailing as it fought to pull the back end up, the tracks attempting to grip as the heavy beast slid sideways.

"Right stick!" Yelled Alex.

Mackey pulled back hard on the right stick, forcing the back end of the tank to swivel left, now tackling the crater full on.

"You've got it. Go for it!"

Mackey powered the engine, and the Chieftain clawed its way back. Twisting to the left, then back on track, where he knew the gap he needed to pass through would be. Faster and faster.

"Bloody move, Mackinson! Left slightly."

Mackey flicked the right stick just enough to get back on track, then pushed the tank and its engine as hard as he could. It screamed in defiance as the anti-tank missile flew overhead. With a range of up to 4,000 metres, the Hind-Ds were not after Alex's troop yet, but were hitting out at the British armour on the western bank who were starting to have an impact on the advancing Soviet forces. The rear of the tank smashed into a young sapling, tearing it down, the right track shredding it as the fifty tons passed over it. Fifty metres into the trees and a Swatter missile, fired by a second Hind-D, having seen Two-Two-Alpha on the move, struck the foliage of another tree, exploding uselessly. They were safe for now. But Alex knew the Hinds would come hunting for them. He had Mackey move them deeper into the trees. Not too far though, as there was a clearing just before you entered the town of Gronau. The birds of prey would be watching that gap.

"Two-Two-Charlie, location? Over."

"*Two-Two-Charlie, outskirts of town, Dotzummer Strasse. Fucking Hinds. Over.*"

"Roger, Two-Two-Charlie. Hold position as best you can."

There was a sudden explosion out front.

"*Two-Two-Alpha. Rapier has just taken out a Hind. Blown the shit out of it.*"

"Calm down. Hold position if able."

"*Roger.*"

Alex tried to contact the infantry and 438s. From the Strikers he got nothing, but the infantry corporal was able to respond.

"*Two-Two-Alpha. We're in the shit here, sir. Managed to pull back to the second line. Multiple casualties. If we don't get out of here soon, we're fucked.*"

"Hang in there. Standby. Two-Two-Bravo, this is Two-Two-Alpha. Over."

Still no response. Alex pushed the turret hatch open, breathing in the fresh air, dragging it into his lungs, a relief after the smell and fumes from the firing of the GPMG and the main gun. He suddenly felt dizzy, exhausted. They had been under attack for nearly an hour now, yet it felt like they had been fighting for a full day. He heard the driver's hatch open, enabling Mackey to sit up, ease his aching limbs, lift his head out of the fridge. Still no response from his third tank though.

"Bravo-Zero, this is Two-Two-Alpha. Sitrep. Over."

"*Go ahead. Over.*"

"Lost contact with Two-Two-Echo call signs and Two-Two-Bravo. Infantry element under severe pressure. Over."

"*Understood. Help on the way. Just hang in there. Out.*"

Chapter 16

Colonel Trusov, now a full colonel, his new rank confirmed by radio an
hour earlier, made his way down a street in the small town of Harsum.
His T-80K was camouflaged in the woods behind him, manned by his
crew and the MTLB-RkhM-K, one of two, his mobile command post, had
gone on ahead, 200 metres to where the regimental headquarters
had been set up in a barn. From the south came the sound of small arms
fire. The West German *Landwehr* were doing battle with Soviet NKVD
forces, along with elements of the *VolksArmee,* the East German Army
and *Grenztruppen,* East German border guards, that had been shipped in
especially to subdue Hildesheim. It would take at least a regiment, if not
two, to take the town, but Trusov didn't much care so long as the enemy
were kept occupied and his men were kept out of it. The follow-on
forces would clear the town at a later date, should it prove necessary. He
passed a T-80 on his left, backed up in a side street. One of the tracks was
laid out to its fullest extent in front, the crew doing their best to make
a repair. He approached the men, and two AK-74s were immediately
aimed in his direction as they heard him approach.

"Sorry, sir," stuttered a sergeant, realising he had pulled a gun
on his Regimental Commander.

"Better you were ready, Sergeant. I may well have been
a Western saboteur. Your repairs going well?"

The Sergeant lowered his weapon and rubbed the back of
a blackened hand across his forehead, leaving a smear of oil and
grease. "This one will be fixed, sir, but we've had to cannibalise
another tank for the parts. When will we get some spares, sir?"

"They're on their way, Sergeant. When will this one be ready?"

"About an hour, sir."

"Good. We need as many tanks as possible operational. Keep up the good work."

"Sir."

He left the men to continue with their task and headed towards his HQ. Command had informed him that spares were on the way. He hoped that was the case. His equipment was now starting to feel the strain of being in battle for over forty-eight hours. The repair list was growing rapidly, and he needed as many tanks as possible ready. Although there was a major air battle for air superiority going on above him, NATO forces were still able to interdict some of the Soviet army's supply lines. And, despite the fact that his regiment was now considered the divisional reserve, he had a suspicion that he and his men would be needed far sooner than anyone expected. Although they had suffered battle losses in material and men, he sensed that this first phase of the war had been easy. Perhaps too easy. In part due to NATO's strategy of trading ground for time, and the fact that they were still flying and shipping reinforcements from the US and the British mainland. The assault that was planned to go ahead shortly would find a very different approach from the British, and their new Challenger tanks would be a formidable obstacle, not that the Chieftains didn't pack a heavy punch. Within fifty metres of his destination, he could hear the steady hum of the generators, powering the lights and the communications systems. As he approached his Regimental Headquarters, two sentries, who recognised him as their Regimental Commander, even in the dim early morning light, saluted and waved him through.

Trusov pushed his way through a layer of blankets that had been suspended from the roof of the open-ended barn. The other end had been closed off in a similar fashion, creating a space inside that could be lit without giving away their location to enemy aircraft that would likely be on reconnaissance missions in the skies above, searching for such targets. The officers and men jumped to attention as they recognised him, and he waved them back down. Lieutenant-Colonel Antakov, the Commander of the 1st Battalion, 62nd Guards Tank Regiment, was standing over a crudely assembled table, a temporary platform supported on wooden crates, perusing the map placed there, familiarising himself with the perceived positions of the enemy and those of his own units.

"Sir."

"Grigory, checking positions or hoping to catch a glimpse of the forthcoming battle?"

"Both, sir," Antakov responded, smiling; coming to terms with the fact that this man was now his senior, and his commander.

Trusov turned as one of the three radios, set up along one of the barn walls, crackled into life as a routine message was passed through. "The next radio transmission I hear that isn't critical to the success of this regiment's operational role, I will personally have the man responsible shot. Is that clear?"

"Yes, sir," all three radio operators responded, knowing that it was not an idle threat.

"We'll have bloody NATO rockets down our throats."

"Well, sir, it's going to kick off in ten minutes," said Lieutenant-Colonel Antakov, checking his watch.

Before Trusov could answer, the blankets were again pushed apart as three more Lieutenant-Colonels joined them. Oleg Danshov, commander of the third tank battalion, Kirill Mahayev, newly promoted in order to take over command of the second battalion from Trusov, and the commander of the unit's infantry battalion, Lieutenant-Colonel Pyotr Lachkov.

"Make yourself useful and sort out some drinks for over here," called Antakov to one of the junior lieutenants hovering on the fringes, watching over the radio operators in the command post. He in turn despatched a sergeant to fulfil the order. A second lieutenant was checking the latest supply returns, while a captain kept track of the radio log.

Another radio message came in and the Captain informed his senior officers. "Artillery strike has started, sir."

Trusov nodded and checked his watch. It was four in the morning. General Abramov had already informed his senior officers that, on the advice of his new Chief-of-Staff, Colonel Pushkin, he intended to bring the artillery barrage and the assault timings forward from the original time of four-thirty. Using the twilight to provide them with additional cover. Should the current wind speed and direction remain steady, a smokescreen would protect the advancing army from the prying eyes of the enemy, but it would also blind the Soviet tanks who would blunder about in the smoke, disorientated and potentially at the mercy of the NATO tanks and anti-tank missiles. They could just make out the thunder of the explosions in the distance, some ten kilometres away to the west. The defenders would now get thirty minutes of heavy bombardment, a deluge of shells, missiles and rockets shaking them to their very core.

"It's started then," said Mahayev, slightly nervously, having not yet fully adjusted to his promotion and higher level of responsibility. The day before he was junior to the other three battalion commanders; now, he was their equal.

"Have there been any changes, sir?" asked Danshov.

"No major changes other than bringing the assault forward. Colonel Pushkin has also convinced the General to hold back the air-assault battalion. He is suggesting we use them when we go for a second push."

"A second push? They've been running like rabbits. There were times when I thought we wouldn't be able to keep up with them," exclaimed Antakov, always the arrogant one. Trusov had already logged that this particular battalion commander was a hothead. Most of the tanks he had lost due to enemy action were as a consequence of his over-confidence. That was a trait that could perhaps be useful at some point in the future. But only when the time called for it, thought Trusov. Antakov was the officer who seemed to resent the change of command the most, believing it was he who should now be commanding the regiment. Trusov suspected that the man had links to someone higher up the military hierarchy, or even a politician. He would have to watch him closely.

"It's been deliberate, Grigory," advised Trusov. "The British make many mistakes, and many of their officers are incompetent. But, they are far from stupid."

There was a noise at the entrance as a sergeant, and a private, followed by his sergeant, brought a battered tray in, arrayed with an eclectic mix of mugs and a large plate of sandwiches: thick dark bread with a heavy layer of *Leberwurst*, no doubt appropriated from the local population.

"Excellent, excellent, Sergeant Tsvilenev. Someone finally knows how to use their initiative." Tsvilenev ordered the private put the plate in front of Trusov and the commander helped himself to one slice.

"They are moving into position, sir," called a lieutenant manning the divisional radio net.

"Put it on speaker," ordered Trusov.

The speaker, on top of one of the wooden tables, crackled into life.

"One-Zero, Six-One. All units in position."

"Roger, Six-One. Five minutes."

Trusov looked at the map, picturing where the 61st Guards Tank

132

Regiment would be forming up. A tank battalion would be moving north-west of Sorsum; the infantry battalion would be preparing to infiltrate Emmerke and provide cover for the battalion as it advanced, using the anti-tank missiles on their BMP-2s to target any British armour that exposed itself. A second battalion would be lying up east of Emmerke, ready to whip around the northern outskirts and go hell for leather south-west. Mine-clearing tanks would lead the way, and bridging units would be quickly brought forward to cross the Rissingbach, avoiding the small marshy area just north-west of Emmerke. The third battalion would be moving into the wooded area south of the high ground, Giessener-berge, ready to respond quickly, when committed to thrusting through a weak point in the enemy's defences.

"*One-Zero, this is Six-Three. Units in position.*"

"*Roger, Six-Three.*"

"They'll be around Giesen then," suggested Danshov.

"Yes," responded their commander. "A battalion will strike for the gap between Rossing and Barnten. The motor rifle battalion will push north of Rossing to cover the regiment's left flank with a tank company from the second tank battalion covering the north around by Barnten. The rest of the battalion will support the thrust through the gap. The third tank battalion will come forward when called."

"Two hundred tanks. The British are going to piss their pants."

"So they might, Kirill. But they have to cross at least three-kilometres of pretty much open ground first."

"The arty fire has stopped, sir," Lachkov informed the Colonel.

They all checked their watches as one. It was four-thirty.

But the reprieve for the Royal Hussars and the rest of 7th Armoured Brigade units didn't last for long. Four SU-25 ground-attack aircraft, with the NATO designation of Frogfoot, weighed down with weapons' loads of 80mm rockets, flew low above the barn, heading towards the front line. They were soon joined by another four. Overhead, SU-27 Flanker fighters and Mig-31 Foxhound fighters provided cover to protect their charges below. At least thirty Mig-27 Flogger ground-attack aircraft carrying 4,000 kilograms of bombs each weren't far behind.

A constant stream of aircraft flew over the barn and the village as the Soviet attack aircraft swooped in to deliver their deadly loads, complete a circuit and either drop the rest of their weapons load or strafe the dug-in defenders with their powerful cannon.

"16th Aviation Army have promised at least 200 sorties during this first hour."

"This has got to work, sir," Lachkov chimed in.

They heard a large explosion, high up and to the west. A Frogfoot had just been taken down by a Rapier missile.

"Let's hope so, Pyotr, let's hope so."

They chatted through various tactics, how they thought the battle would play out, while the air-to-ground attack and air-to-air battle went on around them. Trusov just listened most of the time, starting to get the measure of these men from a different perspective: one of command.

The speaker crackled. *"One-Zero, Six-One. Moving."*

"Roger, Six-One."

"One-Zero, Six-Three. Call sign Six-One-One advancing."

"Roger."

"First battalion on the way," suggested Antakov.

"About three-kilometres to Escherde," mused Trusov.

"One-Zero, call sign Six-One-Four moving."

"Acknowledged."

"One-Zero, call sign Six-One-Two moving. Six-One-Three holding position."

Antakov's hand swept across the map, the other flicking the ash from his evil-smelling cigarette to the floor.

"That's their motor rifle battalion heading for Emmerke and the second tank battalion sweeping north of the village."

"They'll need to be bloody quick with their bridging equipment," suggested Mahayev, his confidence steadily building. "If they get stuck west of Emmerke, they will be wide open to tank fire from Rossing."

"The 63rd will cover their flank," advised Lachkov.

"One-Zero, Six-Three. Six-Three-Four and Six-Three-One on the move."

"There they go." Danshov smiled. "The foot sloggers will push on Rossing, while the real work is done by the tanks."

That brought a laugh from the assembled officers. Even those on the periphery couldn't help but get caught up in the excitement. The group felt like voyeurs, spying on their comrades who were about to go into battle.

Every troop of the Royal Hussars' Battlegroup had been on the receiving end of a Soviet strike, whether by artillery, missiles or the bombs and rockets from Soviet aircraft. At least two of the low-flying attackers had been shot down by Rapier missiles, and one had been damaged by a Blowpipe shoulder-launched SAM. British RAF Tornado, Air Defence Versions (ADV) and a dozen West German Luftwaffe Phantoms called in to support, battled with the Soviet Flankers and Foxhound fighters at high altitude. Their preferred target was the Flogger ground-attack aircraft, preventing them from inflicting damage on the defenders dug in to hold back the massed tank attack that was about to ensue. They shot down five fighters and damaged a Foxhound, losing two Phantoms and a Tornado in the process, before breaking off the attack to refuel and rearm. More NATO aircraft were on the way, a maelstrom of activity forming overhead of the British 1st Armoured Division. But the Soviet air force was also sending in a second wave.

"*Delta-Four-Alpha, Delta-Four-Bravo...movement, 2,000 metres, near high ground west of Giesen. Cannot identify at this time. Over.*"

"Numbers. Over."

"*Delta-Four-Bravo...ah, maybe three, no four. Large, possibly main battle tanks. Over.*"

"Roger, out to you. Zero-Delta, this is Delta-Four-Alpha. We have sighting at grid Charlie, five, nine, five, Echo, eight, two, nine. Unidentified armour, numbers estimate figures four. Over."

"*Roger.*"

Earlier Lieutenant Barrett had provided his squadron commander with a situation report on his troop, and he in turn had received feedback on the state of the squadron. His troop had survived intact. Most of the shells and missiles had landed behind him and the aircraft had not spotted his position. The two Challengers he had pushed forward hadn't been touched. The Soviets had a vast area to bombard and clearly had difficulty in picking out the well-camouflaged British defenders east of the river. Had they spent more time on preparation and completed a more detailed reconnaissance of the defensive positions, the artillery and missile strikes might have been more effective. But urgency seemed to be what the Group of Soviet Forces Germany Commander was advocating, keeping the pressure on NATO, giving them no time to effectively dig in using properly prepared positions.

The squadron hadn't got off scot-free. B-troop, covering the northern section of Escherde, had been completely wiped out. Something had given them away and the Soviet air force had all but flattened the village north of the road, completely destroying all three of the Challengers and killing their crews. One of the tanks of the troop south of the road had suffered minor damage and was already racing west down the road that would take them through Heyersum, the location of the squadron HQ, then north-west to cross the river where the Royal Electrical and Mechanical Engineers (REME) would attempt to work their magic. But of the six tanks defending that stretch, they were now down to two. Combat Team Charlie had received a battering, losing three tanks and one damaged while the units west of the river, although receiving the bulk of the arty and air attention, had lost only two tanks between them, one with minor damage. Still, for a tank regiment to lose eight of their fifty-six, plus three damaged and one broken down, without firing a shot was of concern to all.

"Delta-Four-Alpha! Explosion our north-west. They're breaching the minefield."

"Roger. Is there smoke? Over."

"Negative, no smoke. Can now see figures three, Tango-Eight-Zero, 1,500 metres, north-west my position."

"Delta-Four-Bravo, standby. Zero-Delta, three, Tango-Eight-Zeros, 1,500 metres north-west call sign Delta-Four-Bravo. Request strike, stop line Jackdaw. Over."

"Delta-Four-Alpha, Delta-Four-Bravo. Explosion east of my position. Target 1,500 metres, Bravo-Mike-Papas, possibly four."

"Roger. Out to you. Zero-Delta. Target, 500 metres east of stop line Jackdaw, request strike. Over."

"Zero-Delta Roger."

"Delta-Four-Alpha! This is Delta-Four-Bravo! Eight, I repeat eight Tango-Eight-Zeros 1,200 metres north-west. Ten, I repeat ten, Bravo-Mike-Papa-Twos 300 metres east of Jackdaw. Permission to engage. Over."

"Negative. Hold your fire."

"This is Zero-Delta, to all Delta call signs. Shot out."

"Delta–Four–Bravo and Charlie. Shot out, batten down."

"*Roger.*"

"*Roger.*"

0450 7 July 1984. 62 Guards Tank Regiment. South-east of
Hanover, West Germany.
The Black Effect -1 day.

"*Six-Three, Six-Three-One. Breached minefield. Advancing.*"

"*Six-Three, Six-Three-Four. Engineers through minefield. First
company, moving. Out.*"

"Like a dream," purred Antakov.

"*Six-Three, Six-Three. Under heavy artillery fire! Two call signs
destroyed. No three!*"

"*Call sign, identify yourself!*"

"*Six-Three, Six-Three-Four. It's a cauldron. Over. I've lost contact
with more of my call signs.*"

"*Six-Three-Four, you are relieved of command. Major Petrov, are
you receiving? Over.*"

"*Petrov receiving! Driven through the barrage, lost two vehicles. Once
clear, we hit scattered mines. Request urgent mine-clearing support. Over.*"

"*Understood. Assume immediate command of Six-Three-Four.
Acknowledge.*"

"*Roger. Assuming command. Six-Three-Four-Alpha, Bravo and
Charlie. Move 300 metres west, create smoke and wait for engineers to
clear scattered mines.*"

"Turn it up," ordered Trusov.

The crackle of the speaker became louder, the sense of panic
identical. Voices could be heard calling for help; only the call signs
were different.

"*Six-One, Six-One-One. Under heavy artillery fire. Two units
lost. 1,000 metres east Escherde.*"

"*Six-One-One, expect mines at less than 1,000 metres east of
Escherde. Get your rollers forwards.*"

"*Six-One, Six-One-Four. First company at outskirts Escherde, two
units lost. Second company sweeping north-east.*"

"*Six-One-One, situation? Over.*"

"*Six-One. Two units down, one unit damaged track. Mine clear in
operation. Estimate through scatter mines in two minutes. Over.*"

"*Understood. Urgent you get west of Escherde.*"

"*Roger.*"

"Momentum is being maintained, sir."

Trusov didn't answer Antakov. He was trying to get an impression of the battlefield in his mind. His eyes flickered over the map as more Soviet aircraft roared low overhead. Yes, they had taken casualties from the artillery strike, and they would lose more from the minefield and the scatter mines, but if they could keep pushing on. To get bogged down now, amongst the minefields, they would have no room to manoeuvre and would be at the mercy of any British armour, and if the NATO air force could get through, it would be a disaster.

"*Six-One, Six-One. Contact. Armour in south Escherde. One unit destroyed, one damaged.*"

"*Use your call sign, Six-One-One. Move south, skirt the village.*"

"*Six-One, this is Six-One-Four. First company pushing through Emmerke. Second company entering from the north. Third company bypassing, approaching western edge.*"

"*Delta-Four-Alpha. Contact. One thousand metres. One, Tango-Eight-Zero-mine-roller, two, Tango-Eight-Zero, through minefield. Permission to fire. Over.*"

"Four-Bravo, Four-Charlie. Weapons free."

"*Roger.*"

"*Roger.*"

Chapter 17

0530 7 July 1984. 34th Airborne Assault Brigade. South of
Gronau, West Germany.
The Black Effect −1 day.

Lieutenant Colonel Ivakin tapped his watch, then held up five
fingers to the pilot of the Mi-8 Hip helicopter, the noise making it
impossible to have a conversation, the internal comms system working
intermittently. The pilot nodded, indicating that he agreed that they
were five minutes away from their landing zone. He and his battalion
were finally going to get to grips with the NATO soldiers who
always thought themselves superior to the Soviet conscript army. Here
was an opportunity for his battalion to demonstrate their skills and
show the British just how wrong they were. Thirty-seven Mi-Hook
helicopters were strung out in a line, some carrying BMD mechanised
infantry combat vehicles, others carrying his troops. High above,
Soviet Interceptors were keeping the skies clear of enemy fighters and
bombers, and, ahead and on their flanks, armed Mi-8 Hips and Hind
attack helicopters were smothering the enemy in a blanket of fire. The
companies that had parachuted in earlier had secured the landing sites,
encountering very little opposition.

A second battalion was also on its way and, between the two
of them, they would swamp the British defenders around Gronau,
either forcing their way to the bridge and securing it, or cutting off
any retreating troops if the enemy were able to destroy the bridge.
The remaining two battalions would also be in the air; a mix of AN-
12 Cubs, IL-76 Candids and AN-12 Cocks were at this very minute
dropping the Soviet paratroopers in a ring around Benstort. Two
battalions cutting off Gronau, and two battalions securing the gap
between Salzhemmendorf and Osterwald. The British didn't have
a chance. The two company-sized units had already reported back
that the landing zones they had been sent to capture and secure were

in their hands. For an hour, the guns from two divisions, along with 3rd Shock Army level artillery, had been pounding any location they believed to contain a defending unit.

The Colonel had not yet seen the results, but had witnessed the streaks of the rockets and missiles overhead, and the horizon had been lit up as if a theatre show was in progress. Once he and his men were in position, the rest of their force would be brought in, consisting of artillery, a battalion of D-30s, an anti-tank battery with its 85mm ASU-85s and anti-aircraft support. He was certain they would need it all if they were going to achieve their objectives.

Ping.

A bullet ricocheted off the airframe and the Colonel and the co-pilot looked at each other. The co-pilot looked fearful, but the pilot appeared calm, concentrating on the task at hand, the control stick vibrating in his hands, his feet working the peddles as he banked the helicopter to the right. They had flown south of Gronau, keeping low as the flight passed between Gronau and Banteln, the pilot showing two fingers, indicating they were two-minutes out. A Hind-D raced past them, its rocket pods launching four projectiles at a suspected enemy position, its guns suppressing an infantry machine-gun post, protecting the armada that was rapidly approaching. Ivakin watched as sparks flew off the airframe of the Hind. Not all the enemy units were seeking cover. His men were going to be in for a fight when they landed. The pilot indicated one minute and the Colonel warned his men in the back. The craft jolted as another Hip, flying alongside and slightly back from them, erupted in an explosion. A Blowpipe missile, spoilt for choice there were so many targets, missed the helicopter it was meant to target, striking the engines of a second Hip that just happened to get in the way. The pilot fought with the controls as his aircraft dropped 100 metres, the majority of the passengers, although shaken and some injured, survived.

The Hip Ivakin was in suddenly juddered as the pilot brought the front end up, pulling back on the controls to bring the Hip to a hover, the tail boom close to the ground, before leveling off and touching down, almost gently. *He's a good pilot*, thought Ivakin, intending to mention it to his commander when this was over. His men started to leap out, and he tapped his hand on each shoulder as he counted his soldiers out of the aircraft. Jumping down himself, he looked back, the downdraught causing him to squint as he indicated to the pilot that all his men were out.

Two rows of bullet holes stitched along the canopy. The mangled faces of the pilot and co-pilot were visible as an Infantry GPMG and a Chieftain's coaxial machine gun reminded the Soviet airborne forces that the British were far from beaten and they were very much in for a fight.

0600 7 July 1984. Combat Team Alpha/Royal Green Jackets
Battlegroup. North-west of Osterwald, West Germany.
The Black Effect -22 hours.

Lieutenant Dean Russell sheltered behind his FV432 armoured personnel carrier, the thumps and sounds of combat in the distance a constant reminder that they were very close to the front line. No artillery ordnance had landed in their vicinity, and apart from keeping close to their armoured vehicles just in case they needed to change location, they were using it as an opportunity to get some hot food and a little rest. Although Combat Team Alpha had been hit hard, and was destined to move behind 2nd Infantry Division, which was slowly moving into position behind the two armoured divisions that were currently taking the brunt of the Soviet assault, the 1 BR Corps Commander had made the decision to hold back a small element of 4th Armoured Division. The Corps Commander, General Cutler, wished he had more men, more tanks, more units, but he didn't. He had to make do with what he had. Although more of 4th Armoured Division had survived than expected, some seventy per cent, they were battle-weary and their armour and equipment needed maintenance, refuelling and rearming. But he had made the decision to keep the Royal Green Jackets Battlegroup in the immediate theatre. At sometime in the future, he would thank all that was holy that he had made that decision: keeping a tired, battered unit in reserve. Combat Team Alpha had gone through a major thirty-minute Soviet artillery and missile bombardment in the early stages of the war and had suffered crippling casualties. Following on from that, there was an assault by Soviet T-80 tanks and the dreaded Hind-D attack helicopters. It had ended in a defeat for the British. Although it could be argued that they hadn't been able to put up much of a fight, they had fulfilled their intended mission: held up the enemy for short period of time.

Dean was angry. Some of his men had been killed, while some had been maimed so badly they probably wished they were dead. He heard the growl of an engine approaching from the village of Osterwald.

"Stand to, stand to," he bellowed.

He brought up his SLR, and the rest of his platoon dropped their mess tins and prepared to defend themselves. But all was well. A Ferret scout car appeared from around the corner, one of the occupants the combat team commander, Major Philips. A cloud of dust rolled forward as the four-wheeled scout car came to a halt and the Major leapt down from the Ferret and called Lieutenant Russell over. Dean was there in seconds. He saluted, and Major Phillips flicked him a quick response. "Problem with your 432, sir?"

"No, Dean, this was just quicker. Anyway, I have a task for you."

The Major pulled a map out from the inside of his combat jacket. None of the combat team were currently donned in NBC suits as they were originally being pulled well back to the rear. He placed the map on the front of the scout car, the driver sitting at the front-centre of the small, unarmed reconnaissance vehicle, trying to look anywhere but at the two officers.

"We've got big problems heading our way."

"But I thought we were being pulled out of the line, sir?"

"I'm sorry, Dean, but the entire Battlegroup is being brought back into operation. Here," he pointed to the map. "A Soviet parachute unit has just landed here and one here," he informed Russell, pointing to a location south of the village of Oldendorf, only four kilometres to the south-east of their current location. "And one here south-east of Esbeck."

"What strength, sir?"

"We're not sure, but first estimates say company strength."

"That shouldn't be a problem, sir. They can soon be isolated, surely."

"I wish it were that easy."

For the first time, Dean saw tiredness in his company commander's eyes. He suddenly looked older. Dean felt goose bumps prickle down his back. His men were going to be asked to fight again.

"At least one battalion strength unit is in the process of parachuting in to join the company south of Esbeck, and we anticipate one will join the unit already south of Oldendorf."

"Christ, sir, we can't take on a battalion, not the state we're in."

The Major looked at his Lieutenant, but said nothing.

"Sorry, sir, just tired."

"We're all tired, Lieutenant."

"Sir."

"Right, there's more. A heliborne landing is in progress here, just north-west of Gronau, and Sov helicopters are blasting everything in their path to the south-west. So, we expect another landing there."

"They're after the bridge—"

"Yes, Dean, and it looks like they're throwing a full Air Assault Brigade at us."

"Do we have a full brigade, sir?"

"No, the rest of 11th Brigade are pulling back towards the River Weser, our next stop line."

A rustle of a uniform behind them turned out to be Sergeant Rose.

"Good to see you, Sergeant Rose."

Sergeant Rose saluted. "Likewise, sir. We were starting to feel a bit isolated up here."

"You'll be joined by the rest of the unit shortly. Got your map?"

"Sir." Rose pulled out his map and laid it on the front next to his platoon commander's.

"I'll need to be quick. We effectively have a heliborne assault here and here. East of Eime, south-west of Elze, and east of Sehlde. The first wave is down, and we believe it to be the elements of two battalions. One targeting north-west of Gronau, the other the south-west."

"This side of the river, sir?" Sergeant Rose asked.

"Yes. We expect a second wave as soon as their heli-force can do a turnaround. 22nd Brigade have two combat teams centred on Elze and Banteln, and a reserve combat team in the area of Eime."

"They should already be hitting the enemy from all sides then, sir," suggested Dean.

"Yes, they seem to have responded quickly. The issue is they are cutting off elements of Combat Team Bravo on the other side of the river. Combat Teams Alpha and Delta have been hitting the enemy on the other side of the river as they've tried to flank left and right around Gronau. They have had to reduce this to deal with the more immediate threat."

"Can't they pull them back?"

"Blow the bridge, sir?" added Rose.

"If they pull them back, the enemy will have Gronau and will be threatening the bridge. We may well have to blow it up and leave our men behind, but at the moment Brigadier Stewart is holding firm. His intention is to push Combat Team Charlie straight down the middle, splitting the enemy forces on the ground and actually reinforcing Bravo. Elements of Bravo this side of the river will then cross to support the troops on the eastern bank."

"Who's defending Gronau itself then, sir?"

"Elements of Bravo and a local Bundeswehr unit, a company of about 100 men, maybe more. They'll put up a fight, but can't be expected to hold out for long."

"The RAF?"

"They're in a pitched battle with the Soviet air force at the moment. This area is clearly getting a great deal of attention, Sergeant. Both sides are throwing aircraft into the battle, and until that resolves itself, we can't expect too much help."

"What about us then, sir?" questioned Rose.

"The Soviet airborne west of Benstort and east of Benstort clearly have a purpose. We think it is to hold the gap open between the high ground of Thuster to the south and Osterwald to the north. We expect the westernmost unit, probably in battalion strength when it gets here, to send a large force towards Coppenbrugge, extending their coverage of the gap."

Dean tapped the map in three places. "Push through Gronau, pass around Benstort, and up through Coppenbrugge."

"Exactly. Your task, Dean, and I'm giving you three-platoon in addition, is to hold Marienau. It straddles the road here. Keep that valley open, but watch out as they will no doubt try to flank you."

"Understood, sir."

"What's left of three-platoon, sir? Like us, they're pretty beat up," Rose enquired.

"I have amalgamated their three surviving sections into two. You can use their third 432 for the Milan firing posts, and you have your mortar team."

"Milan won't be much use, sir."

"That's where you're wrong, Dean. The heliborne assaults are landing BMDs, and at least one ASU-85 has been seen with the southern parachute force. I will take two-platoon and Company HQ south-east, towards Hemmendorf. The rest of the Battlegroup will be deploying here at Mehle. Combat Team Charlie and Combat Team Delta will move towards Benstort, and Combat Team Bravo will go south, then swing north-east through Salzhemmendorf."

"Christ, we'll be all over the place. Sorry, sir," apologised Rose.

"I wish I could disagree with you, Sarn't Rose, but you're right.

But, we have to contain them. If this is a full brigade assault, then we'll have over 2,000 heavily armed troops right in our backyard. We have to contain them."

They looked up and to the south as the drone of low-flying aircraft broke into their briefing, all suddenly aware of the chatter of small-arms fire in the distance. Before anyone could comment, the sound of the aircraft, no doubt bringing in more Soviet paratroopers, was blocked out by the roar of 432 engines as the remnants of three-platoon ground their way along the forest track just north-west of Osterwald.

"Your reinforcements, Dean. Both Lieutenant Ward and Sergeant Holland have been killed, so you two are the senior. Congratulations on your promotion, Colour Sergeant Rose."

"Th-thank you, sir," responded a flustered Colour Sergeant Rose. "Although, I wish the circumstances were different."

"Yes, Colour, don't we all. Right, I'll leave you to it." With that, the OC climbed back into the Ferret scout car, and it roared off to take him back to the Company HQ, which was co-located with the Royal Green Jackets Battalion and Battlegroup headquarters.

The three 432s of three-platoon rocked to a halt after they pulled over onto the side of the track, getting as far beneath the trees as possible. Some soldiers immediately started to drag camouflage netting over the roof, to hide the vehicles from above.

"Leave that," shouted Lieutenant Russell.

The soldiers looked across, bewildered. Their Corporal confirmed the order to them.

"Corporal, here," called Colour Sergeant Rose.

The Corporal trotted over. "Sarge?"

"Corporal Jenkinson, isn't it?"

"Yes, Sarge."

"Tell your boys to be ready to move out in five; then get back here."

"What's happening?"

"Just do it, and quick."

The Corporal sped off to instruct his men, and Rose joined his platoon commander by the rear of the platoon commander's 432.

"Congratulations Colour Sergeant Rose."

"Thank you sir, come as a bit of a surprise."

"Not to me. Well deserved. But I think we are both going to have a lot on our plate these coming days. I'm glad I've got you backing me up."

Before they could continue, the NCOs of the platoon congregated around the rear of the 432. The Lieutenant took a deep breath as he looked over the command element of his platoon: his platoon sergeant, now Colour Sergeant Rose; Lance Corporal Burford in command of the mortar team; Lance Corporal Reid had two-section, now with only two men to command; and Corporal Stubbings with five soldiers and the two Milan firing posts. But now he had two additional sections: one of six men commanded by Corporal Jenkinson, and a second one of five men, commanded by Lance Corporal Coles.

"Right, listen in. First, command. We will have five sections in the platoon. One-section will consist of Lance Corporal Reid's and Corporal Stubbings' men under the command of now Acting Corporal Reid. Call sign One-One-Bravo. It will also be the Platoon HQ. I will be One-One-Alpha. Corporal Stubbings, I want you to take command of the two Milan firing posts. They are all the anti-tank weapons we have, so they need to be positioned appropriately and well protected. Understood?"

"Yes, sir," responded the young but most experienced Junior NCO in his platoon.

"You'll be One-One-Charlie. Corporal Jenkinson."

"Sir."

"Welcome to the platoon. Your section is to take control of our three Blowpipe SAMs. One-One-Delta. Got that?"

"Sir."

"You will be our air defence. I doubt we'll have much more help in that quarter."

"Lance Corporal Coles, welcome to you too."

"Sir."

"Yours and Corporal Reid's sections will be our main fire teams. You are One-One-Echo. But, you won't be on your own. We have two mobile mortar teams under the command of Lance Corporal Burford. One-One-Foxtrot. Our air defence and mortar teams will come under overall command of the platoon 2iC, Colour Sergeant Rose, One-one-Golf."

He looked at each of the section commanders. The NCOs from his original platoon seemed relatively calm, considering what they had been through during the last twenty-four hours. The new men, on the other hand, seemed less relaxed and slightly nervous. The loss of their platoon commander and platoon sergeant had hit them hard.

146

"Situation." He pointed to the map pinned up on the inside of the wide-open 432 door. "We appear to have two heliborne assaults north and south of Gronau, on this side of the river. There have also been two para landings. One here, west of Benstort, north and south of the road..." He peered at the map. "The road that links Benstort to Hemmendorf. The second one east of Benstort, north and south of Esbeck."

He looked at his men again, checking their level of attention. He was pleased with what he saw: even the new members of the platoon started to appear more alert and less tense. Maybe they finally had something to occupy their minds with, something to do. Perhaps even the thought of hitting back.

"Mission: move directly to the village of Marienau, here, just south-east of Coppenbrugge. We are to hold and prevent the enemy from moving to Coppenbrugge. Questions?"

Corporal Jenkinson piped up, "What is the air threat, sir?"

"In regard to the Soviet air force and their bombers, I'm not sure. But we know they have Hip and Hind attack helicopters. No doubt they will be sniffing out the route."

"Try and get them as they pass you," advised Colour Sergeant Rose. "Their cockpits are protected by titanium. Even the bloody blades are made of titanium. But if you fire at them from behind, you stand a better chance of hitting the tail boom or the engines."

The Corporal nodded his understanding.

"Do they have tanks then, sir?" asked Corporal Stubbings.

"Not main battle tanks, but they will probably have ASU-85s, with an 85mm gun that could do us some damage. Then they will have their BMDs, the airborne equivalent of the BMP."

"I've got photos and silhouette pictures of both. Once we're in position, we can go through them to refresh all our memories," Colour Sergeant Rose informed them.

"Any more?" asked the Lieutenant. "No? Good. How many mortar bombs do you have, Corporal Burford?"

"Forty in each 432, sir, plus six each of smoke."

"Excellent. We move out in two. I'll lead with One-One-Bravo, through to One-One-Foxtrot. Let's go."

Russell looked back, hanging onto the GPMG pintle. The next 432 in his platoon was following behind, the third further back again. He would be happier once they were dug in. He wasn't comfortable driving out in the open like this, particularly in broad daylight, but speed was critical if they were get to their new location in a timely manner.

Chapter 18

"*Two-Two-Alpha, this is Bravo-Zero.*"

"Bravo-Zero, go ahead. Over."

"*Keep your heads down. You have help on the way.*"

"Roger that, Bravo-Zero. We've heard heavy heli activity to our south. Over."

"*We have numerous air assaults in progress our side of the river. A call sign is coming to bolster your position. Hold tight.*"

"Roger, Bravo-Zero. Out."

"Two-Two-Delta, this is Two-Two-Alpha. Sitrep. Over."

Before the infantry unit to their south could answer, Alex heard another flight of the shells go overhead, again going west to east. *At last, our artillery is finally giving the Sovs some of their own medicine,* he thought.

"Two-Two-Alpha, this is Two-Two-Delta. We're still holding. Heavy casualties. Need urgent medical evacuation."

Alex could hear the thumps of explosions coming from the direction of the enemy troops.

"Two-Two-Delta, wait. Bravo-Zero. Heavy arty fire all along the line. They're pounding the Sov positions. Over."

"*Understood. Out.*"

"Two-Two-Delta. Help is on the way. Will keep you posted. Do the best you can. Out."

He looked down into the turret and spoke into the intercom. "Take us forward, slowly."

The Chieftain lurched forward.

"Left." Alex searched through the vision blocks, finding a gap in the trees. "Right, right, right, forward. About 200 metres."

He searched the skyline, seeking out any Hind-Ds that might

be hovering, waiting for his and any other Chieftain tank to appear.

They crept forward, the sound of the artillery barrage getting louder and louder, plumes of smoke scarring the horizon.

"Fifty metres."

He needed to get them into their alternate berm where they would have a 180-degree view of the ground in front. It was risky going close to an old position, but he needed to see what was happening.

"Stop, stop." The tank ground to a halt. "Keep your eyes peeled, Corporal Patterson."

"Roger that, sir."

Ahead the ground erupted with explosions as round after round fell amongst the Soviet armour. A battery of Abbots had joined in along with M109s, the heavier M110s and the long range M107s. At last, thought Alex, they were getting some support and the enemy was getting a taste of its own medicine. The bombardment stopped, and the battlefield from Betheln to Eitzum was strewn with the wreckage of armoured vehicles. One of the 438s was still operating; a Swingfire missile flew towards a retreating BMP-2. Another brewed up as it was hit by Two-Two-Charlie. Two-Two-Charlie targeted a second tank.

Alex pushed up the hatch cover, ducking as two aircraft, one after the other, flew low overhead. The twin-engined Tornados powered past, splitting up, banking left and right, pulling Gs as the pilots pulled back on the stick, radioing their sighting to their two fellow pilots three kilometres back. The rearmost aircraft each released a Maverick air-to-ground tactical missile. Both, travelling at over 1,000 kilometres an hour, hit home. Guided by an imaging infrared system, the fifty-seven kilogram shaped charges slammed into a T-80 and an SA-9. No sooner had they destroyed their targets when all four Tornados released another round of missiles.

Alex's spirits rose, until he saw one of the aircraft going down after being hit by an SA-6 missile. No sooner had the Tornados delivered their lethal load than a flight of Harriers attacked the Soviet armour north of Heinum. They too lost one of their number. A flight of six SEPECAT Jaguars from the Royal Air Force's No 31 Squadron picked up where they left off. Originally from RAF Bruggen, they had been moved further west due to the rapid Soviet advance and further attacks by Spetsnaz forces. Only now were they able to get back into the fight. More Soviet armour suffered from the onslaught. But the ground-attack aircraft had to disperse after two were shot down by Soviet fighters. The Soviet air force was also taking casualties as two Rapier missiles eventually hit home, once the technicians had fixed the glitches as a consequence of the rough journey the tracked Rapier units had getting into position.

Silence. It was six twenty-five. They had been fighting for less than two hours, but were exhausted. They were in need of fuel and ammunition, and Alex wanted to go in search of Two-Two-Bravo, check on the infantry unit, and get an update regarding their relief. The Soviets had taken a beating, but Alex knew they would be back, with a vengeance. 7th Guards Tank Division, of 3rd Shock Army, had lost twenty-four T-80s and eighteen BMP-2s. For the moment, the Soviet airborne troops were on their own.

Chapter 19

0630 7 July 1984. Combat Team Alpha/Royal Green Jackets
Battlegroup. West of Osterwald, West Germany.
The Black Effect –21.5 hours.

Russell's 432s, fifty metres apart, raced north-west along the forest track to get to their positions. They skirted the edge of the forest, just inside the tree line, the track zigzagging through the trees, a trail of dust steadily building. Above, the tree-covered high ground towered over them, climbing to a height of nearly 600 metres. After two kilometres, his convoy came out of the forest, the drivers tugging hard on the left stick as they careered left onto a minor road, maintaining their speed, the tracks sliding across the loose stones as they swung round and headed south through a small conurbation, Dorpe, arriving at Coppenbrugge a kilometre later.

"*One-One-Alpha, this is Zero-Alpha.*"

"One-One-Alpha, go ahead. Over."

"*You have small packets, high ground, south-west your final location. Over.*"

"Roger. Call signs? Over."

"*Echo-One and Echo-Two. Out.*"

That came as a relief to the Lieutenant. The OC had informed him that two reconnaissance vehicles, probably Scimitars, would be watching the high ground to their right.

He slowed the convoy down and drove at twenty kilometres an hour through the town, the 432s at the front, each with pintle-mounted GPMG. The gunners covered the houses lining the road each side: one gun forward, the next watching left, and the third one right. The village appeared deserted, the rattle of the tracked vehicles echoing through the empty streets. One pair of eyes looked fearfully out of an upper window. The soldier on the 432 elevating the barrel of the Gympy felt Russell's hand on his shoulder.

"Well spotted. They're just civilians. Keep your eyes peeled though."

The military convoy turned left at the T-junction, and shortly they left the village, Marienau, a kilometre ahead. After a few hundred metres, Russell ordered the driver to pull over to the left, beneath a line of trees with large canopies, giving them some cover from the air. He signalled a halt and the soldiers de-bussed, forming a defensive stance around their small convoy.

Russell jumped down, running back to the next APC, and was soon joined by Colour Sergeant Rose. On orders, the NCOs quickly gathered round. They followed him to the lead 432 where he climbed on top and proceeded to scan the area with his binoculars.

Lieutenant Russell had made a quick appraisal of the map earlier and knew where he wanted to deploy his reinforced platoon. He lay down on the top of the vehicle, suspending a map from the top so that it lay flat against the slab sides of the APC. His NCOs gathered around and he pointed at the map that was upside down to him but the right way up to his men.

"This is our area of responsibility. From the base of the Hohenstein to our right, our south-western boundary, where we have recce Scimitars watching over us, to the Nesselberg-Osterwald to our left, our north-western boundary."

"Whew, that's a large area to cover for a company, sir, let alone a platoon."

"I concur with that, Colour, but we are all there is for the moment. Enemy armour can flank us either side, come straight along the main road through the village, or over the top of the high ground."

"What about Osterwald, sir?" asked Colour Sergeant Rose.

"The OC will take care of that with the rest of the company. We also have a Royal Green Jackets' combat team near Benstort." He shifted his position to get more comfortable. "I want your two Milan FPs collocated, Corporal Stubbings. At least then you can provide each other with mutual support, particularly if you have airborne infantry trying to root you out. I suggest you dig in at the junction of the road and the railway line here," he said, tapping a point at the most south-eastern tip of the village. "You should be able to get a good field of fire from there, at least a 180-degree sweep. This is 'Clapham'. How many tubes do you have?"

"Six for each firing post, sir."

"Make sure you change positions the minute you fire. Don't try for a second shot from the same place. If they home in on you and bring down mortar fire, you'll be stuffed."

"Understood, sir."

"Corporal Reid."

"Sir."

"I want you to split your section. I want your gun group and two men with the Milans at Clapham, to give them cover, and three men and the 432 positioning themselves in Gut Voldagsen, 'Little-town'. It looks as if it's made up of half a dozen houses. Warn me of any sightings and only open fire if necessary. If Soviet airborne are going for it, disrupt their advance as best you can, but don't take chances. Get back to Clapham."

"Gotcha, sir."

"Corporal Coles."

"Sir."

"I want your men dug in by the bridge over the water feature. I doubt they'll have any bridging equipment, though they probably won't need it as the water runs straight down the centre of the valley. But if they want to use the road then they will attempt to cross the bridge."

"My full section, sir?"

"Yes. We will fall back through you. 'London bridge', ok. Once we have to give up Little-town and Clapham, we'll fall back to the north-west of the village, where the Milans can cover both flanks. Especially if they try to use the rail bridge. Ah..."

"Little London, sir?" Colour Sergeant Rose laughed.

"Little London it is. Once you have to pull back, Corporal Reid, you will head straight for Coppenbrugge, and we will be right behind you. By then, we may have received some new orders." He heard a cough. "I've not forgotten about the rest of you. Corporal Burford, I want your mortars here. There's what? A 300 metre square plot, with some good tree screening. Better than being in the village having to move all the time."

"Roger that, sir."

"Corporal Jenkinson, leave two men and a Blowpipe here and the other four men, with you, in the village."

"What is the likely threat, sir?"

"We could expect anything, but the Falklands War taught us that Blowpipe won't be much good against fast jets. So only have a stab at those if they are coming towards us and are low and close. It's likely that we'll have helicopters about, probably Hip, Hooks and Hinds. Hips and Hooks, take them head-on. As for Hinds, I suggest you wait until they turn away, and hope you hit the engines. Firing at them head-on will get an immediate response. They might jink to avoid the missile, but you can bet your life one of their buddies will be homing in on you. So, don't do anything rash. You'll just get yourselves killed, and we will lose what little air defence we have. Any questions?"

"Can we set up some pre-planned fire, sir?" asked Colour Sergeant Rose.

"Yes, I plan on doing that now. You take the platoon forward and get them into position, and I'll run through some scenarios with Corporal Burford."

"Come on, lads, let's move," Rose ordered. "I'll leave the AD 432 with you then, sir."

"Good idea, Colour. Corporal Burford, let's move to your APCs."

Lance Corporal Burford led the way as the other units gunned their engines and were soon on their way towards the village they were to defend.

Private Taylor ran towards his NCO and platoon commander. "Sir! Sir, look!"

The Lieutenant spun round. He didn't need to ask for the reason for the shout; he could see it himself. Dark smudges whipped from a flight of troop carriers, wisps of white trailing behind, blossoming into full parachutes as the airborne soldiers swung from their harnesses out of control. More Soviet soldiers were landing three kilometres away, west of Benstort, to increase the number of troops that were slowly upping the pressure on the British soldiers attempting to defend themselves from a push on the other side of the river. Lieutenant Russell pulled a spare map from his pocket and pressed up against the side of a 432, and drew two lines across it with a pencil. The first one ran south-west to north-east, directly through the northern edge of Gut Voldagsen.

"This line, Liverpool. Liverpool-north, hit the open ground north of the houses. Liverpool-south, the road and rail to the south. This one, Manchester, bisects the rail/road bridge. So, Manchester-north, then hit the open ground to the north-east, Manchester-south, then it's the bridge itself. Got that?"

"Yes, sir."

"Anything else and I will give you a grid. But have a fire-plan set up for Liverpool-north and south to start with."

With that, he ran to the 432 and joined the air defence group, and the carrier screamed off at high speed down Route 1, heading for Clapham.

Lieutenant Russell caught up with the rest of his platoon just as British artillery started to pound the Soviet forces. He zoomed in with his binos; the view from Clapham was quite clear. Clouds of smoke and yellow flashes filled his lens as he watched the salvos land amongst the enemy. He couldn't see any soldiers on the ground, but paratroopers were still falling out of the sky. During the occasional lull in the explosions, he could hear small-arms fire as elements of the Royal Green Jackets moved in from Salzhemmendorf in the south and Benstort in the north.

Colour Sergeant Rose came alongside. "Corporal Reid has positioned his Gympy over there, bang on the rail/road junction and has assigned one of his men for each Milan."

"Voldagsen?"

"They've taken over the second storey of a house. Gives them a pretty good view of the enemy if they try and flank us to the north. We just don't have enough firepower, sir. We could do with holding that location. If the enemy occupy it, they could take potshots at us from good cover, or get into the high ground."

Alex looked back, identifying the two Milan positions, one either side of the railway line just before it crossed the road. The Gympy was set up on one side of the road where it crossed the rail line. He beckoned his signaler over and took the handset from him.

"One-One-Foxtrot, One-One-Alpha. Radio check. Over."

"*One-One-Foxtrot. Five, five. Plots in for Liverpool-north and Liverpool-south, over.*"

"Roger, out to you. Hello, One-One-Bravo-Alpha, any sightings? Over."

The unit in Voldagsen had the spare radio. "*One-One-Bravo-Alpha. Negative, no movement. Arty fire still dropping on Grid Delta, seven, one, five, Echo, four, two, five. Over.*"

"Acknowledged. Out."

"I'm going to check the Milans. Then all we have to do is wait."

"I'll be with the AD section, sir."

Russell moved back along the railway line for about fifty metres, coming across the two soldiers acting as sentries first. He talked through the fields of fire with the crews who had set up the FPs, one either side of the double railway line.

"*One-One-Alpha, this is One-One-Echo. I have an unidentified unit approaching my location. Over.*"

"Numbers and intention. Over."

"*Two vehicles and a small tank...could be, wait...looks like one of those Jag Panzers. Probably twenty-plus troops in a couple of Unimogs. Over.*"

Kanonenjagdpanzer, thought Dean. It only had a 90mm gun, but could create havoc with any BMDs, and maybe even an ASU-85, if the Sovs had one.

"*500 metres out, slowing down.*"

"Roger. Hold your fire, but watch yourselves."

"*Roger.*"

"Corporal Stubbings, have one of your Milans ready to swing round. Target the road as it leaves the village."

"On it, sir."

"*One-One-Echo. They've stopped, 100 metres out. Someone walking towards us.*"

"Roger."

They all waited patiently. Dean was confident nothing was amiss. He didn't anticipate it being a Soviet airborne unit behind them. They had seen no paratroopers that far back, or any heli flights in the last hour.

"*One-One-Alpha, One-One-Echo. Over.*"

"Go ahead."

"*There's a box-head officer wants to speak to you, sir.*"

Colour Sergeant Rose, who had just joined his platoon commander in the last few seconds, picked up the latter part of Lance Corporal Coles's message and hissed. "I'll speak to him, sir, when I see him."

"*He says he's Leutnant Burger, sir, come to support us. Over.*"

Dean thought for a moment. If they had wanted to, they could have sent some men forward covertly and taken out Coles's small section.

"Let them through."

"*Wilco, sir.*"

"Standby, lads, just in case," warned Rose.

Within five minutes, the two Bundeswehr trucks and the

twenty-seven ton tank-destroyer pulled up close to the railway crossing.

The German officer dropped down from the cab of the Unimog and saluted Russell who returned the salute. The man, looking to be in his mid to late forties, then proffered his hand and shook Dean's firmly.

"Leutnant Burger, Herr Leutnant. I am with the Landwehr. Our mission is to hold Coppenbrugge, but I think with the unit you have we would be better placed with your men here, if you don't object."

"More than glad to have you and your men alongside us, Leutnant Burger, but I would just like to check in with my HQ first."

"Naturally."

"Colour, would you do the honours please?"

"Of course, sir."

With that, Rose took the signaler to a position about twenty-metres away so they could contact their Company HQ and confirm the identity of the intruders.

"Once you get clearance, where would you like my men?"

"How many do you have?"

"Twenty-four, including myself. Oh, and I have that," he said pointing to the tank-destroyer. "Ugly I know, but it packs a *Wunderbar* punch," he said with a huge grin.

Dean couldn't help but reciprocate, so unused to Germans with a sense of humour. He pulled out his map, knelt down, and flattened it out on the surface of the road.

"Sir," shouted Rose, and gave Dean the thumbs up.

"Seems you are kosher."

"Kosher?"

"Genuine."

"*Gut, gut. Danke.* Now, your map, eh?" He knelt down alongside Dean. "I want to get my men under cover, before they stop," Burger said, pointing to the continuing barrage hitting the Soviet airborne forces to their south-west.

"I've got three men in the village there," Dean said, pointing towards Voldagsen. "It would be better if we could hold that."

The German officer studied the map. "I used to command a battalion in the Bundeswehr until I was invalided out. I have a bit of a limp," he said, tapping his left leg. "Jumped out of a helicopter just as a gust of wind jolted the machine upwards about five-metres. My leg is now more steel than flesh." He laughed. "Yes, we must hold that plot. I could put half my men there with Kanonen. The rest...where would you suggest?"

"We have recce on top of the Hohenstein, but it would be good to have a small force lower down on the eastern edge. You can spot for any enemy approaching and pull back should you need to through the forest, covering my southern flank."

"Yes, I like it. We work well together already, Leutnant."

"Dean, my name's Dean."

"Ah, Dean. Mine is Leon. So, you will pull your men back and reinforce here, yes?"

"Yes."

"Good, I will get my men moving."

Dean watched as the Lieutenant organised his men. Many of them seemed older even than their leader, perhaps as old as sixty. They certainly weren't going to let the Soviets take their country without a fight.

Chapter 20

The Snake hovered behind the trees. Its partner was 100 metres to the right. The rotor blade slicing through the air was keeping it at just the right height, the tail rotor keeping it facing east, towards where the enemy would appear.

"*Viper-One. Zulu-Three. Four Tango-Six-Fours, 2,000 metres my location.*"

"Roger, Zulu-Three."

"*Zulu-Three. Moving past your location figures two. Standby.*"

"Roger, Zulu-Three. We'll watch out for you, buddy."

The pilot tilted his head forward slightly as he spoke through the intercom to the gunner who was sitting in front of the tandem cockpit.

"Our boys will be through in about two minutes. Four Tangos are right behind them."

"I'm ready."

"*Viper-One, Viper-Two, this is Angel-One. I have visual. Behind Tangos are six Bravo-Mike-Papas.*"

Angel-One, a Hughes OH-6, was a kilometre further forward, spotting for the two AH-1, Cobra attack helicopters.

"Roger that, Angel-One."

"*Viper-Two, Viper-One. Four Tangos inbound, right behind Zulu-Three. Over.*"

"I'll take number one. Over."

"*Confirmed. Number two is mine. Out.*"

All the two AH-1 Cobra attack helicopters had to do was wait. Once Angel-One gave them the nod, they would pop up and unleash their TOW anti-tank missiles, hit their target, drop down, move back and go through the same sequence all over again.

Ever since the Soviets had crossed the River Fulda in force, they had been steadily pushing the American force backwards.

Private First-Class Larry Poole started the gas turbine, and Emery turned the turret and the 105mm gun barrel, checking everything was in order. SSGT Lewis was still standing with his body half out of the turret, scanning for any sign of the enemy. A-platoon, Anvil-platoon, were now down to two tanks. They had survived the last attack, but Lewis knew they wouldn't hold out here for long. All they had to do, for one last time, was blunt the attack and race back as fast as they could. The Soviet army had pushed the 11th Armoured Cavalry Regiment, the Black Horse Regiment, back twenty-five kilometres and were now on the doorstep of the Fulda Gap with every intention of thrusting through the gap and speeding the 100 kilometres that would see them right in the centre of the German city of Frankfurt. His squadron wouldn't have to remain here for long. They were just acting as a covering force while the rest of the regiment withdrew completely from the battle area. Not only were the men of the regiment desperate for a break, but so were the tanks. This would be just a short fight.

Maybe even shorter than they planned, should they get hit, thought Lewis with a smile. Two rounds of sabot, fire the smoke grenades, and then hot food and a shower, he kept telling himself. The big battle was to come. The Soviet forces were getting stronger and stronger every day as more and more flooded across the river. But soon they would come up against the 3rd Armoured Division and the 8th Mechanised Division. Then you would see the battle of the giants. That he would like to see. No more running. Those two formations would have to hold their ground until reinforcements, flown in from the States, had drawn their equipment from the POMCUS sites and joined the fight. Bigger units would follow, crossing the Atlantic Ocean.

Thank God AH-1 Cobras were in support, he thought to himself, but they had already lost two: one to the dreaded Shilkas and one to a Hind-D.

"Any US unit, Kerzell area, this is Viper-One. You have at least one battalion, Tango-Six-Fours, heading your location. Going back to refuel and rearm. Good luck, buddy. Out."

"Standby," yelled Lewis.

He dropped into the turret and patted the armour of his beloved M1. "Looking to you to protect us today."

The tank crew would be depending on the M1's Chobham armour.

"See anything, Staff Sergeant?"

"That's a negative."

They heard a distant explosion as a Cobra took out its last Soviet tank before it too had to return to base to rearm.

"Unidentified US tank unit, this is Viper-Two. I'm the last one out. They're 1,000 metres out."

"I see one. A thousand, two Tangos."

"Sabot."

"Up."

"Fire."

The Soviet T-64 didn't see it coming, but was lucky as the sloped armour caused the round to ricochet off.

"Missed!"

"Sabot."

"Up."

"Fire."

This time the long-rod penetrator hit one of the T-64's ERA blocks, the subsequent explosion destroying the penetrator's momentum, leaving it partially fragmented in the armour with the remaining piece dropping away.

"Son of a bitch," yelled Emery.

The target had now fired, but fortunately not at them, but at an anti-tank missile post hoping to get its first hit of the day. The tank was now 800 metres away.

"Sabot."

"Up."

"Fire."

This time the long slender dart did its job, penetrating the tank's armour; then, driven by the sheer force of the kinetic energy, it drilled through the T-80's turret, the residual energy blowing a spall of fragments of armour that peeled off the inside of the fighting compartment, killing its crew within a matter of seconds. The T-64 finally ground to a halt. More tanks appeared, and Lewis knew they would have to bug out soon. There were just too many of them and so few M1s. But he waited for the order. He knew his commander would make the right decision at the right time. Another shot went out as half a dozen T-64s, a line of BMP-1s behind them, appeared at less than 1,500 metres away. If they didn't move soon, they would be over run.

Suddenly, artillery rounds erupted around the enemy tanks, stripping off some of the protective blocks. A round sliced through a section of a T-64, destroying the auto-loader and killing the gunner. The two crew left, the commander and driver, escaped the stricken tank, only to be cut down by a burst from an M1's coaxial machine gun.

"Anvil-One-Two, this is Anvil One-One. Make smoke and bug out. Out."

Lewis didn't need to be told twice. He hit the button and popped smoke.

"Get us out of here, Poole! Now!"

Chapter 21

1800 7July 1984. 8th MotoSchutz Division, 8th Armee, Nationale
Volksarmee. East of Ecklak, West Germany.
The Black Effect −10 hours.

The East German machine gunner dropped to the ground. His
IMGK, a Soviet RPK machine gun, was instantly set up on its bipod
and, within a matter of seconds, rounds were going out, keeping the
heads down of the Bundeswehr soldiers defending the small village of
Ecklak. The platoon commander called his radio operator forward and
spoke to his company commander via the R-126 radio. His motorised
rifle platoon, along with the rest of his Company, was tasked with
keeping the heads of the defenders under fire, while the rest of the
battalion went round the right flank. He bellowed to his men, and a
steady stream of gunfire ripped into the buildings 300 metres away, the
enemy returning sporadic fire. He didn't envy his *kameraden* who were
going to initiate the attack. Not only would they come under fire from
the Bundeswehr and Landwehr soldiers in and around the village, but
also from Bundeswehr tanks on the other side of the canal, 500 metres
north of the village.

The Nord-Ostee-Kanal, that ran across Schleswig-Holstein,
fed from the Baltic Sea in the north-east and from the North Sea
to the south-west, was NATO's second stop line in this sector.
Here, NATO hoped to stop the NVA and Soviet forces thrusting
north to Flensburg and deep into Denmark. They had fought
well, defending the eastern sector of Hamburg and Lubeck on the
opposite coast, but the Warsaw Pact forces were just too powerful.
Once the Soviet and East German forces had broken the line, the
defenders just had to keep moving; otherwise the enemy would
have just rolled up a flank and they would have been surrounded.
Better to pull back where they could prepare better defences. This
stretch was being defended by the remnants of 16th Panzer Brigade

of the 6th Panzer Division. Germans were now fighting Germans.

After the war, the East German Army, the *Nationale Volksarmee* (NVA) came into existence when, in 1955, the Federal Republic of Germany formed its own army to contribute to its own defence in support of NATO forces. The *Deutschland Democratic Republic*, DDR, authorised by their Soviet masters, responded quickly and, by 1962, conscription was enforced. The NVA grew to the 108,000 strong army it was now. Along with Soviet divisions, the 5th German Army had struck at Lubeck, quickly crossing the Elbe–Lubeck Canal, supported by the Soviet 336th Naval Infantry Brigade landing west of Gromitz. With T-55 tanks, BTR-60s and BTR-70s, wheeled armoured infantry combat vehicles, and in the region of 4,000 naval infantry, they quickly overpowered the local defence force, threatening the left flank of the Bundeswehr forces defending Lubeck who were in danger of having Soviet troops behind them. They were forced to make a steady withdrawal. The Naval Brigade, as well as threatening the eastern and northern sector of Lubeck, also struck out for Pansdorf, to cut off the Travemunde Peninsular.

Over time, the Bundeswehr were slowly pushed back, overwhelmed by the sheer size of the Soviet and *Nationale Volksarmee* forces arrayed against them. Schleswig-Holstein-Command had already decided to abandon their headquarters in Neumunster and would need time to get organised at their new location: the town of Schleswig. Their latest defensive position was a line that ran across from Brunsbuttal in the west, through Schafstedt, Rendsburg to the north of Kiel. Landwehr and Jaeger units were still fighting the Soviets in the city of Kiel, the Russian leaders reluctant to commit too many forces to a street by street, house by house battle.

The Bundeswehr's 6th Panzer Division had been fighting for nearly three days and the men were exhausted. Their machines were holding up well, Leopard 1s in the main, but due to heavy interdiction from the Soviet air force, fuel and ammunition was in short supply. The three brigades, one Panzer and two Panzer grenadier, along with a mixture of Jaeger and Landwehr units, had a front of 100 kilometres to hold. They were now dug in behind the Nord-Ostee-Kanal, their mission to hold until the arrival of much needed reinforcements from the Allied Command Europe (ACE) Mobile Force, a multinational force that would not only demonstrate the solidarity of the NATO alliance but could also pack a punch in its own right.

The platoon commander pulled his head down as some stray shots zipped overhead. He needed some heavier firepower and called forward his two remaining BMP-1s, the two others lost to a shell from a Bundeswehr Leopard-1. The two BMPs soon got into the firefight, their 73mm guns and PKT coaxial machine guns putting extra fire down onto the enemy. He only allowed five of the 73mm rounds to be fired from each gun. Ammunition was starting to run low, and he wasn't sure when they would be resupplied. He heard large explosions coming from deeper into the village as the rest of the battalion of the 8th Motorschutz Division got to grips with the enemy within. Every time that word 'enemy' went through his mind, it felt uncomfortable. *These were Germans, like him. Were they truly the enemy?* he thought.

The previous day, he had spoken to some wounded Bundeswehr soldiers, and one of them asked him why they were attacking them. What had they done wrong? He found he couldn't answer. Not because he didn't want to, but because he didn't actually know the true reason himself. The radio crackled, and his radio operator confirmed that the enemy were pulling back. They were to wait ten minutes, then advance. Once secured, the bridging units and additional forces could be brought forward ready to force a crossing the next day.

Behind them, the 9th Panzer Division was ready to exploit the crossing once a bridgehead had been formed. A fast crossing, fanning out west and east, attempting to cut off the retreating Bundeswehr forces, and they would be one step closer to entering Denmark.

1800 7 July 1984. 12 Mechanised Division, 1st Polish Armee.
North of Tostedt, West Germany.
The Black Effect −10 hours.

Colonel Bajek, his black tanker's uniform and badge showing him to be with the Polish army, steadied himself as he rocked backwards and forwards in the turret of his T-55 tank, attempting to steady the map as they raced along Route 76. He needed to be sure when to come off the road, to pick the right time to bear north, passing around the northern outskirts of Tostedt. His orders were clear: don't get bogged down fighting for towns, or even villages; bypass them. Push west and hard. His objective was Rotenburg, less than twenty kilometres from the town of Achim and the River Werdesee. His division had been ordered to secure the east bank of the river by nightfall. An Air Assault Brigade would be assaulting the western bank the following morning. A crossing had to be forced, a bridgehead made, enabling 20th Tank Division, with its more modern T-72 tanks, to break out. He hoped to command one of the T-72 tank battalions one day, if not a full regiment. His own T-55AD2 command tank was old, built in 1976. His battalion had been plagued with breakdowns and, out of his battalion of forty tanks, five had been left behind for repairs.

At the same time he heard the rumble of an explosion up ahead, his radio crackled in his headphones beneath his black-ribbed, padded helmet. *"Zero-Jeden. Shontaktuj."*

"Damn, another contact!" He groaned loudly above the sound of the tank's engine and the rattle of tracks.

He ordered his driver to pull over. He ran his finger across the map. His lead company was about 200 metres up ahead, the other two companies behind.

"What is it?"

"One of those missile panzers again, sir."

"Have you destroyed it?"

"No, sir, it fired its missile then disappeared."

"Hit and run, hit and run," he mumbled to himself. The Bundeswehr Racketenjagdpanzers, particularly the Jaguar 1s, had been hitting his battalion for the last twenty-four hours. They would simply hide, hit the first tank in the column, then race off at sixty kilometres an hour to set up another ambush. Four tanks lost to date. He cursed his senior officers for pushing his unit so fast, diverting the division's reconnaissance for other flanking tasks.

"Lysek, move north. Leave a platoon on the road to cover, then head north."

"Understood, sir, north."

He looked at his map again. "Watch out for the village to your north, Dohren. I'll call in some air support. See if we can't give them a taste of their own medicine."

"When will you release my platoon, sir?"

"Once the battalion is clear of Dohren, they can join up with you. Moroz can take the lead then. Out."

He spoke into his intercom, ordering his driver forward. He turned, hearing his second tank company approaching from behind. Time to move north soon, skirt the town ahead, and press on.

Chapter 22

Baskov, the General Secretary of the Soviet Union, slammed his fist down on the table. The cups, some still full of coffee, jumped. Splotches of liquid leapt upwards, then rained down on the documents in front of the two generals, leaving dark stains as they were soaked into the paper. Baskov pushed his seat back again, for the third time during this session, his patience running as thin as the strength of his temper was increasing. With absolute frustration, he stormed around the room yet again, fiddling with his signet ring, a memento of a 300 day battle he had been in during WW2. No retreat!

On the right of the extended table sat Yuri Aleksandrov, Chairman of the dreaded KGB, the *Komitet Gosudarstvennoy Bezopasnosti,* or the Committee for State Security. In overall power terms, he was probably only second to Baskov, the most powerful man in the Soviet Union. On the opposite side was Marshal Obraztsov, the Commander-in-Chief of the *Teatr Voyennykh Deystviy,* Commander of the Western TVD. His battlefront covered an area extending from Southern Norway, through Denmark, Belgium, the Netherlands, Federal Republic of Germany, Northern France, and even including Great Britain. Nearest the General Secretary was General Zavarin. The General Secretary's rage was such that he had bypassed the *Stavka Verkhovnogo Glavnokomaidovaiya,* STAVKA, the full Soviet military command, responsible for commanding all of the Soviet forces involved in times of war. Instead, he had called in his Chairman of the KGB and the Marshall responsible for the Western TVD. With the Polish, Czechoslovakian, Hungarian, and the Groups of Soviet Forces under his command, this man had the ultimate responsibility for ensuring the attack on the West was successful. The second officer was Army General Zavarin, Commander of the Group of Soviet

Forces Germany (GSFG). His command had the most powerful conventional force in the Soviet Union's armoury and was conducting the bulk of the assault on NATO's Northern Army Group.

"Momentum! That's what we agreed was key to destroying their first echelon quickly. You both sat here and agreed with me. Momentum, momentum, momentum." Baskov dropped back down into his chair, then leant forward on his elbows and locked eyes with his Western TVD commander. "Destroy the enemies covering force, then their first line of defence, before pushing them back to the Rhine. That's what you told me would happen. In this very room, you sat there and told me it would take only a matter of days to have them reeling." His voice got louder and louder. "Did they not, Comrade Yuri?" He said looking at the head of the KGB. The chair was pushed back again and the General Secretary was up on his feet.

Aleksandrov nodded in reply, not wanting to add any more to the discomfort of the two generals sitting opposite him. The two generals also remained quiet, waiting for some of their leader's wrath to dissipate.

"General Zavarin. Third Shock Army would fight on a narrower front, enabling them...what were the words you used?" The General Secretary looked at the transcript of a recording of the meeting when the plans had been discussed. "...to slice through the Northern Army Group's meagre defences. So, tell me. Why is the knife so blunt?" It was a rhetorical question. Baskov had not finished his latest rant just yet. "Why haven't our airborne forces been used yet? I thought our T-80s were a match for any Western main battle tank. Why... haven't...we...smashed them?" Each word was punctuated by a thump on the table as he leant close to the two officers on the receiving end of his wrath. But this time he wanted to hear an answer, this time he wanted a reply, so sat back down so he could look directly into their faces as they responded.

"Comrade General Secretary, we are making good progress," responded Obraztsov. He looked tired, his face almost gaunt, but not as tired as Zavarin who hadn't slept in thirty-six hours, keeping constant control over his advancing armies. "The Northern Group of Forces, led by Comrade General Zhiglov, along with the 5th German Army and the 1st Polish Army, have Hamburg surrounded and are already moving into Denmark and towards Bremen. 20 Guards Army, part of our 2nd Strategic Echelon, are already on the move to reinforce our army and continue the momentum.

Your idea to persuade the West to save Berlin and its population from imminent death and destruction, giving them your word that we would not assault or enter the city, but on the condition that they withdraw their forces back to barracks, has released an entire army. It is safe to leave the encirclement of Berlin to the *Volksarmee*. 2 Guards Tank Army is also advancing on Bremen. To the south, the 3rd German Army are pushing towards the south of Kassel, and 1 Guards Tank Army are hitting the Americans hard at the Fulda Gap."

"Is it time you switched to the southern axis and made that your main thrust?" asked the KGB Chairman, speaking for the first time.

"The north should remain our main strategic drive, Comrade Aleksandrov. Although there is a delay in crossing the River Leine, it is still NATO's weakest front."

"And their reinforcements?"

"The British reinforcements, their 2nd Division, and those reserves that have been called up, are getting closer to their deployment positions, having now crossed the English Channel. But they are taking a beating from our air force."

"The Americans?"

"The American reinforcements allocated for NORTHAG, a full Army Corps, will be sometime before they can be in a position to make a difference. They will not be in time to delay our crossing of the Leine."

"But, now the French have decided to come onboard with NATO, that will surely allow the Americans to release forces in the south to support the north?"

"Not yet, Comrade Aleksandrov. The French have not yet moved into position, and the two Czech armies are already across the Danube. Some forces will have to be diverted to support the Austrians. We expect that to be the French. Our Central Group of Forces will add more weight to that sector."

There was a moment of silence. The KGB Chairman had finished with his questions for the moment, and Baskov was clearly mulling something over.

"But we haven't solved the Hanover problem yet," stated Baskov, almost in a whisper.

Zavarin spoke, for only the second time during the meeting. Up until now he had allowed his commander to take the brunt of the heat from their General Secretary. "Within twenty-four hours, Comrade General Secretary, we will be marching on Minden. The Weser will not be able to contain our advance."

"You say that with confidence, General," suggested Aleksandrov.

"Now we have the release of our special weapons approved and with one airborne division behind them, with a second to follow, they won't be able to stop us. Our numbers, firepower and tactical position will be a guarantee of success."

Baskov searched the man's eyes and face, seeing total confidence and belief in what he had just said. "Very well, General Zavarin, I will hold you to that statement."

Obraztsov interrupted. "The Baltic, Byelorussian and the Carpathian Military Districts are already moving their troops to the front, Comrade General Secretary. Once airborne and ground forces have secured the crossing of the river and a divisional OMG exploits the breakthrough, these additional forces will be able to maintain the forward momentum."

This time it was the KGB Chairman who got up out of his seat and stretched his legs. "What response have you had from the *Volksarmee* as to the use of the special weapons, Marshall Obraztsov?"

The Marshall's response was slightly hesitant, but he was soon in full flow. "They are soldiers like the rest of us, Comrade Aleksandrov, and they take orders."

"Did they agree willingly to those orders?"

"They...ah...had some reservations, Comrade Aleksandrov, but... understood the necessity of their use."

Baskov and Aleksandrov made eye contact, and no more needed to be said.

"Thank you, Marshall Obraztsov, General Zavarin. You are released to continue leading the war against our enemies."

The two officers stood, placed their military caps on their heads, and saluted before heading towards the door.

Just as Zavarin was about to follow his commander out, Baskov called out to him. "General Zavarin."

"Yes, Comrade General Secretary?"

"If the crossing fails, I want the senior officers responsible for that failure shot. Do I make myself clear?"

"Yes, Comrade General Secretary. I will personally carry out the order."

The two Politburo members were now on their own, and

Baskov summoned his secretary to provide fresh drinks and some of his favourite biscuits.

"Well, Yuri? The Germans?"

"There have been grumblings, Comrade Secretary. The use of special weapons on German and NATO positions, where civilians may well be in close proximity, will be an issue. Some of them are bound to be affected, and this is causing them some concern."

"It will save lives in the long run. The sooner we can beat NATO into submission, the sooner we can claim victory and end this war. You need to keep an eye on them, Yuri."

"I have loyal insiders who are reporting back to me."

"What about the Poles?"

"They don't care. They are happy to see Germans killed whichever side they're on. There is no love lost between those two nations. The last war saw to that."

Baskov reflected on what he had just heard. "We need to have some of our forces on standby, just in case."

"I anticipated your request, Comrade Secretary. I am meeting with MVD and NKVD commanders in the morning."

"Good, good, Yuri. I knew I could depend on you. Why don't we forget about this coffee. I have something much better in my cabinet."

Chapter 23

"*Two-Two-Alpha, this is Bravo-Zero. Over.*"

"Two-Two-Alpha, go ahead. Over."

"*You have friendlies moving your location. Over.*"

"Roger that, Bravo-Zero. Call signs and type. Over."

"*Alpha, Charlie, with Three-Three-Delta, and Delta troop moving to south-west of your location. Suggest you recall Two-Two-Charlie. Roger so far? Over.*"

"Roger that."

"*One Jaeger platoon, call sign Foxtrot-One and one tank destroyer Foxtrot-Two. Roger so far? Over.*"

"Roger."

"*Foxtrot-One will move north of your location. Foxtrot-Two, south. Two-Two-Echo are being withdrawn, but stay on your side. Alpha and Delta will cover your west exit. Golf-One and Golf-Two also in position. Over.*"

"What about Two-Two-Delta? Over."

"*Medical support is following Three-Three-Delta in.*"

"Roger that, sir." *Thank god there will be some relief for Two-two-Delta*, he thought. What's the situation to our west? Over."

"*All call signs under heavy pressure but holding. A Landwehr unit is being reinforced by Alpha, and Delta is holding. Charlie will be joining you to your south. But be ready to get out of there quickly, Alex. When we can see how it pans out, you may need to shift.*"

"Roger that."

"*Bravo-Zero, out.*"

Patsy came up alongside him. "Getting some help then, sir?"

Mackey and Ellis joined them by climbing up the glacis. They had been taking a break, stretching their legs, breathing in fresh air, although it always seemed tainted by the smell of something: burning buildings were still smoking in Gronau, explosives' residue, and an almost permanent smell of diesel. The Chieftain's engine was quiet for the moment and, apart the firefight still in progress on the other side of the river, the immediate area was almost peaceful, the quiet before the storm.

"Yes, listen." Directly behind them, about one kilometre away, in between the sounds of gunfire and explosions, they could hear the distinctive sound of Chieftain engines as the drivers manoeuvred the three tanks of the third troop of Combat Team Bravo through the streets of Gronau, a Combat Engineer Tractor following to pull out any tanks that got bogged down in the rubble-strewn town, or threw a track. They tracked the moving vehicles by sound alone. The Chieftains, along with the mechanised infantry section, were moving south. The Infantry would take up positions close to Two-Two-Delta.

"Two-Two-Delta. Friendly Tangos moving your location. Some help on the way for the wounded. Over."

"*Two-Two-Delta. Good news, sir. Are we pulling out?*"

"Not yet, but pull your unit back once relieved and hold in reserve. Over."

"*Will do, sir.*"

"Out to you. Two-Two-Echo, Two-Two-Alpha. Over."

"*Two-Two-Echo, go ahead.*"

"Friendlies moving to your location. Withdraw to the tree line when relieved."

"*Roger that. One unit abandoned, but crew will extract with us. Over.*"

"Understood. Friendlies are not Brit. Over."

"*Box-heads?*"

"Roger that. Two-Two-Charlie, location? Over."

"*Two-Two-Charlie, still same. Over.*"

"Three-Three moving your location. You are to move north of my location. Check on Two-Two-Bravo."

"Can hear them coming now. Estimate figures ten."

Chapter 24

2000 7 July 1984. United States Navy Nuclear Powered Submarine.
Atlantic Ocean.
The Black Effect −8 hours.

The sonar operator strained to pick out the particular characteristics that would aid him in identifying the submarine that had suddenly appeared in range of his sensors, picked up by the spherical sonar array positioned in the bow, along with the conformal array mounted around the bow. The unidentified submarine appeared to be changing depth. It was the move between the thermocline layers that had suddenly brought the enemy submarine to his attention. It had to be an enemy submarine. There were no Brits, French or other US subs in the immediate area, he thought. They were on their own. Well, not any more. A slight smile broke his concentration, but it soon returned to a frown. They were at war, and if this was an enemy submarine... USS Providence, SSN-719, a Los Angeles-class submarine, one of the United States' latest, was patrolling fifty kilometres ahead of a convoy that was heading across the Atlantic from Texas to a port in Europe, where the forty merchant ships could disgorge the supplies it was carrying. It had armour and troops to support the forces already in battle with the Warsaw Pact, along with fuel, ammunition and rations.

Poulton had definitely heard something. Maybe it was an SSN. It certainly wasn't a Boomer. It was the wrong position for it to be in to launch nuclear missiles against Britain or the United States. Poulton examined the Waterfall, one of two octagonal screens in front of him, the display green, showing white noise and snow, the solid line telling him he had something. He was one of four sonar operators manning the BSY-1 Console in the sonar room on the port side of the boat, next to the control room. Larry Poulton was sitting at the console on the far left, his favourite position.

"What is it, Poulton?" asked Commander Clifton, leaning over Poulton's shoulder, peering at the screen. Although as a skipper of a nuclear-powered submarine he had learnt how the sonar arrays worked and was able to use them, it was an art. A dark art, some said; an art that Poulton had studied, practiced until it was almost part of his very soul. He excelled at tracing and tracking submarines, both friendly and enemy.

"Designated Sierra-One, it has to be a Soviet SSN, skipper."

"How far?"

"Two-seven-thousand yards, maybe less."

"Type?"

"Not sure, skipper."

"Your best estimate then?"

"Akula-class SSN, I reckon. What's our speed, skipper?"

"Five knots."

Holder, a sonar operator at the next console, hunched over his screen monitoring the signal from the towed array, the receiving hydrophones at the end of an 800 metre cable towed behind the port side of the boat, piped up, "If we can steer ten degrees port, I might be able to get a better reading, sir."

Commander Clifton glanced at Poulton, his most experienced operator, who nodded. Via the intercom, Clifton gave the order. "Ten degrees port."

"Ten degrees port, aye," responded Control. The 110 metre boat slowly turned until it was on its new course, the seventeen-bladed propeller powering it forward silently, cavitation kept to a minimum.

Holder's head tilted forward and his hand went to his earphones. "It's...bearing two-two-five, sir."

"We need a solid solution. I'm heading back to the Con. We need a good TMA, Poulton."

"Aye, sir."

Commander Clifton made his way back to the control room, immediately next door to the sonar room. He needed full control of his boat if he was to take on the enemy, a possible deadly Akula-class submarine.

The skipper entered the brightly lit control room. It was a compact, squared space, the centre dominated by a raised platform with the two periscopes: the attack scope on the port side with the optical periscope to starboard. On the port side was a bank of consoles for the navigational equipment, NAVSTAR GPS receiver, and, most important, the control station, the helm, controlling the ship's direction of travel and trim. On the opposite side was the centre that managed the submarine's teeth, its missiles and torpedoes, the weapons control panel, BSY-1 consoles and the CCS-2 console. The masts, just behind the bridge position on the sail, consisting of the search periscopes, radar, electronic countermeasures and communications, fed the control room with data from its many sensors.

"I have the Con," he said to his Executive Officer, Lieutenant Commander Joel Granger.

"You have the Con," the XO responded.

"Bridge, Sonar. Definite contact, bearing zero-two-six. Designated Sierra-One. An Akula-class. Range two-six-thousand yards. Course zero-four-five at fourteen knots."

"Every 1,000 yards, Poulton."

"Aye, sir, every 1,000 yards."

The skipper turned to the XO. "All stations ready, Joel?"

"Aye, skipper, they're ready. Been training a long time for this. Didn't think I'd ever see the day, though."

"None of us did, but it's here now."

"Bridge, Sonar. Range, two-five-thousand yards. Can we turn ten degrees to port, sir?"

"Losing them, Poulton?"

"Not yet, sir, but Sierra-One's course has changed. Now heading zero-five-zero."

"OK, Poulton, keep tracking."

"Tracking, aye."

"Ten degrees port."

"Ten degrees port, aye, sir."

"They haven't heard us yet, sir," suggested the XO.

"No, they're going too fast, wanting to get across the front of the convoy, no doubt, and lie in wait."

"Bridge, Sonar. Sierra contact, designated Sierra-Two. Bearing two-three-zero, range two-seven-thousand yards. Course zero-five-zero, speed fourteen knots."

"Damn," exclaimed the XO. The rest of the control room looked up from their stations momentarily, noting that another Soviet SSN had been spotted. Things could get hot.

The skipper turned to the helm. "Maintain course and speed."

"Maintain course and speed, aye, sir."

The XO and skipper both moved across to the port side plotting table, where a young lieutenant was tapping into the Hewlett Packard computer, aiding him in identifying the instant ranges to the, now, two targets.

"We're going right in between them, sir," suggested the XO.

"If we can pass right in between them, get behind their baffles, we could put two each right up their backsides. Helm, initiate zigzag."

"Zigzag, aye, sir."

"Sonar, Bridge."

"Bridge, Sonar," responded the sonar supervisor

"We're going into a zigzag pattern. I want those two pinned down tight."

"Aye, sir, zigzag pattern."

"I hope to God there aren't any more, sir. Keeping track of these two will be difficult enough."

The fire control technician continued to stack the dots, developing a fire solution for both targets, constantly estimating the two Sierras' speed, course and range, the zigzag now helping to firm up the solution. His eyes flickered over the screen, monitoring the targets bearing and the time, the dots giving him a base of time.

"I have solution for Sierra-One, sir."

"Solution for Sierra-One," responded the XO.

"We'll go with an ADCAP XO. I don't want to take any chance of that bugger catching a whiff of us before we shoot."

"Weapons, load two ADCAPs, tubes two and four."

"Two ADCAPs, tubes two and four, aye, sir," responded the weapons officer who was standing at the weapons control console on the starboard side of the control room.

"I have solution for Sierra-Two, sir."

"Solution for Sierra-Two," confirmed the XO.

"Weapons, load two ADCAPs, tubes one and three," ordered the XO.

"Two ADCAPs, tubes one and three, aye, sir," answered the weapons officer.

Deep down in the boat, at the near tip of the bow, the crew followed the orders of the weapons officer. Although they checked the torpedoes, they didn't actually need to load them as they were already in the tubes. The four in the tubes, plus the reloads, gave USS Providence fourteen M-48 ADCAP torpedoes in total. Along with

Tomahawk land attack missiles, with a range of 3,000 kilometres, Harpoon anti-surface ship missiles, with a range of 130 kilometres, and the ability to lay mines, the SSN submarine could punch well above her weight.

To say the torpedo room was compact would be an understatement. With two racks for storage of weapons either side of the ten-metre beam and one in the centre, space was at a premium. Moving weapons to and from the tubes to the racks was like operating a Rubik's Cube: complicated but, once you got the hang of it, it became second nature. Two of the torpedoman's mates connected the A-cable, the data-transmission link, from the back of the torpedo, along with the guidance wire. Once all four hatches were closed, the crew checked the seals were secure and the cables were live. A square sign, indicating a 'Warshot loaded', was suspended from the each of the tubes.

Back in the control room, one of the technicians at the weapons control panel looked on as the status lights lit up, indicating that the tubes were loaded with four Mark-48 ADCAP torpedoes.

"Tubes two and four loaded, sir," he informed the weapons officer.

"Tubes two and four loaded, aye," confirmed the XO.

"We're set then, sir."

"Bridge, Sonar. Sierra-One, two-four-thousand yards; Sierra-Two, two-three-thousand yards. Course steady, speed steady."

"Sonar, Bridge. Aye."

"Tubes one and three loaded, sir."

"Tubes one and three loaded, aye,"

The XO and Skipper looked over the plotting table. It showed they were slowly moving towards the two enemy submarines, in between two deadly killers.

But who was moving into the trap? thought Commander Clifton. Them or us? They were closing in on each other at 1,000 yards per minute. Twenty-three minutes would see them alongside; four minutes after that he would turn and fire. He touched his temple as a trickle of sweat ran down his sideburns. *Was he scared?* No, surprisingly not. Just tension, concentrating heavily on the task ahead. Wanting to destroy these two hunters before they got to the convoy, but wanting to keep his boat and his men alive. If he missed any one of the Akulas, the other would finish them off. The clock ticked, minutes passed, seemingly in slow time.

"Bridge, Sonar. Sierra-One, 4,000 yards; Sierra-Two, 5,000 yards. Course steady, speed steady."

"Sonar, Bridge. Aye."

"Pass the word, I don't want to hear anyone breathe," ordered the XO.

"Pass the word, silent routine."

The sonar room stopped reporting, the technician at the plotting table now keeping the control room up to date. The solution was constantly changing as the three submarines slowly converged.

"Sierra-One, 3,000 yards; Sierra-Two, 4,000 yards. Course steady, speed steady, sir."

"Sierra-One and Two, aye," confirmed the XO.

"XO, you have the Con."

"I have the Con." The XO took control, leaving the skipper free to focus on the imminent battle between the three boats.

"Sierra-One, 2,000; Sierra-Two, 3,000 yards. Course steady, speed steady, sir."

"Sierra-One and Two, aye," acknowledged the skipper.

Apart from the odd rustle of clothing, the control room was silent; the tension tangible.

"Sierra-One, 1,000 yards; Sierra-Two, 2,000 yards. Course steady, speed steady, sir," whispered the technician, sensing how close the Soviet submarines were.

"Aye." Clifford peered at the plotting table, and steadied his breathing as he could feel the adrenalin coursing through his veins, his heart pumping in his chest, a slight throbbing in his ears. He raised his finger to his lips, indicating to the technician to stop reporting. He considered cutting the engine, letting the boat drift as the two enemy boats powered by. But, although the noise they produced would lessen considerably, that sudden change might be enough to be picked up as an anomaly by the Soviet sonar crew. It was too big a risk to take. He would stick with his decision and remain at five knots.

Sierra-One would be passing on the starboard side, at no more than 1,000 yards away from them. USS Providence, an elongated SSN, was a precise piece of engineering. The reactor compartment was sandwiched between the engineering and manoeuvring room at the stern and the galley and cold storage areas. Beneath the sail was the control room. Forward of that lay the sonar room, crew and officers' berthing, the torpedo room and, right at the bow, the sonar dome. The long narrow hull, reducing the drag, assisted the submarine to reach a submerged top speed of thirty knots. Their greatest defence at the moment though was stealth, the anechoic/decoupling coating aiding its ghost-like presence beneath the waves. The carpet of individual rubber tiles attached to the hull absorbed the sound of the boat's internal mechanics. That silence was essential to the survival of the boat and its crew as the Akula, oblivious to their presence, slipped past.

The K-284 Akula, the lead boat in the Soviet submarine class, project 971, and the Delfin, of the *Akula*-class, *Akyna*, meaning Pike, were both Soviet *Akula*-class, nuclear-powered attack submarines. Their mission was to focus all their efforts on disrupting the convoys of military troops and supplies being shipped from the North-American continent to the European continent, sinking or destroying as many cargo and warships as possible. Their primary targets were those fat cargo ships, laden down with American soldiers accompanying a mixture of M-60 and M1-Abrams tanks headed for the battle already underway. Both of the submarine commanders knew they were taking a risk by travelling at fourteen knots but, believing the convoy and any protective screen were some distance yet, they had taken that chance. They hadn't anticipated that one of the US SSNs had been dispatched well ahead, to catch any Soviet submarines doing exactly what these two were doing now. USS Providence had used a tactic of scoot and drift: racing at speed, then drifting, allowing the front sonar and the towed array sonar to do their work.

The Akula-1 class, with a double-hull system, composed of an inner pressure hull and an outer 'light' hull, had more buoyancy than its Western counterparts, but the greater wetted surface area increased the drag. More power was required to push it through the water, ensuring it was not as silent as the hunter-killer that was at this very moment in between the two unsuspecting Soviet submarines. The enemy submarines each had four tubes, capable of firing the Type-53 torpedo or the SS-N-15 Starfish missile. They also had four larger tubes each, for the Type-65 torpedo or SS-N-16 Stallion missile. Built at the Amur shipbuilding plant, the 110 metre long submarine could travel at a top speed of thirty-three knots, powered by its 190-megawatt pressure water reactor. If these two killers got anywhere near the convoy, they could cause devastation until they were driven off or sunk by the convoy's anti-submarine-warfare units: other SSN submarines, ASW surface ships, or ASW helicopters.

Commander Clifford let his breath out slowly, after realising he had probably been holding it for nearly a minute. He took a badly needed deep breath as he looked port side, knowing that, at about 1,000 yards out, a second Soviet SSN was passing by. He thanked his God that the captains of the subs were ploughing through the water at the speed they were, helping to hide his own command from discovery.

He looked at the bridge clock: six minutes had passed; the second Akula must be at least 2,000 yards away.

"Sonar, Bridge. Where are they, Poulton?"

"Bridge, Sonar. Sierra-One, bearing zero-five-zero, course zero-five-zero, range 3,000 yards, speed fourteen knots. Sierra-Two, bearing zero-five-five, course zero-five-zero, range 2,000 yards, speed fourteen knots."

"I have the Con, XO."

"Skipper has the Con," reiterated the XO.

"Hard to port."

"Hard to port," repeated the XO.

"Hard to port, aye," confirmed the helm.

"Weapons, SRA."

"Weapons, Short Range Attack." The XO again mimicked the skipper's order.

"SRA, aye," responded the weapons officer.

The submarine, still maintaining five knots, slowly swung around in a large arc, its bow eventually hitting the bearing the two Akulas were sailing on.

"Ahead."

"Ahead."

"Ahead, aye."

USS Providence was following directly behind the two killers, right behind their baffles, the noise of their spinning screws creating a barrier to any noise the unseen and unheard enemy was creating behind them.

"Sonar, Bridge. Come on, Poulton, talk to me."

"Bridge, Sonar. Sorry, sir."

"Just let me know what's going on."

"Sierra-One and Sierra-Two. Bearing zero-five-zero, course zero-five-zero, range 5,000 yards and 6,000 yards, still fourteen knots."

"Thank you, Poulton."

"We wait, sir?" asked the XO.

The skipper wiped his moist upper lip, suddenly feeling hot. And, he admitted to himself, a little scared, "Yes, I want at least 7,000 yards between us and them before we fire."

"Four miles is good for me too, sir," Granger responded with a grin.

After the allotted time, the skipper was satisfied they were far enough away from the enemy submarines to fire at the still moving targets. He gave the necessary orders. His crew were nervous; he could sense the tension in the control room. It was only natural. They had trained and trained for this. But no exercise on earth could be a substitute for the real action.

"Make ready."

"Make ready."

"Make ready, aye, sir." The weapons officer gave the go-ahead for the torpedoes to be warmed up.

Commander Clifford checked the plot on the plotting table, and got confirmation from the technician that the two solutions were set.

"Make tubes ready in all respects."

"Make tubes ready in all respects."

"Make tubes ready in all respects, aye, sir."

The fire control technician transmitted the data that would be required by the weapons of choice, and the order was passed down to the torpedo room. The torpedo in the torpedo tube, warm and ready to fire, was immersed in water as the tube was flooded. Now they were at their greatest risk. The noise of the water flooding into four tubes would immediately take away their stealth, leaving them exposed, able to be picked up by an enemy submarine. Once flooded, the TMs opened the outer doors, the four deadly torpedoes now ready to be launched.

"Launch ten degrees left and right tubes one and three; launch ten degrees left and right tubes two and four."

"Aye, sir."

"Firing point procedures."

"Firing point procedures, aye, sir."

"Match bearings and shoot!"

"Match bearings and shoot, aye, sir." The weapons officer directly in front of the launch control panel immediately pressed the firing switch, the firing sequence now initiated.

The jet of water at the rear of each of the torpedoes formed a ram and pushed each deadly weapon out of its tube, one by one and into the open sea. With two thin wires trailing behind each advanced capability (ADCAP) torpedo as they snaked, the seeker searched for the target as they sped towards the Akula-SSNs.

"Five minutes to target," called out the weapons officer.

"Bridge, Sonar. Sierra-One and Sierra-Two, cavitation, estimate speed twenty knots. Sierra-One new course two-two-five; Sierra-Two, speed twenty knots, new course one-three-five."

"Bridge, aye," responded the XO.

"Four minutes to target."

The four torpedoes raced towards the two Akula-class, hunter-killer submarines, which at that moment in time were the hunted. The Mark 48 torpedoes were world-class. With twenty miles of guidance wire tucked into the body of the torpedo, it gave the USS Providence the space to get out of the area quickly, reducing the likelihood of the enemy being able to strike back. The swashplate piston engine powered the nearly six-metre torpedo at fifty-five knots, over 100 kilometres per hour. Travelling at nearly two-miles per minute, the enemy had very little time to react.

"Three minutes to target."

"Bridge, Sonar. Sierra-One, twenty-four knots, new course zero-three-five; Sierra-Two, twenty-four knots, new course one-one-five."

"Bridge, aye," answered the XO. "They're racing and zigzagging, skipper."

"Two minutes to impact."

"Bridge, Sonar. Countermeasures deployed, countermeasures deployed."

"Bridge, aye. Calm down, Larry," encouraged the XO. They needed their best sonar operator to be calm and specific.

"Weapons, are the 48s still on target?" asked the skipper.

"Yes, sir. They've got through."

"Bridge, Sonar. Fish in the water! No, wait. Two fish, two fish in the water!"

"Bridge, aye. Hard to port, full ahead."

"Bridge, Sonar. Four fish in the water!"

"One minute to impact."

The Akulas were hitting back. One had fired down the bearing of the torpedoes heading directly for them, while the second had manoeuvred further away, tracking the Providence and launching two torpedoes in the submarine's path.

"Helm?"

"Fifteen knots, sir."

"Sonar, Bridge. Poulton."

"They have four in the water, sir. Fifty knots. First two impact four minutes. Second two three-minutes twenty."

"Thirty seconds to impact."

"Helm?"

"Twenty-five knots, sir."

"Ahead full."

"Ahead full, aye sir."

The XO and Commander Clifford looked at each other. There was nothing else to do or say. All they could do now was hope that the Providence could cut thirty-plus knots, and they could put some distance between them and the chasing Soviet torpedoes. It was likely that they were the Type-65 and, with a top speed of fifty knots and a range of fifty kilometres, it was unlikely the US SSN would outrun it.

"Bridge, Sonar. I can hear popping sounds. Sierra-One is moving towards the surface."

"Bridge, aye."

"Fifteen seconds to impact."

"Helm."

"Thirty knots, sir."

"Engine room, Bridge."

"Engine room, aye."

"We have four fish up our backside and I need all this baby has got."

"One hundred and twenty per cent, aye."

"Ten, nine, eight, seven, six…"

"Helm."

"Thirty-two knots, sir."

"…five, four, three, two, one, impact."

You could have heard the proverbial pin drop. The entire ship's focus was on what would happen in the next few moments.

The USS Providence shuddered slightly.

"Bridge, Sonar. One, no, two explosions."

"Bridge, aye."

"Bridge, Sonar. Sounds of breaking up and rushing water. It's a hit, sir."

The men in the control cheered and the cheering spread throughout the ship.

"Quiet," snapped the skipper. "We're not out of the woods yet."

The remaining two Mark-48 torpedoes, not fooled by the Soviet countermeasures, approached their target: the second Akula. The proximity fuse of each one sensed the large object ahead and two 300 kilogram high-explosive warheads, plus the remaining fuel, erupted with devastating force. The first one ripped the bow off the now stricken submarine, the second one breaking its back, tearing into both layers of steel. The submarine, now a mass of entangled wreckage and dead sailors, sank ungainly to the bottom of the Atlantic Ocean, to join its sister ship that was already ploughing towards the mud beneath.

The boat trembled again as the second submarine was struck.

"Bridge, Sonar," came the excited voice of Poulton over the comms. "Two explosions...I can hear the sound of tortured metal... water has breached...on last bearing...depth increasing...they've been hit, sir."

"Thank you, Poulton."

The control room erupted into cheering and backslapping. They had just blown two of the Soviet navy's best out of the water and done their duty by protecting the convoy.

The XO was about to demand silence again when the skipper indicated no; leave them to enjoy the moment.

"Bridge, Sonar. Torpedoes, two minutes to impact."

"Bridge, aye."

"Standby decoys," ordered the XO.

"Decoys, aye." The weapons officer confirmed he had received the order.

"Bridge, Sonar! Two more torpedoes, right behind the first four! One minute to impact!"

"Bridge, aye," responded the skipper keeping his voice calm, although inside his mind and his heart were racing. "Helm."

"Thirty-six knots, sir. Maybe have one more in her."

"Decoys in five seconds."

Fifty seconds. The crew could now hear the whine of the torpedoes as they got closer and closer.

Forty-five seconds. "Launch countermeasures."

"Countermeasures, aye."

Forty seconds.

"Countermeasure launched."

"Hard to starboard."

"Hard to starboard, aye." The helmsman turned the boat to the right, the submarine tilting slightly as the rudder and planes gripped the water.

"Down 100."

"Down 100, aye, sir."

Thirty-five seconds. The SDC Mark-Two hovered in the water, transmitting signals to mimic a submarine, at the last depth the Providence was at before it turned and dived to lose the chasing Soviet torpedoes.

An explosion, followed by a second, rocked the boat.

"Ahead full."

"Ahead full, aye, sir."

Thirty seconds.

"Bridge, Sonar. Two torpedoes destroyed. Four still on our tail. Second two, forty seconds."

"Bridge, aye."

"Launch countermeasure."

"Countermeasure launched."

Twenty-five seconds.

"Hard to port. Depth 150. Prepare the MOSS."

"Hard to port, depth 150, aye."

The helmsman turned hard left, pushing the boat down further to a depth of 150 metres.

"Ahead full."

Twenty seconds.

"Ahead full, aye, sir."

"Fifteen seconds." A myriad of thoughts ran through the minds of every man on the boat. They were seconds away from survival or seconds away from a horrible death.

The boat shuddered again as the second two torpedoes were lured away by the ADC decoy and exploded.

"Twenty-five seconds," came the reminder that all was not over yet. The last two torpedoes were still tracking them.

"Launch MOSS."

"MOSS launched, aye, sir," responded the weapons officer.

"Twenty seconds."

The MOSS, a mobile submarine simulator, equivalent in size to one of Providence's torpedoes, was launched from its own special tube.

"Fifteen seconds."

"All ahead, stop."

"Stop, aye."

The MOSS moved away from the submarine, travelling through the water at twenty knots, transmitting wildly, generating a strong underwater signature, doing its best to impersonate the Providence.

"Ten seconds."

"Bridge, Sonar. One has gone for it. The lead torpedo is following the MOSS."

"Bridge, aye."

Five seconds.

The sound of the torpedoes screaming through the water was now almost deafening to the crew as the two of them were almost on top of the now drifting submarine.

"Bridge, Sonar. The second one's not been fooled!"

There were two almost instantaneous explosions. The first blasted the MOSS apart; the second blew the stern off the now stricken SSN, the blast and cold flooding water killing many of the crew. The boat, now severely damaged, listing at the stern, powerless and blackened, was at the mercy of the elements. Only the skills of the captain and the crew could save what was left of themselves and the submarine that was now lying silent and stationary.

Chapter 25

The Divisional Commander of the 12th Guards Tank Division, known as the 'Bear' to his men, stubbed out another of his foul-smelling cigarettes, vowing for the one hundredth time he would stop smoking. But then his intake of vodka would likely increase. He smiled at the simple thoughts swirling around his head, yet he and his men could be in full battle mode within twenty-four to forty-eight hours' time. The rest of his command looked on, not wanting to interrupt the Bear as he clearly had something of great importance on his mind. Even the most feared man in the unit next to the Bear, the Deputy Commander and Political Officer, Colonel Yolkin, thought it best to remain silent.

General Turbin looked about the divisional command post, a huge storage area, part of a large mining complex close to the town of Lehrte. He was slightly uncomfortable having his Forward Command Post so close to the Forward Line of Enemy Troops (FLET), but he knew that, when the time came for his division to fullfill their role as an OMG, they would need to move at lightning speed. His main command post was east of Peine, with an alternate main headquarters in Salzgitter. His forward HQ had travelled light, only fourteen vehicles and eighty men, most of those the senior officers of his division. Only a reduced platoon protected the HQ. But it was what was needed. If they got into trouble, elements of the division were not far away, hidden in the forest on the south-western edge of the town. The remainder of the division was scattered around Hamelerwald, Sehnde, Hohenhameln and Peine, waiting to be called forward to fulfil their role in the subjugation of the NATO forces they were up against.

They had not yet been blooded, he thought as he took another pull on his cigarette, blowing a plume of smoke into the air. In some respects, that was a good thing. His men had no real fear of the realities of battle yet, so would go into it with full vigour. The second time round would be more difficult, perhaps. Their armour was fresh and his maintenance teams had kept on top of repairs, so he had nearly ninety-five per cent of his tanks available. Some of those losses had been the result of NATO airstrikes, the consequence of an incompetent battalion commander failing to camouflage his tanks adequately. The yellow-black ring around the man's left eye bore the evidence of the General's displeasure. The entire upper divisional command were in attendance, over thirty officers, ranging from Majors through to full Colonels and the General himself. The junior officers and NCOs, who would normally be part of the HQ staff of the 12th Guards Tank Division, 3 Shock Army, fulfilling tasks such updating maps, manning the radios, helping prepare written orders, and provide refreshments, were excluded from this meeting. The fug increased as the Bear lit up another one of his foul-smelling Belomorkanal cigarettes. Many of his officers also had cigarettes in their hands, but chose a milder option. The commanders of the main teeth-arms and supporting units were present: Commanders of the 48th, 332nd and 353rd Guards Tank Regiments, 200th Guards Motor Rifle Regiment, and the 18th Independent Guards Reconnaissance Battalion; officers from the signals battalion, self-propelled artillery regiment, surface-to-air missile battalion, guards engineer battalion, supply, repair, medical and the chemical defence companies; his Chief of Staff, Colonel Pyotr Usatov, his two Deputy Commanders, one responsible for technical services and the other for operations in the division's rear area; the arrogant Political Officer and Deputy Commander of the Division, Colonel Arkaldy Yolkin, and the Chief of Rocket Troops. The Commander of the Tank Division, Major-General Oleg Turbin was a hard taskmaster, and he pushed his officers and men relentlessly to make his division one of the best in the Soviet Army.

"The Uman Division is going to war," said Major-General Turbin finally. "Our selection as the army's *Operacyjna Grupa Manewrowa* (OMG) has been confirmed." He looked at the faces of his senior most officers, looking for something. A sign. A sign of doubt, fear, nervousness or even pride. He saw the occasional flicker of fear, which was not a bad thing, but overall his officers exuded confidence. Even in peacetime, he had pushed his men and the division hard; honed them into a professional fighting force that would stand them in good stead in the coming weeks. Being able to retain all the conscripted soldiers that were due to leave at the end of their two years' service and the new intake undergoing intensive training ready to act as reinforcements when needed had helped. Their standard of training was high, and there was a good pool of reserves ready to fill in the gaps when they started to incur casualties. They had every reason to feel confident. During the last six months, he and his officers had even tackled the 'grandfather rule', where the *Dedovschina*, the older draftees, ruled the new intakes through fear and intimidation. Even officers and NCOs had been reluctant to tackle that imbalance. But the Bear had struck with an iron fist and ensured that this changed. NCO and officer rule was enforced and NCOs, conscripts themselves, were given additional training enabling them to fulfil their roles in commanding a section or acting as a platoon sergeant. Right across the Soviet armed forces, appropriate authority had been reinstated. Senior officers, Majors, had been shot for various accusations of incompetence, theft of military supplies, and other forms of corruption. If the war was doing anything, it was bringing back the Soviet army to the level it had been at during the successful battles against the Germans in the Second World War.

"There has been a setback," the Bear continued. "Our forces have been unable to cross the River Leine as planned."

The skinny Political Officer, his ill-fitting uniform measured and cut to fit his gawky frame, looking so unlike an officer let alone a senior one, interrupted. "Their failure has not gone unnoticed by our superiors. Their efforts will be redoubled..." He left the end of the sentence hanging in the air.

The look from the Bear would make any officer wilt. The Political Officer, although confident in the legality of the statement he had just made, confident in his authority and support from his political masters, still winced. On a one-to-one basis with the man, Yolkin's confidence was even less. Many of his officers though reflected, knowing that a failure by this division would see them up in front of the dreaded MVD to explain that failure in full. If found guilty of failure, they knew they would likely face an execution squad.

The Bear continued, nonplussed by the Political Officer's statement. "There are currently two main axes for 3rd Shock Army. 7 Guards Tank Division is targeting a crossing at Gronau, and as we speak, an assault brigade is battling with British forces to secure the western bank of the river. The assault from the east will continue tomorrow. The Division is waiting for ammunition and supplies to be brought forward, and an artillery barrage will start early tomorrow. Opposite our location, at Rossing, our 10th Guards will be upping the tempo."

A cloud of foul-smelling fumes interrupted his speech as he puffed on his fortieth cigarette of the day.

"There will be a full assault tomorrow. An air-assault battalion will be landing east of the river, south of Schulenburg. And, there will be a full airborne division assisting us. The 7th Guards Airborne Division will be assaulting to the west of Hanover, holding the ground for our passage through the gap between Hanover and the high ground of the Deinster. They will also disrupt reinforcements and supplies getting to the enemy. With the Air Assault Battalion directly behind the enemy and the 7th Guards Airborne Division attacking from behind and cutting the enemy's supply route, this time we cannot fail."

"We will not be allowed to fail," added Yolkin.

The General's broad shoulders shifted left slightly, ignoring his Political Officer's outburst, and he pointed a finger at Colonel Yuri Kharzin, Commander of the 48th Guards Tank Regiment. "You will be first to move again, Yuri. When the 10th assault and force a river crossing, you need to be ready to roll. You are not to get involved in the fighting until you receive my orders. Understood?"

"Yes, sir. But, if they get bogged down, wouldn't it be best if we lend a hand?"

"Quite possibly, Yuri, but I don't want your men and equipment exhausted, out of ammunition as a result of doing their dirty work. I have it on good authority that the 10th will use every man and tank they have to force a crossing. I know Major-General Abramov well. He is a good soldier and a good leader. He will get us our crossing. We burn them out first. They will throw everything they have at the enemy wall until they batter it down. The more of the enemy forces they destroy, the easier will be our passage through. They will secure a crossing no matter what the cost. Our priority is to exploit that breakthrough. Anyway, with an Assault Battalion and Airborne Division kicking the Brits up the arse, the 10th will succeed. And if needed, they will switch units of the 47th Guards Tank Division from supporting the 7th, to supporting this crossing."

This brought a laugh from his officer corps, as he had expected it would.

"Yes, Comrade General, my regiment will be ready," responded Kharzin.

The General turned to the Deputy Commander 'Rear', who was sitting to his right. "Have the special ammunition stocks been brought forward, Borislav?"

"Yes, Comrade General. They have been kept well away from out troop lay-up points."

"We have one other asset in our armoury. The use of chemical weapons has been authorised, by the Stavka."

Almost as one, the group took a deep breath. They had trained for it and always knew it was an option. In fact, they used chemical weapons whenever they conducted a military exercise, and as a consequence considered it as conventional munitions and therefore could be used in a conventional war. NATO, on the other hand, and the senior officers present were aware of this, saw it as an escalation that warranted a severe response.

"Comrade General, I have already ordered stocks to be distributed amongst the divisional artillery group," the Chief of Rocket and Artillery Troops informed him.

"Good," responded General Turbin. "The brigade of BM-27s from the TVD will also be in support, along with FROG-7s and Scuds. Our own Divisional Artillery Group (DAG), along with the SS-21s, will participate in the barrage tomorrow."

He paused while he lit another cigarette from the one that was now nearly burning his yellowed fingers. "I know that some of our soldiers have slit the underarms of their rubber suits to help keep them cool when taking part in military exercises, so this needs to be addressed. Repairs made or replacements found. Take them from some of the rear units if necessary."

"Abusing military equipment that has been provided for their protection is a military offence that shouldn't go unpunished, Comrade General."

"Yes, yes, I know, Colonel Yolkin. When we come back from this mission, we will take the names of those survivors who have damaged their personal equipment. OK?" He didn't wait for an answer. "So, you need to check all your men. If any suit is too badly damaged then draw fresh from stores. We can worry about the accounting aspects when this is all over. I want our soldiers to be well protected. They are no good to me dead. I want them to fight."

"Will we be using persistent agents or non-persistent, sir?"

asked Akim Yermakion, Commander of the 200th Guards Motor Rifle Regiment. It would be his troops that would be exposed the most, should they need to dismount from their BMP-2s.

"All the crossing points will be hit with non-persistent, as will some areas further east. There are some maps available showing the areas that will be targeted. We will go through these later. One or two areas will be bombarded with persistent chemicals, where we want to permanently deny the enemy safe access. Those are yet to be determined, but will be where they have stocks of ammunition. We will also hit their airfields. The Army's Spetsnaz will be feeding back information over the next twenty-four hours. At least twenty teams of up to ten men each have been dropped behind the British 1st Armoured Division."

He leant forward, adding emphasis to what he was about to say. "We are a unique unit. As the army's Operational Manoeuvre Group it is our task and our honour to be the first unit that completes a full breakout." He thumped the table and then spoke in a strong whisper, his officers leaning forward to catch his every word. "We will not get bogged down. If we come across any stiff enemy resistance and we can get around it, we will. We will wend our way through the weak points in their defences, pushing west." He sat up. "Once in their rear areas, we can tear up their communications centres, supply lines, ammunition depots and artillery. The further we push back their artillery, the harder it will be for them to target our follow-on forces, and it will take away their opportunity to stop and target us. Targeting reserves, unprepared as they arrive in theatre, we will smash all opposition." He stood up and stretched his legs, tipped the contents of the now full ashtray onto the floor and pointed in the direction of Colonel Yolkin.

"Our Political Officer has something to say. Then I want to go through the plans that have been agreed. We will go over them until I am satisfied that you can repeat them in your sleep. Then regimental commanders can return to their units. I, along with my key staff, will change location soon. Those bloody British signallers will think it's Christmas when we start transmitting. But until we get our movement orders, it's radio silence. Understood?"

His officers acknowledged, equally fearful of an air or artillery strike being brought down on top of them.

"Over to you, Comrade Arkaldy."

Chapter 26

2010 7 July 1984. Corps Patrol Unit. South-east of Lehrte,
West Germany.
The Black Effect -8 hours.

Wilf signalled for Tag to come forward, while Hacker and Badger
watched their tail.

"If we go west now, follow these hedge lines, it should take us
to Erich Segen. According to the map, there are just a few buildings
scattered about. There, we can cross the 443 and the railway line
before we push north. I want to follow the railway line for a while,
see what traffic is about. Make sense?"

"Sounds good to me," agreed Tag.

"Fetch the other two."

Tag went back, briefed the other two, then brought them forward
to Wilf's position. Tag took point and, in the evening gloom, guided
the patrol west, the patrol constantly on the alert for Soviet forces,
Soviet rear security and even locals, particularly dogs that might give
away their position. They had spent the entire night tabbing fifteen-
kilometres to circuit the large town of Lehrte, which was now about
three kilometres to their north-west. Travelling east, they kept well
north of the outskirts. On their route, they crossed under the E8/A2
autobahn where they had reported back to HQ the heavy movement
of troops; in particular, lots of heavy artillery. There, they found
cover and waited out the daylight hours until it was safe to move
again. In the meantime, they fed back their sightings to 1 BR Corps
headquarters. Now they were on the move again. It was eight-ten
pm, 7 July. The going was OK, so long as they stuck close to the
hedges. Moving too far off brought them into rutted fields where
the soil stuck to their boots making their tab difficult. There was just
enough light to enable them to see where they were going, but not
too bright that they stood out for all to see. Occasionally they would

stop for ten minutes, and Wilf would scan the area with his image intensifier, enabling him, looking through a green haze, to spot any suspicious movement. The enemy would know they were there, or at least they would suspect that special forces would be snooping around and reporting back, but they hadn't come across any excessive security or patrolling. The Soviets seemed to have one purpose in mind: to push west as quickly as possible. The CPU had to be careful at major crossroads or bridges, or at least the ones still standing, as these always appeared to be guarded well, often with a platoon, at least. Wilf suspected that there were other bridges, military ones, built by Soviet engineers to keep the flow of military traffic moving, particularly supplies needed by the army that must be using them up at a rapid rate. When Wilf stopped, he also checked his sat nav as well as the map. It was important they knew where they were at all times, particularly if a planned air or arty strike was in the offing. He shifted his equipment into a more comfortable position and signalled they move. Although they weren't carrying their heavy forty-kilogram Bergens, they still had a lot of supplies of food, water, ammunition and explosives with them. Once this mission was over, they would return to the Mexe-hide, rest up, and restock before their next task. After about three-kilometres and two hours of tabbing, they could hear the rumble of traffic on the road that was about 300 metres ahead. Tag signaled, and the CPU formed a circle.

Tag whispered to the three men. "The buildings are about 200 metres to our north and the road about 300 to our west. I reckon it's too risky crossing here, so I suggest we move a kilometre south to the small copse that straddles the road. We can cross there."

"Makes sense, Tag. Badger, you take point, then me, Tag, and, Hacker, you've got tail-end-charlie. Let's go."

Badger led them south, his C7 carbine, with its C79 optical sight, following the movement of his eyes, ready to react, knowing they were very close to the enemy at this moment in time. They were a close team and instinctively knew what to do, how to react. Badger would watch their front, to the south, but keeping an eye towards the road; Wilf would watch their left arc; Tag the right arc, where he could hear a steady drone of traffic; and Hacker, with his beloved M-16 A2 with an under slung M203 grenade launcher, would cover their backs. Wilf felt surprisingly secure, and judged that, should it come to a firefight, they would give their best.

After thirty minutes, Badger brought them to a halt at the

edge of a small copse, no more than 400 metres long and less than 150 metres across. He guided them inside, and it was quite eerie to suddenly be in an enclosed area, the light they had been moving by, now blocked out. The copse smelt musty, but with a lingering tang of diesel fumes that had drifted in from the road. Badger knew what he was doing and led them south for a further twenty-metres before moving west towards the road. They formed a circle again and Badger went forward to recce the road. They knew this was going to be a difficult task; the volume of traffic sounded quite heavy.

Badger came back, collected the team and, with two facing away from the road, Wilf and Badger watched the traffic pass by. The rattle of caterpillar tracks got closer and closer, and were soon revealed to be SA-6 surface-to-air missile launchers, six at a time, with radar vehicles, box-body control vehicles, and the occasional MTLB interspersed between them. Just as Wilf was preparing the order to cross, the rattle of tracks grew louder again as a battery of 2S-5s passed them, heading south towards Sehnde. *Convoy lights only, getting ready for a big push*, thought Wilf. *No point in radioing in just yet.*

1 BR Corps was expecting another attack in the morning. As a stay-behind force, it was their task to seek out the Divisional Headquarters and guide the bombers, or artillery, onto the target. As a Corps Patrol Unit, CPU, it was their mission to report directly to the Commander of 1 Br Corps. As members of the 21st Special Air Service Regiment, patrolling behind enemy lines, keeping the British army abreast of what was occurring to their front, was their primary task.

The minute there was a break in the flow of traffic, which lasted for only forty-five seconds, they crossed. A short stretch found them on the western edge of the wooded area, and the unit quickly crossed over the railway line that ran south to north. They turned north, using dead ground to shield themselves from any prying eyes. Their objective was an opencast mining site which, during hours of darkness, should be unoccupied. The team would use it in the hope of avoiding contact with the Soviet military. Wilf felt sure that if they avoided the larger forests and farms, particularly those with large barn complexes, they should be OK. They arrived at the quarry and made their way to the northern edge, and Wilf and Badger scanned the route that lay in front of them; Wilf with his image intensifier, Badger with standard binos.

"We haven't got a fucking inch of cover out there, Wilf. A fucking ant couldn't get across there without being spotted," growled Badger.

"You're right, Badger, it's not looking good. Let's have a look at the map."

They both crouched down close to a pile of discarded rubble, probably from the quarry, and Badger surveyed the map with his red-filtered torch.

"Let's go east. There's nothing on the map, but that track we crossed going north looked pretty well covered. Further up I reckon it will bear off to the left and feed the other quarry complex further north. There should be cover, trees and the like, along the track."

"I'm with you on that. I figure it's our best option. I'll fetch the boys."

Wilf checked his watch: eleven-thirty. They were OK for time.

Once the team were together again, they headed east. At the far end of the mine buildings, they found the track less than fifty-metres away. They followed it north for 200 metres, where, as Badger predicted, it bore off to the left and proceeded to take them north-west towards the other quarry complex that was their main target. Based on the information they had received from 1 BR Corps, and intelligence from an Electronics Warfare unit, that was where the enemy divisional HQ was supposed to be.

The track had plenty of cover so, against all normal standard operating procedures, they followed along the edge of it. After 700 metres, they came to where the track split, one snaking west then north, leading to the western boundary of what they believed to be a processing plant for the quarry, the second heading off north-east, probably passing the plant to the east. But in the centre of the two tracks, for the next 300 metres, was a thick copse that widened the further north it went, its boundary touching the edge of the two tracks either side as they pulled further apart.

The patrol now slowed right down, placing their steps carefully, taking their time, nearly an hour to move the next 300 metres. But it paid off. At the far end, at the southern edge of the plant, they could see, and hear, the generators that powered the electrics and the radios for a possible headquarters. Wilf spent an hour studying the complex, getting his bearings. The green mist of his image intensifier gave him a view of a guard patrolling along the outside of a large shed that was close to 100 metres long, a smaller one opposite. The large shed was close to the track to the west, no more than fifty metres away from it. Probably had an entrance to the plant at the northern end, guessed Wilf. The guard's AK was slung over his shoulder, and he seemed completely relaxed. The building was certainly big enough to house the elements of a Soviet divisional headquarters, although there was a distinct lack of vehicles and security forces. He was surprised they had been able to get so close, so easily.

They heard a cough off to their right, and Wilf despatched Tag and Hacker to check it out. They returned within ten minutes.

Tag whispered in Wilf's ear, "Two men, foxhole."

"How's their security?"

"Crap. Both are having a fag."

Wilf pulled the team together into a huddle. "We need to know what's in that bloody shed."

"If we do a circuit, we're likely to bump into another foxhole, or some other guards. They probably have the complex ringed by a defence company. Let's go straight for it," suggested Tag.

"Makes sense, Wilf," agreed Hacker.

"It's open ground," thought Wilf out loud.

"We could go diagonally from here, north-west, to that smaller building opposite the main one. Skirt round the outside into the trees up against the wall, then straight across to it. It's what, a twenty-metre dash?" estimated Badger.

"It's the best option, Wilfy," agreed Tag.

"Let's do it then. Hacker, Badger, you two stay here and cover our exit." Wilf checked his watch: one-forty. "Give us two hours. If we're not back by then, scarper. Our emergency rendezvous will be the north-east tip of the quarry we came through. Wait thirty minutes and, if a no-show, then we meet back at the Mexe-hide. Got it?"

The two SAS troopers staying behind acknowledged. They were slightly disappointed that it wasn't them that would be doing the full recce, but understood that their patrol leader had to choose someone. Wilf and Tag dropped their packs; then moved west, taking them to the edge of the copse, while Hacker and Badger got into a position where they could watch for the enemy and be ready to cover their two comrades should they have to make a hot exit.

Wilf placed the imaging device in front of his eyes, the green shimmer showing what lay ahead of them. Left, about twenty metres away, was a two-metre high hedge. It followed the left-hand track, running west then curving sharply to the north. The hedge stopped where the track suddenly veered right, about 100 metres away, and ran north alongside the western edge of the complex, where the main entrance was guarded by Soviet soldiers. Somewhere in between the track and their position, Wilf could make out darker shadows, the image intensifier revealing possible box-body vehicles. To their immediate front left were some abandoned civilian vehicles, rusted and rotting and, to their half right, the first building they needed to head for. Wilf signaled, and Tag slipped behind him as they moved towards the box-bodies, turned right, using them for cover, and, after checking all was clear, sprinted across to the smaller of the two buildings, crouching down, controlling their breathing, listening. The hum of the generators was distinctly louder now, probably two or three in operation, indicative that it may well be a Soviet divisional headquarters. Satisfied they hadn't been discovered, Wilf led them west, along the southern edge, for ten metres; then took them right, into the gathering of trees alongside the smaller of the two buildings where they could launch their recce of the larger building opposite. Both moved slowly, testing the ground with the tip of their boots before allowing their leg to take their full weight. The noise of the generators, one occasionally emitting a cough and a splutter, went some way to cover any accidental noise they might make. At the edge, Wilf looked to the left, and about fifty metres away, hidden by the civilian vehicles they had passed earlier, was a Soviet Ural-375 box-body, the shadow of the distinctive twin troposcatter dishes on the top, close by a Kamaz-4310, with its power generator running, and carrying the support equipment for the R-423-1 Brig-1. He knew that this was a tropospheric scatter communications system, used as a tactical means of communication between headquarters and higher command. He had questioned in his own mind the likelihood of a divisional headquarters being so close to the front, particularly considering that its regiments were believed to have not yet been deployed. *Reinforcements maybe,* he thought, *or just second echelon divisions getting ready to take over from the first echelon units.*

His thoughts were interrupted as Tag placed a hand on his shoulder and indicated they had company: the Soviet sentry, who had earlier been patrolling up and down the length of what now appeared to be a ramshackle building made of concrete blocks for a low base wall, corrugated sheets for the sides, and topped with metal sheets for the flattish roof.

The sentry, who still had his AK-74 assault rifle slung over his shoulder, approached the trees and was within a metre of the two hidden men when he stopped by one of the larger trees and proceeded to undo his flies before urinating up against the trunk. Once finished, he buttoned up and moved further along to another tree, on the other side of Wilf and Tag's position, just over two metres away, where he leant against that trunk and lit himself a cigarette. The sentry was humming a tune to himself as he moved around the tree, so he was out of sight of any of his seniors who could potentially catch him smoking whilst on sentry duty. Wilf and Tag waited it out, hoping the soldier would move soon. Time was not on their side. Just as they thought he was about to leave, he pulled out a canteen from his pocket, unscrewed the top and took a swig. Replacing the cap, putting the canteen back in his pocket, he pulled out his cigarette pack, extracting another and lighting it, leaning against the trunk again before taking a deep drag. Wilf pulled Tag in close, held out his wrist and tapped his watch; then drew his right hand across his own throat. Tag nodded and watched as Wilf lowered his M-16 to the ground; then eased off his webbing, taking his time for fear of making a noise. Then, stealth-like, he crept towards the sentry who had moved to the side of the trunk, peering round, down the length of the building he was meant to be protecting, no doubt looking for a sign of the duty NCO or officer.

Wilf estimated that the soldier looked to be no older than twenty. He judged the soldier to be a similar height to his own. The double-edged fighting knife was now in his right hand: the Fairbairn-Sykes fighting knife, his favourite weapon. He didn't relish using it, but from his experiences in the Falklands, he knew it was an effective weapon and a relatively silent method of securing a kill. Taking one step at a time, nudging anything aside with his toecap that he felt would make a noise if stepped on, he moved closer and closer. Less than a metre, the soldier humming away to himself, drawing on his cigarette, the red glow lighting up his young face, oblivious to the stalker that was close behind him. A twig cracked, and the sentry pushed himself off the tree, not sure what he had heard, stubbing out his cigarette in panic in case it was that bastard of a sergeant doing his rounds.

Wilf didn't hesitate. He sprang forward, clamped his left hand over the sentry's mouth, crushing his face, pulling the man's helmeted head tight into the crick of his own neck and shoulder. His right hand pulled back, gripping the commando dagger, and he slammed the blade deep into the soldier's kidney. He felt the young man tense, desperately trying to open his mouth in response to the terrible shock that resonated through his entire body. Wilf pushed the guard past the soldier's own webbing and the seven-inch blade bit deep into his body, using the man's own weight to assist him. As the soldier started to recover from the shock, Wilf withdrew the blade and slammed it in again, before withdrawing it and slicing across the soldier's throat, sliding it in a saw-like motion to cut through the gristle, severing the trachea. Not once did his hand move from the man's mouth. The killing was silent, and Tag came forward to help Wilf lower the body quietly and drag the dying man under cover. By the time they had pushed him against the wall of the building, he was dead. They stripped him of any documentation in his possession, perhaps helping to identify the unit; then left him.

"Nice one, Wilfy, but now we'd better fucking move before he's missed."

Wilf didn't need any encouragement. He collected his kit and led them both back to the edge. A quick scan showed the area was clear, and they ran, hunched down, across the open concrete ground to the main building. They both felt exposed as they moved south along the side of the building reaching the corner where they could see the communications vehicles spotted earlier. There was no one around. The men who manned it were probably sitting in the box-body or even asleep somewhere. The humming of the generator was masking any noise they might make. Turning the corner, Wilf moved west, looking for an entrance, a window, somewhere that would give them a view inside the building. Very soon, they turned another corner and were creeping north on the other side, some trees providing temporary cover.

"It's going to be at the other end, Wilfy."

"Yeah, I know, a real pisser. We have to be quick. Any minute they could be looking to change their sentries." He checked his watch: two-fifteen. "If they change on the half-hour, we have fifteen minutes."

"Let's go then."

This time, Tag took point, and they moved as swiftly as they dared along the full length of the building, slowing down before they reached the north-west corner. On their way, they saw another guard patrolling along the length of a one-metre high wall that ran along the western perimeter, and four more manning the double gate that closed off the entrance. North of the building an array of military vehicles were parked up; spread over a large area, cam-netting draped over them to hide the recognisable shapes from the air. There were box-bodies, a couple of troop carriers and a scattering of MTLBs, a T-64 and two BMP-2s. Engines could be heard starting up, and soldiers were in the process of de-camming one of the BMPs.

Tag indicated they move back and hissed in Wilf's ear, "This is a fucking Div HQ all right, and they're getting ready to move."

"It's not a main though. It's not big enough."

"You're right, probably a Forward CP."

"We need to make it quick. It's five minutes to the half-hour."

The two men backtracked, turned left around the end of the building, watching the communications truck as they moved past it. At the far corner, they halted, and Tag peered around the corner. They would need to stick close to the building for about twenty metres before crossing over to where they had left the dead sentry.

Tag was about to signal Wilf to move when they heard the shout.

"*Vasily...Vasily.*"

"Fuck, Wilfy, they're going to discover he's missing pretty damn soon."

A door banged open from the Ural-375. They too had received orders to pack up and move out.

"We need to move sharpish, Wilf. We're buggered if we hang around here."

"*Vasily, мы где?*"

"What's he shouting, Wilf?"

"No idea."

"I thought you spoke Russian."

"So did I. We'll make a dash for it. Straight for Badger and Hacker."

"*Vasily, мы где?*"

Bent over low, the two men sprinted for the location where they had left the two others, time becoming critical now.

"*Vasily. Кто это?*"

"Shit, run!" yelled Wilf. They sprinted, a 100 metre dash to the wrecked box-bodies and another ten would see them in the trees, their boots pounding on the hardened ground as they raced for cover.

"*Кто это?*"

"*Кто это?*"

Crack, crack, crack.

A three-round burst tore up the ground to the side of the running men just before they whipped round behind the trucks, giving them a breather. Within seconds, they were in amongst the trees and in the prone position ready to return fire.

There were more shouts from the direction of the building, and additional clamour from the direction of the communications vehicle.

"We go east," called Wilf. "Badger, Hacker, take out that foxhole and follow us. We'll wait for you by the track."

"Roger."

"Go."

Badger and Hacker quickly made their way behind the foxhole. One of the soldiers was standing on the edge looking towards the direction of the commotion; the other was inside, his gun at the ready. Badger, using a garrote dragged the choking soldier out of his hole, while Hacker slit the throat of the other. The Soviet conscript soldiers didn't even hear them coming and died not really knowing what the war was all about in the first place. The two men weaved through the trees and met up with Tag and Wilf. They all followed the edge of the trees to the north before dropping down into a gully running east. Fifty metres found them at the track.

Wilf called them together. "This gully continues east. After 200 metres, it splits north and south. We go north, get to the outskirts of Lehrte, then run east back to the railway line. Yes?"

"Sounds like the best option to me," responded Badger. Hacker and Tag also agreed.

"OK, let's go. The minute we get some breathing space, I shall call in."

Wilf led the way, leopard crawling his way through the culvert that crossed beneath the road, a few centimetres of rank liquid mud soaking his combats. Once out the other side, they pushed forward, crouching so they were below the lip of the gully. They heard more shots, but the sound faded the further east they went. They tabbed for nearly two hours and, just before daylight, they were able to hide up.

Once the radio was set up, the aerial extended, Wilf called in. The PRC-319, a fifty-watt microprocessor-based radio transceiver, would pass on the information they had just gathered. Using the electronic message unit, he tapped on the small alphanumeric keys and typed his message for his commander. As it was a burst transmitter, he could send the message data at high speed giving them significant security.

Chapter 27

"*Two-Two-Alpha, this is Bravo-Zero. Over.*"

"Two-Two-Alpha, go ahead. Over."

"*Heavy movement your east. Incoming likely.*"

"Roger, Bravo-Zero. Out to you. All Two-Two call signs. Standby, standby. Out."

Alex called down to Corporal Patterson. "Mask up. Make sure Mackinson and Ellis cover up as well."

"Sir," Patsy shouted back.

Dropping down, he closed the hatch cover and peered through the scopes, turning the cupola to scan the area. Mackey started the engine again and they were ready for action. He felt sick, knowing what was coming this time. They had finally got to Two-Two-Bravo. The crew had been unable to get out of their Chieftain tank, trapped in a potential coffin. For the Gunner, Lance Corporal Owen, it had literally become his steel coffin. His broken arm, crushed ribs and pierced lungs, after being bodily thrown heavily against the solid breech of the 120mm gun, had left him crippled and effectively drowning in his own blood. His muffled screams of agony had gone unheard by his fellow crewmen as the clamour of sound outside the tank, and the noise resonating through the fighting compartment, left him isolated. When Two-Two-Charlie had finally got to them, they discovered the tank on its side, the top of the turret and the glacis pressed up against the side wall of the berm. Deep gouges had been cut into the Chobham armour, such was the ferocity of the shelling. The track, in short sections, barely hanging together by the odd pin, lay draped over the side of the tank, the drive sprockets and bogie wheels unprotected and vulnerable. Two of them were missing, wrenched off by the powerful explosions. Anything attached to the outside had all but disappeared. Baskets, storage bins and the radio antenna were nowhere to be seen.

Corporal Simpson immediately called for help and, within an hour, the unit was joined by an armoured recovery vehicle. While Two-Two-Charlie provided cover, they slowly pulled the giant tank away from the side of the berm, allowing the tank troopers to get access to the turret and fighting compartment. Sergeant Andrews, who had smashed his head against the hard metal of the turret, was conscious, but his smashed hand had swollen to treble its normal size, and he was in severe pain. A jab of morphine and he was carried to the tracked Samaritan armoured ambulance where he could get further treatment before being shipped to one of the field hospitals in the rear.

Trooper Lowe, who had been pinned in the driver's compartment, was well and was soon spouting off about how he was going to kick some arse when he got back in a driver's seat. He too was taken to the Samaritan. They removed Lance Corporal Owen's body, as ceremoniously as they possibly could, manoeuvring him through the second turret hatch, four of them carrying him to the ambulance. Lowe burst into tears when he saw his friend, realising how lucky he had been and wondering why Owen and not he had died.

The tank was dragged further out; then pulled over onto its remaining track and bogie wheels. A Scammel tank transporter had been ordered to assist, so they could recover the Chieftain fully and, perhaps in time, even have it back on the battlefield, although it would be days rather than hours. But they were building up quite a graveyard of battered tanks, so spare parts were becoming easier to find. The barrel, buckled and useless, would have to be completely renewed, as would some of the splintered and shattered vision blocks. Two-Two-Charlie could stay no longer. They had been ordered to move to their new location, but a pair of Scorpions were being sent across the river to act as sentries. The rest of the recce troop, along with a second one, were helping with the battle to keep the Soviet airborne forces out of the town. Lieutenant Baty and his two Scorpions, with their 76mm guns, had already had some successes, knocking out four BMDs. The Soviets were slowly running out of armoured support.

Corporal Carter ran along the line of foxholes, checking on the new section that had recently arrived. He had sent the remnants of his section back into the orchard, about 100 metres behind them, giving them the opportunity of being out of the direct firing line, but available as a quick reaction force should they be needed. He wasn't so sure of how quickly they could react. They were tired and shocked, and had seen their dead and wounded comrades taken away. Ashley, the youngest member of the section, was just a mass of blood, his body peppered with shrapnel from an AGS's 30mm grenade. Against orders, they had used their own first field dressing, bandaging him up to try and stem the flow of blood pulsating from numerous rents in his body. He had just stared at his section commander, a slight smile on his pale face; a smile that said, I know you will take care of me, Corporal.

There was still a second 432 with the Peak Engineering turret. Carter's plan was to use what was left of his section, along with the 432, to block any flanking attacks. The best way to judge when to use them and where, was by remaining on the front line himself. He wasn't trying to be heroic by staying; he just needed to orientate the fresh section to their new location: point out where the BMPs might stop to disgorge their troops; where the AGS-17s could set up and suppress them while they assaulted their defences; where the tanks were likely to come from; blind spots; dead ground...all the pointers that could keep these men alive and maybe even hold their position. He assisted the new section commander, Corporal Lawton, in establishing arcs of fire, where best to position his GPMG, where best to place the Milan FPs. Carter's surviving Milan firing post had volunteered to stay on the line, but his orders had been explicit: he was to pull his unit back unless needed. His platoon commander was with the third section of the platoon, battling with the Soviet airborne troops that were trying to get to the Gronau bridge; adding his leadership to the West German reservists who were doing their best to protect their homes and defeat the enemy trying to take their town, and their country, from them.

Carter keyed the handset of his radio. "Two-Two-Alpha, Two-Two-Delta. Radio check. Over."

"Two-two-Delta. Five, five. Over."

"Roger. Out. Two-Two-Delta-Alpha. Radio check. Over."

"Two-Two-Delta, loud and clear this end. Anything happening, Corp?"

"Negative on that. Will keep you posted but we expect incoming any minute now. Out. Foxtrot-One, this is Two-Two-Delta. Radio check. Over."

There was a delay of about ten seconds before he got a response.

"Two-Two-Delta. We receive you. Can you hear, bitte?"

"*Ja.* With you in *zwei minuten.* Out." He smiled to himself. Fluent in German already.

He checked in with the gun-group before running at a crouch further north, where, with the help of a Royal Engineer digger, they had prepared their defences. He stood by the trench alongside a bespectacled young officer, Leutnant Bieber, who was observing his men adding the last-minute touches to their defensive positions. Further along, he could just make out the rest of the German trenches. Strictly speaking, should Lieutenant Wesley-Jones, who he had come to respect, for an officer that is, be killed, this German officer would be in command. *Over my dead body* were his personal thoughts.

"Ah, Korporal. *Danke.* The...digger, *sehr gut.*"

"You're welcome, mate...ah, sir."

His radio crackled and he listened to the message, a hollow feeling in his stomach and it wasn't from hunger. Radar had picked up the movement of vehicles indicating an attack on their position was likely.

"There's movement out there, sir, I suggest you get your men under cover."

"Yes, Korporal. My men have nearly finished."

They heard the whine of the projectiles as they passed overhead, the detonations shaking the ground as they exploded. Corporal Carter instantly held his breath as another salvo landed fifty metres to their front. Carter peeled his helmet off, picked his respirator from its case and pulled it over his face, tightening the thin green elastic straps as he shouted at the top of his voice. "Gas. Gas. Gas." He then dropped into the trench close by.

Bieber had thrown himself to the ground. Most of his men pressed their bodies as close to the bottom of their hole as possible.

"Get your fucking masks on!" he yelled at the shocked troops. "It might be fucking gas! Masks on... *Jezt,* now. *Schnell.*"

The Leutnant scrambled towards them on his hands and knees,

seeking the protection of their defences. He suddenly collapsed as violent spasms racked his body. A bout of violent coughing ensued, the delicate membranes of his lungs stripped by the burning toxins that were now encroaching on his body. Another salvo rocked the area, the entire quarter to their south being bracketed by the blast of at least twenty 152mm rounds. Bieber was engulfed by a fit of coughing, his body desperate to clear the ever increasing flood of fluid and mucus that was slowly filling his lungs, drowning him. He thrashed about, panic setting in as blood rather than air passed out of his lungs, their facility to give him life-saving oxygen now eaten away.

Carter checked his mask and hood was secure, then climbed out of the trench, crawling over to the stricken soldier. The Leutnant continued to thrash about, arms flailing as Carter, and another German soldier who had joined him, tried to calm him down. The soldier was wide-eyed himself, stricken with fear as he saw the bulging eyes and red foam frothing from his officer's mouth, yet relieved that he had been spared the misery he was now witnessing. Bieber's face turned purple then blue as he fought for air. Small fluid-filled blisters formed on his face as the officer's body gave one final shudder, the last movement before he evacuated his bowels.

Corporal Carter looked at the soldier who had come to assist him, mask-less and already starting to cough and show signs of the effects of the blister agent. The Soviets had chosen well. The blister gas would not kill all the soldiers. Many who were affected would survive, but be blinded, ill and needing urgent treatment; placing a drain on the already swamped British and German medical resources and the soldiers around them. He moved back to the trench, there was nothing else he could do. Man's inhumanity to man was well known, but had not been witnessed first-hand by all. These young soldiers had been confronted by hell, and what they had witnessed frightened them. Some felt ashamed that they had, in the past, sneered at their NBC training, joking about it. Complaining about the itchy suits, the ridiculous over boots, the hot suffocating masks. Now they looked at the consequence of getting it wrong.

Chapter 28

Colour Sergeant Rose checked his watch again, and once more removed the magazine from his SLR rifle. Checking the rounds were secure and the magazine housing was clean, he clicked it back into place.

"It's four in the morning and your SLR is still loaded, Colour."

The sergeant laughed. "This bloody waiting is doing my head in. Why haven't they attacked? Do you think they're having problems near Gronau, sir? Maybe they've been diverted to provide support over there," he said, pointing west in the direction of the fought-over riverside town.

Lieutenant Russell thought for a moment. "There's a pretty heavy artillery barrage in the vicinity of the river. They're certainly up to something. We have them penned in, but the OC says they're pushing back hard. Anyway, there's nothing to stop them coming west towards us. And, beyond that, we're all that's in their way."

"That's a sobering thought. It'll be today then you reckon, sir?"

They heard a rustle behind them as one of the platoon brought them both a drink. Although the weather was mild, there was always something comforting about cupping a mug of tea in your hands; the sugary scent of hot, sweet tea. They were in the middle of a raging war, yet somehow, for a few moments, Dean felt quite relaxed. He and most of his men had got through one battle. There was no reason why they wouldn't get through the next.

"One-One-Alpha, this is Zero-Alpha."

The signaler passed the handset to his platoon commander.

"One-One-Alpha, go ahead. Over."

"We have movement east of Gronau, and the airborne are getting restless west of Benstort. Over."

"Roger that, sir. Do you have a direction? Over."

"Negative. But I suspect they are heading in your direction."

"Numbers? Over."

"Estimate a battalion-minus. Call sign Zero-Bravo are in contact, Hemmendorf. Zero-Delta will try to support you. Over."

"Roger that, sir."

"Hang in there, Dean. We'll get you some backup as soon as we are able. Out."

Dean returned the handset to his signaler and placed his map on the earthen berm in front of him, using a shielded torch as the light was still dim. It was now four-ten.

"Looks like they are going to press ahead in between Benstort and Hemmendorf. Maybe they intend to use the road for a quick move."

"I think you might be right, Colour. It's a shame we don't know how many BMDs they will have. Don't suppose you remember your Soviet order of battle, do you?"

"Parachuting in...I reckon they will have at least a dozen. We are probably looking at a full battalion heading our way. We're slightly outnumbered, sir."

"I think you're right, but maybe nearer twenty-plus BMDs. The RAF and the Rapiers took some of their transport aircraft out, but they seem to have been dropping a fair few."

"Well, judging by the noise coming from Hemmendorf, the Green Jackets are definitely in contact."

"They're trying to expand the ground they hold. They had a bit of a battering from our Gunners yesterday."

"Yes, but Gunners switching to the other side of the river gave the Sovs a breather."

"Too many targets, too few assets."

"At least the Jaeger unit will give them a small surprise when they come our way."

"It's lucky they came along, sir. We should have a company if not a battalion defending this piece of ground."

"We're all there is, Colour, at least for the moment. We'll do all we can."

"I'll call up the troops, sir, make sure they're ready."

Colour Sergeant Rose moved off with the signaler to call up the rest of the platoon, leaving his platoon commander to assess, yet again, the positions of his small unit on the map.

He had to defend a piece of ground from the base of the Hohenstein on their right to the high ground of Nesselberg-Osterwald on their left. His two Milan FPs were dug in at Clapham, the junction of the road and the railway line, the south-west point of the village. They also had a gun-group plus two men to provide cover. By the bridge over the water feature, designated London Bridge, about 400 metres back, he had a section of six men. He also had a Blowpipe team close by and one other team further back in the village. He knew his men would do what they could, but wasn't confident that they would provide them with much support. At least they might put the Hind helicopter pilots off their stride, he smiled to himself. He looked across at Voldagsen, Little-town, glad that a twenty-seven ton tank destroyer, a *Kanonenjagdpanzer* along with a dozen *Jaeger* were in position. Another dozen *Jaeger* were to the south.

Colour Sergeant Rose dropped into the trench, the signaler to the side of him. "HQ, sir."

"Zero-Alpha, One-One-Alpha. Over."

"There's heavy movement on both sides of the river. Friendlies are being shelled to the east of Gronau. On the other bank, they look like they're getting ready to move up."

"Roger that, sir. We've normally had an arty strike by now. Over."

"They're tricky bastards, Dean. They're up to something so keep your men on the alert."

"Understood, sir. Anymore reinforcements? Over"

"Not confirmed yet, but we may be getting some reinforcements to you within the next couple of hours. So hold on as best you can. Zero-Alpha. Out."

Dean passed the handset to his signaler. "Give everyone a warning. Now."

"Sir."

The radio operator carried out his order: informing the units of the platoon to be on their guard as something, although he didn't know what, was imminent.

In the next trench, Private Daly placed his SLR on the top of the berm to the front, scrambled out, and adjusted a thick piece of turf that had been placed on the door, lying flat across one side of the trench. They had pulled the thick oak farm door out of one of the houses, using it, along with a layer of earth, as overhead protection. Placing turfs of wild grass, they hoped it would help to hide their position form the enemy. A shadow caught his eye, and he looked up and back, towards the west, towards Coppenbrugge. He peered into the sky that was slowly gaining colour as the early dawn started to give way to the early morn.

He knew almost immediately they were aircraft. They were flying low and could have been helicopters, but were going too fast.

"Sir, the RAF are coming at last. Them'll give the Sovs something to think about."

One second.

"Get down!" yelled Russell as he held his breath and fumbled for his respirator, pulling off his helmet at the same time.

Two seconds.

He pulled the rubber mask over his face and screamed, "Gas, gas, gas" with what little breath he had left. Quickly checking the straps at the back, the seal around his face, he finally sucked in a deep breath, before pulling his Noddy suit hood over his head.

Three seconds.

"Gas...gas...gas," he yelled again, his voice muffled. He heard mess tins being banged together off to his right, a warning to everyone.

Four seconds.

On hearing his platoon commander's warning, Daly had tried to do two things at once: grab for his respirator and jump down into his hole.

Five seconds.

Russell looked up and back as the two aircraft flew over, a trail of white mist coming from canisters beneath their wings.

Six seconds.

"Oh God," he groaned to himself.

Seven seconds.

Daly slipped and went down on his backside, frantically pulling at his S6 respirator, ripping his helmet and hood off, dragging his black rubber mask over his head, panicking, breathing rapidly, forgetting all of his drills.

Eight seconds.

He'd pulled it too far, the front chin cup sliding over his mouth.

Nine seconds.

He finally pulled it back down and tightened the straps.

Ten seconds.

Daly shouted, "Gas, gas, gas." Instinct told him he had to get into his foxhole, but he knew he was in trouble. His nose had started to run and his chest felt uncomfortably tight. As ordered, he had been taking his NAPS tablets, a pre-treatment to increase his body's defence against low levels of nerve agent, so he should be alright, he thought. Maybe he had missed one or two. What should he do now? He fumbled in his respirator-case, searching for a ComboPen, his eyesight starting to dim and his rubber-gloved hands trembling as he pulled the entire contents out, panic setting in. He was sweating now, drooling at the mouth, and his vision was so bad he could no longer identify the objects laid out in front of him. Feeling nauseous and dizzy, he vomited into his mask, tearing it off before he choked to death, just managing to peel it off as his body stiffened, his muscles cramping, then his muscles jerked in uncontrollable spasms.

Lieutenant Russell clambered out of his trench and ran over to Daly, knowing exactly what had gone wrong, seeing the twitching soldier, his one leg kicking out uncontrollably. Another of his platoon joined him to help. He spotted the ComboPen lying next to Daly. Picking it up, he peeled off the packaging, removed the cap that protected the needle, knelt on Daly's leg to keep it as still as possible, and placed the point against Daly's thigh. He pressed the button on the top and the powerful spring inside ejected the long needle through the soldier's NBC suit, combat trousers and deep into his muscle. The fluid flooded into his upper leg, and Dean moved into a crouch as he was joined by Rose. Daly urinated and defecated inside his combat trousers, his body heaving as he convulsed violently, unable to breath, then his body twitched irrepressibly, faster and faster, one leg kicking out involuntarily, until he went into a coma and death released him. He died close to the men he had drunk with, fought with and now died next to. One pinprick of Sarin nerve agent was all it had taken to kill yet another British soldier.

They didn't hear the sound of the incoming shells through their NBC hoods, but the explosions that erupted behind them were all they needed to encourage them to dive for cover in their prepared holes. A line of explosions erupted along their front, fifty metres away, but they still felt the force of the blast. With his head down, Dean peered at the detector paper stuck to the pocket of his Noddy suit. It was coloured blue. Not that he needed confirmation that they had been hit by a chemical agent after seeing Daly die in such a horrendous manner; the confirmation was there all the same. He was glad that Colour Sergeant Rose had reminded him that, now they were back on the front line, NBC suits should be worn again. That advice had saved many lives that day.

They spent fifteen minutes hunkered down before the explosions ceased as quickly as they had started. A sharp boom came from the direction of Little-town as a tank-round from the Bundeswehr tank destroyer lifted a BMD mechanised infantry combat vehicle off its tracks, a plume of smoke following the surviving Soviet airborne soldiers as they escaped the inferno inside only to be cut down by machine-gun fire from the Jaeger soldiers.

"Stand-to, stand-to."

Dean doubted many of his men had heard him, but it helped to prepare him for the fight that was coming their way. Peering through the fogged lenses of his respirator, he pulled his SLR into his shoulder and aimed it in the direction he thought the enemy would appear.

Brrrrrp, brrrrrrp, brrrrrrp.

The Gympy was already firing at the advancing Soviet airborne soldiers, hundreds of rounds tearing up the ground in front of them, many of the bullets ripping into their bodies. Thank God the gun team had survived both the chemical and artillery strike. This had to be a local attack. *The gas to weaken them*, he thought, *then the Assault Brigade using its own D-30 122mm artillery, parachuted in the previous day, to prepare the ground for this particular battalion's attack.*

Boompf. Another BMD suffered from a 90mm round from the Bundeswehr tank destroyer, as it punched through the MICV's 19mm thick side-turret armour. A plume of earth shot up at Dean's right side as a BMD tried to target the Gympy that was cutting the advancing soldiers to pieces. A sudden flare shot across the front of his eyes as a Milan missile rocketed towards the vehicle that had just fired its 73mm gun. There was no competition. At 1,000 metres away, the Milan warhead struck. The shaped charge tore a hole in the side of the eight-ton vehicle, stopping it dead. The minute the soldiers lost the covering fire of their armoured support, they went to ground. The closest airborne soldiers were now 200 metres away, and Dean took aim. Although he felt shaky, he steadied his aim, controlled his breathing and squeezed the trigger. The powerful rifle kicked into his shoulder and, less than a second later, the soldier that had been in his sights spun around, a fatal wound taking him out of the fight. More and more cracks and rifle reports could be heard as more of the elements of the platoon defending this area picked off other targets. A deafening explosion close to his right ear indicated his signaler was also joining in the fight.

Dean unfolded his map, spread it on the rear slope of the berm and beckoned for the handset. "One-One-Foxtrot, One-One-Alpha. Target. Over."

"One-One-Alpha. Send. Over."

"Grid. Three, nine, nine, seven, two, zero. Four rounds, fire for effect. Grid. Four, zero, zero, seven, two, five. Four rounds, fire for effect. Grid. Four, one, zero, seven, three, zero. Four rounds, fire for effect. Out."

He'd had to shout through his mask to ensure they could hear and that they understood. A mistake and they could be on the receiving end of the mortar rounds that would soon be on their way. But, the Corporal in command would have all friendly forces marked on his map and would quickly know if there was a error in his officer's orders.

Colour Sergeant Rose dropped down next to him and he returned the handset to his signaler.

"Sir. The Sovs aren't wearing NBC kit!"

Dean thought back to the soldier he had shot, and Rose was right. They had no protective equipment on. It had been a non-persistent chemical strike. If they could get a breather, they could decontaminate, change their kit and remain in the village. Dean nodded.

They fought for another thirty minutes before the Soviet airborne troops withdrew, the mortar rounds bracketing their positions proving to be lethal and effective. The company sent forward to probe the defences had suffered badly. They had lost four of their precious BMDs, with twelve men dead and over twenty wounded; the mortar bombs breaking up the attack just as they were about to make a big push.

Dean didn't know how much time they had before the next attack, but he had no doubt it would be the full battalion, and they would try to flank him and his men. It was time to check on his men, then decontaminate and move back to their second line of positions. Looking at the dead soldier across from his trench, he wondered how many more of his men had succumbed to the deadly chemical attack.

Chapter 29

Colonel Trusov was jolted suddenly as Kokorev pulled heavily on the
left stick, the T-80K swerving around a burning hulk of a T-80 from
the 63rd Guards Tank Regiment. Twice, the tanks of 10th Guards Tank
Division had been thrown at the NATO front lines east of the River
Leine, but the Challengers of Combat Team Delta, even after being
battered by a thirty-minute artillery barrage, struck back. Many of the
T-80s encountered the scattered minefields, salvos from 1st Armoured
Division's artillery, and a steady assault from tank-busting aircraft. Even
with ERA armour, the hardened penetrators fired from the superb
British 120mm main gun knocked out tank after tank. As the Soviet
armour got closer to the river, the Challengers, dug in on the western
bank, added their weight to the wall of steel that was meeting the Soviet
tanks as they clawed their way west. It was only when the divisional
commander released the Hind-D tank killers that they were they
able to make progress and force the now battered combat team back
across the river. A few Landwehr units had not retreated, preferring to
fight to the last man, protecting their homes and the families that had
remained behind.

Combat Team Delta was effectively finished as a fighting force.
Out of its original fourteen Challenger tanks, the pride of the British
Royal Armoured Corps, only three had made it back across. Now
part of the Battlegroup reserve, they had been withdrawn to safety,
where they could recover from the horrors of the battle they had
just fought. Feeling secure as they initially crossed the river, their
opinion changed as they passed a regimental aid post. The horror of
the sights they saw sickened them. Lines of soldiers mixed in with
civilians were laid on the ground outside a large house that was now

a makeshift first-aid point. A member of the, Women's Royal Army Corps (WRAC), was helping to triage some of the recent arrivals. One line of soldiers and civilians were covered in blankets and sheets, many killed by toxic gas; either failing to pull on their respirators in time, or shrapnel opening a rent in the NBC kit and combats exposing them to the deadly nerve agents. The civilians, some of them with skinny legs and small feet sticking out indicating they were children, just hadn't stood a chance.

Trusov had been disappointed that his regiment, 62nd Guards Tank Regiment, 10th Guards Tank Division, had been put in reserve and excluded from the main thrust the previous day. Now, he perhaps regretted that eagerness after hearing tank after tank being knocked out, the screams of dying men over the airwaves, the cries for help and, even worse, the burnt and torn bodies, the lucky ones being brought back in the hope that the medical team could keep them alive. Although, seeing some, death would probably be their preferred option once they realised the extent of their injuries.

Major-General Abramov, the Commander of the 10th, the Ural-Lvov Division, had pulled his senior officers together for an urgent briefing, and the look he gave Trusov said it all. Pushkin, the new Chief of Staff and his ex-Regimental Commander, nodded his head once, and Trusov knew immediately that tomorrow was not going to be a good day for him and his men. The division had to succeed. The Operational Manoeuvre Group was waiting to complete its mission. But, to do that, they needed to get across the river.

The briefing had been short and sharp. The General knew exactly what needed to be done and who was going to do it.

"Not only have I had our own army commander sticking his fist down my throat, but General Zavarin has ordered me personally to cross that river." He had said the next bit more quietly. "There is no alternative. I cross it or go down in it." A weak smile broke through, but nobody laughed. They all knew that the General was not joking; the consequences of failure were known to all of them. As senior officers, they would not escape the retribution of the MVD or KGB. "We have four assets to support us in our venture tomorrow. The Independent Tank Regiment has been released and will be under my direct control." He looked across at Trusov. "Colonel Trusov, you and your men will have the honour of making the crossing."

Trusov came to attention. "My officers and men will do their duty, Comrade General." Inside, though, he felt vomit rising to his throat. Swallowing, he contained the bitter stomach acids, feeling true fear for the first time in his life.

"I know, Colonel. That is why I have chosen you." Abramov beckoned the officers forward to look at the map spread out on a large farm table, nearly three metres long, purloined from one of the local houses, no doubt.

"We cross here." He made the mark of a cross on the River Leine, between Schulenburg and, at the high ground, Marienburg.

"Sir—"

"One moment, Pavel, let the General finish," advised Pushkin.

"I know you have lots of queries, Comrade Colonel, but at least allow an old General to anticipate some of your questions." Abramov smiled. "Our motor rifle regiment has one operational battalion, perhaps sixty to seventy per cent strength at the most, and one that is a battalion in name only, which can barely pull together a company. But, they have one last task to complete: they are to occupy Rossing. They shouldn't get much opposition. There are only a few old men there left to fight."

He turned to Colonel Maxim. "Charkov, you have to secure Rossing and bring as much fire as you can to bear on Schulenburg."

"Yes, Comrade General."

"With the death of Colonel Yegor, what is left of the 63rd Tank Regiment I will put under your command, Colonel Trusov. So, with your current strength and what is left of the 63rd, it should give you over sixty operational tanks. The infantry have less than a company, so I shall use them here at Barnten, to the north of Rossing."

His finger moved down the map and he pointed to Nordstemmen. "Although I shall be keeping what's left of the 61st in reserve, I shall need the remnants of your infantry battalion," he said, turning to Colonel Konstantin, "in Nordstemmen. I need our flanks covered. You are to bring your regiment forward to Emmerke to act as the division's reserves."

"Sir."

"Back to you, Pavel. I will call the engineers in shortly, but I wanted to cover your task first. What is the state of your infantry?"

"I've amalgamated the three companies to make two, sir. Pretty much at full strength, but they've not had much time to work together as a consolidated unit."

"They'll have to learn on the job, Pavel. They will be crossing with you. You will also have an independent battalion from 3 Shock

Army under your command. The commander is being flown in by heli and will be here in the next thirty minutes." He held his hand up as Trusov went to speak. "I know this is all happening very quickly, and you are getting very little time to plan. But speed is our best ally. NATO will already be figuring out where we are going to strike next and will be marshaling reinforcements to come to their aid. Their division that has come across from the mainland to slot in behind the British Corps' rear is starting to get organised, and some units are already starting to dig in. Get across this river now, and we can smash right into their rear area. As you predicted Colonel, the first bridge, north-east of Schulenburg, has been blown, along with the second next to the high ground further south. You have to get your tanks across and secure a bridgehead. It doesn't matter how small, so long as it's there."

"GSPs?"

"Yes," answered the General. "Six from the division and another six have been brought forward from 12th Division. You will have two K-61 platoons and PTSs to get your infantry across. Once you have secured the other bank, two pontoon bridges will be laid, one kilometre apart."

"What's the ground like here, sir?" Trusov asked, pointing at the eastern bank of the river.

"Recce and our engineers have checked it out. Although marshy in winter and spring, it is reasonably dry, and capable of taking a pontoon bridge and supporting units."

"Will we be making the initial assault to secure the eastern bank, sir?"

"No, the independent tank regiment has that task. They will secure the bank along a two-kilometre stretch and provide covering fire while you cross. You will naturally have artillery and ground attack aircraft in support. The anti-tank battalion will dig in as well and you will get the majority of the Air Defence Regiment."

"We'll be watching your back, Pavel," added Pushkin. "General Zavarin has personally spoken to the air boys. You should have a constant flight of ground-attack aircraft hitting the west bank almost without a stop. But we can only maintain this level of support for a few hours. You have to press hard."

"You must be at the river's edge by six," continued the General. "The Air Assault Battalion will land on and around the Marienburg at six. 7th Airborne Division will be dropped in two waves. One regiment will complete a heliborne assault west of Pattensen with the second airborne regiment conducting a descent, a parachute assault further west, securing the western end of the gap near the Mittleland Kanal, acting as a blocking force. Stavka have also authorised the release of special weapons, so you will need to ensure your tanks' chemical defences are operational and that your men have full NBC suits available."

"Surely we'll be using non-persistent, sir?"

"Of course, Colonel Trusov, but it may not have all cleared by the time you get across."

"I see, sir. Are there any other actions to keep the British occupied?"

"There will be another push at Gronau," answered Pushkin.

"Has the Air Assault Brigade closed in on the Gronau bridge yet, sir?" asked Colonel Konstantin.

The General frowned. "No, they haven't. It's been twelve hours and they've moved about 500 metres. It seems there were two British armoured units close by, and German reserve units are putting up a stiff resistance at Gronau. The paratroopers have moved west though and should be at Coppenbrugge by early hours tomorrow."

"All in all," added Pushkin, "the British forces are in for a hard time."

The General interrupted before the conversation could continue. "Comrade Colonel, I will leave you to take Comrade Trusov and his comrades through the finer details. I need to speak to the Chief of Rocket Troops."

The group braced and saluted, the General leaving them to reflect on the mission that had just been handed to them.

Trusov instructed Kokorev to position the command tank on the southern outskirts of the small battered village of Rossing, and when he heaved his shoulders through the tank hatch, he could hear the occasional crack of small-arms fire from the centre. The remnants of the divisional motor rifle regiment were clearing up the last bit of resistance before lining their BMP-2s on the western edge where they could launch anti-tank missiles at any enemy tanks they could see across the river.

He called down to his gunner that he was moving to the MTLB-RkhM-K command vehicle that had pulled up behind his T-80. He disconnected the cables from his padded helmet, climbed out of the turret, then down, dropping onto the ground, gripping his AK-74 in his right hand, and ran over to the command vehicle where he was met by Major Chadov.

"They're moving forward now, sir."

They both climbed into the back of the MTLB, and Trusov immediately tuned in to the sounds being emitted from the speaker above his head.

The speaker crackled. *"Six-Two, One-Zero. Salvo on way."*

Trusov nodded to the Major and he replied. "One-Zero, Six-Two. Received."

Trusov nodded again.

"All Six-Two call signs. Artillery on the way."

The units all acknowledged.

Another radio crackled and a Lieutenant passed Chadov a set of earphones. He listened intently before acknowledging the message. "It has been confirmed, sir. Colonel Kharzin and the 48th Guards Tank Regiment have moved into position."

Trusov looked at the map board, secured against the side of the MTLB's slab side. With the two rear doors shut, the space was cramped and the light poor. He pulled out a torch and shone it on the map to get a clearer view,. The leading tank regiment from 12th Guards Tank Division would be dispersed around Sorsum and Escherde, ready to use the main road to speed towards the river crossing, once Trusov and his men had achieved it, that is. Cross over and start to punch through the British lines. Trusov's 62nd Guards Tank Regiment and the independent tank regiment would be thrown at the British lines. A sacrifice to batter the armour and soldiers defending the western bank; their aim to weaken or smash the defenders, using Kharzin's 100 tanks to exploit any gaps and break through. The rest of 12th Guards Tank Division would then cross. The OMG would subsequently do its bit, meeting up with the Soviet airborne forces, racing through the enemy's rear, causing mayhem and destruction, preventing the NATO forces from securing a new defensive line.

Trusov pushed the doors open and stared out over the banks of the River Leine. A pall of smoke steadily expanded along the eastern riverbank between Schulenburg and Marienburg, and BM-21 rocket launchers started to pound the enemy on the opposite bank. A smoke screen was lying along a 500 metre stretch, completely blocking the British view of what was transpiring. Along the section, six Ural-375s positioned themselves about 100 metres apart, hidden from view of the opposite bank. The Ural-375s, were designated TMS-65, as they each mounted a model VK-1F, a modified gas-turbine aircraft engine, mounted on a turntable and swivel. The crew, all wearing their full NBC protective equipment, left their cabs, the engines still running. One operator ran to the trailer that was being towed behind, unhooking it. An SA-9, a BRDM-2 with surface-to-air missiles mounted on top, pulled alongside to protect these vulnerable vehicles. ZSU-23/4s rolled behind them; more air-defence protection. The second crewman pulled the canvas cover off the jet engine, then returned to the cab to turn the vehicle around so the engine nozzle was facing west, towards the river and the opposite bank.

Then the second crewman, after connecting a pipe from the 4,000-litre capacity trailer to the 1,500-litre tank near the cab of the 375, jumped into a cab alongside the turbo-jet outlet. They often used Mig-21 aircraft engines and even sometimes one from a Mig-23. The TMS-65 had been designed as a rapid decontamination vehicle, and two were held with each tank or motor rifle division; spewing out a gas-steam mixture that could be played over armoured vehicles, destroying any toxic agents on the vehicle. These, though, were far more ominous: specially modified, and held in a separate reserve pool for just an occasion like this, the two tanks contained a chemical mixture, the deadly nerve agent Sarin.

At a designated time, the operator powered up the jet engine, turning and raising the nozzle to the required direction and angle. The adaptor on the end of the nozzle, purposely designed so the liquid agent could be forced out as a high-pressure aerosol yet not be affected by the heat, would ensure a steady stream of Sarin nerve-agent gas would be distributed high into the air, the easterly wind ensuring the aerosol would be dispersed along the enemy's line of troops and tanks. At exactly four-thirty in the morning, on 8 July, the six TMS-65s increased the output from the jet engines, and a steady stream of toxic nerve agent flowed up into the prevailing wind and slowly covered the unsuspecting British troops with its deadly poison.

Chapter 30

Dressed in their distinctive camouflaged one-piece coveralls, a blue
and white horizontally striped shirt beneath distinguishing them as an
elite unit, the paratroopers of the 7th Guards Airborne Division were
lined up behind the IIyushin II-76s, designated Candid by NATO.
These four-engined strategic airlifts would take these highly trained
soldiers to their dropping point in West Germany. On arrival overhead
of their target, they would tumble out of the sky and descend on the
British army defenders in force.

The aircraft were in a line, nose to tail, with their rear doors
open ready to receive their passengers for the one-way trip. Behind
each one, a company of paratroopers waited for their orders to board.
A few of the aircraft had Aeroflot markings, commandeered for
use by the military, but piloted by Soviet air force pilots, much to
the relief of the airborne troops. By utilising Aeroflot's fleet of 200
IL-76s, the Soviet air force effectively doubled this size of transport
available to them. On a separate concrete apron, additional Candids
had been loaded with their cargos. This time it wasn't men, but
equipment. A Candid transport aircraft could carry three BMDs,
the paratroopers' mechanised infantry combat vehicle, or three
BRDMs, or three D-30 artillery guns, or even three Gaz-66 utility
vehicles. Even further away, on a third apron, AN-22s were loading
up with more paratroopers, and tucked behind them, the smaller
Cubs. Carrying sixty paratroopers, the Cubs had a special task. They
would be the first to drop their passengers, an advanced element that
would secure the ground ready for the main drop. There were even
a couple of AN-124 Condors, in service with the Soviet air force
for less than three months. They were capable of carrying over 100

223

tons of cargo, but could not be used to carry paratroopers due to pressurisation issues. But, they could carry the military vehicles the paratroopers would need to be an effective force, on the ground, behind enemy lines.

General Zimyatov, Commander of 7th Guards Airborne Division, had been given his mission by the Stavka, the Soviet high command, who were controlling how the battle for the conquest of West Germany would be fought. He had formulated his plan, run it by his senior officers and, after a few tweaks, it had been finalised and approved by the high command. Just as the British army thought they could stop the Soviet army crossing the Leine, his men would change their perspective completely.

0500 8 July 1984. 108th Guards Cossacks Air Assault Regiment,
7th Guards Airborne Division. East of Peine, West Germany.
The Black Effect +1 hour.

On yet another aircraft apron, although really a concrete strip close to an industrialised area, an array of helicopters were being loaded with troops and equipment. The temporary airport, identified years ago by Spetsnaz sleepers, was quickly pulled together for the Soviet airborne regiment's use, one of the many temporary forward bases being utilised for the continued attack on the West.

Colonel Viktor Boykov watched as the last of his men boarded the Mi-6 Hook helicopters. The 108th Guards Cossacks Air Assault, Kuban Regiment, probably had the toughest task of all. His men would be landing the closest to the enemy front line. Theirs was a heliborne assault, their mission to secure two key points: the entrance to the gap between the high ground of the Deinster and Hanover, and an area west of Pattensen where they could move to close the gap and launch strikes against 7th Armoured Brigade's rear. Their sister regiment, the 247th Caucasian Cossacks Air Assault Regiment, commanded by Colonel Vydina, would conduct a descent, a parachute assault further west, securing the western end of the gap, near the Mittleland Kanal.

An Mi-2 Hoplite, a small lightly armed transport helicopter, swooped in, landing close to the control tower. Perhaps a senior officer wanting a last-minute face to face with General Zimyatov, who had chosen to be well forward for the operation about to commence. The General would fly in with the second wave.

Boykov looked again at his own Mi-8 Hip; able to carry twenty-four combat troops or play a close air-support role. Today, though, it would be used as his command helicopter, at least until he was on the ground. Its two stub wings supporting four weapons pylons capable of carrying rocket pods, anti-tank missiles or machine guns, looked bare. The weight of the communications equipment and his immediate HQ staff created too much weight to allow a weapons load to be carried.

An airborne officer of the *Vozdushno Desantyne Voyska (VDV)*, Lieutenant-Colonel Stanislav Yezhov, battalion commander of one of the BMD assault battalions of the 108th Airborne Regiment, came up alongside his regimental commander.

"I don't need to ask if your boys are ready."

"I would describe their mood as impatient, sir."

Boykov smiled. He understood their feelings. They had been geared up, wound up and prepared for a major assault on a number of occasions, only to be stood down at the last minute as the ground forces had failed to get close to making a breach in the British lines. Both attempts at crossing the river at Gronau and Schulenburg had failed. Stavka had considered committing the airborne forces to facilitate a crossing of the River Leine, but relented. The purpose of the airborne divisions was to facilitate the advance of the Operational Manoeuvre Group, enabling the Soviet forces to bite deep into the British rear area; not to help the main ground assault. Should they be committed too early, and the 10th and 7th Guards Tank Divisions fail again, they could find themselves isolated by NATO reserves, and slowly destroyed.

Boykov responded, "Well, Stani, we'll know soon enough whether or not our Motherland's confidence in our skills is warranted."

Chapter 31

0630 8 July 1984. 108th Guards Cossacks Air Assault, Kuban Regiment, 7th Guards Airborne Division. West of Pattensen, West Germany. The Black Effect +2.5 hours.

One of the tasks of the Group of Soviet Forces Germany's 16th Tactical Air Army was to protect an area from south of Gronau to Sarstedt in the north, to a depth of nearly thirty kilometres. For once, surface-to-air missiles suddenly became silent on both sides such was the density of aircraft in the combat zone above them. As a consequence, the fighters and ground-attack aircraft from both sides became so intertwined that, on occasion, an aircraft from either side was shot down by their own missiles. NATO and the Warsaw Pact, recognising that a surface-to-air missile no-go zone had been established, deliberately kept their fighters within a 100 square kilometre area. To support the air assault by the 108th Guards Airborne Regiment, the Soviet air force maintained small formations of fighters over their intended landing zone, a ten-kilometre diameter sector around the town of Pattensen, accomplishing local air superiority. Not without cost. NATO air forces reacted quickly, and a steady trickle of attrition affected both sides as they continued to battle for command of the air above the intended target. NATO air forces were struggling to prioritise their targets, the requests for support now coming in thick and fast.

Other aircraft, such as the Soviet Flogger close-support aircraft blasted the ground with bombs and rockets. Mig-29 Fulcrums dropped cluster bombs, weakening 7th Armoured Brigade's defences ready for the impending attack; their targets: any armour, troops or reinforced positions that were in the path of the air armada that was following close behind. They strafed dug-in troops with cannon fire, and any quarry that resembled a communications vehicle or headquarters complex, and any refuelling activity. They had to clear an area where their comrades were soon to land. These pilots were not so lucky. Deemed as safe targets, in that there was less chance of one of the NATO aircraft being hit due to the low levels the attacking aircraft were at, even the poor performing Blowpipe shoulder-launched SAMs finally had some targets to go for, and in 7th Armoured Brigade's area of responsibility, shot down two Flogger Js. Rapier missiles accounted for three more: two Floggers and a Fulcrum. One flight of Flogger Ds had a particular target in mind: the British ground-to-air defence. Backed up by aircraft with Electronic Counter Measures (ECM), whose role was to disrupt the British ground-based air defence radar, the Flogger aircraft attacked with anti-radiation missiles. The ARMs homed in on the transmissions of both wheeled and tracked Rapier air defence units, destroying the systems radar and missile launcher. The Rapier units soon learnt to turn their radars off when there was the threat of an ARM attack, turning them back on when the threat was gone. A flight of twelve SU-25s, with the NATO designation of Frogfoot, and regarded as the Soviet equivalent of the American A10-Thunderbolt, flew in fast and low, destroying FV432s, Chieftain and Challenger tanks; their orders: to clear a path for the helicopters that would soon be entering the battle area, and to deliver the troops destined to secure the entrance to the gap.

They didn't have it all their own way, though. Four British Phantoms swept in behind them. Of the twelve, only nine made it back to their base. It was a costly attack for the British forces on the ground, but the Soviet air force also paid a heavy price.

Colonel Viktor Boykov looked over the shoulder of the pilot of the Mi-8 Hip-G as they sped low over the West German countryside at a speed of just over 300 kilometres an hour. His view through the large perspex canopy was of blurred fields, trees, houses and roads flashing by as they headed towards the landing zone. Ahead of the air armada was a vast array of helicopters. On the outer perimeter flew eight of the deadly M-24 Hind attack helicopters, targeting anything they deemed to be a threat to the airborne force now transiting through enemy territory. In the lead of the main force were eight Hip-Es, following closely behind a Hip-K, attempting to jam the British forces' communications. A further thirty-two Hips followed behind them, each one carrying twenty-four combat troops. Fifty-four Mi-6 Hook helicopters trailed even further behind, protected by four more of the deadly Hinds, this time Hind-Fs. They carried a full airborne battalion, along with their BMD mechanised infantry combat vehicles.

The 108th Guards Air Assault Regiment had a tough task ahead of them, though. Colonel Boykov's men would be landing very close to the enemy front line, landing west of Pattensen. He had to block the entrance to the gap between the high ground of Deinster and Hanover, take away the enemy's freedom of movement, disrupt their supplies and reinforcements. At exactly the same time, the 247th Air Assault Regiment was already parachuting onto the western end of the gap, closer to the Mittleland Kanal, a barrier NATO would no doubt use as a defensive position. The role of the 7th Airborne Division as a whole was to secure a passage for the 12th Guards Tank Division. As soon as 10GTD broke the British lines, opened up a gap, the 12th GTD would flood through, linking up with Boykov's men, then pushing towards the Mittleland Kanal and heading for the River Weser.

The Hip-Es swooped down towards the landing zone, one plastering the entire area with over 190 55mm unguided rockets. A second one followed its leader in, sanitising the ground even more. A third caught a British platoon in the open, their 432s swerving left and right as they tried to make themselves a difficult target. They didn't stop, using their speed to their advantage, but another batch of rockets engulfed them, blocking them from view and the explosive warheads obliterated their convoy. If there were any survivors, the 12.7mm gun soon finished them off. A fourth Hip was not so lucky. Out of four Blowpipe missiles launched from different directions, one hit home, striking the Hip's wing pylon, still containing a full weapons' load. The helicopter flipped over and plummeted downwards, hitting the ground where a second explosion completely destroyed the aircraft, killing all those on board. The fifth and sixth were given targets further out, looking for British outposts, forces diverted to counter the airborne assault. The rapidly depleted Rapier force took out one but was destroyed itself as a Hind-D swooped in, bracketing the area with rockets, destroying the launcher and killing the crew.

The first of the Hip troop transports started to land, disgorging the airborne soldiers. Landing in angled lines of four, they touched down hard, the troops jumping out of the door immediately behind the cockpit, running at a crouch to get away from the helicopter before throwing themselves down, seeking out cover and any potential threat. Some of the Hips didn't even touch the ground, but moved slowly at the hover while soldiers dropped to the ground. As soon as their passengers were dropped off, the Hips were in the air, flying east to refuel and pick up a second wave of airborne soldiers.

As soon as they had cleared the ground and headed on a wide curve to clear the airspace, the big boys started to land. So far the landing operation had taken a little over five minutes, the British forces completely stunned by the continuing suppression attacks from the escorting helicopters. Two Chieftains moved into position to bring direct fire to bear on the landing area, anticipating the destruction of some of the helicopters and their troops through the use of High Explosive Squash Head (HESH) rounds.

The Hind-F, the latest attack helicopter in the Soviet's armoury, hovered nearly 2,000 metres away. An AT-Spiral anti-tank missile flared at the helicopter's wing tip launcher rails. The ten-kilogram high-explosive anti-tank warhead was guided to its target by its laser seeker, the weapons operator having illuminated the target with a laser designator. The first hit was unsuccessful, the Chobham armour protecting the crew, but a missile launched from a second Hind destroyed it. His companion triggered the smoke dischargers either side of the turret and, under a cloud of smoke, quickly reversed back into cover.

The fifty-four Hooks came in to land in waves, clouds of dust and debris blocking them from view as their powerful engines and rotor blades whipped the ground with enormous force. The flight required a sector of half a square kilometre as a landing area. With their two rear doors swung open, troops and vehicles were quickly offloaded. BMDs, BRDM-2 Sagger's and two BRDM-2 SA-9s added to the force that was steadily building up. Within a matter of minutes, the second flight of Hooks were landing as the first flock of helicopters vacated, lifting off to return across the River Leine to pick up its second load.

Boykov's Hip landed in amongst the Hooks, and he was soon gathering data on the disposition of his forces. He had a clear plan. One battalion of over 400 men and their thirty BMDs would secure the perimeter, providing protection for further flights that would be coming in. His four BRDM-2 scout vehicles would go west, seeking out the enemy so he could call in targets for his artillery when it arrived. His thirty D-30 122mm artillery guns would come in on the second wave. He had two priorities: disperse his men before the British started to bring down artillery fire, and ensure that small packets of soldiers, with the Strela-3 shoulder-launched SAM, designated SA-14 Gremlin by NATO, were spread throughout the area in readiness for the attack from the air that was bound to appear. His second battalion would strike east, hitting the British forces defending the River Leine from behind, and the third battalion would push west, blocking reinforcements and supplies getting to the NATO forces and opening a gap for 12GTD to pass through.

The local British Combat Team Commander, desperate to do something to interfere with the air assault, ordered four of his available Scimitars forward in an attempt to disrupt the Soviet airborne operation. At first, their 30mm RARDEN cannon had a massive impact. Moving in fast and close, they picked off helicopters, armour and airborne soldiers with ease, destroying four Hooks and one Hip that had malfunctioned and was still on the ground. Their victory was short-lived however as the Hind-Fs pounced, their 30mm cannons puncturing the reconnaissance vehicle's armour, destroying two, before the remaining pair, popping smoke, fled the battlefield. All the time, the Combat Team Commander was bringing in more of his forces to try and box in the airborne force. Initially, just from the north and the west. As his was a mechanised combat team, with only one troop of tanks, now with only two Chieftains in support, he was finding it difficult to pin the enemy down, without actually having his own men ending up trapped and pinned down themselves. The Soviets were already deploying the ten ASU-85 assault guns that had been landed.

Boykov chattered on the radio as his BMD-KSh command vehicle bounced over the open farmland, the entire area a patchwork of cultivated fields. He needed to get his men organised. He probably had nearly 700 men on the ground already, but knew that, within thirty-minutes, he would loose his helicopter support. Hips were already flying back east, their weapons' loads depleted and fuel running low. The Hind attack helicopters would not be far behind. The next wave, at least an hour away, would bring his artillery, the rest of his ASU-85 assault gun battalion, another BMD battalion, more BRDM-Saggers, and more SA-9s and additional supporting weapons, such as RPG-7s and the deadly AGS-17 grenade launchers.

Even with the BMD closed up, he heard the noise of the explosions as the British local force commander brought artillery fire down onto this rapidly expanding force. Although most of the Hooks had left, two of the slower ones were still on the ground. Although not destroyed, they were sufficiently damaged that they were unable to take off.

He would just have to take whatever the British threw at him, expand his perimeter, and complete his mission.

Chapter 32

There were three battles in progress; artillery, air and the ground battle.
An artillery duel between the British and Soviet artillery, with both
sides committing heavily to counter-battery fire. The consequence to
the British Gunners, and the Soviet artillery, was the need to constantly
move once they had fired, before they too became the target of the
British and Soviet long-range guns. Even so, there were still enough
Soviet weapons to pound the British forces between Schulenburg
and Marienburg, and surface-to-surface missiles took their toll on the
defenders. But the 10th GTD was not getting it all its own way. The
British Gunners still found the time and resources to hit back at the
Soviet tank formations advancing on the River Leine.

Outside of the artillery barrage area, and outside of the dense air-
combat zone, missile smoke trails, from both sides, flew upwards at
speed seeking out each other's aircraft, as fighters and attack-aircraft
flew into and out of the combat area. The number being launched
by the Soviet forces was significantly higher, with SA-9s, SA-8s, SA-
13s, SA-6s and SA-4s all joining in to provide a protective cap for the
forces in the process of crossing the River Leine. Sometimes aircraft
were shot down by their own side's missiles, such was the density of
the aircraft in the air and the number of missiles being launched. The
Soviet air force was flying too high and too fast for the ineffectual
British Blowpipe, and Rapier had so many targets that it couldn't
maintain a high enough rate of fire to do significant damage to the
attacking aircraft.

Much higher up, Soviet and British, American and German
fighters locked horns, both trying to get mastery of the skies, the
sound of the aircraft's afterburners often heard above the sound of

the explosions below, such was the volume of aircraft being sucked into the battle along a fourteen-kilometre stretch of the River Leine. Losses were high on both sides, but at the moment it was stalemate. Good for the invading Soviet Army; bad for the defending NATO forces.

Dissatisfied with remaining in the back of an MTLB and trying to run the battle far back from where the action was, Trusov had returned to his trusted T-80K. Major Chadov and the other officers of his command group following close behind in two MTLBs and some box-bodied Zil-131s. Tucked in behind the forested high ground that was topped by Callenburg Castle, now occupied by a reconnaissance platoon of the division's reconnaissance battalion, Trusov kept a tight control over his forces.

Major Chadov was sitting on the edge of the turret, communication lines linked to the MTLB alongside.

"Six-Two-Six, this is Six-Two-Zero. Commence. Over." He waited for the acknowledgement.

"Wave one, two and three are crossing now, sir."

Trusov nodded. *Well, the engineers are on their way. It's started now,* he thought.

Under heavy cover of smoke and an almost constant bombardment to keep the British Brigade's soldiers' heads down, he had given the go-ahead for the first three waves. Although the depth of the river was acceptable, the flow speed wasn't perfect at just under four metres per second. But they would have to deal with it. He had split his 500 metre section of the River Leine into three. From Sector one in the north and Sector three in the south, he was sending over PTSs, tracked amphibious vehicles, capable of carrying a BMP along with motor rifle troops. In addition, K-61s would carry troops across. Hip helicopters had already landed a small force, accompanied by engineers to check for minefields. Hind-Ds, like demons from hell, ranged up and down the river, firing at anything that moved. Bullets ricocheted off their protective titanium shells, making them feel invulnerable. Their confidence was dented slightly when a lucky shot from a Blowpipe missile took off the tail of one of the hovering demons. The aircraft pilots were a little more cautious, but still made it difficult for the British tanks and Milan FPs to respond.

Sixteen Hinds were supporting the crossing. British forces, reeling from a forty-minute bombardment and coming to terms with the numerous military casualties as a consequence of the chemical strike from the TMS-65s, reinforced by the use of chemical artillery shells, had spotted them through the smokescreen that was slowly diminishing. They soon had the engineers pinned down, but with the arrival of the PTSs carrying BMP-2s, and the constant fire from attack-helicopters they were the ones ending up being pinned down. A British tank troop sent to reinforce, was ambushed by the Air Assault Battalion that was now on their flank, and slowly moving behind the NATO forces to link up with the bridgehead. To make matters worse, the first wave of the 108th Guards Air Assault Regiment had also landed, diverting British troops from the defence of the river and threatening to cut them off. The opposite bank was lined with fifty tanks from the independent tank regiment, T-12 anti-tank guns, and troops with AGS-17s. The minute the British troops raised their heads and were seen through the smokescreen, the tanks were able to bring direct fire against them. The barrels of the tanks became hot as they poured round after round into the opposite bank, being careful to aim high so as not to hit their own men.

In Sector two, the middle point, the river crossing consisted of GSPs, two tracked amphibious units amalgamated as one, to form a ferry capable of carrying a main battle tank. Two mine-clearing tanks, mounted with KMT-5 mine-clearing devices, along with four of Trusov's T-80s, were on their way across.

Trusov knew he was taking a chance sending across heavy armour so soon, but felt it was best to hit hard and quickly. The clock was ticking and he was becoming impatient just sitting there, knowing that the General would be watching his actions closely. Trusov knew the smokescreen would disappear very soon, blowing back across the British units and exposing his own men. Then NATO air and artillery strikes would come again.

"Second wave is moving, sir," Chadov informed him.

Thank God, he thought. More troops to cross, including BRDM-2 Sagger missile carriers and BMPs. Another area of Sector two would also start rolling. Tanks would be wading across, using the BROD-M snorkeling system, allowing them to ford depths of up to twelve metres. BMP-2s, although they had an amphibious capability, would have to cross on the GSPs. The water speed was too fast and there wasn't the time to bring in engineer support.

The Major handed the headset and mike to his Commander.

"Six-Two-Zero, Six-Two-Zero. Artillery fire in sectors one and

two. *One K-61 and one PTS destroyed. One BMP destroyed on the bank and one T-80 hit and stranded. Over.*"

"Identify yourself!"

"*Sorry, sir. Six-Two-One.*" Lieutenant-Colonel Antakov, the Commander of the 1st Battalion, 62nd Guards Tank Regiment, sounded flustered.

"Has the smoke cleared? Can you see a bridgehead?"

"*Smoke has cleared. Small bridgehead, maybe 300 metres, out to 200.*"

"Get your men ready. Six-Two-Zero. Out."

"We're across then, sir?" asked the Major.

"We are for the moment. Get back to your coffin, Major. We're going forward. I want those Hinds covering, understood?"

"Yes, sir." The Major swallowed, then dropped down to join the crew of the MTLB and follow his lunatic commander closer to where the fighting was.

"Kokorev, take us to the river. We're heading for Sector one. Barsukov, you direct him." Both acknowledged and the T-80K made its way down to the water's edge, half a kilometre away.

"Six-Two-Two, Six-Two-Four, this is Six-Two-Zero. Situation report. Over."

"*Six-Two...Zero...Six-Two-Four...I have a full company across... heavy...casualties...five BMPs, two PTS and three K-61s destroyed. Two...BRDM-Saggers operational...holding. Over.*" The sound of gunfire and explosions were audible in the background.

"Hold your ground, Pyotr. Tanks are on their way to you."

"*We're not...going anywhere...sir.*"

"*Six-Two-Zero, Six-Two-Two. One mine-clearing tank destroyed, two T-80s, one lost in the river. Sector two and Sector three secure. Four T-80s just landed, will link up with Six-Two-Four. Over.*"

"Excellent, Kirill. I shall be coming to you. Just hang in there."

"Sir," called Barsukov. "We're approaching Sector one. It's under fire."

"Keep going."

"Six-Two-Six, Six-Two-Zero. Pontoon ferries ready? Over."

"*Three. Over.*"

"Are they in the water?"

"*All three are ready.*"

The T-80K came to a halt and Trusov pushed the hatch open above his head as he heard a metallic rap on the top, and was met by Major Chadov.

"Division have been on, sir, screaming for an update. I told them we were across and that you would update them soon. They... ah...weren't too pleased that you were so far forward, sir."

"Never mind that. I want the NBC recce platoon across next. This sector. There should be enough PTSs left. I need to know how much contamination is left. It must be murder for them fighting in NBC kit. You stay here. I'm crossing at Sector two."

"But, sir—"

"Just do it. Make sure the BRDM-2 RKhs get across. Start moving elements of the anti-tank battalion across as well, in case they counter-attack. That will release our tanks to move forward. We need to expand the bridgehead. Oh, and get some SA-9s across. Let's beef up their air defence."

"Sir."

With that, Trusov pulled the hatch back down as a bullet whined as it spun off the top of the turret. A second ping could be heard hitting elsewhere.

"Left stick. Along the river. Sector two. And quickly."

Kokorev spun the tank on its tracks and they were soon speeding south, Sector two only 200 metres away. Barsukov turned the turret so that the main gun was pointing west, across the river, just in case a juicy target came into his sights.

"Stop, stop." Trusov was up and out in a matter of moments, running across to where he could see the command tank of Lieutenant-Colonel Oleg Danshov, Commander of the 3rd Tank Battalion. The thump of tank rounds being fired across the water could be heard all along the entire east bank of the river as the independent tank regiment gave the crossing fire support. Once Trusov was satisfied the other bank was secure, he would unleash them on the British forces. At whatever cost, he would make sure that these additional tanks would make progress west. There was also the sharper crack as the T-12s fired blindly across the water, firing sometimes too close to their own men. But the risk was worth it.

Oleg was beside his tank, doling out orders to the unit commanders around him.

"Sir, am I glad to see you." The response was genuine. Trusov, in his eyes, was now very much the Commander of the 62nd Guards Tank Regiment.

"The pontoons are on their way, sir. That will give us nearly a company across in one swoop."

"The GSP?"

"We've lost three here, but still have three operating."

"Well done, Oleg. You should have your entire battalion across by ten."

Before the Commander of the 3rd Battalion could respond, their voices were drowned out by the rush of air and clatter of rotor blades as two Hind-D attack helicopters positioned themselves either side of the two command tanks. Six other Hinds hovered over the river itself, picking off any targets of opportunity that presented themselves.

"Guardian angels, ay, sir?"

"Angels of death, more like," responded Trusov. "But welcome all the same."

"Down, sir!" screamed Oleg has he threw himself at his Commander, dragging him to the ground between the two tanks.

Barsukov whipped the 12.7mm turret-mounted machine gun round, spinning it to follow the low-flying Harriers as they came down the line of the river from the north. Two of them swooped low, rockets firing at the tracked ferry vehicles crossing the river, laden down with BRDM-Saggers, SA-9s and T-12s. One GSP was hit immediately, sinking, taking its cargo down with it. The crew, still in their vehicle, were mainly drowned, only one lucky soldier escaped.

The first of the Harriers was torn apart as two ZSU-23/4s fired round after round into the aeroplane, its fuselage literally disintegrating as the 23mm shells tore into it. The wingman escaped, pulling up out of the devastating fire, ready to come around for a second time to use the two 30mm cannons. A second pair of Harriers targeted the armour on the riverbank, destroying a T-80 and a BMP as they passed. They also didn't escape scot-free, as two SA-9s launched their missiles at the same time as an SA-13. The rearmost aircraft had its tail blown off, and the Harrier plummeted to the ground, the pilot ejecting safely. After another two passes, strafing the Soviet forces with their cannons, the remaining two Jump-Jets left the area, amazed that they had survived, their thoughts already switching to the two men they had just lost.

Trusov got back up. "God we've been lucky so far."

"They can't hurt us now, sir."

The officer would have bitten his tongue off had he known what was coming next. Northern Army Group (NORTHAG), desperate to hold back the mass of Soviet tanks that were pushing their armies back all along the line, had chosen to use all the forces at their disposal. Sixteen Hawk aircraft, in four flights of four, each aircraft carrying three 200 kilogram bombs, swooped down on the Soviet bridgehead and the tanks preparing to cross. Of the company of nine tanks that had just landed on the west bank, three were destroyed. Two T–80s snorkeling across were also hit, as were four of the tanks belonging to the independent tank regiment. They then returned and strafed the ground with their 30mm Aden cannons, destroying more equipment and men, tearing apart one of the PMP pontoon ferries as it crossed the river with three tanks on board. The ferries were punctured in many places and the tanks ended up, along with their crews, on the river bed.

Out of the sixteen brave pilots, seven were shot down. Of those pilots, only four managed to eject in time, the rest hitting the ground with their crippled aircraft.

"Oh God," groaned Oleg. "We're finished."

"Get a grip, Danshov," snapped Trusov. "This is good news."

"Good news?" asked the stunned officer.

"They have just thrown the last of their air force at us. If they have had to use their converted training aircraft, it means they have done it out of desperation. Keep those pontoons working. We must have nearly a company of tanks across by now."

He climbed the tank and met with Barsukov reloading the red-hot machine gun.

"Well done, Barsukov, you will be rewarded for that."

"I don't think I hit anything, sir."

"But you tried." Trusov grabbed the radio transmitter. "Two-Two-Zero-Alpha, Two-Two-Zero. Over."

"Are you OK, sir? That last attack was right over the top of you," blurted Major Chadov.

"Yes, yes. Now listen, damn you. Get both the PMP units up here now. One to go to Sector one, the other to Sector three. They need to hurry. We have a breathing space, but it's short."

"Understood, sir. Over."

"Also, I want the rest of my regiment across now. All of them. All GSPs and PMP pontoons are to be allocated to my tanks. Got that?"

"Yes, sir."

"Right, see to it. Out."

"One-Zero, this is Six-Two-Zero. Over."

"Go ahead, Pavel, we've been waiting for your call. What's the situation? Over."

Pushkin. He recognised the voice of his old commander, now the Chief of Staff. "We have secured a bridgehead. Am sending the last of my tanks over now. The PMPs are being brought forward. Once my tanks are across, I will send the independent regiment either by ferry or the bridge if complete. Now is the time to commit. Over."

"How deep is the bridgehead?"

"I don't know."

"You don't know? We can't commit without a secure bridgehead."

"Now is the time, sir. It's now or never."

There was a delay before he got a response.

"Colonel Trusov, you think we should commit all now?"

"Yes, sir. They have thrown the last of their air force at us. It will be at least an hour before they can turn around and hit us again. The troops on the ground are still reeling. With my regiment across, the independent tank regiment following and two bridges laid, our committed unit will succeed. Over."

Trusov took a deep breath. Once the PMP battalion arrived, he knew that he could get a PMP-bridge, capable of carrying tanks across, up and ready in less than an hour. If he and the other tank regiment could continue to push the enemy back, 12th Guards Tank Division, the OMG, fresh, fully fuelled and armed, with masses of support behind them, could break through.

"Pavel."

"Yes, sir."

"They have been released. Make sure you have a route across. Do you understand?"

"Yes, sir."

"Out."

Trusov put the handset down. He'd done it now. If he didn't hold the bridgehead, or the bridges weren't laid, he would end up with the elements of a division stranded on the east bank, and elements of a division on the western bank with nowhere to go. Easy pickings for the next airstrike.

Chapter 33

1200 8 July 1984. Combat Team Bravo (+). Gronau, West Germany. The Black Effect +8 hours.

"Two-Two-Alpha, this is Bravo-Zero. Over."

"Two-Two-Alpha, go ahead. Over."

"They have broken through to your north. Elements pushing south to cut you off. Pull back now, I repeat, pull back now! Acknowledge! Over."

"Roger that. All call signs, I repeat, all call signs?"

"Yes, all Two-Two call signs. Make it fast, Alex. They want to blow the bridge, and it's only your forces preventing them. Make it a quick dash. Out."

"Corporal Patterson, we're getting out of here. Tell Mackinson that, when we move, it's quick and there is no stopping. Nothing gets in our way. Got that?"

"Yes, sir."

"All Two-Two call signs, this is Two-Two-Alpha. Withdraw immediately, I repeat, withdraw immediately. Acknowledge. Over."

Each call sign responded in turn; the sound of battle could be heard in the background.

"Roger, all Two-Two call signs. Make it fast. No stopping. Two-Two-Alpha signing off. Out."

"Target," yelled Patsy. "Tango-Eight-Zero, 2,000 metres. Sabot."

"Up," confirmed Ellis once he had loaded the sabot round.

"On. Fire."

The breech shot back.

"It's a hit," confirmed Alex as he tapped the switch for the smoke grenades. The remaining launcher rearmed. Smoke trails shot out from the Chieftain tank and, out to the front, it was immediately blocked off from view by a growing cloud of smoke.

"Back, back, back. Mackinson, get us out of here."

"One-One-Alpha, this is Zero-Alpha. Over."

"One-One-Alpha, go ahead. Over."

"How are you holding up? Over."

Russell watched as the 432 he had sent to pick up the Bundeswehr soldiers sped behind his position, the Kanonenjagdpanzer following close behind.

"About to move to our secondary positions. Over."

"Roger that. You have to hold your location. I repeat, you have to hold your location. Acknowledge. Over."

"What's happening? Over." A slight nervousness in his voice.

"The line is moving back. Friendlies will be passing through your location. Over."

"Understood. Over."

"You have to hold, Dean. If you don't, friendlies will be trapped. Do you understand?"

"We'll hold, sir."

"Good lad. Zero-Alpha. Out."

"You get the gist of that, Colour?"

"I did, sir. I'll round up the boys then and we can get set up again. At least we've still got the box-heads with us. Sir?"

"Sorry, Colour. Yes, they will be needed. Let's go."

Chapter 34

1230 8 July 1984. 62 Guards Tank Regiment. South of Schulenburg, West Germany.
The Black Effect +8.5 hours.

Major Chadov pressed the wad of bandages against Colonel Trusov's upper arm, the sleeve of his tank coverall wet with blood. Trusov constantly pushed him away as he sat in the back of the MTLB, his damaged T-80K parked alongside, his two crewmen surveying the damage. They were lucky to have got out alive, a strike by a Milan missile hitting the glacis low, below the protective array of ERA blocks, but low enough that the chamfer at the front end took the force of the explosion, reducing the missile's effectiveness. Trusov, who had been standing up in the turret, directing soldiers around the PMP bridge, had been hit by a hot piece of metal that had cut a deep gouge in his upper arm. Kokorev and Barsukov, although badly shaken and partly deaf, had survived.

"The first of Colonel Kharzin's tanks are crossing now, sir." Informed Chadov.

Trusov looked back along the length of the accordion-like pontoons, now supporting Colonel Kharzin's 48th Guards Tank Regiment as they crossed to prepare for the next assault on the battered British forces. Tank after tank clattered off the ramp at the end, a cloud of smoke as they accelerated up the gentle slope, powering forwards to do battle with the slowly withdrawing British force. Two pontoon bridges, 500 metres apart, had been quickly laid, the engineers building them at the rate of seven metres per minute; an ingenious system where the truck carrying the pontoons braked at the water's edge, causing the large pontoons to slide into the water. The pontoons opened automatically and, once turned around ninety degrees by the powerboats in the water, were quickly connected, section by section, forming a continuous strip of floating roadway.

While the remainder of Trusov's regiment and the surviving tanks of the independent tank regiment continued an almost suicidal battle to push the enemy further and further back, the tanks of 12GTD were crossing the pontoon bridge at twenty-five kilometres an hour. The second bridge had been destroyed, but there were so many surface-to-air missile defence systems in place now, further attacks on this bridge had failed and proven costly to British, US and West German pilots. A second pontoon bridging company was already en route.

Chapter 35

1300 8 July 1984. 1 British Corps Alternate Headquarters, deep in a bunker-complex, west of Monchengladbach. The Black Effect +9 hours.

Although well lit, the room in the concrete bunker felt cold and dark. Even when occupied, a musty smell seemed to hang in the air. A small group sat around a large metal table covered with a layer of hessian and topped with a map of the 1 BR Corps area of operations. The plastic-coated map had various tokens on it, representing the numerous British units now deployed to stem the Warsaw Pact forces pushing west. In attendance were Lieutenant-Colonel Stevens, SO1 G2 Intelligence, Major Colin Archer, the SO2 G2 Intelligence, Major Bill Castle, SO2 G3 Operations, Major-General Clifford Renshaw, Deputy Commander of 1 British Corps, and the Commander of 1 BR Corps himself, Lieutenant-General Sir Edmund Cutler. The General also had his aide, Captain Mallen, with him.

"They've gone and done it, sir, a full-scale chemical strike right across NORTHAG's and CENTAG's FLOT. Not only has it disrupted the forward line of our own troops, killing many, but thousands of German civilians have been caught up in the strikes. The German politicians are furious."

"We knew it was coming, Clifford," responded General Cutler, his well tanned face at odds with the cold, whitewashed walls. "The Soviets have always trained as if they intended to use chemical weapons in a conventional war, so we shouldn't be surprised that they've done just that. It's just part of their normal conventional arsenal." He turned to Bill Castle. "Major Castle, what are the casualty rates looking like for the Corps?"

"Better than we had expected, sir." He checked the figures in front of him. "We've had about 400 killed as a direct consequence of the chemical strikes. That's including our rear areas and airfields. The

243

airfields and weapons stores have been hit by a powerful, persistent nerve agent. It's going to take some time to decontaminate those areas."

"And the Corps area?"

"At least 120 killed so far, sir. And we estimate over 200 wounded. The field hospitals are coping, but with the Soviet's latest big push still in progress, they now have an influx of standard battle injuries. On top of that, there are hundreds of German civilian casualties and they are swamping the local hospitals and looking to our Field hospitals for aid."

The General was quiet for a moment before turning to his SO1 G2. "What's the latest on the Soviet advance?"

Colonel Stevens pointed to the River Leine. "They've crossed here, sir, south of Schulenburg. Our forces have pulled back, but they have an airborne regiment right behind them."

"Just the one?"

"Yes, sir. Immediately behind, that is. A second regiment has also been dropped north-east of Bad-Nenndorf. But the forces across the river are also swinging south, moving forces further south. They clearly intend to threaten Gronau from the north. The Soviet Air Assault Brigade west of Gronau has increased its tempo and is now aggressively attacking Gronau from the south. They are also pushing a battalion here, towards Coppenbrugge."

"What do we have around Coppenbrugge?"

"Just a beefed up platoon and some German reservists in Marienau."

"Christ, how have we let that happen?"

"We were lucky to have them, sir. They are part of the Royal Green Jacket's Battlegroup. 1st Division decided to keep an element of 4 Div in the local area as a reserve."

"Just as well they did. How are they doing?"

"They've repulsed the first attack and are now pulling back into the centre of Coppenbrugge. The Soviets' intention is to cut Gronau, and our forces there, off."

"What have we got in that area?" the General asked his deputy.

"22nd Brigade is responsible for Gronau, but the 14/20th are under a lot of pressure. We need to get their forces back across the river and pull everything back to Coppenbrugge."

"What do you make of the enemy's intentions in general, Colonel Stevens?"

"I think they're after these three gaps, sir: here, between the high ground of Deinster and Hanover, the route through Coppenbrugge, where they can push for Bad-Munder, and then Bisperode south-east of Hameln."

"That would take them across the Weser and head for Osnabruck?"

"Yes, sir. They have the option of going north or south of Osnabruck."

"Or both."

"Yes sir."

"Won't 3rd Shock Army have run out of steam by then?"

"Undoubtedly, sir, but with 20th Guards Army in the fight, the Soviets will probably go for where we are at our weakest. They would be less than 100 kilometres from the Dutch border. I'm not sure of their intentions to the south, but in the north they've made it pretty obvious. An airborne regiment has parachuted close to the Mittleland Kanal, and a second landed by helicopters west of Pattensen here. A bridgehead has been secured on the Leine, and an armoured division is crossing it now. Through one of our Corps Patrol Units, we've identified it as the 12th Guards Tank Division, of 3 Shock Army. This has to be an Operational Manoeuvre Group, sir. We believe it has been training for this very role for some years now. Its objective, once across the Leine, is to link up with the regiment at Pattensen, push through to the Mittleland Kanal, linking up with the second airborne regiment, and then crossing over the Weser and getting deep into our lines, sir. Once across, they will go wherever we are at our weakest. They won't be looking for a fight. That OMG will want to get as far west as possible. Then, of course, we will have their second echelon coming at us. We know 20th Guards Army is on the way and their Military Districts, their 2nd Strategic Echelon, are bound to be moving their forces west."

"And the other two gaps?"

"I'm not so sure about those two, sir. Once they're across at Gronau, they are likely to push a division up through Coppenbrugge and then to Bad-Munder. As for Hameln, we're not sure at the moment. But we need to know what the 20th Guards are up to."

"The CPU can help us with that. Clifford, what do we have covering this gap by Coppenbrugge?"

"Just that reinforced platoon from 4th Armoured Division. We have the remnants of the Battlegroup in the area still."

"Two Div?"

"The 15th Infantry Brigade, with five battalions, is in position, along with the Queen's Own Yeomanry recce. Three battalions of the 49th Infantry Brigade are digging in along the Weser. 49th Field Regiment with their FH-70 guns are in position."

"The rest of the 49th?"

"The last two battalions are en route."

"Four Div?"

"Apart from the Battlegroup left to act as a reserve, they are currently resting around the area of Petershagen."

"What about the Territorial battalions?"

"Three have been brought across, sir. Two have been hit quite hard on the way by Soviet interdiction and a Spetsnaz ambush. They have no armour, just soft-skinned trucks."

The General remained quiet for a moment, clearly running through his options. He would have liked to have his divisional commanders here from the 1st and 3rd Armoured Divisions, but to take them away from their units at this moment in time would be madness.

The 1 BR Corps Commander turned towards his aide. "Make a note. I want a stop line along the Mittleland Kanal. Raven. That will run south towards Hameln. I need to go through the plans with the Brigade commanders before I finalise the stop-line further south. The second one, Magpie, will be the Weser. The 24th Airmobile Brigade will deploy, with the 1st Battalion Duke of Wellington's Regiment and the 1st Battalion King's Own Royal Border Regiment, south-east of the E-36, from here at Wunstorf to Bad-Nennendorf. I'm going to assign the parachute battalion to the brigade, but we'll hold them in reserve. I'll talk through the final dispositions with the Brigade Commander when he gets here. I want a blocking position in that area. We can liaise with 1 German Corps and get them to plug the gap north-west of Hanover. You say they'll take the weakest route, possibly using 20th Guards. Well, let's give them a fight in the north of our sector; encourage them to deploy 20th Guards further south. 3rd Division are still pretty intact, so if we can push the Soviets to go up against them, we may hold them up at least. Pull 1st Division back. We need to set up a Stop-Line though, to slow the Soviets down and give the division a chance to regroup. Blackbird will run from…" He tapped the various points on the large map. "Hameln, Bisperode,

Coppenbrugge, Eldagsen, Springe, Volksen, Bredenbeck, Gehdren and Seelze."

"Units sir?" Asked the deputy commander.

"I'll work out their positions once I get an update on the situation down there. Clifford, I want you to take a heli ride to the front. I need to know the true situation down there. I need to take action before it all falls apart. I want a Brigade from Four Div on alert for moving to plug any gaps. I want 15th and the 49th to be left alone to dig in."

"I'll leave as soon as we've finished here. What about the Kanal? Who are we going to put there?"

"Those three infantry battalions. Move them there immediately."

"But, sir. They probably haven't recovered from their recent attacks, nor had time to orientate themselves."

"Clifford, none of us have time. We need good defences along the Weser. I need to leave those brigades to get on with their preparations. Find me a good Colonel from Four Div, make him acting Brigadier and put him in command of those troops, but get them on the Kanal"

"Understood, sir."

The General turned to Major Castle. "How far away is the American Division?"

"Probably two days, sir. Advance elements could be here in twenty-four hours, if pushed."

"Right, I'll get NORTHAG to release them to us. We have to put in a counter-attack as soon as possible."

"Counter-attack, sir?" responded General Renshaw.

"The Soviets will be stretched, and we need to hit them before their 2nd Strategic Echelon gets to the front." He turned to his aide again. "Start the preparation for a warning order for Four Div. They will be in action again sooner than they think. Oh, and one more thing: release one Helarm to 1st Division, but keep the second one back for the 24th Airmobile Brigade. They may well need it."

"How will we retaliate, sir?" Major Archer asked the General. "To the chemical strike, I mean."

"A good question, Major. The answer to that is being discussed by the powers-that-be as we speak. Right, Clifford, you have a Lynx to catch."

Chapter 36

How do you protect your family from a nuclear attack?

BUILD A FALLOUT ROOM — *You need to protect your family against the heat and blast of a nuclear explosion. Choose the right place. It could be on the ground floor, but a cellar or basement would be better. Keep as far away as possible from an outside wall or the roof.*

HOW TO STRENGTHEN YOUR FALLOUT ROOM — *Strengthen the weak points, such as doors and windows. One way is to fill bags with sand or earth and stack them outside your windows. If those materials are unavailable to you then push a large bookcase or a wardrobe up against the space you are trying to block off. If you have enough time, you could board up your windows on either side, filling in the gap with earth or sand, or, even better still, brick the windows up completely.*

THE CORE — *Inside this fallout shelter build a 'core' to protect your family further. It could be a lean-to up against one of the walls, protected with sandbags. Or you could use a cupboard beneath the stairs, making sure you have a layer of sandbags on the stairs and the surrounding area of the cupboard.*

Protect your Family - Handbook 2

1400 8 July 1984. Chanticleer, United Kingdom Government Emergency War Headquarters, Corsham.
The Black Effect +10 hours.

The Prime Minister took her twice-daily walk through the main areas of the complex where she had spent a good part of her days and nights since the launch of the Warsaw Pact invasion of the Federal Republic of Germany. Her circuit of the underground bunker, followed at a distance by one of her close protection team, always started from Area 14, the Prime Minister's office. It was also the home of the Cabinet Office, Chiefs of Staff and the War Cabinet. No one ever thought the day would come when the Government Emergency War Headquarters

(GEWHQ), situated in between the village of Corsham and Lower Rudloe, would ever be used in earnest.

The Prime Minister walked down the corridor, Area 21 on her left, the home of the Government Communications Centre and, on her right, the British Broadcasting Centre studio, along with the Home Office and local government departments. The BBC studio was far from what the news presenters were used to back at Broadcasting House, now having a space no bigger than three-by-three metres. She turned right and was now walking underneath West Road, which was thirty metres above her head. She could hear the footsteps of her CP officer resonating on the solid floor of the large concrete, and sometimes brick-lined, corridor of the bunker. The sounds were not so hollow now as they competed with other sounds of activity as Britain's Cold War underground headquarters had now come to life to meet the threat on the other side of the English Channel. The dank, mildew smell that had previously tainted the air had also changed. The odour now consisted of a mix of sweaty bodies, ablutions and machinery, mixed in with freshly baked bread and the smells of stale cooking. Although Harriet Willis still scrunched up her nose slightly on occasion, she, like the rest of the 4,000 occupants, was getting used to the environment and its nuances. She turned right onto Main Road, now with Area 15 on her right and Area 8 on her left, looking up as one of the fluorescent tubes above her head flickered. If she missed anything, apart from seeing her children naturally, although adults now, it was natural daylight. She didn't think she would ever get used to this unnatural glow. Large conduits lined the ceiling, taking cables and pipes to various parts of the complex. New cables had been laid outside of the casing, quickly put into place to ensure that the site was fully operational.

She moved over to the left as one of the yellow battery-powered vehicles, carrying four people, whirred past. A red one came from the opposite direction, a driver taking supplies, piled on the platform at the rear, to another part of the bunker. She popped her head through a door, the buzz and clatter as the operators on the two General Post Office switchboards connected and reconnected numerous cable plugs, putting various departments in contact with the outside world. The two switchboards, set on a black and white tiled floor, backed by the clinically white walls, were fully manned. One was a huge forty-position oak unit, while the other had fourteen positions dealing primarily with international communications. In the background, a bank of teleprinters rattled noisily. One of the exchange supervisors started to get up, acknowledging the Prime Minister's presence, but Harriet Willis waved her down and carried on with her tour. Her journey took her past the central stores, Ministry of Transport, Ministries of Power and Agriculture, and, finally, the kitchen and dining rooms before arriving back at Area 14.

Willis made her way into the conference room where a reduced War Cabinet was to meet. The demands of the war were pulling her ministers far and wide. Four men stood up as she entered. One was Lawrence Holmes, the Secretary of State for Defence, his shock of greying hair swept back at the top and sides looking lank. Finding the time to groom oneself was not easy. He attempted a smile, but the deep lines in his face barely moved. If he was lucky, he could snatch two to three hours of sleep a night, but the strain was now starting to show. "Prime Minister, we're ready when you are. Your stroll highlight anything?"

"Thank you, Lawrence. Only the lack of daylight," she responded. The Prime Minister had managed no more sleep than anyone else, but still contrived to look fresh and alert. Her pale blue, one-piece woolen dress was at odds with the surroundings, and she exuded confidence and command. Even Cabinet ministers who had often been at odds with their leader now found they welcomed her leadership, recognising that she truly was the person, if anyone, who could get them and the country through this crisis. Some were even glad that the full responsibility for running the country in a time of war hadn't landed on their shoulders. She sat at the head of the conference table. Jeremy Chapman, her Home Secretary, a pearl of sweat running down his forehead, was sitting to her left on the other side of the Defence Minister.

She looked across at the two uniformed soldiers sitting to her right. "Thank you for joining us today, gentlemen. I know you have lots of other duties you feel you need to attend to. We shall be as brief as possible, but information is one of our greatest assets at the moment."

Thomas Fletcher, Chief of the Defence Staff, the most senior uniformed officer of the British forces and Alistair Hamilton, Chief of the General Staff, were both dressed in disruptive combat uniform, but still with red tabs showing on their shirt collars beneath. The time for full dress uniform would have to wait until the time was appropriate.

"Will you start us off with an update, Lawrence?"

"Yes, Prime Minister."

The Defence Secretary picked up the latest report he had been given and scanned it briefly. "The Soviet chemical strike has been confirmed as being launched across the full length of the German Federal Republic. The Germans are hopping mad and are calling for an immediate retaliation."

"What are they looking for? Chemical, tactical nuclear or a full-blown nuclear exchange?" Harriet Willis responded sharply.

"They have had a considerable number of civilians maimed and killed, Prime Minister."

"As we have lost many of our brave soldiers, Lawrence. This is not the time to lose our heads."

"How have the Americans responded?" Jeremy Chapman, the Home Secretary, asked.

"They are also mad as hell," answered Holmes. "They are asking for an agreement that we at least respond in kind."

"General Fletcher, do we have those particular munitions available and close to the assets that will use them?"

"Yes, Prime Minister. We can have our artillery units so armed within four hours."

"A conference call is being convened with all NATO leaders within the hour. I'd like you to attend that with me."

"Yes, Prime Minister."

"And the front, General?"

"It is not going well, I'm afraid. We are about to lose the line we had along the River Leine. The size of the Soviet forces up against us is vast. They have already pushed an Operational Manoeuvre Group across the river, so we are having to adjust our lines accordingly."

"Retreat, you mean."

"We are just moving into a better position where we can keep our line together until we are able to counter-attack."

"Counter-attack?"

"Yes, Prime Minister. NORTHAG has a reserve American Division that will be with us in less than two days. Using that division, elements of our own 4th Armoured Division, and a Panzer battalion from the Germans, we hope to hit them back hard."

"Hope, General?"

"The Soviets have to be where we want them. Our troops have to be where we need them. Then we can strike."

"I see. And the bigger picture?"

The General frowned, knowing he had more bad news for his

Prime Minister. "The Soviets have surrounded Hamburg and are pushing towards Bremen in the west. The lead division is Polish. In the north, they are already at Nord-Ostee-Kanal, threatening Denmark. A DDR army and a Soviet army will push for Denmark any day now."

"Any good news, General?" asked the Home Secretary.

"The ACE mobile force has been released. By placing them into Denmark or Husum, they could set up a defence line for when the Schleswig Holstein forces have to withdraw."

"Wouldn't it be best to bolster up the forces already there?" asked the Defence Secretary.

"No, sir. They wouldn't be able to hold them. We need time to prepare and for the Danish troops to sort themselves out, because they will need to fight as well if they are to protect their own country."

"The Danes happy for ACE mobile forces to pass through their country?"

"More than happy, Prime Minister," answered Holmes.

"As for the rest of NORTHAG, the Dutch, Germans and Belgians are slowly withdrawing."

"The Americans in the south?"

"They were holding well, Prime Minister, but the chemical attack has thrown them into disarray. They too are having to pull back."

There was silence in the room. "Do you have any better news for me, Jeremy?"

"I'm afraid not, Prime Minister. We've had some major disturbances in London, Bradford, Manchester and Birmingham. They are demanding a ceasefire and that we negotiate with the Russians for a peaceful settlement."

"Do they not appreciate that the Soviet army has just killed thousands of German civilians with their chemical strikes?" The question was rhetorical; just Harriet Willis releasing some of her frustration. "We're fighting a war that we did not start; our soldiers are being killed by the hundreds; our very existence is being threatened by a monster-led regime. Have the newspapers been reminded of the D-Notices? We don't want word of these riots being plastered all over the news, encouraging more to break out."

"Yes, Prime Minister, they have. The announcement later today will only make matters worse, I fear. We have to introduce major rationing. The Soviet submarines are sinking too many of our merchant ships, and food supplies are running low."

"What action have you taken?"

"Police officers are already working shifts of twelve on and twelve off, seven days a week. I have asked General Hamilton to provide some troops to provide additional support."

"And has that been offered, General Hamilton?"

"Yes, Prime Minister. Four battalions that were due to go to Germany have been held back to give that support to the police."

"Has the call-up process started, Jeremy?"

"Yes, Prime Minister. That will provide us with more resources, but ideally they should be shipped to the Continent to reinforce our troops over there."

"Are our key points protected?"

"Yes, Prime Minister. Power plants, bridges, communications buildings have all been assigned either police or reserve forces to guard them."

"How many attacks so far?"

"The current count is twenty-four," answered the Home Secretary. "We know that at least eleven were the work of Spetsnaz units. We've also had attacks on RAF bases and airfields in general. Again Spetsnaz."

"We believe that some of the special forces' units have been dropped off on our coast by submarines," added the Defence Secretary.

"What about the wider picture, Lawrence?"

"Well, in Spain and Turkey, it is stalemate. The Soviets aren't making any moves at this time, but we daren't move any of our allies forces to help out further north; otherwise that might just provoke them to attack. We have enough on our plate as it is. The French have finally come off the fence, and some of their divisions are being sent towards Austria. The Soviets are across the Danube and making progress. I've also had reports that there are at least twenty-one Soviet warships in the Norwegian Sea. Danish air reconnaissance shows there to be two Krivak-class guided missile frigates and a Kashin-class destroyer. More importantly, there is a Kynda-class cruiser which we believe to be armed with nuclear missiles. No doubt there will be Whiskey-class and Foxtrot-class submarines in support. Also, supply ships and amphibious landing ships. We have a task force on the way now to intercept."

"Our nuclear option?"

"All available Resolution-class submarines are on the high seas."

"And that is how many?"

"Three, Prime Minister: Resolution, Renown and Revenge. Repulse is undergoing a major refit and couldn't be made ready for at least one month."

"Is three enough?"

"More than enough. Each has sixteen Polaris missiles."

"And our tactical nuclear option, General Fletcher?"

"Our missile regiment has been deployed. We have four batteries, each with three missile launchers. Those batteries have been dispersed across 1 BR Corps' area of operation."

"Well, let's hope we never have to use them. Who knows what will transpire once those are launched."

"We've already had grumblings from the Germans in regard to the Americans' use of MADMs," the Defence Secretary informed her.

"MADM?"

"It's a Medium Atomic Demolition Munition, hence the acronym. An eighty-kilogram charge."

"Ah yes, of course. They use them to destroy particularly large bridges and block narrow passes."

"Yes, Prime Minister. The German Chancellor is concerned that the use of these weapons could escalate to the use of tactical nuclear weapons by the Soviets."

"Likely?"

"I doubt it. But, if necessary, the Soviets could use it as an excuse to launch a pre-emptive strike. Tactical, yes, but it would have devastating consequences."

"Right, right. I will raise it with the NATO council. How is Berlin coping?"

"They are still very much on alert. As agreed, all troops have returned to barracks, but men and equipment have been dispersed around the barracks in case the Soviets change their mind and bomb the hell out of them."

"Food?"

"Berlin has significant reserves, Prime Minister. Up to six months at least."

"So there is no let-up from the Soviets..."

"None," responded General Hamilton. "On the contrary, they seem even more determined to take West Germany. The use of chemical weapons supports that."

"Then we must fight them. I must speak with the NATO ministers. We meet back here in four hours."

Chapter 37

From a distance, it could have been mistaken for any tented military complex. As you got closer, the sights, sounds and smells told a different story. Erected under a thin screen of trees, the dressing station was well laid out and organised. But the line of bagged bodies and the cries from some of the wounded and the almost manic, yet purposeful, actions of the soldiers manning it were indicative that their workload was high. The five treatment bays were in full swing, as were the two surgical teams. Capable of dealing with 450 casualties in twenty-four hours, they were currently having to manage twice that number, many of them civilians, children who had been brought to the station by desperate parents. Many of the German civilians were suffering from the effects of being exposed to chemical agents used by the Soviet army to target airfields and logistical depots of the NATO forces. The military personnel reluctantly turned away as many as they could, telling them they must use their own hospitals, even though they too were overflowing. On occasion, they relented.

Two vehicles from the evacuation troop, a 432 ambulance and a 1 Ton Land rover pulled up close to a treatment bay. The stretcher cases were quickly taken off for triage. A Royal Army Medical Corps (RAMC) medic completed the triage quickly, needing to know the state of each casualty so she could allocate them to the correct treatment station. The Land rover then sped off to the Chemical Decontamination Cell (CDC). Two further stretchers were slid out from the top and bottom rack on the rear right-hand side. Both were quickly carried into the first section of the tent where absorbent powder, bleach and slurry were used to remove any remnants of contamination before they removed the casualties' clothing. Even as the two soldiers were being decontaminated, another 432 pulled up alongside, more casualties from the front. The surgical teams, some of them with doctors from the Territorial Army, had already had a long night and a long day.

As the Soviet Western TVD continued its thrust west, respite was not on the horizon.

CPSIA information can be obtained at www.ICGtesting.com
Printed in the USA
LVOW07s0128030214

371939LV00004B/126/P